COME NO
FURTHER

MICHAEL ZACCARIA

PINNACLE PEAK MEDIA
SALT LAKE CITY, UTAH

COME NO FURTHER
First Paperback Edition: March 2015
Copyright © 2015 by Michael Zaccaria
Published by Pinnacle Peak Media

Book Layout & Design ©2015 - BookDesignTemplates.com

Cover art by Weston Woodbury and Jalena Gajic
Title design by Shawn Hight

ISBN-13: 978-0-9904385-0-2
ISBN-10: 0990438503

This book is dedicated to Ann and Dave Zaccaria. Thank you for all of your love and support.

PART ONE

COAL AND GOLD

1

900—In his stern, coal-blackened hands, George Hendricks held an object worthy of immeasurable admiration. It was a figurine, about the size of a fist, forged in gold and fashioned by a skilled craftsman centuries earlier to resemble a Great Horned Owl with its wings spread and its brutal talons extended—thirsty for the soft flesh of an unsuspecting prey. It was one of the most beautiful things that he had ever laid eyes on. Though, relatively speaking, a lump of coal could be considered attractive in light of George's dreadful smell and appearance. His face and hands were covered in coal dust. He wore an unkempt beard, blackened trousers, an equally blackened jacket—although many of the buttons had long since fallen off—and a pair of worn rubber boots.

In his defense, only two hours prior, he had completed a twelve-hour shift laboring underground in the Rainville No. 4 mine, where he earned roughly two dollars per day. At the end of his long and toilsome shift, he had clambered onto one of the coal trains that ran twenty miles due west to the town of Helper. It was here that he had an opportunity to acquire the golden owl figurine, which he was holding in his filthy hands for the first time.

Helper's Main Street was lined with brick buildings that had been erected over a decade earlier. The brick structures were two, three, or four stories in height and were raised only six to ten feet apart from one another on both sides of the street. When seen from a distance, an unknowing traveler could easily mistake the numerous buildings as one massive structure. Most of the buildings were hotels or flophouses that accommodated the coal miners and railroad workers who wandered in and out of the neighboring coal camps. The town had been established as a freight terminal for the railroad and had been settled for that very reason, along with the prospect of easy access coal. But, most importantly (in the humble opinion of many of its inhabitants), Helper was the only town in thirty miles that possessed a suitable brothel. The Royal was a place befitting of a man who sought drink or the comfort of a young woman. In most cases, the type of man who wandered into the Royal sought both.

Edmond Kelly was a man who unquestionably desired both. He desired them so much that he desired little else in his sad and meaningless life—aside from the currency required to sustain such an existence. He sat opposite George in a private room that smelled of charred cigarettes, sweat, and the mold that had accumulated for two decades where the spring's rainwater slipped through the shoddy mortar work of inexperienced masons. The room in which they sat was typically reserved for sexual intercourse, though the overhead lighting was more akin to that of a police interrogation room. It created an atmosphere that exemplified transgression as opposed to ecstasy. It belonged to the whore that Edmond had been screwing, inadequately so, for the last two weeks. She allowed Edmond to use it for thirty minutes for his meeting with George. Naturally, she had a stake in the meeting, too. Edmond's money was partially her money thanks to Edmond's roaring sex addiction. There was a small bed with tousled sheets and blankets centered against the far wall, and near the door was a circular table with two chairs. This is where George and Edmond sat. An oak dresser with a large oval shaped mirror was opposite the bed with a brass chandelier hanging above it. There were black and white and sepia tone photographs encircling the room—photographs of lawmen, outlaws, and laborers from decades past. Behind the photographs was the egg-shell-colored wallpaper, yellow and stained.

The golden owl figurine was the property of Edmond Kelly, and it was property that he neither appreciated nor valued. Edmond was a simpleminded man, and his hygiene was even worse than George's. Dirt and sweat encrusted his long hair and scraggly beard, and his russet-colored cowboy hat was caked with perspiration stains. He had not bathed in well over a month, though he was ignorant of his vile scent.

Edmond spent four months laboring underground with George, George's father, Joe, and Joe's closest friend, Remo Parelli, before wandering into the Royal one night. Two weeks later, he was still there—balls deep in Irish whiskey and whores. Without a job, and thus, an income, it didn't take long for Edmond's money to run dry. When he realized that this was inevitable, he decided to sell the golden owl—an object that he had stumbled upon three months prior when his Ute mother died in her sleep. When he heard of her death, he felt neither pain nor sorrow. Instead, he regarded her passing as good fortune, and he hurried to her home to ravage her possessions. He was not in search of sentiment, but value. It was strange, but the only slice of nostalgia that struck him at the time of his mother's passing were vague memories of his Irish father, Charles Kelly. Charles had abandoned his family when Edmond was only ten-years-old to pursue a silver prospect in northern Idaho—a journey that he never returned from. Little did Edmond know that his father had formed a claim on fifteen acres of land that would one day produce a great deal of silver; however, a week after staking his claim, he was found face down in a creek with a gunshot wound to the chest. Not long after that, his claim was mysteriously wiped from the local land records. The killing had been carried out by corrupt town officials who in turn were linked to the gluttonous mine owners who had been buying up all the silver bearing real estate in the area. The chance to increase their fortune was always worth the life of some bothersome outsider.

Edmond had no treasure hunting ambitions of his own. Not because of a lack of interest, but because of a lack of willingness to put forth the required effort. To be frank, he was a lazy slug who was constantly looking for a free ticket through life.

Edmond unfolded a goatskin parchment map and slid it across the table for George to view. The map was at least one hundred years old. It portrayed a mountain region, the circumference of which was roughly fifty miles. A Great Horned Owl was depicted largely and imaginatively on the map—a mirror image of the golden figurine. The features were matched and blended into the shapes and features of the mountain terrain. There were two lakes depicted, illustrated asymmetrically as the eyes of the owl. Beyond the eyes in both directions were two curved sets of mountains that were integrated into the owl's wings. Directly centered on the map was the beak, which was labeled *El Corona del Rey*—The King's Crown. The beak depicted on the map looked more like a crown than a beak, though one would have to pay close attention to notice.

George, who was still holding the golden owl figurine, flipped it around and found another phrase stamped over the length of the owl's wings: *el ala derecho*—the right wing.

It was all terribly unusual. George didn't speak nor understand a lick of Spanish outside of "sí," "gracias," and "siesta," but in his impressionable mind, the peculiar phrases only contributed to the authenticity of the objects. Equally, it made him nervous. To cope, he removed his favorite luxury of life, an Aura brand cigar, to settle his nerves. His right hand shook as he struck a match and raised it to the cigar dangling from his lips. He sucked in the tobacco then exhaled a puff of smoke. Then he looked the objects over again.

A grin arose on Edmond's face, revealing his mustard-colored teeth. He could sense the enormous interest that George had in the owl and the tattered map.

George knew how desperate Edmond was to sell the objects and understood that he had buttered up many of the details. Despite this, the sheer intrigue of the owl seemed to make its way into his consciousness through some strange mesmeric power. He wanted the golden object, and he couldn't help but feel like the golden object wanted him, too. It was a sensation that had never smitten Edmond Kelly, who was becoming increasingly impatient by the second. The longer George's money remained in his pocket, the longer it kept Edmond's tongue from being saturated with more of his beloved Irish whiskey.

"The map goes along with the owl. How it works, I dunno, so don't ask," said Edmond in a loud voice, attempting to overcome the rowdy patrons who hollered and screeched on the other side of the skinny wall. To persuade George to make a hasty decision, he threatened, "Either ya take it now err I'm sellin' it to another fella first thing in the mornin'."

George didn't register the warning. He was still troubled by a sense of uncertainty. His desire to obtain the golden owl began a week earlier when Edmond boasted to George and five other men about how he could make any one of them a potential millionaire, as long as they were willing to cough up enough money to satisfy such a proposal. The other men dismissed Edmond's blathering by laughing in his face. Who could blame them, George thought at the time. Edmond Kelly was just one of hundreds of drunks living in the coal camps who could deem the Royal or some other brothel or tavern their second home. But George didn't see the harm in at least investigating Edmond's claim. He told him that he might be interested as long as he could look the objects over first. Edmond agreed.

George held the golden owl inches from his face. He stroked his black beard like a pondering old man then subtly lifted his gaze to Edmond.

"Well," he muttered. "It's color all right."

He lowered the owl, and the golden hue faded from his eyes, leaving only a shale gray.

"That's eight ounces," Edmond said. "I oughta git me somewheres round a-hunnerd 'n forty dollars. I gotta fella offered me hunnerd 'n sixty fer it. I'm sure I could git more but fer a friend I'll let it go fer a-hunnerd 'n fifty like we talked about. I still don't think ya could pay it though. That's alotta money fer a muckman."

The thought of parting with one hundred and fifty dollars induced a tingling in the pit of George's stomach. He indeed possessed such a sum of money after saving as much as he could throughout a decade working underground. In fact, he had saved exactly two-hundred and eighty-four dollars and seventy-three cents. It was money saved to provide a better opportunity for himself and hopefully for a family later in life. Now, he was about to surrender more than half of it in one sitting. The more he deliberated, the more the tingling in his stomach evolved into a formidable nausea. He inhaled a long drag from the Aura cigar and then exhaled a plume of smoke. It alleviated the sickness in his stomach and calmed his nerves a little.

"What else can ya tell me about it?" George asked.

Edmond replied impatiently, "Hell, I already told ya all ya needtuh know. I know I got it from my Ma and that it's Spanish gold. Them sons-a-bitches had all kindsa mines up there. Had 'em all over the damn country for cryin' out loud."

While the two men stared at one another, George thirsty for more information and Edmond reluctant to give any, a poorly performed version of "Just One Girl" erupted from an out-of-tune piano on the other side of the thin wall. This only annoyed Edmond further, but it wasn't long before the disgruntled patrons jeered and booed and the butchering of a fine composition came to an end. When it did, the patrons roared with approval.

"That's all ya can tell me?" George asked, dissatisfied by Edmond's response.

"That's all I know about it."

George shifted uncomfortably in his chair. "I've been lookin' for a reason to get outta Rainville for some time," he said. "If ya say there's gold on that mountain, then I'd like to think there's gold. I'll take it. I ain't got much choice."

That was true. He had spent half his life underground, and because a coal miner was ceaselessly exposed to the potent coal dust that contributed to Black Lung, collapses, explosions, suffocation, and the buildup of various hazardous gases, such as carbon monoxide, methane, and hydrogen sulphide, he would be lucky to see the age of forty—a milestone that was only five years off.

He removed a stack of bills from his pocket and tossed them onto the tabletop. Edmond snatched the money as if the table itself were a cauldron of fire that would sear the bills into a pile of ash. As he counted the money, he looked at George suspiciously. "They payin' ya triple over there at Rainville are they, er maybe yer runnin' in some kinda outfit?"

"You think I stole that money?" George asked.

Edmond grinned as he counted the bills. "Money's money. I don't give a goddamn where it come from. And if ya stole it from Wolf Blankston, then that's all the better."

"Wish I could say I did," George replied as he exhaled a plume of smoke. "You member Jari Ronni, dontcha—that Finnish fella with the long hair?"

"Sure I do. I worked with 'im a coupla days. He was a good help, a hell of a good help."

"Blankston canned 'im this mornin'. Said Jari was kickin' up too much of a fuss over his brothers dyin' in the mine. Loada shit as far's I'm concerned. A man who loses two brothers underground oughta be able to kick up all the fuss he wants."

Edmond made a strange mumbling sound as he continued to count the money. He then looked up at George for a split second as though he had forgotten he was sitting across the table from him. "Somebody oughta lick that Blankston and lick 'im good," said Edmond as he finished counting the cash. He then wobbled to his feet with his left hand gripped on the back of the chair for support. "You already told yer Pa yer leavin' 'im to go yer own way?"

George carefully rolled up the old map, refusing to make eye contact with Edmond. "No. I think it's better he don't know about it."

George's father, Joe Hendricks, had owned a general store in Colorado with his wife, Alice. George, their only child, was never educated in the local schools. He was instead employed full-time at Joe's store where he acted primarily as a courier for local deliveries. When the bigger mining companies swept through and bought out the majority of the operations, they built their own general stores, which were much more adequate establishments than the ramshackle stores, such as Joe's, that had served the community before the company's arrival. The only sensible action for Joe to take was to sell his store to the encroaching company, which he did. With the money he made and the money he had saved over the years, he bought two hundred acres of land near the Elk River in the spring of 1889. There, he attempted to convert himself and his family into ranchers—something he knew very little about. He spent every dime on an established homestead, over two hundred head of cattle, and a dozen horses. By October of the same year, more than eighty percent of the animals were lost to disease. Joe tried to sell the remaining animals, but the towns-folk refused to buy them. The Hendricks family watched helplessly as their future as well as their livelihood disap-peared with the passing of each animal. By November, their entire livestock was gone. Joe had no choice but to sell the ranch so that he and George could seek employment in the nearby silver mines.

The worst was still to come. Just over a month later, Alice Hendricks died of pneumonia on the frigid New Year's Day of 1890. The following day brought with it a nasty snow-storm that forced Joe and George to shovel through three feet of snow and through another six feet of ice-hardened soil to bury the beloved wife and mother. George would never forget the numbness in his pink fingers or the tears that were frozen on his cheeks and eyelids. None of it mat-tered. The pain that he felt in his heart outweighed any-thing that he could possibly bear on the surface. Even after Alice had been buried and covered with icy soil, George and his father stood in the midst of the treacherous white-out—bewildered and weary—unsure of themselves and their future. It was there in that ferocious storm that George remembered that he had lived a happy childhood. He thought of the streams that he had once played in and of the friends that he had once shared laughter with. But those memories were now vague in his troubled mind. The more he reminisced, the more he realized that he had not been happy since, and he feared that he would never be happy again.

Joe sold his ranch property in March at a discount and then turned to drink. Less than a month later, all of his money had evaporated into card games or whiskey bottles and even the occasional whore that he thought would help alleviate his pain, though it never did. And that's how it had been for the last ten years—jumping from operation to operation and sleeping in a shack or a tent or even in the dirt just to make enough money to afford something to eat and a bottle of booze to shroud the horrors of the past. With each passing day, Joe slipped deeper into the void of infinite gloom. Little by little, he tried to pull George into it with him. But George fought it the best he could. He secretly started to save his money. And he had to keep it a secret; otherwise, his own father would steal it to fuel his gambling outings.

Edmond sensed the tension that his question had unmasked and swiftly changed the subject. "When ya leavin' town?" he asked.

"Day after tomorruh," George stated.

Edmond looked at George with an empathetic expression. "I shore hope there's some gold in that mou'un fer ya. If there ain't then ya can always turn a profit on that owl. That's a-hunnerd 'n forty dollars' worth-a-gold. I'm sure ya could find some dumb bastard who'd pay two-hunnerd fer it, maybe more. Some-a-them Chinese fellas'd pay jist about anything fer gold."

George and Edmond shook hands, and then Edmond disappeared into the shadowy, smoke-filled brothel. George sat alone in the room and smoked his cigar. The nausea had set in once again, and this time, no amount of Aura cigars or cheap whiskey could repel it. It was there to stay.

What stood out to George was Edmond's suggestion that he could resell the golden owl or smelt it down if something went awry. It was unfortunate that this suggestion was presented after George had already coughed up the money because it seemed to suggest that deep down, Edmond was doubtful of the map's legitimacy. As for George, he had taken an enormous risk. The pressure of it had already started to weigh him down with an astounding force. Nevertheless, it was a risk that he had long prepared himself to take. He had to follow through with his intentions to pursue a life of his own satisfaction—to separate himself from the millions of laborers around the country who were enslaved by corrupt businessmen.

Within the golden owl figurine, George saw a life of meaning and achievement. He saw a mining operation that he could call his own—a place where he could wear an extravagant suit and smoke box after box of his glorious Aura cigars. He saw his friend Remo, one of the most skilled laborers that he had ever worked with, taking on the role of mine foreman. He saw retirement and suitable medical treatment for his ailing father, whom he loved dearly but had grown apart from over recent years. But to George, it was nothing a stroke of good fortune couldn't fix.

In the palm of his hand was a ticket to a grand yet enigmatic venue. Long before the passing of George's mother, she had once told him, "The golden rings of opportunity present themselves once in a lifetime—take hold of them or they're forever lost." What Alice failed to mention was that not all golden rings of opportunity were genuine in nature. Nature has its own way of deciding who is worthy and who is not. At the heart of a self-indulgent society, the majority of these golden rings were rings of deception, and greed served as the potent fuel that kept the wheels in motion.

2

The midnight trains hissed as George drew near the depot. It had been two years since he and his father were hired at Rainville, and in that time, he had memorized the routes of all of the trains that traveled to and from the Rainville camp. The shorter coal car locomotives, typically one or two cars in length, would be sent from Helper to the coal camps and from the coal camps back to Helper. One of the two car locomotives would be departing for Rainville three times that evening to collect the coal extracted by the night shift. The train responsible for this task was the No. 38.

He had to be careful. The depot employed a night watchman who was in charge of keeping people from hopping the trains at night. Many years earlier, there was no penalty enforced for riding the night trains, but on a summer night in 1896, a drunk who labored at the nearby Placerton mine climbed aboard one of the trains. Halfway to his destination, the man slipped and fell, and the iron wheels of the train severed his left leg. A week passed before the man's body was found. The severed leg was never discovered. It was assumed that a mountain lion had dragged it off and eaten it. Because of this incident, hopping trains at night was prohibited.

George crept through the rail yard. There were oil burning lanterns throughout it, and he had to avoid them to the best of his ability. He hid behind one of the boxcars and poked his head out to get a look at the depot, which was a huge structure that looked like a Victorian style home. A wooden sign above the door read: "HELPER." George could see the night watchman sitting in a chair near the door. There was an oil burning lantern resting on a table next to him. Its faint glow provided just enough light to reveal that he was asleep with his head resting on the building behind him. George could even hear him snoring.

He made his break for the No. 38 locomotive with light and hurried footsteps. He put both hands on the rim of the boxcar and set his feet on the iron wheel. He then leaped and held his bodyweight with his biceps while he carefully maneuvered his legs into the car. Once both feet were touching metal, he exhaled a breath of relief. He had been as quiet as a cat.

After a couple of minutes, the mechanism of the No. 38 hissed, and the great beast progressed into a monotonous crawl. The sound of metal on metal pulsed as the train accelerated. George looked up at the stars in the brilliant, cloudless night.

The invigorating air touched his rugged face, bearing with it the aroma of the sagebrush and junipers. It would be nearly an hour's ride back to Rainville, and during the ride, he would be consumed only by his ambivalent thoughts. He tried to think of the golden owl and of the future, but the only thing he could think of was the abandonment of his father. Part of him wanted to invite his father to join him on the journey to the mountain, but he knew it was out of the question. Joe's damaged knees barely allowed him to get to and from the mine every day. But, more than anything else, it had been ten years since Joe's company could be regarded as pleasant. Nothing quite wore a person down like persistent negativity, and George had endured it for twelve hours a day for the last decade. Enough was enough. It was time to make something of himself. It was time to break away.

•

The drab industrial lamps of Rainville emerged in the distance over the top of a rolling hill. George dismounted the train one hundred yards before it arrived at the tipple (the place where the train was scheduled to stop) because it was a quicker route to the residential area where he lived on the adjacent hillside.

As he walked toward the residential area, he heard a critter scamper through the brush. It scared him a little, but then he realized that it was only a mouse. An owl screeched overhead. It was scouring the hillside for the small critters that George could hear stumbling about. He surveyed the dark sky in an attempt to spot the creature, though his attempt was unsuccessful. He tried to listen for it, but all he could hear were the chattering crickets and the idle hum of the No. 38 locomotive, which had stopped at the tipple.

George walked another two hundred yards before he reached his stone miner's cabin, which was owned by the Wolf Blankston Mining Company and occupied by George and his father, Joe. The rent was withdrawn from their paltry paychecks once a month.

The wooden door of the stone cabin creaked open, and George emerged from the night into the dim glow of a small hearth.

The room, which reeked of Joe's flatulence, was just over one hundred and fifty square feet in size. The decor was sparse, including only two bunks that were contaminated with coal dust and dried sweat and a small table that had been battered and beaten from years of use by rugged miners. A thin strand of nickel wire was secured to the wooden ceiling planks and hung loosely above both cots where a half dozen pairs of unwashed socks were draped—socks that had once been white and clean but were now black, crusty, and rank. The red glow of the hearth lit the ashen stone walls that were littered with pots, pans, pickaxes, a woodcutting axe, crowbars, hammers, jacks, shovels, a light jacket, a set of cotton caps, several boxes of bottled pickles and tomatoes, coffee tins, biscuits, and canned beans. It also lit a man who was snoring raucously on the bunk closest to the fire. This was Joe Hendricks, who was a mirror image of his son, George, though Joe's hair had long since lost its blackish hue to a pallid gray, and his leathery skin had sagged and wizened.

George unbuttoned his jacket and hung it on the wall as quietly as he could. But as he took a step forward, his foot connected with an empty whiskey bottle that was lying on the floor next to Joe's bunk. The bottle spun violently and skittered across the brick flooring until it slammed hard against the base of the stone wall. George froze in fear. His eyes remained locked on his father, as though waiting for a sleeping grizzly to rise ferociously from the cot and maul him to death. But Joe didn't move a muscle. His eyes remained closed, and his odious snoring continued. George realized that the bottle he kicked had likely been full a few hours prior. When Joe got drunk and blacked out, nothing could wake up him up. Even if a locomotive were to roar and scream through the center of the room, the old fart wouldn't have a clue.

George walked to the opposite side of the cabin to his bunk. He kicked off his boots and laid down. His joints and muscles ached from shoveling coal, and his scalp was amassed with cuts and bruises where the ceiling rock had fallen onto his inadequately covered head. If his head were to meet the pillow, he would slip directly out of consciousness.

But all he could think about was the golden owl. He couldn't help but recover it from his pocket and savor one last glance at it. He held it to the light, and his eyes reflected both the golden figurine and the orange flame from the hearth.

What a marvel it was. A Greek laborer had told him once about the Owl of Athena—a symbol of knowledge and wisdom. *Maybe the owl will teach me something important about life*, he thought to himself; however, he was unaware that many cultures around the world, including several Native American tribes, believed the owl to be an ill-omen—a harbinger of death and a vessel for evil forces.

George had zero interest in the ideology and symbolism behind the thing. He only cared about where the owl would lead him—to wealth, to ruin, or to something in between. And equally, he couldn't help but wonder how the curious object had made its way to him. There was no doubt that the golden owl had once been important to someone long ago.

3

Incandescent light pierced the sky and lit the marvelous Book Cliffs that ran nearly two hundred miles in a snake-like pattern from western Colorado into eastern Utah. Composed primarily of sandstone from the Cretaceous Period, these unique ranges were aptly named due to their multiple layers of water erosion, which resembled the tiered pages of a withered book—geological remnants of the ancient lake Bonneville. The year was 1733—the pinnacle of the Viceroyalty of New Spain—one hundred and thirty-two years before the birth of George Hendricks. It was a year of drought and death.

A weathered deer skull laid dormant in the dirt near a skimpy sagebrush plant. It was quiet and calm, yet eerie—lifeless. A light breeze picked up and caused the sagebrush to sway gently from side to side. Soon after, the sound of slow trotting horses became audible, ridding the land of its mysterious silence. It was a Spanish expedition: thirtyfold, whose physical appearance suggested that they had traveled to Hell and back. Thirteen of the thirty men were Spanish soldiers who donned elegant tricorne hats fashioned with gold laced trim, though they had long since abandoned their woolen military coats. All that remained were white long-sleeved shirts that were various shades of yellow and tan due to a collection of dirt and sweat, their torn and tattered britches, and their scuffed boots, the soles of which had almost worn through.

There were fifteen Native American slaves, most of whom were carrying cumbersome provisions fixed to their backs and shoulders. The slaves who were not carrying provisions were leading horses that were overburdened with mining picks, shovels, hammers, and jacks. The slaves had been brought along to ensure that no one of Spanish blood would have to labor within the narrow mine. The slaves were the designated labor force, and the soldiers were there to act as overseers and slave drivers. There were nine Pueblo and six Navajo. They were all tribesman who had been captured on various battlefronts and returned to Santé Fe to be used in any way the Spanish pleased. Becoming a slave under the authority of the Spanish crown meant that captives could keep their lives, which wasn't necessarily the best option given that it meant a lifetime of enslavement and malnourishment.

The expedition made its way through the scattered flora of Narrow Leaf cottonwood, sagebrush, Rocky Mountain juniper, and Douglas fir, all of which were wilting in thirst from the intense summer heat. The men traveling in the group were exhausted and filthy. Wind had battered their faces, dust had encrusted their eyelids, ears, and hair, and their lips had dried and cracked under the ruthless foreign sun. Half of the Spanish soldiers rode on horseback, and the other half paced behind the slaves armed with rifles, pistols, short swords that hung from their hips, and daggers that were tucked into their leather belts. Those who were armed yearned for any reason to make use of their deadly weapons, but they were directed only to kill if a prisoner attempted to flee. This frustrated the witless, bloodthirsty soldiers.

The fifteen slaves and thirteen soldiers comprised twenty-eight of the thirty members of the expedition. The remaining two were a Franciscan priest and a fearless leader, who strode proudly at the head of the caravan.

The Franciscan priest who paced second from the front was a stout, well-fed man named Father Diego Rodriguez. He carried a large wooden crucifix that doubled as a walking stick, a divine symbol to guide his rugged path. His short, silver hair spiked outward and formed a circle around a large bald spot on the top of his head. It was as if a bolt of lightning had struck the center of his scalp and disintegrated the hair it touched and frightened the rest, leaving only an ashen crown. He had a ragged silver and white beard, and he was bound in a chocolate colored robe that fit comfortably around his sphere-like belly.

It was customary for a Franciscan priest to navigate an expedition by the light of the divine authority, but this task was far more treacherous than any other. It required a vanguard that was as ruthless as he was acumen. Such a leader was Esteban Garza, a battle-hardened man of war who had a nasty scar that ran from the height of his forehead, down and over a black leather eye patch that shielded his left eye, and across his cheek nearly to his jaw. He was also missing his left hand and the bulk of his left arm, which was lost a decade earlier during a quarrel with the Apache. In place of a hand, he wore a metal hook. He sported a thick black beard and a yellow long-sleeved shirt that was unbuttoned nearly to his stomach. With his eye patch, his hook, and his black beard, he looked like a pirate of the desert. His one good eye was a rich amber color, uncannily similar to the shade of gold. In fact, it resembled the gold that had been used to forge the golden owl figurine, which had been crafted in Santé Fe that same year—1733.

The golden owl was knotted around Esteban's neck with a thin strip of leather. It bounced rhythmically against his chest with the progress of his footsteps.

Esteban was the only one in the group who appeared to be unaffected by the inhospitable conditions. He strode on with bewildering vigor and perseverance. His features were stern, and he carried an air of unquestionable authority.

Eleven days prior, he was gifted *El Mapa del búho,* or, The Owl Map, which was a goatskin parchment map intended to be used in combination with the golden owl figurine. Used together, they would reveal the whereabouts of the gold-bearing mine. The Owl Map, as stated by the sovereigns of Santé Fe, led to one of the most affluent gold mines in the western United States. But, with such an esteemed reward came a momentous risk. According to *El Mapa del búho,* the precious resources were located further away from Santé Fe than any other documented resource, making the excursion into The Mountain of the Owl the most dangerous of all.

The Spanish had developed hundreds of mines throughout the southwest. The purpose of these hearty expeditions was to track down a mine, drudge it for a particular length of time, and then return the precious cargo to Santé Fe. In the twilight of summer, merchant ships loaded with gold, silver, copper, indigo, jewels, tobacco, and other valuables would join the war galleons in Havana, Cuba, to form the treasure fleet so that the wealth could be protected en route to the Spanish crown. Though, regrettably for Spain, these ships were often separated due to poor weather or inexperienced seamen. Thus, a considerable amount of the resources were either seized by pirates or entire treasure ships were lost in the midst of ocean storms.

The vessels, such as the Atocha, the most infamous Spanish treasure ship, were generally lost in the hotbed of Mother Nature's fury—the region known today as the Bermuda Triangle. Whether the source of their disappearance stemmed from weather phenomena, deep sea phenomena, supernatural phenomena, or just plain rotten luck is unknown.

Esteban Garza knew nothing of the Bermuda Triangle, for in his time, there was no such place with that name; however, he did know of the strange phenomena that had been previously documented by men who returned from *La Montaña de la Lechuza,* The Mountain of the Owl, with their lives intact. The superiors of Santé Fe had given Esteban some of the journals from past expeditions. They all told of a powerful, malevolent force that was present there. It controlled the land, the elements, and the wildlife. There were also accounts of strange sounds, blood-red skies, and bizarre mist-like beings. Naturally, there was only one explanation. *La Montaña de la Lechuza* was the home of the devil. Esteban was instructed to keep the information to himself. The last thing they wanted was to scare the daylights out of the men before they even left Santé Fe. The secret of The Mountain of the Owl was safe with Esteban. Furthermore, being the audacious man that he was, he couldn't wait to face the devil head on.

The meandering route through the Book Cliffs was the core path to the gold-bearing mountains. The Spanish had already passed through Pueblo and Navajo country with little incident, and now that they had travelled into eastern Utah—no more than two miles from where the Rainville coal mine would be established sixteen decades later—they had entered Ute territory. They had arrived swiftly thanks to the grueling pace that Esteban Garza commanded.

The dry climate sparked a tickle in the back of Esteban's throat. He retrieved a leather canteen that was draped over his left shoulder and wedged it under his half amputated arm. He removed the cork with a sharp tug of his right hand and then tried to satisfy his parched tongue with a swig of warm water. When he lifted a depleted canteen to his lips, he grew angry. He turned to his companions and shouted in Spanish, "Does anyone have any water?"

The other men looked on, downcast and terrified of their stoic Captain. They all shook their heads. Esteban looked at each of them. He could detect their distress and uncertainty.

"We are several hours from water," he said coldly. "If we cannot be resilient now, this desert will be our grave."

When he finished speaking, he scowled at the priest, Father Diego Rodriguez, as if he were the one personally responsible for the lack of water. And, in actuality, he was.

The priest dipped his head.

The men responded little. They feared that they would never survive long enough to see such a water source. Worse yet, they feared that no water source existed at all in such a wretched, alien land.

A huge mountain range loomed in the distance over the top of the Book Cliffs. It looked like the teeth of some mas-

sive mythological creature jutting from the Earth. The caravan dragged on toward it, leaving a powdery layer of dust
floating in the dry canyon. The men, who struggled to walk
through the flour-like dirt, had embarked on the journey in
the name of duty and honor for Spain, but those coura-
geous sentiments had long faded. All that was left was
hopelessness.

4

As soon as Esteban Garza's expedition entered the foothills, one of the Pueblo slaves collapsed and died of heat stroke. The men had little choice but to carry on without burying the body. They had to reach a water source by nightfall; otherwise, the slaves would start dropping like flies. Father Rodriguez would have preferred to bury the man, but the perished slave didn't have a drop of Spanish blood. Furthermore, after eleven days of persistence, the fallen Pueblo had not accepted the priest's religious teachings. Thus, according to Catholicism, there would be no recoil from the Almighty for letting the slave's corpse rot under the burning sun like a deer or a rabbit.

The flora of the desert gradually dwindled as they started through the red willows, cottonwoods, elders, kinnikinnick, hop vines, and grass that grew as high as their hands. Each man watched their surroundings. More than anything else, they observed each other—their fellow pale, fragile, and demoralized companions whose ribcages showed through their sunburned flesh, most notably the Native Americans, who had received far less in rations than those of Spanish blood.

Despite the unsettling imagery, the vegetation had become more fertile, and the temperature dwindled as they traveled deeper and higher into the mountain, giving the men a glimmer of hope. The stillness of the high desert had passed, and the singing of the birds and the mundane humming of the insects swelled through the foothills. A tranquil calm settled in. There wasn't a single cloud in the liquid blue sky, and each individual—soldier and slave— was coaxed into a dreamlike phenomenon. They all stared in wonder at the green, grassy pastures, the tall, dense pines, and the distant sunlit peaks. The mountain encapsulated a state of supreme comfort and solace—a place where no evil could ever intrude and enforce its wickedness. The burden of fear was lifted from the travelers, allowing them to press onward confident that a water source existed, and that they weren't far from it.

Suddenly, the tranquility vanished with the sound of a loud thud. Esteban turned sharply to see that one of his soldiers had fallen from his pinto and was lying face down in the mountain underbrush. Father Rodriguez was the first one to the fallen rider. He flipped the man over to reveal a pale, lifeless face. The priest tried to revive him by shaking him. When that didn't work, he resorted to prayer, though that, too, was of no use. He moved his hands from the man and embraced the crucifix that drooped from his neck.

The fallen rider had been hunched over the horse's neck since morning and could have easily been dead for more than an hour or two for all they knew. He had suffered from severe heat exhaustion the previous day, and without a water source, it was only a matter of time before his life came to an end. He was also the sole reason why the rest of the group had nothing to drink. They had squandered a great deal of water in an effort to preserve the man's life the previous night. The order to use the water had come from Father Rodriguez, who claimed to be doing what the Lord told him to do. Nonetheless, the irrational action displeased Esteban Garza a great deal, regardless of where the order came from.

The welcoming mountain grew silent as the desert below had been, and the rest of the wavering expedition followed suit. Not even the horses made a peep. They, too, had grown disheartened.

The soldiers and slaves looked at Esteban and waited for his instruction; however, it was Father Rodriguez who spoke first.

"You men," he said as he pointed at a group of slaves. "Retrieve the shovels and arrange this man a proper burial."

The natives looked on with confused faces, unsure of what the priest had said. The group's translator was a short, stocky man with a jet-black moustache and a receding hairline who went by the name of Del Rio. Del Rio echoed the priest's request in Pueblo. Right away, the Pueblo slaves retrieved shovels from the pack horses, and the Navajo mimicked their actions.

Esteban watched heatedly for a moment before turning to regard The Mountain of the Owl. He then turned back with his customary scornful gaze. "Del Rio," he boomed, which frightened both the soldiers and the slaves. "Tell those men to return the shovels to the horses and to take the reins of this fallen man's horse at once. We leave the body, as we left the other."

Rodriguez, Del Rio, and the other soldiers were stunned. This was no meaningless savage. This was a fallen man of the Spanish crown, and to abandon him without a proper Christian burial would certainly unleash the Lord's wrath upon them.

Esteban regarded each man cautiously, prepared to take action if needed by readying his right hand near his silver-plated flintlock pistol. "If we stop to bury him, then we might as well hollow out twenty-eight more graves while we're at it."

This statement sent a chill through the men who were now forced into the unfortunate position of choosing between the will of the Lord and the will of their imposing leader. Their conviction of faith commanded that an indecorous burial would be an absolute, unforgivable sin. Not to mention a disgrace to the departed soul.

Rodriguez gulped hard and prepared to stand his ground. "We bury him," he stated with his holy crucifix exposed on his chest.

The thick vein on Esteban's sunburned forehead bulged in anger. "We carry on, or you reside in the ground with him!"

A rush of fear came over the priest. The impression that he assumed all along had finally displayed itself. Esteban Garza was no man of the Lord. He was a man of something much darker. He possessed a black heart, a black soul, and an eye of gold. The abnormality of Esteban's eye forced the priest to look away for a moment. When he did, his wandering eyes met the other soldiers who returned a scrutiny of uncertainty and fear. Perspiration began to flow from the priest's face. It had become a tug of war between good and evil, of light and dark, and of gold and God. Neither man seemed to be willing to capitulate.

As the priest continued to leak sweat, Esteban remained calm and vigilant. He even unleashed a wry smile as if to inform Father Rodriguez that he already knew the outcome of the confrontation, which he absolutely did. In the end, the sheer presence of Esteban Garza was too much to endure. The priest backed away from the dead man and echoed Esteban's request to have the slaves return the shovels to the horses.

Father Rodriguez was defeated, though he convinced himself that he had relinquished for the sake of the other travelers and for the ongoing religious conversion of the slaves—a noble cause. But in actuality, the priest had stood down to protect himself from certain death. He knew that another minute of defying Esteban would have resulted in a bullet through his head. Whether he was guided by a hallowed deity or not, Father Rodriguez was an obstacle in Esteban's destined path. That much was apparent.

Esteban moved his hand away from his pistol, turned, and then marched forward. The rest of the caravan half-heartedly followed. They were cast as tiny beings against the huge mountainside, which looked like a great prehistoric beast hungry for the souls of foolish and ignorant men.

From then on, Father Rodriguez elected not to walk in the second position from the front. Instead, he found himself near the tail of the caravan where he could speak in private with the other soldiers who supported his attempted stance against Esteban Garza. "He leads us to death and nowhere else," muttered the priest to a handful of soldiers.

The soldiers chose not to respond. They were fearful that siding too convincingly with Rodriguez would encourage

Esteban's wrath. Instead, they simply listened and kept to themselves.

"Unless we find water soon, he dies, and I lead us the rest of the way," said Rodriguez as he eyed the men to gauge their interest or lack thereof.

One soldier nodded his head, another scowled, but the others elected not to display their sentiments and remain neutral.

5

By the late afternoon, two more slaves had been claimed by the summer heat. Like the other men, their corpses were left to rot under the burning sun. One of the fallen was a Pueblo teenager. The other was a middle-aged Navajo. They were both men that Esteban regarded as important laborers who would still be alive if their water rations hadn't been wasted by Father Rodriguez the previous night.

The caravan arrived at the first marker. There were twelve fist-sized stones arranged in a circular pattern, and inside the circle were two large stones leaning against each other. There was a carving on each stone. The first looked like a wagon wheel, and the other was a capitalized letter B.

The group rested near the marker in the shade of an aspen thicket. Half of the soldiers tried to sleep, while the other half kept a close eye on the distraught captives, the numbers of which had dwindled from fifteen to twelve. Father Rodriguez was seated near the soldiers eating a piece of bread and scribbling in his journal. His journal contained daily accounts of where the men had camped, what they hunted, the routes they traveled, the rivers and streams they crossed, and the tribes that they met or avoided along the way. With each entry, Rodriguez felt that it was his duty to be as descriptive as possible so that his journal could be used by future expeditions to locate the legendary gold mine in a much more informative manner than the Esteban Garza expedition.

Esteban confirmed the marker on the map and then climbed some twenty feet up the slope. He knelt at the base of a slate boulder with a sharpened knife in his good hand. With it, he carved an impression in the stone that displayed the year, 1733. He regarded his creation proudly before sharing a contemptuous glance with the priest. Father Rodriguez's eyes dropped to the bread he was holding, and he took a bite in an attempt to ignore the hostility between them.

There was a comforting stillness in the air accompanied only by the cheerful singing of Mountain Chickadees and the buzzing of the flies, which were delighted by the wretched smell of the filthy men, though some had more interest in the priest's bread. The view from Esteban's position revealed a seemingly infinite valley below. In the other direction, the taller peaks awaited the presence of the disgruntled expedition with open arms against a cloudless sky. Esteban was close to cracking a smile, which would have been the first since the journey started, but at that moment, he noticed a narrow column of smoke escalating over the tops of the towering aspens.

"Look," he said as he pointed at the smoke that rose into the mountain air.

Rodriguez and some of the soldiers were the next to see it, and there was a flurry of panic as they realized they were likely near a Ute encampment. If the Utes were to catch a glimpse of the expedition, then it would only be a matter of time before the Spanish were stalked, ambushed, and slaughtered. At least that was the conclusion the majority of the Spanish had reached, including Esteban. None of them had ever bumped heads with the Northern Ute. For all they knew, the people may be peaceful and welcoming; however, the land did not belong to the Spanish, and their key reason for scaling the mountain was to obtain resources from someone else's acclaimed province, an undertaking of such deviltry that one could only assume death would be the sentence.

The bloodthirsty Spanish, who had been fighting Native Americans for well over two centuries, had no intention of being diplomatic with a people they believed to be ruthless savages of inferior birth. Certain that they would be unwelcome and outnumbered, the expedition proceeded calmly and subtly, camouflaging themselves amongst the trees.

•

Further up the mountainside, the sounds of life and rustling trees once again displaced the uncomfortable silence. Esteban remained at the head of the caravan, while the other travelers staggered faintly behind, separated from and uncertain of their leader.

Esteban came to a stop at the pinnacle of a mountain ridge. An amused smile spread across his face as he looked back at the other travelers. His off-white smile, while imperfect, was distinct against his tanned and leathered flesh. The other soldiers and slaves glanced at one another with puzzled faces. They increased their pace, curious to observe the sight that was compelling enough to alter Esteban's character in such a profound way.

When they reached the ridge, which overlooked a broad mountain valley, they spotted the key to their survival—a small lake enclosed by pines and aspens. They could see that there were rapidly moving streams running from the easternmost portion of the lake. It was there where the drinking water, as well as the fishing, would be the most abundant. The men roared with delight as they charged down the slope toward the lake. Esteban held his ground proudly at the summit of the ridge and watched his revitalized men with an enduring, self-assured expression.

•

A pink sunset reflected on the water where the thirsty soldiers, slaves, and horses drank until their bellies nearly burst. The lake, which was nestled into a hillside, was like a secret—a place completely uncontaminated by an insatiable civilization.

Father Rodriguez attempted to pray at the base of an aspen for the souls of the men who had perished that day, though he struggled to concentrate amidst the splashing and shrieking of some of the men who were swimming in the stream. At the end of his frustrated devotions, he glared uneasily at them. They reminded him of young children, ignorant of any evildoing. He watched one man splash handfuls of water onto his face as another floated on his back, gazing upward at the rose-colored sky. Another soldier submerged himself, inhaled a mouthful of water, re-emerged, and then spat the contents back into the lake through a thin stream created by his front teeth and his bottom lip. They were comfortable at last, and they were jubilant. To Rodriguez, it was clear that they had all but forgotten their dead companion. Their leader had led them to a water source. Because of this, Rodriguez feared that Esteban had once again gained their trust and allegiance. This both irritated and demoralized him.

Several fish were jumping out of the water to feast on insects. A few slaves were fishing in the stream with crude fishing poles under the supervision of some of the soldiers. A flock of ducks flew overhead, quacking harmoniously while holding true to their uniformed, v-shaped aeronautics. For the second time that day, the travelers felt a surge of tranquility. Everyone but the troubled Father, who felt that he was losing any support that he may have gained earlier. Though, truth be told, Rodriguez's influence remained perfectly intact. Now that the men had recovered from the spellbound trance that eleven days of the fervent pace had unleashed upon them, some of them could see that the furious pace that Esteban demanded was responsible for the deaths of the three men and that it could have easily killed more. On the contrary, there were others who felt that Father Rodriguez was the one to blame.

Esteban sat contently at the base of an aspen, leaning his head against the slender, whitened trunk. He guzzled half of his canteen, wiped his mouth with his forearm, and then dumped the remainder of the water on his hair and face. The twilight of a scorching day spawned a gentle breeze that sifted through the leaves of the aspen overhead. Esteban watched the soldiers delight in the water source and quickly grew annoyed.

"Del Rio," he shouted, which drew the attention of the entire expedition. "Take the slaves into the grove and have them harvest some firewood before the light fades."

Without delay, Del Rio echoed the instruction to the captives. The naked soldiers stumbled awkwardly out of the water and then hurried for their clothing that was piled on the shore. In less than a minute, they were in their clothes and in the thicket with the slaves walking obediently in front of them. Father Rodriguez scurried after them to avoid being left alone with Esteban, who unfolded the map that accompanied the golden owl and rested it on his muscular thighs.

The colors and details were far more defined than they were when George Hendricks would acquire it a century and a half later. The eyes of the Great Horned Owl illustrated on the map seemed to regard Esteban welcomingly, and Esteban regarded the owl in a similar fashion. He ran his filth encrusted fingers across the owl's right wing and then moved them toward the center, stopping at the owl's beak, which read: *El Corona del Rey*—The King's Crown. A yellow grin emerged through his thick raven-colored beard. He felt the power of the owl surging within him. It was a force that had grown stronger with each step closer to the legendary gold mine.

6

The expedition formed a circle around the campfire that had been built near the lake. It was a cool night, and for the first time in over a week, the soldiers were forced to retrieve their woolen military coats to keep themselves warm. One of the soldiers had shot a fair-sized buck at dusk. The animal had been torn to shreds, cooked, and devoured by the merry soldiers, who continued to gorge themselves deep into the night while they swallowed mouthfuls of the cool mountain water. But, despite their thirst and hunger being satisfied, they remained wary of Esteban Garza.

The friction between Esteban and Father Rodriguez also continued. The two men had a common hatred for one another. It all stemmed from the fact that they disagreed wholly on the core objective of their mission. Father Rodriguez desired to confer with the Native Americans in order to convert them to what he thought was the "one true religion." Esteban wanted no part of it. He feared that it would jeopardize their chances of carrying out what he believed to be the chief goal of their mission: to obtain a substantial amount of precious gold and return it safely to Santé Fe. Despite their differences in judgment, Rodriguez could forgive Esteban for the intense pace and restless travel, but Esteban's refusal to bury the Spanish soldier remained an intolerable sin. It was an offense that the priest felt he would personally have to make amends for at some point, either in this life or in the hereafter. Esteban's wrath toward Father Rodriguez stemmed from his orders being superseded by supposed requests from the Lord God. To Esteban, each and every instance of alleged divine intervention instructed only foolishness. Such foolishness had peaked the previous evening when the day's water was squandered and three valuable slaves died of dehydration as a result.

The full moon was abruptly veiled by a sheet of cloud cover, causing the previously illuminated mountain backdrop to mutate into a deep black. The sudden darkness forced a measure of uneasiness upon the camp. Each man eyed the shadows of Esteban and Father Rodriguez in the lost moonlight. As the light faded, so too did the comforting sounds of the surrounding wildlife—the distant cries of the coyotes, the chirping of the birds, and the shifty movements of the large insects and rodents. It had grown uncomfortably quiet, and the weak fire's glow revealed nothing but dim and ominous faces.

A breeze picked up and caused the underbrush to sway and rub together. It sounded as if some huge invisible creature was moving about the camp in all directions. Some of the larger tree branches began to waver as the wind picked up. So did the campfire, which wisped violently back and forth. It was as if the grand force of nature had drawn closer to the camp and delighted in tormenting the weary travelers.

As the wind picked up, the leaves of the aspen trees overhead began to chatter, producing a sound that the men likened to the laughter of some heinous, ancient being. Most of the soldiers and slaves were overcome by a feeling of dread as the smoke from the campfire climbed into their nostrils, though some of them were ignorant of the strange phenomena. That was, until they heard a loud moaning sound from a neighboring area that caused the heart of every man to sink into their stomachs. The sound persisted for a moment, then its pitch shifted, and every pair of eyes looked upward. It sounded as if there were some massive being hovering above them emitting a strange humming noise that probed deep into their consciousness as if scanning their petty thoughts. But as their eyes surveyed the night sky, they saw nothing but an infinite cloud of darkness. Not a single star nor the moon was visible. As quickly as the strange sound had come, it was gone, and an unsettling silence returned.

The men looked at one another in search of an answer, though no one had one. Something incredibly unusual had occurred, and they all knew it. It was one of the Pueblo who broke the silence and spoke, though only the other Pueblo and Del Rio could understand him. He finished his passionate discourse, paused, and then attempted to speak again when he was struck in the mouth by one of the soldiers and ordered to keep quiet. This caught the attention of Esteban, who had not muttered a word since the camp was set three hours prior.

"What did he say?" Esteban asked in a patient voice.

Del Rio swallowed hard and then looked at the Pueblo, who was pressing his left hand against his bloodied lower lip. "I—I don't know that it would be appropriate, Captain. The words of this savage do not seem...practical."

"I did not ask for your opinion on what is practical and what is not," Esteban snapped. "Tell me what he said!"

"Well, Captain, the savage said...that an apparition has made its presence known within the camp and..."

"And what?"

"I'm sorry, Captain. With all due respect, I believe the savage is trying to instill terror into all of us. It is a trick."

"Answer me, Del Rio. Or you'll be laboring hand in hand with these slaves, and treated as one!"

"Forgive me...he says...that the apparition is the essence of a man, and that he has come to warn us of what lies ahead."

Some of the soldiers couldn't help but chuckle at such gibberish, though others were clearly frightened.

Esteban's face remained stoic. He hushed the giggling soldiers with a cold stare. "Carry on," he instructed.

Del Rio looked to the ground, embarrassed by having to repeat the Pueblo's words. "He says...that it is probably the spirit of one of the men who perished today...and—"

His words were interrupted by the Pueblo who once again spoke passionately and fearfully, though his words were difficult to understand because his hand was still pressed tightly against his bloodied lip.

When he finished speaking, Del Rio's mocking expression turned sour. "The savage claims that we'll never make it back to Santé Fe."

"Blasphemy," retaliated Father Rodriguez.

But as soon as he had spoken, he was overwhelmed by a sense of apprehension. Strangely, he knew that what the Pueblo said was true. By not burying the dead, they had unleashed an ill omen upon the entire group—one that would have to be paid with Spanish blood.

The darkness brought the giant spruce trees to life. They appeared to inch closer to the camp as they moaned and swayed in the evening breeze. Their branches scraped together, producing the sounds of creatures, real or not, that scurried threateningly around the camp and forced every soldier to put their hands near their weapons in anticipation. It was the perfect atmosphere for the ancient spirits to roam and share their forgotten tales of woe with things both living and dead. It was the force of the mountain, Nature's Wrath, just as it had been described in the earlier Spanish journals. The nocturnal wraiths haunted the mountain on that night and haunted it compellingly. The poor, wretched souls—they refused to admit that they were dead. Instead, they attempted to continue their lifecycle on their prior level of existence.

The Pueblo did not speak again. He sat timidly amongst his people with his scrawny arms shrouding his face.

A handful of the soldiers jeered and snickered at the Pueblo's outlandish talk, but Father Rodriguez was deeply troubled by it. He looked to Esteban for a response but was not granted one. Esteban remained silent and still with his golden eye occupied with the heart of the fire. It was as if Esteban had not even bothered to listen to Del Rio's translation, or as if he already knew of the inauspicious presence within the camp and accepted it wholly.

7

Two hours had passed since George returned from Helper with the golden owl figurine, and in that time, he still hadn't closed his eyes. He found that it was impossible to sleep with the promise of gold weighing on his mind, so he had stayed up admiring the object with nothing but a few Aura cigars and his father's monotonous snoring to keep him company. George was expected in the depths of the Rainville No. 4 in less than three hours. The thought of working his twelve-hour shift on only three hours of sleep made him sick to his stomach. He put out his Aura, forced his eyes closed, and tried to salvage what little sleep he could.

After only a matter of seconds, he heard the hoot of an owl. It sounded as if it were right outside his stone cabin. He sat still with his heart throbbing in his chest and listened carefully, but all he could hear was his father's snoring and the chirping chorus of a thousand crickets. The wind was blowing hard outside. It caused the rickety wooden door of the cabin to rattle. Then, with a loud BANG, the old door blew open and scared the hell out of George. Joe, on the other hand, continued to snore. He looked like a bear in hibernation.

It wasn't the first time the door had blown open. The vicious desert wind had blown it open a dozen times over the last two years. Still, it nearly gave George a heart attack every time it happened. George got out of bed and walked to the door. Just before he closed it, he heard the hoot of the owl again. He stood under the door frame and inhaled the clean, cool air. He felt that his intuition had heightened a great deal. His eyesight was keen, as was his hearing and his sense of smell. *Maybe it's a dream*, he thought to himself. *I must have fallen asleep. But it can't be a dream.* He could feel the cool night air caressing his face, and he could hear the bustling night shift crew hauling two loads of coal to the tipple. He listened for a moment while looking in the direction of the adjacent canyon, hopeful that the owl would reveal its position; however, before it could, something else caught his eye. It was the figure of a human being descending the hill in the pale moonlight.

As the figure drew closer, George could see that it was a woman. She had jet black hair, and she was not walking; she was floating, and the dress she wore was the color of snow. Many of Rainville's residents spoke of this woman. Her name was Thelma Ambrosius, and she had become somewhat of a local legend. George had only observed her once previously, but it was from afar. Now here she was, coming right at him and no more than thirty yards off. He decided to hurry back into his cabin, but when he tried, his muscles wouldn't let him. He was paralyzed by some unknown force. *It's a dream*, he reiterated to himself. But it wasn't. He was wide awake, and the phantom woman was drawing closer. George's heart was pounding. The sheer terror began to suffocate him. He felt as if he were about to pass out.

There was an ethereal quality about Thelma Ambrosius, who was now within ten feet. Her flesh, as well as her gown, were nearly transparent. She held in her hand an oil burning lantern, which was also transparent, though the flame that it housed appeared to be an actual flame. She was a beautiful young woman, though her beauty was somewhat hindered by a barrage of tears that were streaming down her pale face.

George could see that she was completely ignorant of his presence once she drew within five feet of him. Her black eyes stared directly through him. She floated right by, moaning and sobbing, and continued toward the larger buildings on the opposite side of the camp. Her luminance faded as she drifted away until all that was visible was her dim lantern, which finally disappeared altogether only fifteen yards from her destination—the mine office.

She couldn't see me, George thought. *I must not exist where she is, but she exists here.* He wondered why. Regardless of the answer, there seemed to be a formidable meaning behind it. The owl had lured him from his home because it wanted him to see that woman up close. But, why? The answer would not reveal itself on that night, and after seeing the lifeless face of Thelma Ambrosius, he would not sleep a wink.

8

The muted light of dawn revealed itself on the jagged hills and scattered plateaus. A maze of canyon badlands sprinkled with Rocky Mountain junipers and sagebrush was the home of the Rainville coal mine, which was built at the base of a robust canyon wall. The camp was made up of ramshackle cabins—some made of stone and some made of wood. George and Joe Hendricks had lived in one of the stone homes for nearly two years. There were also more than fifty tent homes erected far away from the cluster of cabins. The tents were raised on the low flatland in parallel, uniformed order, as opposed to the cabins, which were constructed erratically on the deforested uphill slope.

Also straggling the hillside was a tipple, which was elevated a good twelve feet above two sets of train tracks that passed underneath. The train tracks were owned by the Denver and Rio-Grande Railroad and connected Rainville to Helper, Helper to Springville, and Springville to places the miners didn't know existed.

There was a small, crumbling wooden shack near the tipple that served as the Rainville church. The pastor was always adamant about preaching the correlation between coal mining and the Lord's divine plan, as if Heaven Almighty was powered by coal.

Near the church were company owned stores, a schoolhouse, a jail, a pool hall, five bunkhouses, and an infirmary. Last, and certainly not least, was Wolf Blankston's large and luxurious home. It was three stories, and it was built upon the tall hillside—just a two minute walk from his office up a winding dirt road. None of the laborers had ever been inside of Wolf's home, but one of his maids and a cook had shared information about his estate. Inside, there were four bedrooms, a kitchen, a dining room, a large living room, and a massive study that contained his most prized hunting trophies and more books than a person could possibly read in a lifetime. All of the rooms were decorated with Wolf's two favorite colors, red and gold, and they were complete with walnut flooring. The staircase was also made of walnut with hand carved wooden balusters, and on top of the newel post was a bronze statue of a knight in shining armor.

Late in the day, the sun would move behind Wolf's home and project a massive shadow on the residential camp below. It was a constant reminder that Wolf Blankston towered over them, and that their hard work was fueling his lavish existence.

Further up the hillside and carved into the jagged rock was the entrance of the Rainville No. 4, braced by timbers from the neighboring pines. The main entrance of the mine was called a "portal." The name sounded like something from Science Fiction, and in a way, it was. The portal was a gateway to a strange subterranean world—a world of strange sounds and strange beings. Above the portal was an oblong, flat stone. Etched into it was the mine's title: *No. 4 Mine. Est. 1899.*

The oldest employee at the Rainville mine was Martin Paulson. He was fifty-nine-years-old, though he looked closer to ninety. He was frail and worn cruelly by decades of insatiable doses of tobacco and whiskey. On this morning, as he did every morning, he approached the portal of the Rainville No. 4 in the grayish dawn wearing his black mining trousers secured by suspenders that ran over the top of a white long-sleeved undershirt and a filthy, worn-out cowboy hat. He walked slightly hunched over with a limp as he scratched his prickled beard. He spat a healthy chunk of tobacco grit onto the ground then looked into the nether of darkness that waited to devour the men whole.

The iron cart tracks ran all the way through the mine like the giant veins of a subterranean beast. They twisted all the way down the hill and into the tipple where the coal was weighed and charted in order to calculate pay for the miners. It was then dumped through a chute into the boxcar of a transport locomotive.

Martin Paulson unloaded another mouthful of tobacco grit onto the ground as he arrived at a large brass bell just to the east of the mine's entrance. He set his feet, grabbed the bell-bar with both hands, and then pulled with everything he had. Shortly after, a sharp, melodious ring echoed through the cabins, tents, and bunkhouses. He set his feet once more, steadied his arms, and released another grunt. The bell discharged another piercing ring, which meant that the night shift had ended and the day shift was about to commence.

There was no set time limit on how many hours the men had to work as long as each crew pulled their weight. It could be anywhere between five and twelve hours a day depending on the demand for coal. At that time, the demand was high.

The tents and cabins began to open, and the coal miners within began to stumble out, willing to answer the dawn's reverberating call. Some of the men were already dressed in their blackened coal mining apparel with their tools in hand, needing only to fix a minor detail such as to button their jacket or fasten their headlamp to their cap. Others fumbled their way out of their homes trying to walk while slipping into their pants or rubber boots.

The headlamps that the men secured to their cotton caps were teapot lamps that burned sunshine wax—a product of the Standard Oil Company. Sunshine wax was a combination of wax and oil that would ensure that the lamps would burn through the duration of a long day. Though, every man did carry candles in case of an emergency. They used oil and wax to maintain a constant flame mounted to a cotton cap on their head. In essence, that was the extent of the safety regulations in the year 1900.

•

George sat at the wooden table in his stone cabin eating a bowl of breakfast oats, waiting for his father to rise. He wore black mining trousers, black boots, and a black jacket, and on the table was a black cloth mining cap with an iron oil-wick teapot lamp fixed to it. He held a spoon in his right hand, and to the left of his bowl was an opened book with an illustration filling the page. It was an image of two miners using a powerful drill together. A caption below the illustration read: *pneumatic drill.*

He swallowed a spoonful of oats and then stood and approached the lone window in the room, which faced the entrance of the No. 4 mine. He gazed out and saw two dozen men climbing the hill. George himself had climbed that hill every morning for the last two years. He would climb it for the final time on this day.

The bell on the hill rang again. George looked across the room to see that Joe was still asleep. George took the golden owl figurine from his pocket and gazed at it one last time before dropping to one knee. His eyes remained locked on Joe as his right hand hovered just above the brick flooring. Joe let out a loud, deep snore. As he did, George reached for a loose brick on the ground and lifted it free with his overgrown fingernails. He then reached for another brick, and it was also loose. He removed another, and another, until six bricks had been displaced. Underneath the bricks was a wooden cigar box that read *Aura Cigars* in black, faded letters. In a smaller font just below the brand name was the saying: *crafted the real way, the genuine way.* He retrieved the box from the hole and opened it. It was full of money, both paper and coins, amounting to nearly one hundred dollars—his life savings. What was left of it anyway after he had spent more than half of it the previous night on the golden owl figurine and *El Mapa del búho,* The Owl Map. There were also a few assorted knickknacks, such as a faded handwritten letter from his grandfather who had long since passed, a wooden spinning top, and a black and white photograph of his mother that was taken in 1885. George put the golden owl figurine inside the Aura Cigar box, put the box back in the hole, and then covered it with the crimson-colored bricks.

Once the bricks were in place, George returned to his chair. The bell on the hill sounded once more. But Joe didn't move a muscle.

"Come on, Pop," said George in frustration, trying to pronounce the words as stridently as possible without shouting.

Joe began to move subtly. He then let out a displeased grumble, indicating to George that he had awakened.

George closed his book titled *Modern American Mining Methods* and placed it at the top of eight other books that were all related to the subject of mining. They were books that he had purchased over the last ten years in an attempt to educate himself somewhat, though he often found fifteen minutes of reading to be more tiresome than twelve hours of underground labor.

Old Joe groaned once more, this time much louder. He then shot up to a seated position, cutting a loud, deep fart in the process. The aroma was repulsive. It was tainted with sour whiskey. Joe lifted the sleeves of his long-sleeved shirt to the elbows. Right away, his mind labored to remember where he was and what duties he was obliged to fulfill. He knew that he was being summoned to work underground, but he didn't know if it was to extract silver, salt, or coal— or if he was in New Mexico, Utah, or Colorado. It all ran together in his jumbled brain. His skin was pale, and his stout fingers were nearly worn to the bone. He was drenched in a cold sweat, and his hair was oily and shambolic.

George looked on without amusement. This had become a routine that he no longer regarded with pity or shame. With each passing day, his father died a little more internally, and as Joe died, some dark and angry thing within

George steadily grew. He had wasted precious years dragging his father by the seat of his pants from state to state just so they could afford to eat for a couple of months before Joe drank too much and wasn't able to perform a day's shift, and was let go because of it. And yet, it seemed as though the vicious cycle was nearing its end—a resolution that would propel George into the world to accomplish something of his own. He would leave his anguished past to be forgotten in the winding canyons of Rainville.

George retrieved his worn, filthy pickaxe, his jacket, his jacks, and his lunch pail from the wall and then turned to Joe. "Do ya need a hand this mornin'?" he asked.

"I'm fine," Joe snarled.

Joe lurched to his feet using the limp mattress as leverage. Immediately, he began rubbing his damaged knees with stiff movements. His knees, as well as his back, had been severely damaged from crouching in a dark hole every day for the last decade. He had a difficult time moving above ground, but it was even more difficult for him to maneuver through the tight confines of the mine.

"Ya goin' to the Town Hall tonight to hear what Blankston has to say?" George asked.

It was the talk of the town that Wolf Blankston had a presentation to make that evening at the Town Hall. The subject matter of it was still unknown to everyone except Wolf's entrusted circle, though the townsfolk feared the worst.

"I don't give a damn what he has to say!" Joe growled.

As Joe groaned and grimaced, George opened the door and shut it behind him—numbed to any compassionate feelings.

Poor Joe was a snippet of what he once was. He used to be a worthy, conscientious man who never settled for mediocrity. But ill-fate and sorrow had reduced him to someone who genuinely didn't care whether he lived or died. This dire outlook on life had affected George profoundly. George was by his mother's side the night she died, and he spent the next five seemingly endless days by his father's side as Joe wept until his eyes could no longer produce tears. When Joe purchased the ranch by the Elk River, it was supposed to provide a measure of redemption after he had lost his general store. It was supposed to be a place the Hendricks family could enjoy for decades to come—a place that would allow George to have a wife and a family and a place where Joe could live vicariously through the triumphs of his son's bright future. But when the animals began to die and the anticipation of a dreamlike future began to crumble, both Joe and George couldn't help but accept that fate had turned its back on them. *How could it be?* George often thought to himself. *How could we have lived such lives of honesty and diligence only to be kicked to the ground while so many despicable human beings slithered around dishonestly and were rewarded for it?*

As the years drifted by, George had transformed from a well-mannered, compassionate person to a man who barely spoke and who had grown cold and empty inside. He was angered by the misfortunes of the past. He had long felt that something was owed to him and his father for having to endure so much adversity. As more time passed, the more it seemed impossible that they would ever be compensated. With each day, the anger within George spread like wildfire.

To George, Wolf Blankston symbolized all that was soul-less and corrupt in the world. Wolf was a man who knew nothing of pain and suffering and who, at least to George's knowledge, had never had to toil for anything in his life. He was a rich, arrogant dignitary who used transients and immigrants as slaves so that he could enjoy a gluttonous existence. That was the way George saw it. It had been foolish of him to think that fate would reimburse those who had suffered. And yet, he had believed it with all his heart for many years. It was finally becoming evident that there were no patron saints or fairy godmothers that would make right all that was cruel and unjust in the world. The world was unjust, and it would always be unjust. There were only the consequences of his assertive actions.

George stood in front of his stone cottage and watched the men stagger from their tents or cabins and walk lazily up the hill destined for one of the four Rainville mines. He could hear some of them sharing profanity laden theories of what Wolf Blankston would announce at the Town Hall later that day. George took a deep breath, inhaling the aroma of the junipers and the morning dew, and then forced the particles of shame and anger through his nostrils. Satisfied, he started to walk in the midst of a dozen other men who would reach the mine's entrance before the sun peaked over the mountain and filled the valley with tilted shadows. The magpies squawked annoyingly in the dawn as they pillaged the hillside for something to gorge themselves with, and the whistle of an approaching locomotive echoed off the canyon walls.

George heard footsteps next to him, walking in sync with his. But when he turned, he saw nothing. He paced onward. Much to his dismay, the footsteps continued. He looked again, this time tilting his head further downward. There was a six-year-old boy dressed in full mining attire with a brunette-colored smoking pipe in his mouth. The boy's face was still mottled with coal dust from yesterday's shift, most notably around his mouth and on his lips, like he had eaten a handful of coal for breakfast. He took a drag from the pipe and exhaled a little cloud of smoke. All the while, he kept his youthful, suspicious eyes on George.

"Hurry up, Jimmy," called an adult ten paces ahead.

The child took the pipe out of his mouth and smiled at George, revealing four missing teeth, two of which were right in front. He then ran forward to catch up with his father.

By law, a child had to be at least fourteen to work in the mines, but this law was almost always ignored. It was a win-win scenario for the parents of the children, who would reap the rewards of the extra income, and for Wolf Blankston, who didn't have to pay them as much as a legal laborer. Thanks to the fact that Wolf Blankston was old friends with the state mine inspector, children were allowed to labor in the depths of Rainville as much as they and their families pleased. Obviously, having young children laboring underground was highly dangerous, so they were usually hired as a Nipper or a Spragger—positions less likely to get themselves or others killed.

To George's right was one of the bunkhouses where more ragged coal miners stumbled out prepared for a hard day's work. Since these men were unmarried immigrants or drifters, the majority of them looked far more ragged than those who lived in the cabins and tents. There were a total of five bunkhouses—one for the Italians, one for the Finnish, one for the Greeks, and two others for everyone else.

Each bunkhouse housed roughly twenty men who were packed into the tiny space like sardines. Inside, it reeked of sweat and coal—a stench that was almost ten times more intolerable than George and Joe's rotten smelling cabin. The space looked much more like an army barracks than a company bunkhouse. There were tightly crowded, under-sized bunks that were stacked three high. The only place where a man could keep his personal effects was in an apple box that was hammered into the foot of each bunk. Most of the laborers who lived in the bunkhouses owned very few possessions, but they knew that if they were to leave something in the apple box during their shift, then that object would be long gone by the time they returned.

The vision of the bunkhouse disappeared, and a different building came into view—the main company store where some of the women from town were already assembling after their husbands had disappeared underground. It was payday, and the women had gathered at the company store in order to redeem their husbands' paychecks. They had little choice. If their dimwitted husbands got their hands on the paychecks first, then they would likely blow it all later that evening on booze and gambling and force their wives and children to suffer through another week of malnour-ishment. Of course, no man wished such privation to afflict his family, but the narrow chances of doubling one's money outweighed virtually any consequence.

A night out in a coal camp worked in a reckless yet accu-rate progression. The first and second drinks generally con-tributed little. The third tended to insert a hint of audaciousness, and the fourth was likely to instill a measure of comfort. The fifth was accompanied by a permanent grin and a warm, gentle tingle, and the sixth and seventh tended to ensure that any money the patron entered the premises with would be gone by the end of the night. After a seventy-hour work week, no solace existed like that of a whiskey bottle, a blackjack table, or a whore's bed.

Next, George approached the tipple, the place where the coal was weighed and charted so that the company knew how much to pay their laborers. The tipple boss maintained a clipboard where the weight of each load was recorded. But, like everything else, there was a catch. The miners were not allowed to see what the tipple boss wrote on the clipboard. He always called out the weight, but the miner never knew whether he was lying or not. Those who were assigned to Wolf Blankston's "shit-list" often found that they were being cheated on weigh-ins. Most of the men knew the weight of their loads just by looking at them, especially the old timers, and when they were cheated, they were fully aware of it; however, kicking up a fuss was futile as long as they wanted to keep their jobs at Rainville.

Many of the laborers could recall the man who once argued with the tipple boss about a weigh-in. Wolf's highest ranking goons, Leonard Pearl, Carter Hirsh, and Walker Thompson, had him beaten and thrown in jail for a whole month—on top of being fired. Those who committed only petty missteps against the company would be cheated five to ten percent of their payload for a week or two, but those who really angered Wolf would be cheated as much as twenty-five to thirty percent for several weeks, if not months, and there wasn't a damn thing they could do about it.

After passing the company store and the tipple, George advanced toward a large stone structure. There were two rectangular brass tags on the door of this building. The first read: WOLF BLANKSTON, and the second, RAINVILLE MINE OWNER. On the building itself, stamped in bold black lettering was the title: WOLF BLANKSTON MINING COMPANY. Reading Wolf Blankston's name on the building every morning only added to George's disdain of the man who profited so greatly from all of his back-breaking labor. Most of the men who walked by the mine office wanted to run upstairs and give Wolf Blankston a feisty kick to the ballsack, but they knew the consequences would be too severe. George eyed the building, looked away in disgust, and kept walking.

Next up was the Rainville cemetery. It was enclosed by a white picket fence, though the paint had nearly flaked off entirely and moisture had severely warped the wood. All of the graves were mixed and matched. Some were given a headstone, and others were given a simple wooden cross. The headstones, some fancy and some basic, were purchased by the deceased's still living relatives. The wooden crosses were for the miners who died and had no family or money left behind. There were over fifty bodies buried in the cemetery—fortunate souls whose mortal remains were salvaged from the countless disasters. There were at least fifteen skeletons in the hill that would never be retrieved because it was too dangerous to do so. Within the abandoned tunnels, the spirits of those men were said to be wandering for eternity.

From the top of the ridge just above the mine's portal, a Finnish man by the name of Jari Ronni feasted on a green apple. He had long, oily auburn hair and a scruffy beard. He was dressed in black work pants with red suspenders that ran over a white long-sleeved shirt.

He began to holler at the miners in a heavy Finnish accent. "Be careful down there everyone. Lord knows more of this hill will come down as long as that son of a bitch keeps pinching his pennies!"

No man slowed his pace. They hardly had a choice. If Wolf Blankston himself wasn't keeping an eye on Jari, then one of his spotters were. A "spotter" was an employee that Wolf paid a little extra to keep their eyes and ears open for those who might be looking to cause trouble. But Wolf's spotters were asked to report much more than that. They were to report those who were badmouthing Wolf or the company, even when they were off the clock. In fact, most of the men who received Wolf Blankston's wrath were those who had too much to drink and spoke their mind to a small group of trusted friends within the comfort of their own home. No matter where you were, there was always a spotter listening. Nobody knew exactly how many of them there were. Rumor had it there were between ten and twenty of them—a number that was quite troubling for a town of just over two hundred. It was almost impossible for anyone to say anything negative about Wolf Blankston anywhere in the Rainville camp.

To acknowledge Jari Ronni would be to oppose Wolf Blankston. Those who opposed Wolf Blankston would end up on the shit-list. So instead of acknowledging Jari, the men walked with their eyes fixed on the portal. Still, every man couldn't help but glance at Jari with the utmost subtly, enough to assure Jari that they were actually listening. This granted him the courage to persist with his condemnation.

"Look at all of you," Jari continued, "walking blindly into that mine like a herd of cattle walking into a slaughterhouse! Wolf Blankston doesn't give a goddamn about any of you!"

Even though Jari was pleased that some of the men were listening, he expected more. He had walked to the mouth of the Rainville No. 4 with the intent of starting a revolution. He was frustrated by the lack of patronage. He spiked his half-eaten apple directly into the ground and gritted his brown and yellow teeth together. He then yelled, "How many more have to die before you yellow-bellies realize we have to do something?"

His words were much more pronounced, and his face was the color of blood. George allowed the words to sink in, but he chose not to provide him with a knowing glance.

"You're all a lot more fortunate than I am," Jari cried. "I have two brothers buried in that cemetery over there!"

Jari and his two brothers, Timo and Veli, had come to America with their families from Finland ten years prior and eventually found themselves at the Rainville camp along with a dozen other countrymen. Unfortunately for Jari, two of the four men who had been killed within the last two months were Timo and Veli Ronni. Veli had been the latest victim. Three days earlier, he had inhaled a lethal dose of carbon monoxide in the Rainville No. 2 mine.

"I told Wolf Blankston where he could stick it, and he let me go for it," Jari continued. "Something must be done or that criminal is going to keep walking all over you like dogs! Do you hear me?"

This statement stopped George in his tracks six feet from the portal. When his curious eyes met Jari's, dozens of other men looked at George as though he was guilty of some great crime. Realistically speaking, he was.

"George!" Jari pleaded. "Tell them, George. They'll listen to you. They respect you. Stand with me here and now!"

George dipped his head for a moment and then looked at Jari with a face full of sorrow. "I'm sorry, Jari. What's happened to you and your brothers ain't right, but I'm nobody."

George retrieved a box of striking matches from his pant pocket. He struck a match, lit his teapot lamp, shook out the flame, and then discarded the castoff match in the dirt beside his feet. He secured the teapot lamp to his cotton cap and then paced forward.

"George, wait! You're wrong!" cried Jari.

His words faded as George entered the portal and was swallowed whole by the darkness. Nonetheless, Jari's words had hit home. The fury inside George amplified the more he thought about Jari and his fallen brothers—lives donated to increase Wolf Blankston's fortune.

Once he was underground, the hillside rumbled and echoed overhead due to the incredible mass that was held up by crude cuts of lumber. The timbering cried and creaked. It sounded like wailing specters and forgotten souls. Dozens of men had lost their lives in Rainville's dangerous tunnels, but their ghostly presence remained, scouring the gloomy depths for things uncertain to the living mind. As an underground miner, accepting death as a job disclaimer was not only a formality but a necessity. And though George was facing death, he had a much greater problem on his hands.

9

From the second level of the large stone building, the mine's owner, Wolf Blankston, had pushed the drapes aside to look out the window and watch his men enter the mine's portal like ants scurrying into an ant hill. He glared uneasily at the men he depended so heavily upon. Specifically, he had been paying close attention to Jari Ronni's charade. He had watched George Hendricks stop and mutter something to the foul peasant. One of his spotters had certainly heard what was said between the two men, and Wolf would expect a report by lunch time. When he received this report, he would find that George and Jari's conversation was fairly harmless. Still, George had voiced that what Wolf Blankston had done "ain't right" and that he was sorry for Jari. That was more than enough for George to find his way onto the shit-list.

Wolf, who was the only child of an English father and a German mother and was named after his German grandfather, was smoking a fine cigar and was dressed in a stylish striped suit with a black top hat and a pair of horn-rimmed spectacles. Most men had to tilt their head down to look into the eyes of Wolf Blankston. He was only about five foot six inches in height. He was also one of few men in the Rainville camp who packed a protruding gut—he was a well fed, fat man.

His office was cluttered with material possessions—furniture, model trains, small statues, plaques, clocks, broken telegram machines, and unused kerosene lanterns. Hanging on the wall behind his desk was the focal point of the room—a large oil painting of himself in a gray patterned suit, standing in front of the fireplace at his home. He looked like a great emperor in the painting, like Napoléon Bonaparte, and less like a man who owned a mining operation located somewhere outside East Jesus.

Wolf was making good money, but he felt that he should have been making more. He was dissatisfied by this reality. He often mused, *if it wasn't for these careless, lazy peons, we'd double the production, or perhaps triple it.* Right when a measure of consistency settled in and the men started to produce significant quantities, there would be another accident that would damage the structure of one of the mines and force that particular mine to idle, thus cutting off twenty-five percent of the entire operation's production.

Circling the blood red walls of the room were a total of twelve mounted deer heads. They all seemed to stare bemusedly at Wolf, the man responsible for their termination. Their lifeless heads were the essence of the eldritch office, but to Wolf they were comforting. Perhaps they were the only friends within the Rainville camp that he had to his name. Of course, the spirits of the dead animals would probably protest to the idea of being Wolf's pals, but their cosmetic remains were unlikely to object. Wolf would see to it that the antlered heads would favor his verdicts each and every time, no matter how flawed or uniformed or regardless of the mess they would eventually cause. The deer never disagreed, they never talked back, and he didn't have to pay them a dime. They were such glorious creations! If only they were capable of mining the tunnel walls!

The deer heads would sometimes shriek. This was not a sound that Wolf feared, but a sound that he delighted in. It was not actually the sound of wailing animal spirits. It was the sound of metal on metal—the screeching coal carts being schlepped to and from the tipple just beyond his office. It was the sound of his fortune growing.

Even though Wolf was a hated man, there was one human being who interacted with him on a daily basis and in fact shared an office with him. In the corner sat Stanton Pierce, the mine's superintendent and longtime family friend. Stanton was the second oldest of three children who belonged to Rodney Pierce—Wolf's former classmate and closest friend of all who had made a name for himself in the oil business. When Wolf ventured into eastern Utah coal, Rodney Pierce agreed to invest a great deal of money in Wolf's coal company. In exchange, Rodney's second oldest son, Stanton, was to become heir to the Wolf Blankston Mining Company upon Wolf's retirement. Rodney's oldest son, Andrew, was to inherit his father's oil business.

When Stanton arrived, he quickly learned that Wolf would have to die first. He would never retire. He was far too gluttonous to pass the reigns to someone else, no matter how old or sick he became. He was like one of those U.S. congressmen that clung to their positions for forty or fifty years—like a rotting apple clinging to an apple tree—

unwilling to relinquish the money and power after hoarding it for over half their life.

It would be a stretch to claim that Wolf and Stanton were pals. They tolerated one another. Ultimately, they used one another for their more prominent interests. Wolf had trained Stanton to never say no, to never ask why, and to never repeat a suggestion after Wolf dismissed it the first time. It was Wolf's grand show, and Stanton was his marionette—one of hundreds of marionette's that belonged to Wolf Blankston.

Stanton was generally well-liked by the men. He was friendly and genuine, and he always remembered everyone's name. He was so friendly that Wolf often scolded him for it. To Wolf, friendliness was weakness. He feared that if Stanton was too gracious then the men might try to take advantage of him. Stanton was a thin, clean man who was two decades younger than Wolf and seventy-five pounds lighter. His hair was freshly cut and dirty blonde, and he wore a moustache that was combed downward, covering his upper lip completely. His suit was not as extravagant as Wolf's, nor was his roll top desk, which was packed tightly into the corner as though Wolf was trying to hide the man who chewed through most of his busy work on a daily basis. Stanton's loyalty to Wolf was that of a middle-aged dog's loyalty to a rotten master. On occasion, he wanted to defy his master, but he knew that a wrong move may result in an empty bowl or a smack on the behind.

Wolf knew that the residents of his camp disliked him, but he didn't care. He was a profitable businessman, and he did what he had to do to keep his operation running, no matter what. He provided a livelihood to the miners and their families, regardless of how sad those lives were. Because of him, people could eat. He believed that was all a human being could ask for in those days. As the old saying went, "Don't bite the hand that feeds you."

George had nibbled on that hand, so to speak, by acknowledging Jari Ronni's blathering. It didn't matter to Wolf what was said between George and Jari. Jari was the enemy, and he was to be ignored. Even though George planned to leave town the next day, Wolf was historically a vindictive man. It wasn't unlike him to bring suffering upon an entire family for one person's actions. If he did decide to seek revenge on George, then there was a possibility that he would make Joe suffer as well, which—depending on the severity of the punishment—was something that could foil George's plan to escape Rainville.

On a positive note, this was an important day for Wolf Blankston. Later that evening, he was to host an event at the Town Hall and announce something momentous to the residents of Rainville. With that being the case, there was a chance that George's misconduct could be forgotten. Wolf kept a tight lid on the topic of his big announcement. He knew that everyone in the camp feared for their jobs, which in turn made them fear for their lives and the lives of their families. This provided him with a twisted air of authority.

10

Esteban Garza's team survived the seemingly endless night with very little sleep. Their eyes were indolent and red, their bodies were fatigued, and their muscles and joints were tender and taut. Regardless of this, they pushed on toward The Mountain of the Owl in the weak morning light, diffused as it was by a blanket of cloud cover. There was an unsettling vibe emanating from a thin layer of fog that hung about the grassy terrain. Each man felt as though every movement, every action, and every thought was being analyzed by some supreme force of nature. Whether or not the uncanny ambiance was linked to the ghostly presence that was allegedly in the camp the preceding night remained to be determined.

The person who was most intrigued by such a correlation was Father Rodriguez, who walked near the Pueblo who had spoken of the phantasm the previous night. The slave's cut lip had hardened and colorized into the shade of a ripened beet. Rodriguez eyed every move the slave made, as though attempting to read the intentions of the spirit through the slave's body language. His newfound curiosity toward the Pueblo and the wandering spirit was problematic to say the least. He had been interested in tales of ghosts and spirits at a young age, but through the teachings of the church, he learned that any interaction with a nonphysical entity, besides the Lord God, was considered to be akin to interacting with the devil himself.

The Spanish undoubtedly likened the Native American beliefs to devil worship, which couldn't have been further from the truth; however, they spread the word of Christianity to the American tribes because they felt it was "for their own good." And now, Father Diego Rodriguez was convinced that a stalwart of Satan was amongst them, and that the Pueblo had the power to converse with it.

Much to the disappointment of Father Rodriguez, the Pueblo didn't say a word all day. Even though the bizarre tone of the early morning suggested that something was awry, the Pueblo declined to acknowledge that anything was out of the ordinary.

•

The group was trekking through a thicket of aspen trees when they stumbled upon a Great Horned Owl eating a large critter. The expedition came to halt and watched in sheer wonder as the owl used its claws to hold the critter against the ground while its beak ripped the flesh from the carcass. The Great Horned Owl looked up at the men with its beak covered in blood, but it held its ground. Esteban drew his pistol and crept toward it. He came to a stop twenty yards from the owl, steadied his pistol, and then fired. Just as he pulled the trigger, the Great Horned Owl darted upward unscathed. They watched as the owl flew away. It was headed for the mountain in the distance—The Mountain of the Owl.

Lying on the ground was the corpse of a large brown hare. Its head was completely detached and half eaten. One of the eyeballs had been pried loose from its socket and the spine was protruding from the decapitated body.

●

Many hours later, they reached a landmark of considerable importance. It may not have looked like much, merely a four foot tall heap of rocks, but the cairn was the gateway to *El Corona del Rey*. It was here where the goatskin map became irrelevant and the golden owl figurine became everything. There were four canyons ahead of them—some close, some miles off—one to the north, one to the northwest, one to the west, and another to the northeast. According to the map, only one of the canyons would lead to the mine. The golden owl and the cairn stone were needed to reveal which canyon was the correct one.

Esteban turned to his men with a smile.

"This is it. We're close." Then he approached the cairn.

The top of it was covered with a random assortment of rocks that seemed to bear little meaning, but then Esteban seized one of them with his good hand and dropped it on the ground beside his feet. He repeated this action with another rock, and then another, until it became apparent that the first layer of rock was concealing the true secret—a large, flat stone containing additional carvings and Spanish writing.

He removed nearly thirty small rocks before the entire face of the "keystone" was revealed. The keystone was a slab of red shale that had been carved on by a Spanish expedition of years previous. There was a thin layer of mud covering the top of it, but it was wiped clean by Esteban's good hand. Centered on the keystone was an indentation of the golden owl figurine. Next to it was the phrase *muestra el camino*. At the bottom of the stone was a large N, indicating the direction north.

Esteban took the golden owl from his neck and put it face down in the indentation. Running the length of the golden owl's wings was the phrase *el ala derecha,* and it rested next to the phrase *muestra el camino*. After eleven days of grueling travel, the final path was about to be revealed.

Esteban's amber-colored eye found the right wing of the golden owl. It pointed toward the valley below—the direction they had just come from. Esteban swallowed nervously. It made little sense that the map would lead them all the way into the high mountain, only to instruct them to descend it again. It was a clever ruse, but Esteban saw through it. He knew there was one more secret to unlock and that he was in need of his compass. He put the compass on the stone with the dial facing upward, gripped the cairn plate with his right hand, and then gave it a firm tug. The shale keystone scraped hard against the underlying stone, and the entire face shifted slightly. When it came to a stop, Esteban re-adjusted the compass so that it once again pointed north. He repeated this action until the N on the cairn plate mirrored the N on the compass. When it did, the right wing of the golden owl pointed toward the entrance of a narrow canyon to the north by northeast.

"The right wing reveals the way," Esteban said to himself.

•

When the travelers arrived at the narrow canyon entrance, they found adjacent walls that were almost thirty feet in height. They also found that the passageway was nearly blocked by a massive boulder. The positioning of the boulder was odd. It didn't seem to have fallen from anywhere in proximity. It was as if it had been placed there by some trick of levitation, or by the brute strength of some towering giant in order to warn trespassers of the wickedness that awaited.

A lizard scurried from the underlying shadows of the boulder and came to a stop at the pinnacle of it. The creature gazed mockingly at the men and even stuck out its forked tongue, as if to demonstrate how foolish they were for thinking they could pass through unscathed.

The emaciated slaves slipped between the canyon wall and the huge boulder with ease, as did the fit soldiers. The only man who struggled to get by was Father Rodriguez, whose bulging gut rubbed on the rock before he was able to squeeze through. The horses presented a much greater challenge. The first horse slithered through unharmed, though it was thinner than the second horse, which raked its ribs against the boulder leaving a small lesion that bled lightly. The third and fourth horses slipped through unscathed, as did the sixth, but the final horse was the largest and the oldest. Because of the animal's considerable bulk, it seemed impossible that it would make it through.

"This horse will not fit," declared a soldier.

"Yes it will. It is smaller than Hugo," said another soldier, referring to another large horse that had already passed through.

"No," argued yet another soldier. "This animal is much wider at the ribs, it will not make it."

"Perhaps there is another way?" Del Rio proposed.

Esteban had enough. "Another way?" he scoffed. "We will not veer from our destined path and risk getting lost for the sake of a horse. Tell the slaves to force the beast through!"

His instructions were echoed by Del Rio. The slaves eyed one another. They were certain the large horse would not fit. Two of them took the reins of the horse and pulled, but the horse only anchored its weight into the ground and released a loud shriek—expressing its doubt and disapproval.

"Pull harder!" Esteban boomed.

Del Rio echoed the order.

The slaves dug in and pulled the great beast with all their might. The horse finally lifted its front legs and put them on the base of the boulder.

"You see, it's working," Esteban bragged.

But the soldiers and slaves remained skeptical. The horse had no choice but to try and leap over the lower part of the boulder. When its iron horseshoes came down on the hard rock, the animal lost its footing, and its mass came crashing down. The intense impact had broken two of the horse's ribs and left the beast wedged between the boulder and the tall canyon wall, shrieking in both tremendous pain and horror. The men worked furiously to try and pry the horse free, but it only slipped further into the crevice. The grim realization set in that even if they were able to pry the animal free, it would no longer be of use to them.

The cargo was redistributed to the backs of other horses and slaves, and then the old horse was put down by Esteban's flintlock pistol.

"This is not a good omen," said Father Rodriguez.

Esteban looked at the priest with distain. He didn't believe in omens or luck or karma. He only believed in actions and consequences.

•

The clouds darkened in the west and appeared to be headed their way. Esteban demanded his customary hurried pace, hoping they would outrun the storm. Every minute or so, the soldiers turned their heads to keep an eye on the dark clouds as they rumbled and stirred. They all secretly hoped that it would catch up to them soon so they could set up camp early for the night and get a much needed extended rest. But when the storm finally arrived, it brought with it a mere shower that sprinkled their hair and faces. It was nowhere near enough for Esteban to constitute a halt in progress. So they kept on—deeper into the strange, remote canyon.

•

They hiked next to a thick barrier of pine trees while a blood-red sunset flashed on and off of their faces. The sun disappeared and then reappeared as they strode past each pine trunk. With each step, the massive globe of light would follow, like the watchful eye of the mountain.

It had been hours since anyone in the group had heard the chirp of a bird, the buzz of an insect, or the skittering of a rodent. The only sound that was present was a light breeze that whispered through the trees, bringing them to life. The eeriness of the isolated canyon crept into the stomach of every man. The force of nature was potent on The Mountain of the Owl, and the rashness of the Spanish team had allowed them the courage to invade it and to even utilize it for its rich minerals.

We shouldn't be here, Father Rodriguez thought to himself.

Simultaneously, every soldier and slave was thinking the same thing. But something much more dark and influential stirred inside of Esteban Garza. An impish grin blossomed on his face. As it did, the clouds seemed to darken, and as he brushed his arm forward, the intensity of the wind seemed to pick up simultaneously. Overhead, a Great Horned Owl flapped its wings. The soldiers and slaves heard the flapping and looked up, but they were blinded by the shafts of light that bled through the red clouds above.

Now that Esteban was so close to the legendary mine, he would stop at nothing to find it. Obsession had latched onto him, and such an obsession would never let go.

•

The blue twilight shined on Esteban's scarred and weathered face. His coarse hands caressed the dried bark of a dead tree with a crude carving of a Great Horned Owl. This was it, and each man couldn't help but rejoice in the fact that twelve days of tireless travel had come to an end.

The density of the pine trees wavered at that spot. By looking at the trees, the Spanish could tell that the bottom branches had once been cut to create a path to a mountainside on the opposite side of the thicket. Esteban went first, and the others followed. They all had to duck and dodge a few errant branches, but soon they emerged from the thicket into a small clearing against a steep incline.

The entrance of the mine was dug into the mountainside. It was so small that the men would have to crawl on their hands and knees to enter it. It looked more like a bear's den and less like one of the wealthiest gold mines that the Spanish had developed. Above the opening was a large rock formation that resembled a King's Crown, similar to the depiction on Esteban's map. Despite the unthreatening size, there was something wicked about the entrance of the gold mine. Darkness secreted from it like an evil force, creeping onto the surrounding terrain. It was a force that Esteban was already well acquainted with. It had been growing within him for days. Now that he had arrived, he felt entirely at its mercy. There was also a foul stench in the air, one that Esteban recognized immediately.

"This place reeks of blood," he said.

•

They finished setting up camp just before the darkness set in. Even though they had traveled all day for twelve days in a row, the slaves were already in the mine extracting the precious ore. Esteban sat in front of a campfire and smoked tobacco from a clay smoking pipe while a breeze ruffled the pines. Esteban eyed every sound suspiciously, as if each one were the encroaching Ute ready to launch their ambush.

Just as he relaxed, a loud snapping sound sent a jolt of terror through his heart, causing him to drop his clay pipe and draw his flintlock pistol. When a pine cone the size of a fist fell into the radius of the fire's light, he grew ashamed of himself for allowing such a silly thing to scare him so potently. But that was how eerie the atmosphere of The Mountain of the Owl was—eerie enough to frighten even the fearless Esteban Garza. Who could blame him for being afraid? The wind rustling through the trees sounded like the wailing of a thousand tormented souls, and the thin air had restricted the flow of oxygen, creating a lethargic state of mind—one that made it difficult for the members of the expedition to maintain their grip on sanity.

Esteban holstered his pistol and then picked up his pipe and put it back in his mouth. He set alight a twig in the fire and used it to reignite his tobacco.

Del Rio emerged from the entrance of the mine with a chunk of earth in his hand. He presented the sample to

Esteban, who repositioned himself closer to the fire to get a better look at it.

It was igneous rock with a hint of quartz and an impressive streak of gold. The gold glistened as he rotated it from side to side. His amber-colored eye shifted in color to the equivalence of the gold, and the power of it surged within his body. But the sample that he held was inadequate compared to what The Mountain of the Owl truly beheld. He had heard rumblings of those in Santé Fe who spoke of "enough gold to finance a military capable of world domination with plenty left over to pave all of Spain with golden roads." He was confident that the mountain was full of gold. He felt the power of the rich mineral whispering to him—sharing its greatest secrets—and suggesting that the wealth that was to be extracted over the coming months could be his entirely, if he wanted it.

11

As George walked through the main level of the Rainville No. 4 mine, the lamps and candles of other men surfaced and then vanished as they moved through the bends and turns on the way to their assigned coalfaces. Around the first bend were the underground stables where the burros were kept. The stables smelled of urine and feces and were tended by a teenage boy who happened to look and behave like a burro. His hair was the color of copper, and his eyes were small and dark. Each morning, he would smile at every man who walked by. When he did, his raised upper-lip would reveal large, square teeth. On occasion, he would even let out a weird laugh that was always mistaken as a squeal from one of the burros.

As the sounds of the burros faded, a solitary light drew closer. With it came the sound of an old man singing in a rugged and raspy voice:

> *"You could look at the rib or the face or the top,*
> *Never a sign or a laggin' or a slap or of prop;*

Someday I expect that old mountain to drop
And come down, down, down."

The lyrics played over in George's mind. He had listened to the singing of that old man every day for the last two years, but on this day, something about the singing troubled him. It was all too likely that George would become the old man singing in the mine if he stuck around too long, and he knew it.

As he walked further down the tunnel, he felt a shortness of breath. He stopped and took a deep, soot-filled inhalation. The ventilation throughout the Rainville No. 4 was primitive to say the least, as was everything else. There were no safety helmets, no safety training, no high-tech ventilation, no heavy steel roof bolts, no steel-toed boots, no methane meters, and no durable timbering. Wolf Blankston could certainly afford the latest and best accommodations, but he had no interest in dumping money into such things. What the miners *did* have was a canary—the canary in the coal mine—and if the canary, or perhaps even a coworker dropped dead, then one knew he needed to get out.

As George gasped for air, he heard a ruckus coming toward him.

"Clear out!" yelled a voice from the ensuing darkness.

George stopped and leaned against the rib to allow the muck train to pass hopeful that it wouldn't smack his shin or his knee cap, which was something that had happened to him nearly a dozen times during his career underground. The muck train—which was simply a burro pulling a loaded coal cart—passed, and so too did the burly men who were leading it through the passageway.

George arrived at a rickety ladder that led down a winze a good twenty-five feet below. He steadied his hands on the uppermost rail, but before his foot touched the first step, he heard a deep groaning sound coming from further down the tunnel. A paralyzing fear shot through him. He had heard many sounds underground over the last decade. While he had grown accustomed to most of them, he had never heard this particular sound in his life. It sounded like the groaning of a human being combined with the wailing of some kind of animal.

George stared fearfully into the darkness. The hair on his arms and neck stood tall. The mine was chockfull of strange sounds that often couldn't be identified, but the noises that were generally blamed on wandering spirits usually had an explainable origin. There were certainly some sounds in the mine that were so outlandish that even the most esteemed scientists and engineers would be left baffled, at least initially. Could there be sounds that had no explanation? After all, the darkness was capable of hiding secrets of time, space, and the vast unknown. At least, that's what the superstitious miners liked to think.

George had experienced too many strange incidents underground to comprehend them all rationally. In fact, most of them were utterly incomprehensible. He had felt the presence of people wandering through the tunnels—people who were not human beings. They had spoken to him, and he spoke to them. He had heard their laughs, whispers, and cries, and he had even felt their icy touch against his own flesh. Had the wraiths of the past made their presence felt once again? George did not know. He wanted to believe that the groaning sound was the timbering rubbing together with tremendous force, but he couldn't ignore the fact that three men had been killed within the same proximity during his stint in Rainville.

The sound did not return, so George steadied himself and climbed down the ladder. Each step released a muddled creak. He hopped off without the aid of the last three rungs, and his boots made a loud thud as a ruffle of dust lifted into the air. The smell of the surrounding earth had grown less obvious to George over the years. When he made his first descent underground a decade earlier, he had been overwhelmed by claustrophobia and the smell of earthy dampness. But now the scents of the mine were as natural to him as the scent of manure was to a cattle rancher. George too had grown accustomed to the smell of manure. Those damn burros shat where they pleased. Some of the miners did, too.

At the base of the ladder was the No. 2 drift where men had recently been complaining of headaches, and their lamps burned low because of the poor ventilation. It was also the drift where George had labored for the previous eight months. He could hear the canary chirping, and the further he wandered into the No. 2 drift, the more prominent a splashing sound became. It was coming from the coalface where a lone, soft light shone along with the silhouette of a human being. As George drew closer to the light source, the splashing grew louder. It sounded like a steady stream of water freefalling into a puddle. When he finally crept into the radius of the lamp, he found his father's favorite gambling buddy, Remo Parelli, known to the majority of the men as "Shit-Pants," urinating on the rib.

The nickname "Shit-Pants" was fairly self-explanatory. At least five times over the last two years, Remo had drank too much during his shift underground, passed out, and shit his pants. A lot of the men called him Shit-Pants, but those who respected him–George included–always called him Remo. Remo was born in Italy and had been brought to America by his parents at the age of six. English had become his primary language though his dialect still had hints of Calabrese. He stood only five and a half feet tall and was married to a girl half his age. It was a marriage that had been arranged eight years earlier when Remo's wife, Antonia, was sixteen and Remo was thirty-four. Remo received Antonia, and in return, Antonia's father received three goats and two heifers.

Remo had striking eyes, was clean shaven, and now that he had reached his forties, his skin had begun to unwind a little. His jet-black hair was sprinkled with gray and white and had begun to recede. He walked with a slight hunch, favoring his right side, and the form of his body was unlike anyone that George had ever seen. He had a cowlick and a window's peak on his small, rounded head, which didn't seem to fit his stout body that sat atop skinny legs.

"What the hell'd ya do, sleep down here?" George asked, grimacing as he caught a whiff of the urine that smelled like a night of drinking—laden with dehydration.

Remo looked at George with wide, startled eyes. In his right hand was a tenth sized bottle of bourbon that was a quarter of the way empty.

"The baby's waking up early again," said Remo.

The splashing slowed to a trickle and then stopped completely.

"Hey George, what's this?" Remo asked as he reached for a basic scoop shovel.

"A shovel," George replied halfheartedly...it was another one of Remo's games.

"No, it's not a shovel."

"A muckstick."

"It's not a muckstick. What is it?"

"It's a goddamn shovel."

"No, George. I'm telling you it's not a shovel."

"What is it then?"

Remo leaned the shovel against the rib—the scoop facing the wall. He made sure the handle was tight against the rib. He then wedged a piece of wood under the handle so the shovel wouldn't slip, and then he sat down on the back of the scoop. "It's a chair," he said, incredibly amused with himself. He then took a hit of bourbon. "How's Joe? Boy, he went out on a bash last night."

"Could barely get outta bed this mornin'," George replied.

"It ain't my fault the old man's slowing down, George— slowing down faster than this two-bit operation."

There was a small wooden table near the coalface that contained a worn set of mining hammers and jacks, some small and some large, and a wooden box labeled: *High Explosives—Dangerous*. Remo retrieved one of the hammers and a smaller jack. He held the sharpened tip of the jack against the coalface and smacked the opposite side with the hammer in order to bore holes into the soft coal. Once the holes were drilled, they would be packed with dynamite.

Their canary, which they had named Lemon because his little round body looked like a lemon, was housed in a wooden cage that hung from a nail driven into the timbering. Their last canary, named Durango for no particular reason, had died two weeks earlier from a lethal dose of carbon monoxide, which had alerted George and the others to get out. Little Lemon had been on duty ever since.

"What time didja bring 'im back last night?" George asked.

"Around twelve-thirty, I guess. Say, where were you any-way?"

"Took a train over to Helper and had a drink with an old friend," said George, sounding rather coy.

Remo smiled and continued to drive the jack into the coalface with his worn hammer. "Ain't nobody hops a train just for a drink. Why don't you tell me you went down there and had yourself a woman?"

There was a brief pause as the hillside rumbled above their heads, causing the timbers in the drift to moan and sprinkle bits of coal and dirt onto their caps.

"I'm right, ain't I?" continued Remo with a grin on his coal-dusted mug. "Of course I'm right."

George chose not to respond. He situated his withered and blackened tools on the wooden table. He retrieved a hammer and a jack of his own and then began boring an-other hole into the coalface.

The appropriate title for what they were doing was called "single jacking," which was a job for a singular man as well as a lesser hammer and a lesser jack. "Double jacking" de-manded a much higher level of concentration and skill. The double jacking method, which was much faster and was generally performed after a hole was already started with the single jacking method, involved three men—one to hold the large jack, which was made of solid iron, and two other men to alternate hammer blows with the greatest level of attentiveness. When the holes were bored and the dynamite was packed, the coalface was blown so that the mineral was much easier to shovel into the coal carts.

When George and Joe first started working in the Rainville No. 4, the two of them, along with Remo, alternated between holding the jack and swinging the hammers. But one day, Joe, who had polished off a fifth of whiskey, took an errant swing and pulverized Remo's left wrist. From that day on, the typically sober George was designated to permanent hammer wielding duty.

George and Remo enjoyed talking politics. The hot topic was the upcoming presidential election between incumbent William McKinley and his counterpart, William J. Bryan. But above all, they talked industry: steel, oil, and coal. George would share with Remo what he read in books and newspapers. It was well-known to Remo that George had much higher aspirations in life than mucking coal until his lungs shut down. George desired to own and operate a mine of his own. Whether it was coal, silver, or salt didn't matter. He had experienced them all and had not found one to be more satisfactory than another. Remo made it clear that if George were to one day establish an operation of his own, then he would be proud to work for him. George always considered Remo to be one of the most skilled laborers that he had ever worked with. A few months back, George told Remo that he would hire him as foreman if his dream was ever realized. Remo also had a desire for more than mucking coal. He hoped to someday save enough money to open his own grocery market, something that might compete with Wolf Blankston's establishments. But he had thrown away far too much money on booze and gambling, which weren't just mindless habits; they were deep rooted addictions that developed long before he was married and had children.

After they talked of presidents and industry, their discussions would slide into criticisms of Wolf Blankston. Just as they started to speak of the inadequate tools, the deficient timbers, and the abuse of the immigrants, they heard the creak of the ladder. The sound was accompanied by impatient groans. After nearly a full minute of struggle, a pair of boots plopped into the dirt at the bottom of the ladder followed by dragging footsteps and heavy breathing.

When Joe entered the light of Remo's wall lantern, he looked like a reanimated cadaver, hunched over and drained of life. He frowned at George and Remo, and then looked over at the chirping canary.

"Top o' the mornin', Lemon," he said as he tipped his cap to the little bird. Lemon's head twitched around, and his little black eyes watched the three dirty humans. Joe then looked at George and Remo again. "What were ya damned fools chatterin' about?"

If there was one trait the old man still possessed, it was the gift of outstanding hearing, which was highly unusual for an underground miner. Most men who toiled underground experienced quite the opposite. The gift of hearing was one of the few courtesies that Wolf Blankston had bestowed upon his labor force, although entirely without his knowledge. Wolf elected not to install compressed air throughout his mine. With compressed air came deafeningly loud pneumatic drills that were notorious for shattering ear drums.

It seemed as if every technological advancement that was introduced in order to maximize the payload only presented a new and life-threatening danger for the miners themselves—the ones who actually had to use the technology. Dynamite was introduced long ago, but since its inception, hundreds of thousands of people had lost limbs, had their skin charred, or had been rendered deaf, blind, or both. Then there were the cart tracks, which made it easier to move paydirt. But sometimes a miner would be smacked in the knee cap or shin, or maybe a couple of toes would be severed by the dense iron. There were even times when a man would push a loaded cart alone through the tunnels and lose his grip at a downhill slope, causing the cart to pick up momentum and crash into an unsuspecting crew and seriously injuring or killing one or two of them. Then there were the pneumatic drills, which were called "widowmaker drills" for good reason. Not only were they deafeningly loud but they also produced a mass of coal dust that increased the risk of contracting Black Lung one hundred fold. At least the laborers of Rainville had been spared of that much. Still, George wanted one. The jacking methods were meticulous and exhausting.

George and Remo were reluctant to continue with their censures of Wolf Blankston. They knew that Old Joe would oppose such reckless thoughts and ideas being blurted aloud for one of the spotters to hear. But on this morning, there was an air of confidence that George had not felt in years. For the first time in a long time, he didn't care if he angered Joe. He was leaving the next day anyway.

"We were talkin' about compressed air drills," he said. "I was tellin' Remo we oughta have one down here."

Joe was taken aback by his son's confession. He had grown accustomed to George simply ignoring him. "Blankston ain't gonna listen to us bitch and moan," Joe scoffed. "He'll just replace us with some immigrant fresh off the train who'll keep his damn mouth shut. We're grunts,

George—peasants. That's all we've ever been, and that's all we're ever gonna be."

"Am I not supposed to have an opinion of my own?" George challenged.

"You can have yer damn opinion," Joe grumbled. "Just keep it to yerself for cryin' out loud. This mine, hell, this whole stinkin' country's run by rich folks. You don't play by their rules then they'll find somebody else that will. If ya don't see that by now then yer a lot dumber than I thoughtcha were."

George watched his father hobble in pain, fighting his damaged knees to the wooden table where he rested his ancient tools. Challenging Joe while he was hungover was a poor idea. Joe was generally bitter and moody, but when he was hungover, he was one mean bastard.

"Jesus," said Joe. "Smells like piss down here."

A silence set in. All three of them were afraid to say anything more.

The sound of offbeat hammers resonated through the small chamber as the three men bored holes into the coalface. They went on working that way for some time. The only sounds were the rumbling hill and the singing Lemon. The silence was the most difficult to tolerate for Remo because he loved to speak, and he loved for people to listen to him speak. But he knew better than to blabber in the early morning while Old Joe's head throbbed and his stomach turned. All that Remo could do was offer his bourbon until the pain in Joe's head ceased, and that's precisely what he did.

Joe guzzled a fifth of the bottle before handing it back to Remo. The pain immediately began to subside.

George disapproved of the drinking that went on within the No. 2 drift. Not because he found drinking to be immoral, but because he found it to be hypocritical of his father to forbid speaking nastily of Wolf Blankston for fear of losing their jobs while simultaneously engaging in behavior that was much more likely to get them all fired. Not the simple act of drinking, but the inconsistencies that would stem from their drunkenness. If Wolf Blankston fired every man that drank underground, then he would be left with fewer men than he could count on his hands to work the four coal mines.

It was impossible for Old Joe to survive a day underground without doing it shit-faced, and the more he drank, the more his health deteriorated. It would only be a matter of time before Old Joe kicked the bucket. George was well aware of this, and he knew that his father wished for such a conclusion on a daily basis. George didn't want to be present when the death of his father arrived. Every morning that George awoke, he expected to find Joe dead; however, the discovery of his dead father was not what troubled him most. It was the fact that Joe's remains would be put in a wooden box to be forever sealed in Wolf Blankston's overcrowded cemetery. He knew that Wolf would make a quick and deceitful appearance at Joe's funeral to show that he was a man who cared. In fact, he would fill the position of divine minister himself and spit out the same biblical verse he always did when a soul was claimed within his community, only to forget about the departed life after he washed down a few glasses of Scotch and settled back into his office. It was likely that Wolf would celebrate Joe's death. Joe was an old, worthless laborer—an old tool—primed to be replaced by a new tool capable of performing at a higher level.

These were the thoughts that motivated George to depart from Rainville as soon as possible—grim thoughts, but realistic nonetheless. Despite all the emotional frustration, a much greater power had begun to stir within him that he had not previously anticipated. It was the influence of the golden owl figurine. It had already begun to lure him into its twisting nether. It had triggered emotions of wrath, greed, and vitality that he hardly realized were instilled within him, and perhaps they weren't; however, wrath, greed, and vitality were three traits carried by a nefarious man who possessed the golden owl figurine long, long ago.

12

It had been a month since Esteban Garza and his team reached the gold-bearing mine, and they had since taken many strides in order to maximize their payload. A framework for crushing quartz had been developed. It consisted of a tree cut to a stump at four feet in height and rounded so that a tree branch eight feet in length could be hinged on the top of the stump like a lever. At the end of the tree branch was a boulder the size of a large watermelon secured by a rope. Two of the men would use all their strength to raise the boulder into the air, while a third man would situate the gold-bearing quartz directly underneath it. Once the quartz was in place, the two men would drop the lever, and the boulder would come crashing down, pulverizing the quartz so that the samples of gold could be exposed and separated.

The summer heat caused the horses to lie in the shade for the greater part of the days. Father Rodriguez and the horses were the only ones who didn't have to work. Rodriguez spent most of his time exploring the surrounding area and scribbling journal entries. His entries were mostly detailed accounts of the landscape and travel directions. He also documented the vile force of the mountain, the wicked Esteban Garza, and the ongoing conversion of the native slaves. As for the horses, they were simply too large to fit into the mine.

The Spanish had managed to remain hidden from the Northern Ute during their time on the mountain. They concluded that whatever evil force of nature resided within that particular mountain region had kept them away. *Why* it kept them away remained to be seen, but it was a fearsome thing to consider. There had not been a night in which the ghostly winds did not sift through the pines and compose a lament of spellbinding horror. When the wind would pick up, the souls of things unimaginable would begin to stir in the darkness. Some of these creatures were small and skittered through the underbrush with shifty movements. Others sounded like gigantic beasts blundering around in the surrounding woods. Then there were the half-humanoid half-specters whose groans and cries chilled the blood of the Spanish far more than the other creatures. Whatever it was these beings had experienced during their time in the mortal realm, it must have been gruesome and horrifying. That is, if they were actually real. Nobody really knew if what they were experiencing was real or if it was all generated by their tired minds.

Despite the wickedness that swirled around the camp at night, the men found the most disturbing sight within the camp itself. When the soldiers slept, or at least tried to sleep, they would often awaken to find Esteban's golden eye staring directly at them. More times than not, a wry smile would be on his face. It was as if Esteban were one of the sleepless creatures of the night, keeping a constant eye on those who might think to defy him. But when the darkness faded and the illuminant sun shone over the eastern horizon, the creatures retreated into their forgotten pasts, and the region returned to normalcy—apart from the symphony of the wind and the loathsome scent of blood, which seldom ceased.

For the soldiers, contemplating what was happening on the mountain was something that they, as well as the slaves, had little time to do because Esteban pushed them ceaselessly in the mine. Their labor would begin at daybreak, and they would work throughout the night with very little sleep and nourishment. The soldiers worked in shifts as per Esteban's orders. Some of them would work as slave drivers in the mine, while others manned the smelter or the quartz crusher. Three soldiers were assigned to stand guard in case any of the Ute came around, though they never did. As for the slaves, their only hint of freedom came when they were turned loose once a week under the supervision of the soldiers to hunt, fish, and restore the water supply for the camp.

•

A thin stream of smoke lifted into the air, rising above the smelter that had been erected by a previous expedition so that the gold could be melted and formed by the extreme heat. On June the twenty-sixth, there were twenty-six golden bars locked in a sturdy chest within Esteban's tent. With each finalized gold bar, the force inside Esteban Garza escalated a little more. There was much more gold within the mountain, and the output from the men became increasingly inadequate. Though there were plenty of summer days left, thoughts of autumn swirled in Esteban's mind. He had been briefed in Santé Fe as to how much gold he was to return with in order to reap the honors and accolades of the noblemen, but he wanted to return with far more than what was expected of him. The problem was that there was no sensible amount of gold that would satisfy his craving. The slaves could unearth every ounce of gold in the entire mountain range and it would still not be enough.

The wind hissed much more menacingly than usual, and the clouds were as dark as the smoke that rose from the campfire where Father Rodriguez sat tending a cauldron of rabbit stew. The priest inhaled the mountain air. It was resonant with the ever-present stench of blood. Everyone had grown accustomed to the scent for the most part, but there were certainly times when it was more pungent than usual and one couldn't help but notice it. Father Rodriguez held his journal in his left hand and a fountain pen in the other as he scribed the following entry:

"I awoke at sunrise with yet another pain in my stomach. I estimate that I have now lost thirteen kilograms since we arrived at this hell-stricken mountain. Yet, despite the pain that ravages my body, I must remain vigilant for the sake of the soldiers and the slaves. Without me, the poor souls would be concealed from the Lord God, whom our thoughtless Captain does not regard. I remain fearful of Captain Garza. I fear for what he will do, and I fear for what he has become. The more I yearn for Santé Fe, the more I realize that I will likely never return to my beloved home. My only hope is to continue to examine the Pueblo. Del Rio has agreed to translate another conversation between the Pueblo and me. We have found a new place to meet in private. There is a large, fallen tree nearby that is concealed by a barrier of rock. The progress with the Pueblo has been slow. He simply will not accept the Lord's

teachings. Therefore, I must abandon his conversion for the time being to learn of what is happening on this mountain. To this point, all the Pueblo has chosen to share is that we have inhabited "bad land." Unfortunately, "bad" does not convey its true, dire state. The minions of Hell continue to present themselves, and with each passing day, I suspect that they grow stronger. I am relieved that I will not spend the afterlife in such a place. This place is for the children of Lucifer—a place for Captain Garza. It warms my soul to know for certain that I will spend the afterlife with you in heaven, O Lord. I vow that I will continue my attempts to reform the Pueblo as well as the other captives. But first, I must concern myself with escaping this wretched land so that the soldiers and I can return home with our lives intact. By your light, I will take whatever actions are necessary to ensure their safety."

The dark clouds rumbled a melancholy tune as a drop of water plunged downward and struck the priest's journal, causing a portion of the ink to blot. He shut the journal and tucked it into his robe to keep it dry. There was a flash of lightning followed by another rumble of thunder. The wind picked up simultaneously, and the pines began to sway and hiss. Father Rodriguez stood and roused the soup. He watched the pines suspiciously as their branches gently swayed. He was all alone in the camp, and this made him nervous.

He then heard the shouting of two soldiers followed by a loud gunshot that frightened the priest, causing him to drop the spoon into the cauldron of soup. His eyes widened as he heard the scampering of feet through the underbrush.

Esteban emerged from the mine almost immediately with his flintlock pistol drawn. His amber-colored eye was glowing more brilliantly than ever. There was another distant gunshot followed by a scream and then another shot. Then, there was a silence. By the time Esteban and Rodriguez arrived at the scene, they found one of the soldiers with an arrow through his heart. Face down in the underbrush was one of the Northern Ute, and close to him was another Spanish soldier who knelt by the corpse of the native, stricken with fear.

"What happened?" Esteban demanded.

The surviving soldier cowered in fear in the presence of Esteban before speaking nervously. "This should not have happened. It was a mistake. We frightened each other. I don't think we would have shot otherwise."

"How many were there?"

"Three."

"Where are the other two?"

"They have fled."

"Who shot first?"

The soldier dipped his head. "I did, Captain."

Esteban felt compelled to kill the soldier for putting the whole expedition in jeopardy, but he yielded because he knew he needed every man. The Northern Ute would return and return in greater numbers.

"Well, that's it then," stated Rodriguez with a voice that almost sounded relieved. "We have no choice but to abandon our mission and return to Santé Fe before we're overrun and killed."

"Nonsense," said Esteban. "We have only one month's worth of gold. If that's all we return to Santé Fe with, then I can assure you, Father, the two of us will be hanging for blundering our mission. At least here we can fight for our lives."

"You have pushed these slaves until they are no longer able to stand," said Father Rodriguez. "You've extracted enough gold in the last two weeks alone to make the sover-eigns of Santé Fe drop to their knees at the sight of you. We will not be hung for returning now; we will be revered."

Esteban eyed the priest. "Then return to Santé Fe, Father Rodriguez. It is no secret that you wish to abandon this campaign at any cost. Go now, and take what cowardly sol-diers want to go with you. I have no use for those without a spine. I will stay on this mountain, and when the inhabit-ants of this land seek their revenge, I will fight, and I will win. And when I return to Santé Fe with tales of heroism and a mountain of gold, we will see who is revered, and who is not."

"Very well," said the priest. "The men and I will leave at dawn. Though I can assure you, Captain, I doubt that you will enjoy managing the slaves by yourself. They'll kill you the first chance they get."

Esteban chuckled. "I only wish I could see your face when you wander into Santé Fe and tell them that you've aban-doned your quest without a single bar of gold. They'll hang you for it. The fact that you're a priest won't save you."

The two men exchanged an icy stare before Rodriguez turned and walked back to the camp.

"Are you really going to allow some of the men to leave?" asked the soldier who was kneeling at the side of the fallen native.

"No," Esteban replied.

The rain started to fall heavily, but there was an even greater storm on the horizon. One that was likely to involve a great deal of bloodshed.

13

George, Joe, and Remo sat under a juniper fifty yards from the portal of the No. 4 mine. They had detonated their dynamite, and it would be at least two hours until the dust settled in the No. 2 drift and they could return to a safe, workable condition.

Joe and Remo were both asleep when a breeze picked up and ruffled George's messy hair and long, scruffy beard. As he looked at the tipple, the mine office, the bunkhouses, and the residential camp, he suddenly felt rather melancholy. He thought of the friends that he had made and of all the hard work that he had poured into Rainville. Most of all, he thought about his father. Rainville was home to George and Joe. But now his days there were at an end. A new chapter was about to begin—one that wouldn't include his father. He felt a tightness in his chest and found it difficult to breathe. He was beginning to have second thoughts. There was a level of comfort in Rainville. Even with the poor conditions and the lack of safety and pay, there was comfort in the routine of day to day life. Leaving Rainville and pursuing something of his own held only uncertainty. Thus, there was a reluctance to commit.

•

They returned to a hill of loosened coal with two empty coal carts. In order to get the carts to the No. 2 drift, they had to haul them on the long route through the main level where a steep incline connected every drift in the mine.

George picked up the large chunks of coal by hand and lifted them into the cart while Remo wielded his shovel (or his chair, whichever he preferred it to be) and scooped up smaller pieces. Joe swung his withered pickaxe with quick, jerky motions and knocked loose pieces from the coalface onto the ground.

Remo could only stand holding his tongue for so long, and the more he drank, the more he yearned to be listened to. Enough time had passed that he knew Joe was feeling better and that the early morning argument was long forgotten. Therefore, he spoke loudly and proudly.

"Do you remember talking to Bill last night?" he asked while staring at Joe. "That stupid son of a bitch—boy, I tell ya—I says to him, I says, if you want to go ahead and believe the papers then that's all fine and dandy, but I sure as shit ain't votin' for Bryan. One of these days a nice Italian is going to run for president, get elected, and set this whole mess of a country straight."

Joe just looked at him with a sour expression. Remo turned his attention to George and then back to Joe again, hopeful that either one of them would acknowledge him. But as neither one did, he did the only thing that made sense to him—he kept talking.

"I heard they started a ball club over in Placerton. Boy, I wish we had a club. I bet there are enough fellas who'd like to play, too. When I was younger I used to play for a coupla guys down there workin' the railroad. Those sons-a-bitches used to say to me—"

His words were interrupted by a sharp groaning sound—the same sound that George had heard earlier that morning. A chill rushed through all three men. They stopped what they were doing and stared into the blackness with frightened eyes.

"Did you hear that?" Joe muttered, which surprised George and Remo. It was the first time in almost an hour that he had spoken.

The mine was still except for Lemon's chirping and the massive overhead radiating a deep, grumbling hum.

"Oh Jesus, she ain't comin' down on us, is she, Joe?" Remo asked.

Joe took the oil lamp from his cap and then bent over and held the flame between the cart tracks.

"Air's goin' the right direction," he said.

He stood up straight and fixed the lamp back to his cap. He then pointed his right ear toward the darkness in order to maximize the use of his catlike hearing.

George stared at his father, hopeful that the wily old timer would be able to recognize the sound and put their minds at ease.

"What is it, Pop?" George asked.

Joe took a deep breath then said, "Tommyknocker."

A Tommyknocker was interpreted differently by various bodies of thought. Most miners believed that Tommyknockers were the benevolent spirits of men who had died underground and continued on in the afterlife warning living miners of forthcoming accidents. On the contrary, there were also plentiful tales of malevolent Tommyknockers who knocked tools from the hands of men and snickered about it. In fact, the Whispering Ridge mine twenty-six miles south of Rainville had experienced an incident in which their No. 3 mine was idle for two weeks because the men were too afraid of a spirit that was allegedly laughing, spitting, and hurling rocks at them.

Joe listened for a moment more and then turned to George and Remo with a troubled expression. He spat out a chunk of tobacco and then wiped the sweat and grime from his forehead.

"I heard it earlier," George admitted. "I thought it sounded like the timbers."

"That ain't no damn timbers," Joe snapped. "That's a Tommyknocker, all right. Best keep our eyes and ears open from now on. Might be tryin' to tell us somethin'. Hearin' a Tommyknocker's one thing but seein' one's goddamn different. If ya see a Tommyknocker ya better drop whatever yer holdin' and run like hell. Few men see one and live to talk about it."

This, of course, was not new information to George or Remo. Anyone who worked one day underground had heard a story about a Tommyknocker. But Joe had a way of treating them like mindless children.

"What about Thelma Ambrosius?" George asked.

Mrs. Thelma Ambrosius, the spirit that George had come across the previous night, was the wife of Paul Ambrosius. They were Greek immigrants who had settled in Rainville three years earlier. Paul was quiet and private. When he didn't show up for work for a few days, nobody knew why and nobody asked why. But then one day there was a rumor floating around that Paul Ambrosius was dead. That rumor turned out to be true. He had died of blood poisoning from an accident underground that nobody really knew anything about. Paul had kept the accident a secret because he was afraid of being fired and even more afraid of being indebted to the camp doctor. The Ambrosius family was barely scraping by as it was and couldn't have afforded the added expense. After his death, Thelma sought compensation from Wolf Blankston since the accident had occurred underground, but compensation was not granted. Wolf argued that nobody could cite the source of the blood poisoning. Therefore, it couldn't legally be justified as mine-related. When it was all said and done, Wolf didn't offer the poor woman a nickel. Thelma had no money and no means of supporting herself and her infant daughter. A few of the Rainville women provided her with bread and milk when they could afford to do so, which was rare because few people in the camp had a surplus of anything.

Thelma did not request a lot from Wolf Blankson. All she asked for was enough money or the resources to travel back to Greece so that she could be with her still living parents. No matter how hard Thelma tried, Wolf Blankston would not budge. But that was Wolf Blankston. If he were to offer Mrs. Ambrosius some form of compensation, then, at least in his mind, he would have been admitting that he was the one at fault.

A week after Paul died, a group of laborers stormed into Wolf Blankston's office and demanded justice for Thelma, but their actions were too late. That same morning, Thelma was found hanging by the neck from a noose tied to the ceiling of her cabin. Her infant daughter, Mary, was discovered face down in a stream up the adjacent canyon. Thelma

Ambrosius had killed herself and her child because they had been left to die in that horrid canyon. She felt as if she had no other choice. Thelma and Mary were buried on the hill next to Paul, and those who stormed into Wolf Blankston's office in protest were fired, as they were deemed "troublesome" and "riotous."

It was six weeks after the suicide of Thelma Ambrosius when many people in Rainville began to see the ghostly, hovering figure of a woman. The ghost would appear high up the adjacent canyon—the place where she drowned little Mary. From there, it would move toward the mine office. When it reached the door of the office, it would vanish into thin air.

George, Remo, and Joe had all witnessed the ghost of Thelma Ambrosius. They accepted her existence as they would accept the existence of a housefly menacing about. But that didn't stop the rumors from spreading around the coal camps. Some people told of a ghost that wouldn't harm anyone—a compassionate spirit who remained on Earth to illustrate a need for a change, not only in Rainville, but all over the world where so many men and women were being exploited. Others told a much different story. A story about a malevolent spirit that remained in the physical realm to see to it that Wolf Blankston paid for his crime.

Whether her spirit was good or evil, no one could be certain. How could they be *certain*? There were many people who claimed to be *certain* that the ghost of Thelma Ambrosius was an elaborate hoax created by the laborers of Rainville as a tactic to degrade the Wolf Blankston Mining Company. The dozens of people who had witnessed the hovering soul with their own eyes had a problem with that theory. Whatever was happening, it was a touchy subject that smart folks chose not to discuss within a company owned facility (which was damn near everything) unless they wanted negative attention from Wolf Blankston.

Meanwhile, George had taken the chance to bring it up, and he had taken Remo and Joe by surprise. But even more surprising was the fact that Joe chose to reply to such a controversial topic.

"It's different all right," said Joe with a convinced expression. "Tommyknockers are trapped down here and always will be. That woman ya speak of can wander around all she wants. I tell ya, it's different."

It was the most passionate that Joe had been in some time, at least in front of George. George couldn't help but think that the subject of spirits, and to an extent, death and the afterlife was something that swam potently through the old man. The subject had set him off like a stick of dynamite, and for the first time in a long time there was a little color in his face.

"One of the old timers told me once that a spirit is stuck in a moment," Joe continued. "They just keep livin' the same pattern over and over. Pattern might last thirty seconds or it might last a month, but that spirit'll keep livin' some event 'til God knows how long. Hell, a spirit can wander, too. Have ya heard of that headless fella over at the Sweetland mine?"

George and Remo both shook their heads.

"Well," Joe continued. "Fella lost his head in the mine. Damn thing came clean off. Folks over there'll tell ya they've seen the ghost hikin' clear up by Millpoint. Hell, that's thirty miles from Sweetland. Lookin' for his head— that's what folks say he's doin', but I reckon the son of a bitch could be doin' anything. Might think he's the president of the United States for all we know."

Neither George nor Remo could devise a response to such weighty speculation. They instead tried to listen for the Tommyknocker. But after nearly a full minute, they gave up.

"Let's get this cart up, Remo," George insisted, feeling as though the silence needed to be broken.

"I'll take it with Remo," Joe snapped as he rubbed his aching knees.

"Ya sure, Pop?" George asked.

"I can take it up myself, Joe. Don't go hurting yourself," said Remo.

"Could use the fresh air," Joe barked.

Remo and Joe took hold of the coal cart and pushed it in the direction that the horrifying groan had originated. The wheels creaked and moaned as the cart rolled away. Then the sound gradually trailed off, leaving George alone in the dim radius of Remo's wall lantern. Lemon chirped away, and George watched him for a moment. The little black eyes looked back at him.

Upon being left alone, George immediately felt fear. He dreaded whatever thing was lurking in the surrounding blackness. To ease his mind, he took hold of Remo's "chair"/shovel and began loading the loose coal into the second coal cart. A sharp clank of metal on rock rang out as he drove the shovel into the mound of coal, causing a glistening of orange sparks to shower and scatter. Seconds later, a loud thud rumbled as the coal was dropped into the basin of the empty cart. He shoveled hard and fast, trying to stay focused on the task at hand, but suddenly his eyes met a stunning element on the ground.

He leaned over to have a better look at the specimen. He picked it up, spit on his thumb, and wiped the object clean. What he held in his hand was an element that was next to impossible to stumble upon in a vein of coal. It was gold, a truly impressive sample of it. He stared at it with an awed smile and large eyes. He looked down again and saw that there were at least a dozen more samples of gold on the ground. His heart quivered as he thought of the previous load of coal that Remo and Joe had wheeled out. *How much gold did we just hand over to Wolf Blankston?* He wondered. But then again, he had not recalled seeing a single sparkle, and Joe had not said a word when his lamp was two feet away from the freshly blown coalface. It was all terribly odd. If there had been gold mixed in with the previous load, then Remo and Joe would surely realize it by the time the daylight hit it.

George suddenly had the compulsion to start picking up as much gold as he could before Joe and Remo returned. If there was gold in the previous load, then it would raise a lot of attention, enough to attract Wolf Blankston himself into the mine. One by one, George picked up little chunks of gold and stuffed them into his pocket with mesmerized eyes and a cunning grin.

Why, I'll leave right now, he thought to himself. *If Wolf Blankston comes into the drift to find gold, he might check my pockets. I'll make a run for it before he even gets the chance. What's mine is mine; I found it. I'm responsible for this miracle.* He tucked the bottom of his pants into his rubber boots and then dropped samples into the pants so that the mineral could accumulate around his ankles.

He began to sift through the coal, picking up more samples of gold and studying them as he lifted them into the light of his teapot lamp. It was gold. There was no doubt about it. He pocketed only the gold and discarded the coal. He lowered his head to the ground so that he could get a better look at what was in front of him. His hands pushed and pulled coal back and forth. Just as he had lost all under-standing and awareness of where he was and what he was doing, the loud groaning sound rattled his bones and ech-oed through the drift.

Tears of fright collected in his eyes as he sat paralyzed in fear. On the two previous occasions that he had heard the sound, it had disappeared almost instantly. This time there was a strange ruffling sound that accompanied it.

His heart raced as he kept his eyes on the imminent blackness. It was a Tommyknocker. He was sure of it. He waited for the spirit to show itself so that he could sprint out of the drift before the whole thing collapsed. The ruf-fling sound continued, but only a spherical darkness stared back at him. He stood up straight and listened intently.

The second he let down his guard, a birdlike creature shot from the darkness and flapped its wings just above his head. George screamed at the top of his lungs and fell to the ground in an attempt to evade the bird. As soon as his back slammed against the iron tracks, the sound of the bird disappeared, and the No. 2 drift was silent, apart from little Lemon's chirping.

The impact had knocked the wind out of him. He gasped for air but all he sucked up was disturbed coal dust, which made him choke. When he finally collected himself and sat up, the creature was nowhere to be found. It had flown to-ward the coalface that was floodlit by Remo's wall lantern. The flame of the lantern swayed as if a breeze was passing through.

The creature was an owl; George was sure of it. A large, vicious owl with its wings extended and its sharp talons ready—a perfect match of the golden owl figurine.

George was terrified. He wanted to run out of the drift, but then he remembered the gold in his pockets. He reached into his right front pocket to admire it once more, but when he removed his hand, he held only scraps of coal. He then reached into his other pocket, but there, too, he found only coal. He pulled the bottom of his pants free from his boots, and coal trickled out and piled onto the ground. Finally, he rushed to the wall, retrieved Remo's lantern, and shined it directly on the pile of coal that had been blasted free. Coal was all that he found. There was no gold. There never had been. It was a cruel trick. But who or what was responsible for such a trick?

14

The fog lingered in the early morning on The Mountain of the Owl, as it did most mornings, and so too did the smell of dampness from the previous night's rainstorm. It was cool, and the chilled air brought with it a breeze that sifted eerily through the massive pines.

There was hardly a sound when the first arrow pierced the neck of the Spanish soldier who stood guard at the smelter. Before his life was drained from him, he steadied his rifle and fired an errant shot in the direction he believed the arrow had originated. His shot was well off the mark. Nonetheless, it was of monumental importance because it had drawn Esteban and the rest of the soldiers from the mine. It was a crucial turning point in the engagement if the Spanish were to stand a chance. If they had not heard the shot, then the attackers would have had the luxury of taking their unknowing enemies by surprise in the dark passages. Instead, the Spanish soldiers were able to flee and seek the cover of the pines. Their eyes quickly adjusted to the daylight thanks to the fog and the overcast sky.

The attackers moved swiftly and subtly—barely showing themselves as they ran and ducked for cover in the underbrush or behind the thick pines. There was a ghostly quality about them. They moved so swiftly that not a single Spanish soldier was able to get a decent look at one of them.

The battle started with a wicked crossfire of shadowlike arrows, stones, and knives that were hurled and crude bullets that were fired at things that moved and things that only seemed to move, which was nearly everything thanks to the hastening wind. It was as if the force of nature was excited by the violence and grew even more enthusiastic as blood was spilled on the mountain soil. The strange stench of blood that had enshrined the region over the last month suddenly became more loathsome than ever.

Father Rodriguez scurried into the mine and watched the battle from the shadows of the entrance. He closed his eyes and prayed for his countrymen to prevail. The Pueblo and Navajo captives, on the other hand, were hopeful that the Spanish would fall. They knew that such an outcome would be a rare opportunity for freedom.

Del Rio was slain by a charging combatant, and so were Vega and Ramos, two of the higher ranking Spanish soldiers who had tried to flank but instead walked into a volley of arrows. It seemed as though the Spanish were losing ground, but as Esteban looked around the foggy terrain, he saw that many of the attackers had been struck with bullets and were lying dormant in the underbrush.

The wind continued to cry, and the rain began to fall so hard that the sound of feet clomping through the foliage was barely audible. There were muddled shouts and cries all about the camp. Some came from wounded men who called out desperately, hoping that some miraculous act would save them from their dying breath. Other sounds were tactical commands, and both sides shouted them with poise as they presumed that their adversaries would not be able to understand their foreign tongues. Visibility had also become an issue. Not only was there fog, but the wind began to blow so violently that the rain fell horizontally, propelling water directly into the eyes of those who raised their heads.

There was a brief stalemate as both parties were wary of plunging into the unknown. It ended when Esteban caught a glimpse of a fledgling warrior scurrying against the tree line. Esteban fired a shot that hit the young man's left shoulder and brought him to the ground with a shriek of pain. Soon after, there was another blast from a Spanish rifle that brought down another attacker. This one tumbled head first down the ridge after being struck in the center of his chest.

There was another high pitched sound as an arrow was cast from a bow and struck the left thigh of one of the Spanish soldiers. Much to Esteban's disappointment, this reduced the number of able-bodied Spanish to only four, counting himself. Through the fog and the trees, Esteban saw shadows menacing about, the numbers of which were double that of the Spanish. He then looked into the eyes of the last three soldiers. In them, he saw only the trepidation of death. They were outnumbered, and their foes held a stronger strategic position. Still, the remaining Spanish hid in the seclusion of the pines and loaded another round into their rifles and pistols.

With his flintlock pistol loaded, Esteban emerged from the pines and fired a shot that killed another attacker. The other three soldiers fired shots, though only one was on target. Before they could retreat to their hiding place, another Spanish soldier was struck in the neck with an accurately fired arrow. Only Esteban and two soldiers remained. On his hands and knees, Esteban crawled and recovered two pistols from his fallen combatants. Despite only having one hand, he loaded them quickly and readied himself for the subsequent volley; however, much to the surprise of the invaders, Esteban—with two pistols tucked into his belt and a third in his right hand—flanked hard to the opposite side of the pines. With two shots, he killed two opponents who had not heard him coming because of the blaring wind and chattering rain. Esteban took refuge behind a pine trunk and reloaded the pistols. As he peered subtly from behind the tree, he saw two more attackers who were bewildered and clueless as to where the previous shots had originated.

Lightning struck no more than one hundred yards away, and with it came a crash of thunder that provided the ideal cover for Esteban to re-emerge from his hiding place and fire a bullet through the head of one of his enemies. The other turned and lifted his battle knife, but he was too late. Esteban had driven his hook into the neck of the man. He was an older tribesman with tanned and leathered flesh. He hardly gave a response to being mortally wounded at the hand of Esteban's hook. He did not shout or tremble, and he did not wince or become stricken with anguish. He stared into Esteban's golden eye with no emotion, as if it had not happened at all.

The shock and horror did not originate from the wounded man. It instead came from Esteban, who saw something dark and horrible in the gray, hazy eyes of the old warrior. They were the wrathful eyes of some ancient, enigmatic creature—the rightful owner of the territory in which the Spanish had so insolently intruded. The grayness suddenly began to evolve in the old tribesman's eyes. He then fell to the ground with a thud as Esteban removed the sharp hook from his neck. The old warrior laid on his back in the mud. His eyes slowly grew darker and darker, until they were jet-black in color.

Another foe who had been watching from a neighboring pine began to flee. Esteban ran after him. When he reached the top of a small ridge, he saw that all seven of the remaining invaders were retreating for the lower mountain. Against all odds, the Spanish had won the battle—at least, Esteban had.

15

Esteban returned to the camp and sat on a massive log with an expression of discontent. The other two soldiers as well as Father Rodriguez cowardly emerged from their hiding places and approached their Captain.

"Have we defeated the savages?" Rodriguez asked with a timid voice.

Esteban sat still with his head pointed toward his boots. "Those were no savages," he said. "They were the wraiths of the netherworld."

Father Rodriguez's face was colorless. His eyes scanned the wet ground and soon met the corpse of Del Rio, his trusted friend and translator. At that moment, he knew that he would never understand the strange phenomena of The Mountain of the Owl.

He dipped his head, took a deep breath, and then said, "Our time here is finished. Pack the horses. We leave at once."

"Are we taking the gold with us?" one of the soldiers asked.

"Yes," Father Rodriguez replied, causing Esteban to look up at the priest.

"We are here in the name of Spain to work this mountain until the end of September," said Esteban.

Rodriguez's pale skin grew flush. "You're a madman," he said. "You can stay as long as you wish, Captain, but these men and I are leaving, and we're taking the gold with us."

Esteban drew his flintlock pistol and pointed it at the soldiers who were holding the chest containing the golden bars.

"You can leave if you want," said Esteban. "But you will not take a single bar of gold, or a single slave, or a single horse."

Rodriguez and Esteban glared at one another while the soldiers put the chest on the ground. The soldiers then prepared themselves to act by moving their hands near their sword shorts.

"Very well," said Father Rodriguez. "I'll retrieve my personal effects, and we will be on our way."

Rodriguez moved across the camp to the tent that had been his home for the last month. Inside, he retrieved his satchel, which contained his dearest personal effects, including his journal. He also retrieved his blanket, his canteen, and his walking stick. When he re-emerged from the tent, he found Esteban waiting for him.

"Perhaps you could spare us one slave, Captain—to carry some of our supplies?" Rodriguez asked.

"Not one slave. Not one horse," Esteban muttered.

"Your love for Spain is honorable, Captain, but your judgment on this matter is foolish beyond my comprehension. Spain has led us to death."

"We are all led to our deaths by those in power."

"But we have a chance to live. When the savages return, you will be killed, and Spain will never see a shred of this treasure. If you truly loved Spain then you would send the gold we have extracted thus far with us, so that we can return—"

"I shall return it myself," Esteban snapped. "And when I return with a fortune unlike any other, then I, too, shall become a nobleman of Santé Fe, and I will see to it that you and these men are executed for treason—for abandoning your pledge to Spain!"

"Captain," said Rodriguez in a patient voice.

Esteban replied with only a questioning stare.

"You are putting your life in considerable danger. I wouldn't be fulfilling my obligation to the Lord unless I said a prayer for you. May I do that now?"

Again, Esteban didn't speak, though his prying stare seemed to probe a little deeper.

Father Rodriguez put his belongings on the ground and then took a few cautious steps toward Esteban.

"That's close enough," said Esteban when the priest drew within five feet.

The priest gave a knowing glance to one of the soldiers, who in return acknowledged him with a slight nod of the head. Father Rodriguez dipped his head and performed the sign of the cross. Then, he began to speak.

"Blessed God, how I dread this mountain so. I dread it because it is the domain of the devil himself. He is the ruler of this mountain. The rightful owner of the gold we seek.

He controls the minds and hearts of both men and creatures that inhabit these jagged slopes and green pastures,
and his power has done nothing but increase because of
our arrival. Forgive us, O Lord, for that was not our intention. But please, spare us the embrace of Lucifer, and show
our brother Esteban your light and your love. Amen."

At the conclusion of the prayer, Rodriguez looked up at
Esteban and smiled. "I apologize for our differences, Captain. I pray that you return to Santé Fe with this fortune as
you have said. I will pray for it each and every day."

"Your words will not save you from my wrath, priest."

"Please, Captain. I forgive you for our differences, perhaps you could forgive them as well."

Rodriguez offered his hand to Esteban, but Esteban's only hand was occupied with his flintlock pistol. His hook
rested against his left hip. It was still dripping with Ute
blood. His golden eye studied the priest suspiciously. Ultimately, he chose not to recognize the priest's gesture.

Father Rodriguez, in complete desperation, leaped forward and grabbed Esteban's wrist with both hands, causing
him to drop the flintlock pistol. Esteban swung his hook
wildly. It sunk into Father Rodriguez's shoulder, and the
priest let out a shriek of pain. One of the soldiers retrieved
his short sword and drove it through Esteban's back.
Esteban grimaced, but then he used all of his weight to
propel the priest to the ground. He then withdrew his own
short sword and jammed it through the heart of the soldier
who had stabbed him.

Father Rodriguez quivered in the mud as Esteban's gaze
met the other living soldier, who held his hands in the air.

"My loyalty is to you, Captain, I swear it," the soldier
pleaded.

Regardless of this confession, Esteban's sword pierced the bosom of his fellow countryman, killing him instantly. All that remained were Esteban, who had a short sword protruding from his back, and Father Rodriguez, who squirmed in the mud like a pig about to be harvested for its ham and bacon. Esteban pulled the blade out of his back and blood streamed from the wound like a waterfall. Nevertheless, there was a wicked grin on his face.

Father Rodriguez felt the wound on his bicep, looked up at the sky above, and then closed his eyes and put his hands together.

"O, Lord in Heaven, open your gate."

Esteban looked up at the sky, too. There was nothing but dark clouds and falling rain. "I see the gate, priest. I see God. He rides a golden chariot. It seems He has a taste for gold, just as I do."

"Joke all you wish. It will not help you."

"I'm not the one who needs help."

"You will be soon. I will be in paradise, and you will be in hell."

"You display a great amount of fear for someone so certain," said Esteban. "Maybe you've got it backwards. Perhaps it is I who will be in paradise."

"In a dream, Captain Garza."

Esteban grinned, and then lifted the short sword high into the air and brought it down hard over Father Rodriguez's throat, cutting halfway through the esophagus. The priest gasped for air as blood seeped from his flesh. A second hack from Esteban's blade tore all the way to the throat, and the priest was lifeless. Two more hacks were needed to cut through the boney spine, and one final hack detached the head completely.

The rain and wind intensified as Esteban picked up the detached head of Father Rodriguez and lifted it high above his own head as if it were a trophy. He let out a wicked laugh and allowed the rain and the priest's blood to drip onto his face. But then he started to feel faint from the loss of blood. He lowered himself to the ground and put the head of Father Rodriguez on the ground next to him. Esteban's bloodstained smile shone brightly against his dark skin. The golden owl figurine hung around his neck. With his good hand, he embraced it.

•

It was dusk when three dozen Ute crept into the Spanish camp. They found nothing but dead bodies and Esteban Garza, who was leaning against the mighty log in the center of the camp. He was still alive, though barely alive, and encircling him were thirty-six gold bars and the head of Father Rodriguez.

Only one of the Ute advanced toward him, and cautiously so. Esteban heard the leaves crunching under the Ute man's feet, and he lifted his head feebly to see that he was no longer alone. He looked long and hard at the Ute man. Then, with a crazed, bloodstained smile, he said, "When the owl cries, the Indian dies."

The natives looked quizzically at one another, unable to comprehend the Spanish.

Esteban's smile began to fade, and so, too, did the spirit within. His head dropped and then his arm, and he was motionless.

One of the natives warily advanced toward Esteban in order to verify the death of the strange, one-armed man. But as he drew close in the fading twilight, he was mesmerized by the golden owl figurine that hung around Esteban's slumped neck. As carefully as he could, the Ute man took hold of the golden owl and pulled it hard toward himself, causing the dried leather band around Esteban's neck to break. He looked at the golden owl and then at Esteban Garza. The pitiless leader of the Spanish expedition was dead, but his golden eye remained wide open. It was glowing more radiantly in death than it did in life.

PART TWO

ESCAPE FROM RAINVILLE

16

An orange sunset floodlit the Rainville camp at day's end. The bell on the hill sounded, and those assigned to the night shift came stumbling out of their cabins and tents. The day shift men trekked down the hillside headed for the residential camp below. There was not a single man not covered in powdery soot, and there was not a man who was not physically and mentally exhausted. Because they had spent the day underground, the sunlight beat down with ten times the intensity, forcing them to squint and shade their eyes with their hands and forearms.

The men had started their day by disappearing into the subterranean darkness, and they would conclude it by re-emerging into the blinding white void of daylight. The brightness was initially unbearable, but as they drew closer to the camp, their eyes adjusted, and the vision of Rainville returned in sharp focus. The smell of sagebrush was intense but comforting, for the scent represented the smell of freedom—a bookend to a grueling yet rewarding day's work.

A clean and polished Wolf Blankston, who was only an hour away from his grand announcement at the Town Hall, stood outside the mine office puffing on one of his expensive cigars. Next to him stood an equally adept Stanton Pierce, who was always chipper on payday, for his pay exceeded that of the entire Rainville No. 4 labor force. In front of Wolf and Stanton stood a crowd of nearly sixty people, thirty-six of whom were men hopeful to work underground. The others were women, children, and elders. The majority of them were immigrants who held in their bare hands what little they owned.

"Ya playin' tonight, Shit-Pants?" called someone from a group of men behind George, Remo, and Joe.

Remo turned with a scowl but saw that the group contained ten men. He wasn't sure which one had spoken. "Yeah, I'll be there," he said. "And if I see you later, I'll pop you in the goddamn mouth!"

"You just try Shit-Pants," said a tall, stringy guy with a protruding Adam's apple, a scraggly auburn moustache, and eyes that were so close together that only the bridge of his nose kept them apart. This man was Walker Thompson. Walker paced in stride with the No. 4 mine's foreman, a hulking man by the name of Leonard Pearl. Next to Walker and Leonard was a bony old man named Carter Hirsh. The three men formed what everyone knew were Wolf Blankston's most trusted informants and assailants. The top spotters.

Realizing who it was, Remo chose not to retaliate any further. He simply looked away with a humiliated look on his face.

"What's-a-matter, Shit-Pants? Ain'tcha got somethin el-setuh say?"

He just kept walking, looking defeated.

"I'll make this quick," Wolf Blankston stated as he addressed the crowd of new arrivals.

George, Remo, Joe, and several other men slowed their pace to hear what Wolf had to say to the collection of newcomers.

"I'm burdened with far too much to be wasting my time with you," Wolf continued. "I'm looking to hire ten men and only ten. I won't employ any more than that—end of story. Anyone with at least one year's worth of experience, step forward."

George and the other men looked bemusedly at one another. They had never seen Wolf hire more than two or three men at a time. Were they about to be replaced by a batch of immigrants so that Wolf could cut wages and fire ten men who were already employed? That was certainly a possibility. It was the assumption that each man began to brood over.

The crowd shuffled and grumbled. At the end of their grumbling, only twelve men had stepped forward. Those who did not step forward looked on with concerned faces. Wolf began to pace in parallel with the men who had stepped forward so that he could get a thorough look at each of them. He made one complete pass without saying a word or without showing any emotion. On the second pass, he came to a stop in front of an old man who had leathered skin and a handful of missing teeth.

"You," Wolf stated as he glared at the man.

His cold eyes then began to scour through the other eleven men. He came to a stop at another elderly gentleman who had long greasy hair and stood slightly hunched over.

"And you," he concluded.

Wolf turned once more and addressed the two men who he had called out.

"The two of you"—he then pointed to the men in the back—"and the rest of you back there—get lost!"

There was more grumbling within the group, though most of them simply looked at one another with disappointed faces.

"If you're desperate for work," Wolf continued, "then follow the road another eight miles to Red Flats. They may be looking for some new men, though I can't promise you anything."

The relatives of those who were picked stayed put. Those who were not picked turned and sluggishly continued down the dirt trail to embark on the eight mile trek to Red Flats. They walked with aching feet and empty stomachs and with only the slightest hope of finding work. George watched them walk away. He felt terrible for them.

As they departed, Wolf looked over and saw George and the others listening in.

"Christ Almighty," he bellyached. "Beat it, you mutts!"

Everyone just stood there staring at Wolf like frightened dogs.

"Are you all deaf? I said beat it!"

George, Remo, Joe, and the others continued toward the camp like obedient children. But George didn't like how Wolf had spoken to those people. He swelled with rage, and he couldn't help but glare at Wolf as he walked away.

That was the man who was talking to Jari Ronni, Wolf remembered. *And now he has the nerve to glare at me like that.*

"The ten of you I picked," Wolf announced as he returned his attention to the new men. "Find a bunk. If there isn't a bunk available, then you're just going to have to tough it out until one presents itself. With the way things have been going around here lately, it will only be a matter of time before that happens."

Wolf turned frigidly, extinguished his cigar in the dirt, and then disappeared into his office, leaving the new recruits under the supervision of Stanton Pierce.

Joe and Remo, along with nearly a dozen other men, veered from the path that led to the residential housing and onto the trail that led to the bunkhouse reserved for those of Italian descent. It was Monday, and Monday meant blackjack. It was an ugly thing, that Monday blackjack. There was always a lot of drinking and arguing and oftentimes a fist-fight or an occasional shooting. Two months back, a man named Burt Calloway had been knifed to death. Joe and Remo, drunker than skunks, carried his body to the infirmary, but it was too late. The man who killed him fled town and was never heard from again.

The upcoming night would be the last that George could have spent with his father. Instead, Joe would be absent until the weary hours of the morning playing blackjack. It wasn't like the two of them had spent heartfelt evenings together anyway, as Joe was always out blowing his entire paycheck on card games. Nonetheless, watching his broken down father limp away made his heart ache. But sadness was not the only thing present in George's heart. There was also a feeling of desire—a growing hunger for the golden fruit of the mountain.

As he watched Joe and Remo march off, he could see the mountain on the horizon. The sunset was casting a golden light onto it and onto George's face, forcing him to shield his eyes with his forearm. He began to think of the minerals that the mountain contained. He would begin his journey the following day, and once he arrived, he would spend the summer uncovering a fortune in gold—an amount of wealth that would wash away years of heartache and physical pain. Oh, the pain—how it lingered. His back ached, as did every muscle and joint. But from that moment on, George Hendricks would feel no more pain, physical or emotional, that was not for his own self-interest. Joe could no longer bestow emotional suffering upon him, and Wolf Blankston would no longer reap the rewards for his toil underground.

George had debated throughout the day whether or not to attend Wolf's announcement. But as he watched his father hobble away, he decided that he would attend simply for the sake of knowing what Joe's future had in store for him. So, instead of returning home, George walked to the Town Hall. He wanted to be one hour early because he knew that Wolf's announcement would draw a big crowd and that seating would be limited.

17

The Town Hall was a wooden construction that, at least by appearance, could have been mistaken for the withered shack that was the Rainville church. Only forty people could fit comfortably within the one-story square-shaped room, though well over seventy had packed into it while another twenty stood outside in the darkening twilight huddled around the narrow entry in order to hear Wolf Blankston's announcement.

The wooden floors creaked and moaned as the residents shifted uncomfortably. It was utterly miserable inside that sweltering box. It smelled of dust, sweat, and coal. Though the sun had gone down, it was still eighty-five degrees outside—on top of the nauseating body heat that radiated from the tightly packed crowd.

Fortunately for George, he had arrived early enough to claim a seat near the front of the room. Just ahead of him seated with amused expressions, were Wolf Blankston, Stanton Pierce, and Harvey Bloomstein. Harvey was the state mine inspector who graced Rainville with a quarterly presence to ensure the laborers and the state department that he had completed a "vigilant and rigorous examination of the coal mines." With each of his reports, Bloomstein would claim that the Rainville mines were "up to standards" and that Wolf Blankston was "doing everything in his ability to comply with the law while providing safety for his employees." He also stated that "the timbers used within the mines are good for all purposes" and that "there is no problem with gas or dust in any of the Rainville mines." Of course, this was all a fabrication of the truth. Harvey Bloomstein and Wolf Blankston were old friends, and not a single Rainville employee could ever recall Harvey actually setting foot underground. Ultimately, that was because he hadn't, and that was the way Wolf wanted it. Harvey Bloomstein agreed to stay out of the Rainville mines. In exchange, he received a quarterly bribe from Wolf Blankston himself.

Also seated at the head of the room to the left of Wolf was a short, bulky man with a clean-shaven face. In fact, there was still a remnant of fresh shaving cream on his cheek. He was dressed in a United States Naval Officer's uniform, and he was fidgeting, shifting his weight and twiddling his thumbs impatiently. It was as if he couldn't wait for the meeting to adjourn so that he could return to wherever it was he had come from. Wherever that was, it was a place that kept him clean, stress-free, and well-fed. His protruding belly extended nearly four inches further than his sagging man-breasts.

To the officer's right was a tall, thin journalist with a pressed suit and polished shoes whose short brown hair was greased and combed. He leaned against the wall next to a photographer who stood with a large camera fixed to a wooden tripod. The photographer was nearly two decades older than the journalist. He was skinny, though, oddly, a fair amount of skin hung loosely from his face and neck like a turkey's gizzard, as though the man had lost a considerable amount of weight at some point or another.

It was difficult to hear anything over the chorus of bickering, but when Wolf Blankston rose to his feet, the room grew quiet, and every pair of eyes locked onto the feared mine owner. A smile arose on Wolf's face, and then he lifted both hands into the air as though he was about to deliver some divine prophecy.

"I know that you're all afraid for what might be happening," Wolf boomed. "But fear not. This is a marvelous day for Rainville, and a marvelous day for all of you. To my left is Lieutenant W.H. Adams of the United States Navy. He is here tonight to represent the Navy's new partnership with all of us here at Rainville. The contract was signed last Thursday. It's a tremendous honor for me, and I'm sure for all of you, to serve our men in uniform and to contribute to strengthening our proud nation. Mr. Bloomstein, the state mine inspector, has assured Lieutenant Adams that our mines are amongst the safest in the state, and that our workforce is more than capable of keeping up with the Navy's demands."

"And what are the Navy's demands?" shouted a voice from the back of the room, causing the chattering amongst the audience to grow.

Wolf and Lieutenant Adams shared a knowing glance, and then Wolf displayed a large, fraudulent smile. "As most of you already know, the Rainville operation produces six hundred tons per day."

This was another lie. The Rainville operation produced nearly one thousand tons per day, but Wolf wanted the men to think that production was down at all times and that it was because of their lack of effort. He found that the men would fear for their jobs if they thought production was down. If they feared for their jobs, then they would be inclined to work a little harder.

"For the first six months," Wolf continued, "we'll provide the Navy with five hundred tons per day."

The grumbling within the crowd picked up slightly, but then a man yelled, "And how much after six months?" The crowd began to stir, this time more boisterously. It forced Wolf to wield his hands in an attempt to quiet them.

When they finally settled, Wolf stated, "After the first six months, our contract states that Rainville will provide one thousand tons of coal per day."

The crowd roared with confusion.

"That being said," Wolf hollered, forcing the crowd to quiet a little. "It is my esteemed pleasure to announce the openings of the Rainville numbers five and six mines within the next two months. If everything goes as planned, within the next six months, the numbers seven and eight mines will be underway."

The chatter amongst the congregation picked up once more even though Wolf continued to speak, and he had to speak progressively louder as the residents grew more and more bewildered.

"We're doubling the size of our operation," Wolf continued, "which means double the opportunity and double the expectation."

The room grew silent. No one wanted to miss a detail, but they had also become terribly confused. The announcement was the furthest thing from what they expected. It was no secret that most of them had arrived expecting to lose their jobs, but Wolf Blankston had thrown them a much bigger bone to chew on—one that left nearly everyone speechless.

"That concludes my statement," said Wolf with an air of confidence. "I'm sure that you'll all have a lot of questions. Quite frankly, I don't want to hear a single one of them. If you do have a question, then ask Stanton or ask your foreman. I've already shared our plans for the future with them, and they'll be able to answer your questions just as well as I could."

Wolf sat down in his chair and put a cigar in his mouth. The chatter grew louder than it had all night.

"Mr. Blankston," shouted the journalist who leaned against the wall. "May we take a photograph?"

"Who is it for?" Wolf snapped as he lit his cigar.

"The Tribune," the other replied.

Wolf grew uneasy. The Tribune was the largest newspaper in the state. His eyes began to dance across the room. It wasn't long before they met George.

"You, there," he said. "Come up here for a moment."

George broke out in a cold sweat. He was reluctant to rise, but when he did, everyone in the room looked at him.

Wolf nodded at the journalist, who, along with his photographer, prepared the large camera for the picture. Wolf arranged for himself to stand in the center of the photo and instructed George and Lieutenant Adams to shake hands in front of him while he put a hand on the shoulder of each man. Stanton Pierce stood by George's side, while Harvey Bloomstein stood next to Adams.

"George, is it?" Wolf asked.

"That's right. How'd ya know?" George asked.

"Why—I know all my employees, George," said Wolf, loud enough to ensure that the Lieutenant and the newspapermen could hear him.

When the photograph was taken, George knew that he had been used as a prop in order to boost Wolf Blankston's image. When the article was printed in the Tribune, it read that the community of Rainville was in full support of Wolf's plan and that they were excited about the prospect of growth. Wolf also made it known that he cared for his laborer's first and profit second, and the photograph of the filthy coal miner shaking hands with the Navy Lieutenant only helped to support that notion. In reality, the majority of the townspeople were not sure what to think or feel about the expansion. Some were intrigued by the possibility of growth. Perhaps there would be better schools for their children, or perhaps additional stores would open in town and the competition would drive prices down; or maybe with the backing of the Navy, the rate of pay would go up. Though, knowing Wolf Blankston, that was unlikely. Equally, others were terrified of change and growth, for they brought uncertainty. Would their humble community become another Helper, the population of which was nearly four hundred, or would the Navy contract Rainville for more and more coal in the years to come and propel Rainville's population into the thousands, if not tens of thousands?

George leaned toward the likelihood that growth would be a positive thing for the small community and, more importantly, for his father. What George feared the most about leaving Rainville was the possibility that Joe might lose his job at some point and not be able to care for himself as a result. But, doubling the size of Rainville meant that Wolf Blankston would need double the men. Most of the new men would likely be inexperienced, so it would be difficult for him to part ways with those who had years of experience.

The crowd began to dwindle as the attendees made their way out of the humid room and into the night. George shook hands with Harvey Bloomstein and Lieutenant Adams before shaking hands with Wolf Blankston.

"Thank you, George," said Wolf as he gripped George's hand.

"Sure thing, boss," said George nervously.

He had brooded over Wolf Blankston for years, but for the first time, the two men were speaking face to face. The sheer presence of Wolf Blankston turned George into a blathering fool.

"Could you do me a favor?" Wolf asked.

"What's that?"

"Well, there's a reason why I asked you to come up here for this photograph. I'd like for you to come to my office first thing in the morning before you head underground. As you know, we have plans for expansion here at Rainville. We'll need our skilled laborers more than ever, especially those who are responsible."

"What exactly do ya wanna speak with me about, sir?"

"I'll be perfectly frank. I've heard good things about you. The men tell me that you would make a respectable leader. In fact, they tell me that a leader is something you truly desire to be. I'd like you to be the foreman of the No. 6 mine when it opens in a couple of months. I don't expect an answer now. Mull it over tonight, and come have a chat with me first thing in the morning."

"All right," said George with a dumbfounded expression.

"Oh, and George," said Wolf. "If you're worried about your father and his friend, Remo, is it? Well, I would be happy to move the two of them to work under you. I wouldn't want to separate you and your team. I know you've been working together for some time."

"That's very kind of ya. Thank ya again, boss."

The two men shook hands. As they did, Wolf studied George's eyes.

"It's true what they say," said Wolf. "A fire burns in your eyes. I can see it. I have a hunch you'll be an important part of this company for many, many years."

George's reaction was lukewarm. If Wolf's proposal had come one month earlier, George might have accepted it.

Wolf sensed George's ambiguity and put a hand on his shoulder.

"Look. I'm sure you've probably heard a lot of rotten things about me. I want to assure you that none of it is true. I'm a fair and reasonable man, and I take care of those who take care of me. The ones who complain about the way I run this operation are usually the ones who aren't holding up their end of the deal. It's funny how people are. Men come crawling into my office begging for work. 'Please, Mr. Blankston,' they say. 'I'm desperate. I have a family to feed. If I don't get this job my whole family will starve.'" Wolf chuckled. "So, I give them a job, and then guess what happens? Within a matter of weeks, this same person starts complaining about the pay, or the tools, or the hours, or God knows what else. Then they go around the camp bad-mouthing me when all I've done is given them exactly what they asked for. They forget that they were the ones who came to me and not the other way around. You would think they would be grateful, but they rarely are. Instead, I'm made out to be some kind of villain. It doesn't seem fair, does it, George?"

"No, sir."

Wolf patted George on the back. "You're a bright young man. Your hard work and your loyalty hasn't gone unnoticed. Take the night to think about my offer, and I'll see you first thing in the morning."

"Yes, sir. Thanks, again."

George staggered out of the room and into the moonlit eve. He was not at all honored or humbled by Wolf's offer; he was angered by it. George could sense the vindication on Wolf's face and in his words. It was as if he knew all about George's plan to leave Rainville and wanted to make it difficult for him. What worried George the most was having to look Wolf Blankston in the eye and reject his offer. The rejection would only anger Wolf. It would also give him a reason to seek revenge through Joe, and even Remo, if George was no longer around.

18

George's face and arms were still coated with soot, though he had since changed into a clean linen shirt. He was still wide awake even though it was nearly midnight and the start of the day shift was six hours away. He had been sitting at the wooden table in his stone cabin since Wolf Blankston's assembly adjourned five hours prior. The goatskin map, *El Mapa del búho,* was unfolded on the table, and the golden owl figurine was resting strategically on top of it, as if by placing the two objects together some hidden secret of considerable importance would be revealed. But if there were such a secret, then George was blind to it. His eyes danced a hypnotized, arbitrary dance in an attempt to memorize the landscape in case his map should be lost or compromised along the way. A lantern rested on the table to illuminate the map, while a fire burned in the hearth. He had worked late into the night knowing well that it would be his last in Rainville.

He was to meet with Wolf Blankston in the morning, and the thought of it troubled him. He had not decided what he would say to Wolf. Whatever it was, it was going to make Wolf angry, and George knew it. He could try pleading with Wolf, begging him to take care of his father; he could try to be stern with him and show Wolf that George Hendricks was a man to be respected. Maybe, he could promise Wolf a small share of the gold that he would soon find on the mountain in exchange for Joe's well-being. It was no use. No matter what George said, did, or promised, Wolf Blankston was not a man to refuse. Those who had refused him in the past had felt his wrath and then some. When Wolf wanted something, he got it. No matter what.

To George's left was Joe's empty bunk. The fact that it was empty was not out of the ordinary. Old Joe often stumbled in around two or three in the morning blaring slurred and meaningless words that he would forget by the time he awoke for his shift. He would often holler at George about anything that warranted hollering. Usually it was about the hearth. That was Joe's favorite thing to gripe about. If George built a fire on a warm night, then Joe would complain of it being too hot. If George did not make a fire, no matter how hot it was outside, then Joe would complain of it being too cool. Every time it happened, Joe would see to it that George felt as guilty as possible for making his father uncomfortable in his own home.

There was a knock at the door just then that rattled George from his concentration. He was quick to fold the map and conceal it, along with the golden owl figurine, in his front pocket.

"Come in," he said.

The door creaked open, and there stood a barely conscious Joe held up from behind by Remo. George hurried to the door and took hold of his father's legs. They battled Joe's sweat and his stink to get him to his cot where he drifted, almost immediately, into a deep sleep.

"You heard about Blankston's announcement by now I guess?" George asked.

"Yeah," Remo replied. "The whole goddamn town is talking about it."

"Whaddya think?" George asked.

"Doesn't make much of a difference to me," said Remo. "Boy, that son of a bitch Blankston would make one hell of a blackjack player, wouldn't he? He had the whole town jumping around like frogs in a pail. Old Bill Johnson was so sure he was out of work that he packed up his whole family and hiked up to Red Flats looking for another job. He even took those funny looking pigs with him. I'm sure he'll hear the news sometime tomorrow and try to come back, but his cabin will be long gone by then—stupid son of a bitch. Boy, some people get worrying about stuff, and they take it to an extreme. I heard about some other fellas who were going to barricade themselves in one of the bunkhouses in protest if they got canned. I don't know what they thought they would accomplish sitting in a bunkhouse. Blankston would probably just set the damn thing on fire. Or maybe he'd just wait it out. There ain't ever anything to eat in those bunkhouses. I doubt those fellas would last more than a couple days before they got hungry and walked out."

"I'm glad it didn't come to that," said George.

"Hell, I'm not. I'd like to see something like that. There hasn't been a damn thing exciting happen in this godforsaken desert in a long time."

"Sounds like there'll be plenty goin' on the next few months," said George.

There were dark circles under his eyes, and they looked like they were struggling to stay open.

Remo wiped the whiskey-laden sweat from his temple with his forearm and then looked at George. He could tell that he was drained.

"What's the matter with you?" Remo asked.

"Just tired," George replied.

"Well, I won't keep you." Remo staggered toward the door. Once there, he turned and looked at Joe and then at George. "I'm sorry, George. I try to slow him down, but he doesn't listen. He just gets riled up and tells me to mind my own goddamn business."

"It's all right. I know how Pop is."

"I just feel rotten about it is all. I know how much you hate seeing him like this."

"He's a grown man. He does what he wants, and nobody can ever talk him out of it. I tried once a coupla years back. He busted my lip, and I ain't tried since. I know ya do all ya can. You've been a good friend to 'im."

"Thanks, George."

"I'll see ya in the mornin'."

"Okay. Goodnight."

Remo walked out of the cabin and closed the door behind him.

Joe was already snoring loudly. As George regarded his dilapidated father, he felt compelled to do something that he swore he would not do. Against his better judgment, he hurried out the door in an effort to track Remo down. Once he was outside, he called Remo's name. Remo stopped ten yards from his cabin.

The glistening moon floodlit the camp as it had the night before. The crickets were chirping, and the Killdeers were yelling, "Kill-deer! Kill-deer!"

"I wanna ask a favor of ya, Remo," said George in a cautious tone.

"All right," Remo replied.

George freed a muted sigh. "I'm leavin'," he said.

Remo's eyes narrowed. He tried to sober himself enough to grasp the importance of what George was saying. "What do you mean?"

"I'm leavin' in the mornin', and I ain't plannin' on comin' back."

Remo was far too drunk to be having such an imperative conversation. "You and Joe?" he asked.

"No. Just me. I'm gonna leave Pop here."

Remo looked on with troubled eyes. He was concerned for his friend Joe. The concern was so compelling that it sobered him a little. As for George, sharing this news with his father's closest friend struck a nerve within his heart, almost as if he had been saying it to Joe himself.

George said, "I think it's better he don't know 'til after I'm gone."

The two men listened to the crickets and the distant trains crying out in the night.

"He'll be happy I left," George continued. "I'm sure he's sick-n-tired of me treatin' 'im like a child."

George faltered as the memories of his once loving father rushed back to him. He and his father had been happy once, and they had been hopeful that the future would bring with it some degree of solace. It hadn't. It had brought only pain and suffering. Through that, George and Joe had been pulled apart.

"He's had a hard life," George continued. "I don't blame 'im one bit for becomin' the old rattlesnake he is today."

"I think you're being selfish," said Remo in a confrontational tone. "You're all he's got left. He won't be able to afford the cabin by himself if you desert him for Christ's sake. He'll have to go live in the bunkhouse with the animals. God knows they'll take everything he has."

"I'll leave 'im some money so he can keep the cabin."

"You really think he'd use that money on the cabin? Hell, he'd blow it all in a week. You know it; I know it. It ain't about money anyway. Your old man deserves better than this."

"I deserve better'n this, too."

"Boy, I oughta pop you in the goddamn mouth."

"Do it if it'd make ya feel better."

Remo looked long and hard at George before he gathered his wits. "I'm sorry," he said. "I know you've been talking about these sorts of things for a while now. But son of a bitch, George. I never thought you'd leave Joe all alone—you'll break his goddamn heart."

"He's done nothin' but break my heart for the last ten years," George replied. "I can't sit around and wait for 'im to die no more. He might live another three months, or he might live another twenty years. I ain't so young nomore, Remo. I stick around here much longer, and I may never leave. I got this horrible feelin' in my gut that if I stick around, the hillside will come down on me soon. It's hard to explain, but I feel like death is just around the corner. Like it's waitin' for me to drop my guard just a little. I need to get outta here while I still can."

Remo knew the severity of George's will. He knew there was nothing he could say to stop him. George had spoken of such things from the first time they met two years earlier.

"What's this favor you need?" Remo asked.

"I was hopin' ya might look after Pop for me while I'm gone."

"Of course I will, but what do you want me to tell him after you've gone?"

"You can tell 'im that tomorrow mornin' I'm headed to Rabbit Gulch to buy some supplies and a burro. From there, I'll take the Old Horseshoe Trail about three miles passed Moonlight Lake. I hope to find some gold somewhere around there. Tell 'im that when I do find some, then I'll write the two of you. If I can find enough, then I'll buy some land and start a minin' company of my own and hire a couple dozen men. I don't know if I'll start in coal or silver, but when I do start, I'd want the two of ya to come-n-work for me. You can tell Pop every word—it's the truth— just don't say nothin' 'til after I'm gone."

"Can you write down what you just told me?" Remo asked. "If you don't, then I won't remember a word of it come tomorrow morning. Me and Joe would like to know where you are. If it turns sour around here with the expansion, then who knows? Maybe we could find you."

"Pop'd have a hell of a time tryin' to make it up that mountain. Just hold off 'til I'm able to find somethin'. I might even open a mine somewhere around here and put Blankston outta business."

"But what if something happens? What if we lose our jobs?"

"I'll tell ya what...I'll make ya a map. But promise me ya won't get no ideas about bringin' Pop up there unless it's an emergency or a last resort. If the two of ya lose your jobs, then I'd prefer it if ya looked elsewhere for work before ya come lookin' for me. Now that ain't nothin' against you and Pop. You know I love my Pop, and I consider you a close friend. I just need to be alone for a while...I need to find myself."

Remo nodded in understanding and then extended his right hand. "I'm sure you'll find what you're looking for, George, and after you find it, me and your Pop would be damn glad to come work for you. Damn glad. Good luck."

The two men shook hands.

"Remo..."

"Yeah?"

"This might sound a little silly, but...why do you do this? Mine coal, I mean."

Remo deliberated for a moment. "So my boys don't have to. Why?"

"Ask me that same question."

Remo asked, "Why do you mine coal?"

"I've asked myself that question every night for the last six months while I've been lyin' in bed. I really don't have an answer. I guess it's cause me and Pop have done it so long we don't know nothin' different. Just don't seem like a good enough reason to spend my entire life doin' it."

Remo nodded his head, patted George on the shoulder, and then walked to his stone cabin.

George could sense a hint of disappointment and doubt in Remo's demeanor—disappointment in George, disappointment for his close friend Joe, and doubt that George would ever find such a treasure. But on the contrary, George could tell that Remo was a little intrigued. George knew that Remo fantasized of a better future, just as he did. The difference was that George didn't have a wife and three children to care for. It was impossible for Remo to disappear into the mountain without some vast savings of money; otherwise, his family would starve. If Remo ever had an excuse to leave Rainville and pursue a better life for himself and his family and the means to do so, he would do it in a heartbeat. That is, if he could ever muster the willpower to stop throwing away the majority of his income on liquor and card games.

Right away, George began to berate himself for opening his mouth. Not because of an awkward goodbye or a fear that someone would catch wind of where he was going and try to follow him, but the shame that he would feel while observing the sadness in his father's eyes if Joe were to find out and confront George before he left. It would be the kind of guilt that could convince him to stay, and that was unthinkable. Though, who actually knew how Joe would feel? He might be pleased by his son's decision. But he could just as easily be destroyed by it. Joe had become so volatile over the last few years that George hardly knew who he was anymore. In fact, Joe hardly knew who Joe was.

George stood alone under the full moon. The chilly night air began to sift through the trees, causing the leaves to chatter together. He took a step toward his cabin when the flapping of some large fiend sent a scare through him. When he turned to face it, he could hear wings fluttering. Even though the creature could not be seen, George knew it was the Great Horned Owl. It wasn't simply some bird in a tree. Its presence felt more like the presence of a ghost. He could feel the creature, and he knew the creature could sense his fear.

"Hoot-hoot-hoo-hoo-hoo," cried the mysterious owl, giving away its position at the top of a nearby juniper tree.

As George looked up, the eyes of the owl opened wide. They were a glowing amber color, enhanced by the blackness of the night. The owl's eyes were locked onto his, and inside his head he heard a noise unlike any he had ever heard in his life. It was high-pitched, though strangely quiet, and it felt as if it originated deep within his brain. It was as if he were under the control of some indomitable force. He tried to move and tried to look away, but he couldn't. His muscles would not let him. The power of the owl would not even allow him to breathe. The golden eyes seemed to probe deep into George's mind and continue through his soul like some sort of scanning procedure. It was as if the owl was taking a thorough look into what made up George Hendricks inside and out—who he had been in the past, who he was currently, and who he was destined to become. Satisfied with the knowledge that it had gained, the Great Horned Owl flapped its wings and disappeared into the night.

George stood where he was, scared and clouded by what had happened. His body felt drained, like the owl had siphoned every ounce of energy he had. As he collected himself, he was certain of something. The owl had spoken to him. It had communicated telepathically. It was a hard thing for a simple coal miner like George to swallow...an owl...talking to him. Certainly, he could never tell anyone. They would think he was some kind of goddamned looney. But the owl had talked to him. It told him that it wished for him to ascend The Mountain of the Owl, and that the wealth to be found there had long been destined to be his.

19

The next morning brought with it an icy chill and a thick, overcast sky. Like the previous day, the bell on the hill echoed through town and woke up everyone except Joe Hendricks. Joe was lying on his stomach with his shirt off and his mouth open. He looked more sickly than usual. His flesh was yellow-green, which was normal, but on this morning, it seemed much more distinct. It had rained a little through the night. The cabin smelled of dampened coal, dirt, and Joe's revolting gas, which was always laden with the scent of sour whiskey.

On a sheet of paper, George had scribbled a rudimentary map with the directions to his potential fortune. On the other side of the paper, he had written detailed instructions on how to get there. He folded it and put it in his pocket so that he could give it to Remo.

"Come on, Pop," said George.

Joe grumbled and then awoke violently—cutting a loud, deep fart as he shot up to a seated position.

•

It was raining when George and Joe walked out of their stone home. Remo was still hugging and kissing his family goodbye in the doorway of his cabin, which meant that his newborn had allowed him to sleep in for a change; otherwise, he would already be underground, as he had been the previous day. George and Joe stopped and waited for him. As he approached them, he looked at George as though he expected him to be gone already. Joe turned and took the first step toward the mine without saying a word. As he did, George took the folded note from his pocket and handed it stealthily to Remo, who quickly stuffed it into his own pocket. Remo then put his right hand on George's shoulder and gave it a caring pat, as if he expected George to make his break for the mountain that very moment.

The rain started to fall harder as they passed the mine office. Reading the huge, bold words "WOLF BLANKSTON MINING COMPANY" reminded George that Wolf Blankston had asked to meet with him. He had almost forgotten. He decided the previous night that he would ignore Wolf's request and attempt to scuttle out of town without having to deal with him. Surely Wolf would be upset with George, but George felt that sparing Wolf the rejection would bring with it a lighter consequence. To walk into the man's office and turn him down to his face...Lord knows what might happen.

The foreman of the Rainville No. 4, Leonard Pearl, stood at the mouth of the mine. By his side were a few of the new laborers that Wolf Blankston had so warmly welcomed the previous day. Leonard towered over them at a height of six feet and four inches. He had blonde hair, blue eyes, and a steady jaw. Despite such charming features, Leonard was one mean son of a bitch. His incredible height and hulking biceps made the new laborers look like small children in comparison. Leonard grabbed the collar of an eighteen-year-old Greek immigrant and jerked him forcefully to the front of the group.

"This is yer crew," Leonard instructed in a military fashion.

He glowered at the group of men who approached—four men from the Finnish bunkhouse. When they were close enough, Leonard informed them that the young Greek would be joining their ranks. The Finnish men greeted the young Greek halfheartedly before they were all swallowed by the mine's opaque entrance.

George, Joe, and Remo were the next to progress toward Leonard Pearl. As they did, Leonard grabbed the shirt of a scrawny farmhand in his early thirties.

"This here's Ron Garfield, he'll be joinin' ya," said Leonard.

With a light shove, he propelled Ron toward the men. Ron was one of the few new men who was not from a foreign nation, thus Leonard Pearl was willing to use his name. Leonard never tried to pronounce the outlandish names that the majority of the immigrants had. It seemed like a waste of time to him because everyone, including himself, would forget it anyway. Ron Garfield had traveled to Rainville from Texas. His stern face and hard features suggested that he had been through a lot. He hardly seemed pleased with his new partners. He looked coldly at them and didn't bother to say a word. This pleased Joe. A man who could keep his trap shut was right up his alley.

The sky seemed to darken at that moment, and the petrichor rose from the dry canyon soil as it became moistened by raindrops. It was the kind of storm that humbled a human being, simply by reminding them that Mother Nature was a force much more powerful than they. As the thunder rumbled, they felt entirely at her mercy.

Overhead, a shriek was released from a Great Horned Owl. It was flying just below the storm cloud. George and the others looked up in time to see the owl disappear over the top of the canyon wall. Soon after the creature had vanished, a golden spear of lightning crashed downward and lit the foreboding faces of those who had not yet made the descent underground. Whether it was the owl or whether it was the storm, or perhaps a combination of both, a strong feeling of apprehension began to permeate through George. With his heart in his stomach and a cold sweat forming on his temple, he began to slow his pace, allowing the others to move slightly ahead. It was time to make his move.

Before they disappeared into the mine, George cried out, "I forgot my jacks."

He had left his jacks in the cabin on purpose. Joe and Remo were too hungover to notice.

It was enough to immobilize Remo and Joe. Ron had already made it halfway into the portal. He waited there—on the rim of both worlds.

"Go on ahead. I'll go back and get 'em," said George.

Remo was attuned to what George was doing and his face filled with sorrow.

George looked into his father's questioning eyes. He thought about embracing him with a hug, but such tender delicacies had been absent from their interactions for too long. As fast as he realized that any form of affection would be questioned, he turned and hurried down the hill and never looked back. Nonetheless, George's delicate eyes had related to Joe that something was amiss.

"We'll see him in a minute," said Remo.

They took a few steps toward the portal before Joe turned and saw his only son for the last time, though George was already halfway down the hill. Joe returned his gaze to the darkness and then dipped his head. Slowly, he and Remo were engulfed by the underworld.

At the base of the hill, George hurried passed the mine office without a second thought until someone from behind him shouted his name. George stopped in his tracks. When he turned, through the blanket of rainfall, he saw Wolf Blankston standing in the doorway with a fat cigar burning between the thumb and index finger of his right hand.

"Hurry up, George," said Wolf. "I haven't got all morning."

Wolf held the door open in anticipation of George passing through it. George hesitated, and he could see that this annoyed Wolf. To keep him from being further annoyed, he hurried through the pouring rain and into the shelter of the mine office.

•

The bottom level of the office was for the secretaries and bookkeepers. Wolf Blankston's office was on the top floor—at the peak of twelve wooden stairs.

20

George had never been inside Wolf Blankston's office in his two years at Rainville, and he was immediately drawn to the deer heads that encircled the room. They stared grimly at him, and they seemed to suggest that only grim things happened within the blood red walls of Wolf's office.

In the corner of the room, Stanton Pierce sat at his roll top desk pounding away at an Underwood typewriter. Wolf was sitting behind his large walnut desk scarfing down his breakfast of three eggs, ham, bacon, fresh bread, milk, and a hot cup of coffee. He looked up to see that George was admiring his trophies.

"I'm quite the marksman," he said as he wiped egg yolk from his mouth with a napkin. "I tell you, I have one hell of a fancy for sport. What do you think of them?"

"They're beautiful animals," said George.

"I think they're marvelous."

Wolf dropped his napkin on the table and stood up. He then walked to the buck closest to George and stared into its lifeless eyes. "These creatures are truly a metaphor of life," he continued. "Some of us are the collectors of heads, but the majority of us are headless, scrambling through life brainless and blind—wandering from one thing to the next with the false hope that salvation will fall from the sky right into our lap." Wolf turned to George and put his hand on the back of George's shoulder. "Do you believe in fate?"

"I suppose so."

Wolf smiled. "Well, you shouldn't. Fate is a polluted word. It implies that our destiny will just appear out of thin air—that just sitting around waiting and hoping is just as valid as getting out there and putting effort into something. It's a child's way of thinking. Good things don't come to those who wait. Good things come to those who are willing to take them. Those who sit around waiting for fate to intervene are likely to be waiting until they're dead." Wolf smiled and then walked to a walnut cabinet in the corner of the room. "Scotch?" he asked, though he already started to pour two glasses full of the liquid, so George felt too uncomfortable to resist.

"Thanks," George replied.

There was a flash of lightning that lit the dark eyes of every deer head in the room followed by a rumble of thunder.

Wolf carried the bottle over and sat it down on the desk. He handed George a Scotch and then sat in his plush leather chair, causing it to creak under his bulk. He then instructed George to sit in the simple wooden chair opposite his desk, which served as another one of Wolf's metaphors of life: the boss sits in the comfortable chair, and the inferior sits on the dirty piece of wood.

"Do you smoke?" Wolf asked.

"Auras," George replied.

"Auras make me sick to my stomach," said Wolf sourly. He then extinguished his own half-smoked cigar in an elegant yellow ashtray, as if just thinking of one had turned his fine cigar into a rotten Aura. "George, I've heard good things about you," Wolf continued. "Some of the men I spoke to have suggested that you're one of the best men I have working for me. The production of your team is always amongst the top, and as I mentioned last night, there are some rumors floating around that you're interested in becoming a leader. So, here you are. All of your patience and diligence has finally paid off. On top of that, there's plenty of room for growth. If you succeed as foreman, then who knows what you'll be capable of?" Wolf looked to Stanton, who had stopped typing for a moment to rub his aching fingers. "Perhaps someday you'll be working in this very office with Stanton as his superintendent."

Stanton chuckled. "How are you, George?"

"Fine, Mr. Pierce."

"I'm sorry to have to rush things along like this," said Wolf, "but I have some people coming here within the hour, and I need a straight answer from you. Do you accept the position of foreman of the No. 6 or not?"

George's heart began to race. He took a swig of Scotch to settle his nerves.

"Well, Mr. Blankston...I think—"

"Yes or no, George," Wolf snapped.

George wavered for a moment, feeling insulted by Wolf's impolite interruption. He took a deep breath and then sat up in his chair.

"No," he said plainly.

Wolf's eyes narrowed a little just before a mocking grin spawned on his face. Then, he snickered.

"Really?" he said. "Why is that?"

"I plan on leavin', Mr. Blankston. In fact, I was hopin' ya might find a replacement for me as soon as ya could. I hate to leave Remo and my Pop shorthanded."

Wolf slammed his glass on the table. He did not appreciate this foul-smelling man walking into his office and making demands.

"For what?" Wolf asked bitterly.

"Well, Pop don't get around like he used to, and Remo—"

"That's not what I'm asking. I want to know why you're leaving."

The rain began to fall harder. As it splashed against the corrugated iron roofing, it released a loud, metallic thump, which sounded more like pebbles crashing against the iron as opposed to raindrops.

"Plannin' on doin' some diggin' of my own," said George.

"Prospecting, you say? And to think, you could have been a foreman—steady work, a raise in pay. Instead, you choose some hopeless prospecting excursion. You're a bolder man than most."

"Maybe I wasn't exactly straight with ya before," said George as he sat up in his chair. "I may know where I'm goin', and I may have a reason to believe it'll be worth my time."

"You want to dig, do you?" Wolf asked in a monotone. "Well, there's a mine here in Rainville no more than two hundred yards away from us. You can dig there all you want. There's no need to go on some wild goose chase."

"I didn't come here to argue with ya, Mr. Blankston. I'd just appreciate it if my Pop and Remo weren't left short-handed, that's all."

"I pay you and your father well, yes?" asked Wolf as he retrieved a handwritten account from his desk and began skimming through it.

"It don't have nothin' to do with pay," George assured.

But Wolf didn't bother listening. He just kept flipping through the pages.

"Ah yes, here it is," said Wolf. "More than two dollars per day. Why, that's ample, don't you think? Plus, as I've already mentioned, you'd certainly receive an increase in pay as foreman of the No. 6."

"Like I said befo—"

"Let me guess," Wolf interrupted. "The timbering? The ventilation? Did Jari Ronni get to you yesterday? That's right, I saw you speaking to him—the goddamn mutt!"

George suddenly realized that Wolf actually desired confrontation simply because George had refused him. Wolf wanted George to stay. George was a good worker who had two years of experience in the depths of Rainville. He was a valuable asset that Wolf didn't want to lose. Still, Wolf Blankston was not a man to refuse. He owned an entire town after all. He was the king of the canyon!

Wolf's attempt to anger George and inflame the confrontation was working. George swelled with a venomous rage that washed over his chief purpose: trying to escape Rainville without putting his father at risk.

"He has a right to feel the way he does," said George icily.

Instantly, he knew that he had made a terrible mistake, and he wished more than anything that he could take it back.

"I figured that would be it," said Wolf. "You aren't the only one to share your distain for the way I run this operation." Wolf stood and carried his glass of Scotch to the window where he peered down at his operation. "Say you strike it rich. What will you do then?"

"I don't know. Maybe I'll start an operation of my own."

"Is that right? Coal?"

"I don't know."

"Do you plan on hiring some men?"

"Sure."

"Well, then I should share something with you first. There are fifty-three men buried in that cemetery over there, and every person in this camp blames me for every death. It's a difficult responsibility to bear."

"I ain't worried about that," George replied.

"Oh, but you should be." Wolf turned from the window and faced George. "Do you want to know who I blame for those lives lost?"

George did not yield a response.

"I blame you," said Wolf as he walked toward to George. "I blame your father. I blame each and every man that walks through that portal every morning. Ultimately, I blame carelessness." Wolf stopped two feet away. "It's too easy to blame someone else for our shortcomings. I find that to be a shameful characteristic of this country. Nobody takes responsibility for their own actions anymore. It's so convenient to point a finger at someone else like some kind of goddamned child!"

Despite the increase in anger, George knew that what Wolf was saying was true. He started to reminisce about his father and Remo. The two of them were hard workers, but there were surely times when they had displayed a great deal of carelessness. For instance, the time that Joe had shattered Remo's hand with a hammer. George was aware that their alcoholism had been the cause of dozens of blunders and inconsistencies. There were many instances in which George himself had to suppress their miscues in order to save them a good scolding from Leonard Pearl, or worse.

"I want you to think about something," said Wolf as he finished his drink. "As you already know, this mine is not producing the way it should be. We should be producing double, if not triple, what we are now. Everyone knows that production is down, yet you all blame me for the lack of tools and safety, and in that, the morale plummets. The fact of the matter is, without the workforce producing the way they're supposed to produce, then there are no profits, and there are no improvements."

"You mean to tell me you don't make no profit?" George asked suspiciously.

"Why do you think I contracted the bloody Navy? I needed their help, George, before this operation goes under."

"I figured ya signed a contract with 'em to make more money for yourself."

"You mutt. You're just as ignorant as the rest of them. Why—the government and military are the beneficiaries in this deal. They help all of us here at Rainville stay afloat, and in exchange, they get their hands on some cheap coal, don't you see?"

This was likely an exaggeration, though George was in the dark on the specifics of the Navy contract, so he chose to do battle on a different front.

"And what about the timberin'?" he asked.

"What about it?" Wolf scoffed. "Am I the one who physically climbs the hill, cuts them down, and installs them?"

"No."

"But it must be my fault, George. I'm the owner. It must be my fault that they aren't installed properly—hah!" With a swipe of his hand, he knocked a large stack of papers from his desk and onto the floor. "None of you mutts ever bother to question each other. You know, from the day I hired you and your father, I always thought that you were determined, hardworking people. I never took you for the type of man who would come to me in such poor judgment."

Silence enveloped George as the rage within him stirred. He was absent of a suitable reply, and the lack of dialogue frustrated Wolf.

"Speak, damn it!" Wolf snapped.

"I know how much my crew pulls outta that hill," said George. "I also know how much your tipple boss cheats us. You wanna sit here and tell me this mine loses money while ya sit up here in your fancy suits smokin' your expensive cigars?"

"The tipple boss cheats no one, he's a reliabl—"

"He's a skunk, Blankston, and so are you!"

Wolf's face swelled with rage. He walked calmly up to George, paused, and then struck him hard on the left eye with a vicious right hook. George's Scotch glass fell to the floor, but George managed to keep his balance in the chair. His right hand involuntarily found his wounded eye. George then shot to his feet. Simultaneously, so, too, did Stanton Pierce. Stanton eyed both George and Wolf, ready to act if either one made a move for the other.

"You lay a finger on me, and I'll see to it that you're escorted to the jail," Wolf threatened. "And you'll stay there until your beard touches the goddamn ground, do you understand me?"

George calmed a little and then sat down. His temper had already cost him any hope that Joe would be well taken care of after he left, but he was conscious enough not to allow Wolf to take his excursion into the mountain from him.

"I don't think you've listened to a word that I've said," Wolf stated. "This whole country thrives on one thing and one thing only—profit, profit, profit."

The pain in George's temple was incredible. It throbbed harder with each passing second.

"Fifty-three men are buried in that cemetery. Eight alone in the last six months," said George. "You coulda done somethin' about that."

"Not when they're drinking on the job," Wolf replied with a hostile stare. "I see your father and Remo stumble down that hill when the shift changes; do you deny that?"

The anger inside George nearly peaked. He knew that he had to leave the office before anything irrevocable occurred. He stood and turned in the direction of the door.

"If you leave," Wolf threatened, "then your father and his pal Remo are both out of a job. So wherever it is that you're going, I hope you plan on taking them with you."

George looked to Stanton Pierce. He could see the shame on his face. Stanton would have stood up for George. He would have supported his decision to lead a life of his own, but not at the cost of being the future owner of the Wolf Blankston Mining Company. If it were Stanton who ran the Rainville operation, then leaving would not be a problem. George liked Stanton, as did most of the men, and it was a pity not to stick around long enough to work for him.

A flash of lightning frightened all three men, and then a blast of thunder echoed through the canyon. Both the wind and the rain picked up dramatically at that moment. The heart of the storm had arrived, and it brought with it something wicked. There was suddenly a light tremble of earth that softly shook the foundation of the mine office. Seconds later, there was a massive blast that rattled the office and knocked three of the taxidermy deer heads off the wall. Wolf and Stanton took refuge under their desks—George in the doorway.

As quickly as it had come, it was over, and it was quiet. Then, as soon as the men relaxed a little, a huge thud on the ceiling almost stopped their hearts. They all looked up to see what was left of a coal cart penetrating halfway through the ceiling held up only by a splintered wooden beam. It was a miracle that the damn thing didn't break through. If it had, it would have landed right on Wolf Blankston and killed him.

The three men looked at one another in shock. The rumbling had felt like a moderate earthquake. But they all knew that it was no earthquake. The unmistakable sound of the blast, as well as the coal cart poking through the ceiling, had turned the stomachs of all three men.

21

It is difficult to fathom the terror and anguish of those who had become grieving widows and orphans in an instant. Those who were soon to be bereaved had been drawn from their homes by the sound of a thunderous blast. When they emerged into the rousing thunderstorm, they were pelted by filthy, coal-laden raindrops, which had painted the entire camp black.

George dashed through the waves of thick smoke and disoriented miners to reach the top of the hill. He found that the entrance of the No. 4 had collapsed and that it was almost completely blocked by a heap of dirt, coal, and splintered timbers that had been belched out during the explosion.

"What happened?" George hollered.

No one heard him. The yelling and screaming, the chattering rain, and the deep reverberation of the hillside had drowned his hysterical plea.

Stanton Pierce was also in the thick of it. He had hustled to the mouth of the No. 4 with George because he was concerned for those who may have been involved. Wolf Blankston, meanwhile, had only made it to the door frame of the mine office where he watched the chaos from afar. The rain was pouring down, and he didn't want to get wet. He, too, was concerned. Not about the lives of men, but about the profits lost in such a terrible accident. In particular, he thought of the Navy. If the No. 4 was severely damaged, then it would likely be shut down for a while, making it impossible to keep up with the Navy's demands.

As George watched the dark smoke pour from the mouth of the Rainville No. 4, he noticed that some of it was coalescing into the size and shape of a human being. The head and the torso were clearly the shape of a man, though the rest of the body had a faint, mist-like quality about it. *It was a Tommyknocker. It had to be*, George thought. But perhaps it was something else. A Tommyknocker was supposed to warn the living about a forthcoming accident. The appearance of this supposed Tommyknocker was far too late to save anyone's life. Given the intensity of the blast, the chances that anyone survived were one in a million. But just then, a man emerged from the bottom of the rubble near where the strange Tommyknocker figure was hovering.

It was Leonard Pearl, Foreman of the No. 4. His face was virtually unrecognizable because it was covered in a deep black. Leonard, the lucky bastard, had stepped outside just minutes before the blast to smoke a cigarette. It was fortunate that he hadn't been standing directly in front of the portal; otherwise, the coal cart that shot from the mine and landed on Wolf Blankston's roof would have blasted right through his body. He was only feet from the entrance when the explosion knocked him to the ground and covered him with dirt, coal, and broken timbers.

"It's the No. 2 drift," said Leonard in a loud, hysterical voice. "I felt it under my feet. I think the blast brought the whole son of a bitch down. Might have brought down the three and four, too."

George swallowed hard as his heart sank into his stomach. Joe and Remo were both dead. So were a dozen others, if not more. The trials of Rainville had run their course. There was nothing left for him to do but scramble to his cabin and collect his belongings so that he could begin his conquest of the mountain. As he walked through the rain and the dense cloud of dust, he passed dozens of crying widows and orphans who would never see their husbands or fathers again. He felt horrible for them. He wished there were something he could do to ease their pain.

His train of thought was suddenly diverted by the sight of Antonia Parelli, Remo's beloved wife, and two of their young children who each held one of their mother's hands. Antonia's large brown eyes met George, and there was no need for words. Simply by interpreting his demeanor, she knew that her husband was dead. She dipped her head in an attempt to hide her tears and then released the grips of her children and embraced George with a hug. When she released him, George looked at her children. They were dirty and hungry, and they were wearing rags. Their expressions were completely empty. They had no idea what was going on. Antonia took their hands once more, and then the three of them ventured into the cloud of dust. George watched them until they disappeared and then continued down the hill.

He passed the mine office and looked up at the coal cart penetrating through the roof. It was hard to believe that the force of the blast was strong enough to carry it down the canyon like that. As for Wolf Blankston, he was nowhere to be found. The prick was lucky the coal cart hadn't crushed him.

George was convinced that whatever caused the blast was the direct result of Wolf prioritizing profit over safety. He put the lives of every man who went underground in jeopardy because of it.

In his cabin, George gathered two burlap packs and a fresh box of Aura cigars from underneath his bunk. He loaded the box into one of the burlap packs along with his clothing, tools—a lot of them—a canteen, a few books, and as much canned and bottled food as he could possibly fit. He then rolled up the blanket from his bunk and used a piece of twine to secure it, as well as his pillow, to one of the burlap packs. He took his father's rifle and his fishing pole so that he could hunt and fish while he was on the mountain. He had planned on purchasing a rifle and fishing equipment of his own, but now that his father was dead, he figured he might as well take them before Wolf Blankston did.

All the while, George's frantic pace made him sweat. At the same time, his anger and frustration continued to mount. His father and Remo were dead, and it was expected that two dozen more were dead, too. It was all because of Wolf's appetite for more, more, more.

"Who will be the collector of heads, and who will be the headless? Good things do not come to those who wait. Good things come to those who are willing to take them!"

George looked at his father's empty cot. It would never be occupied by Joe again. For the first time in George's life, he was completely alone. His father had been by his side for thirty-five years, and now it was over. It was a crushing thought that forced him to battle a barrage of oncoming tears. He threw the burlap pack on the ground and then fell to his knees. He drove his fist into his mattress and began to sob quietly. His father had let him down for nearly a decade, but deep down, George loved him because he knew how much pain he was in. At least Joe didn't have to suffer anymore.

George sobbed for his father and for Remo. He sobbed for Antonia and the children, and he sobbed for all of the broken families of Rainville. He also sobbed for himself, for a life hard-lived—a life unforgiving. A life, at least to that point, that had carried with it the same gloom that had crushed his father. But tears were not the solution, at least not for George, and he knew it. He couldn't follow in his father's footsteps...he couldn't let the cruelty of life squash him like a meaningless insect. He would find the meaning of his life, and he would find it on the mountain.

He gathered himself and began prying the bricks loose from the floor. Once the Aura cigar box was removed from the crevice, he retrieved the paper money from it and separated fifty dollars, which he then put in his front pocket—leaving forty-six dollars in the box. The box was then closed and stuffed into one of the burlap packs.

He then wandered to the lone window in the room and looked out to see the massive soot cloud growing progressively as haze continued to seep from the entrance of the Rainville No. 4. He had looked out that window every morning for the last two years. In that moment, he knew he was looking out the window for the last time. He had watched so many men climb that hill—most of whom were dead now. So many dead...so many broken families. It made George angry. He gritted his teeth together and then drove his fist into the window, causing it to crack like a spider's web.

•

The storm had settled a little by the time George reached Remo's cabin. Inside, he found Remo's infant son, Sal, wide awake in his crib.

"Hello, Sal," said George.

The infant saw George standing in the open doorway with the rain pouring and the dark clouds hovering behind him. There was no light inside the cabin, not even a lantern, and it was difficult for little Sal to distinguish anything more than a shadowy figure in the muted daylight. George tickled Sal's little feet and made him smile, which made it impossible for George not to smile, too.

George took the fifty dollars from his pocket. He was about to put it on the table when he thought about the night shift men. A few of them, especially the teenaged kids, might probe the cabins for something to steal while the rest of the town was occupied. George looked around the room for somewhere to hide it. He had to put it some place where Antonia would find it quickly. His eyes met baby Sal. He removed the dirty light blue blanket that was covering the toddler and tucked the money into Sal's cloth diaper. He left the ends of the bills poking out so Antonia couldn't miss them. He also placed them on Sal's left hip, hopeful that the money wouldn't be ruined by shit or piss. He covered the toddler with the blanket and then kissed him on the forehead.

"Take care of your maw, Sal," said George before he disappeared into the waning thunderstorm with a burlap pack in each hand.

Fifty dollars was a lot of money. He took comfort in knowing that Remo's wife and his children would be able to afford a trip to wherever they had family; however, he felt sick for the dozens of other families who would not be able to afford the same luxury. The families would likely be compensated eventually, in some way. But how much would they be given, and how long would it take for them to get it? He thought of Mrs. Ambrosius, who had taken her own life for that very reason. If only there was some way for him to ensure that the widows and orphans would be cared for.

Perhaps there was.

•

There wasn't a single soul in town or anywhere near the mine office. The entire camp had fled to the mouth of the No.4, the proximity of which was engulfed in a thick black cloud. George looked to the left and then to the right. The coast was clear apart from a thin and dirty Cocker Spaniel rummaging through some empty boxes outside the company store. George slowly turned the knob of the mine office door and crept inside.

He could hear the light, inconsistent tapping of a telegraph machine coming from one of the main level rooms. He crept across the floor and peeked inside. There was only one man in the room, but his back was turned and all that George could see was the back of his brown suit and the back of his bald head. The man was frantically crafting his report of the terrible tragedy. It was a plea for aid destined for the nearby Placerton mine.

George crept back into the entry and sat his burlap packs on the ground. He then untied the twine from one of them and withdrew his trusty pickaxe (the handle was already protruding from the top of the bag along with the handle of his shovel, the handle of a woodcutting axe, and the butt of his father's rifle). He eyed the rifle for a moment, but then he remembered how loud it was. The last thing he wanted was to cause a commotion. As tenderly as he could, he walked up the wooden staircase wielding his trusty pickaxe with both hands.

When he reached Wolf Blankston's office, he saw that the door was wide open and that Wolf was facing away from the door. He was leaning over the table filling a glass with Scotch. When the glass was nearly full, he drained the entire thing in one swig. As he filled it a second time, George crept into the office. *Creak*, groaned the hardwood flooring under his feet. George stopped where he was.

"Stanton...I want you to send a telegram to Harvey Bloomstein," said Wolf, mistaking the footsteps behind him for the footsteps of Stanton Pierce. "I want you to tell him what happened. I want you tell him that we need him here right away."

George knew that he needed to make it quick, before Stanton really did return to the office. He lifted the pickaxe and drove it downward into Wolf's back. On impact, blood gushed all over the place, primarily on the desk, although there was a little that splattered onto George's face and shirt. Wolf fell forward and smacked his face on his desk before falling to the floor in a frozen heap. A pool of blood began to form underneath him. The color of it matched the red walls of his office.

George pulled the pickaxe from Wolf's back. He needed it for the mountain, after all. When the metal tip exited the flesh, a stream of blood began to flow from the wound and onto the floor where it instantly doubled the size of the pool underneath him. The blow from the pickaxe had sent Wolf into shock, rendering him unable to cry out in pain. Even though he was silent, his questioning eyes stared eerily at George as he battled for life. Before George could force himself to leave the room, he noticed the mounted deer heads. They were Wolf's trophies and, in Wolf's own words, they were "truly a metaphor of life." It was bizarre, but the creatures actually appeared to be... smiling at him, as though grateful that George had avenged them. In a state of bewilderment, George hurried out of the room and down the wooden stairs.

•

It had stopped raining, but it was still overcast, and the town was covered in a goopy mud. As George ran through the vacant residential camp with his burlap packs in hand, he spotted a small stable that housed a single burro. The burro belonged to Wolf Blankston. The only reason it was outside as opposed to underground was because it was either hurt or sick. Whatever was wrong with the creature, George had to hope it wasn't severe. He needed the means of transporting his supplies into the mountain and his vast wealth off of it. He had planned on taking a train to Rabbit Gulch in order to purchase a burro and additional supplies, but that plan was foiled now that he would soon be a fugitive of the law. He feared that a telegram would be sent to the neighboring towns to keep a lookout for him. Thus, he decided it would be best to avoid towns from that point on. Everyone in the state would have a picture of him, after all.

He was on the front page of the Tribune shaking hands with Lieutenant W.H. Adams. In the photograph, Wolf Blankston's hand was resting on George's shoulder.

•

In a matter of minutes, he was hiking away from Rainville with the reins of the burro and two loaded burlap packs. The burro seemed to be fine apart from a slight limp and a sporadic fussiness. As long as the creature did nothing to further injure its ankle, then George felt it would be more than capable of enduring the trek into the mountain. It was probably a less daunting task than what the poor creature was forced to carry out every day underground.

George slowed and then turned to look at Rainville one final time. His heart had grown cold and empty, but he promised himself that he would not become some broken-down and bitter old-timer like his father. He would take what was rightfully his at any cost.

•

Soon after Stanton Pierce discovered Wolf lying in a pool of his own blood, he sent a telegram to Doctor James Meyer—Wolf's personal doctor who was considered to be the finest in the state. Word spread quickly through the camp that Wolf Blankston had been severely wounded and wouldn't likely survive the night. The first name that Stanton Pierce presented to the Sheriff was the name of George Hendricks. Stanton had been present for George and Wolf's ugly argument that had included physical harm. He had also overheard George speaking of his desire to prospect, though he was clueless as to where George planned on going. Wolf's henchmen were deployed to search the camp for George. They returned nearly an hour later to communicate that George was nowhere to be found; however, a burro had been stolen from Wolf Blankston's lot.

PART THREE

THE MOUNTAIN OF THE OWL

22

The storm clouds moved swiftly to the northeast until they disappeared into the peaks of The Mountain of the Owl. It was as though the mountain itself had swallowed the gray clouds whole, harnessing the vile energy within its depths so that it could be channeled into some other nature of wickedness whenever it desired to do so. The storm that had ripped through Rainville left thirty-six dead coal miners in its wake. Of course, the storm itself could not have been responsible for an explosion that occurred underground, or could it? There was still not an answer. There had been a great static charge collected within those dark clouds. They were truly something to marvel at. When the residents of Rainville had observed them and cowered at the brilliant bolts of lightning, they felt that such a storm might be capable of anything. Maybe it was.

The darkness had passed, and the skies opened wide, allowing the rays of the summer sun to touch down on the wet soil. As George pulled his stolen burro through the jagged rock canyons of the Book Cliffs, his pace was decelerated by a wave of unbearable humidity. He was leaking a sticky sweat, and his lungs were dissatisfied by the lack of oxygen in the humid summer air.

He shielded his eyes and squinted to evaluate the undulating terrain ahead. He knew that he had to press on despite being fatigued. Someone had certainly found Wolf Blankston by now. It would only be a matter of time before the pieces of the puzzle were collected, assembled, and a clear image of George Hendricks materialized.

In the distance, he could see a homestead nestled into the crook of a canyon wall where three tall willow trees provided a measure of the land with shade. The homestead consisted of a small, dilapidated cabin where a freshly killed pig hung from its hind legs near the front door. A corral was occupied by four sleeping horses that snoozed in proximity of one another, wired chicken coops housed nearly a dozen chickens, a ramshackle barn that was twice the size of the house contained three ancient cows resting on beds of straw, a small, round windmill released a high pitched creak as it gently spun, and there was a water well, the base of which was constructed with dark brown stones.

The property was occupied by only one man. He was a quiet and serious old timer who wore a straw hat that he made himself. His long, ashen beard was riddled with bodily oils, and his face and hands were covered in dirt. He worked the land alone, though it would not be assumed by the look of the place. The upkeep was flawless, as if a dozen groundskeepers worked it around the clock to ensure that not even a single blade of grass was left unattended. On his property, there was always bread, corn, beans, meat, water, and milk, and on occasion, a few gallons of ale or porter. He sold George some cold water, coffee, bread, matches, a shovel, a gold pan, a bucket, a horn spoon, and an iron spoon—all in exchange for seven dollars.

The rancher counted his money while George fixed his new goods to the burro. The rancher could tell that something wasn't quite right with George. His flesh was pale, his eyelids were heavy, and he was drenched in sweat.

George lifted his new shovel to the burro so that he could secure it. As his arms were raised, the rancher noticed a splotch of dried blood on George's shirt just underneath his right arm. It was the size of a fist.

"You been hurt, Mister?" the rancher asked.

George looked down and saw the blood. "I hadn't noticed," he said timidly.

"I've got some bandages in the cabin. Be happytuh dress that wound fer ya."

"That's all right. I've got some bandages in my pack. I'll take care of it."

"Don't put me out none. Looks like a fairly serious wound. Ya oughta have it dressed."

George put his hand under his shirt and pretended to feel the wound, but he knew damn well it wasn't his blood—it was Wolf Blankston's blood.

George said, "It's all right. I'll take care of it."

"Okay," said the rancher. He was suspicious, and he felt inclined to pry a little. He extended his right hand. "Well it was a pleasure meetin' ya mister..."

George hesitated for a moment, and then he, too, extended his hand.

"Joseph," said George. "Al Joseph."

It was the first thing that had come to mind. Al, short for his mother Alice, and Joseph, for his father.

"Be safe up that way, Mr. Joseph," said the rancher. "Terrain's hell, and it's mighty easytuh git lost."

"Thanks for your hospitality," said George as he smiled and turned. He then stopped in his tracks and faced the rancher once more.

"One more thing," he said. "How much for that hat?"

•

A minute later George disappeared around the canyon bend wearing the rancher's straw hat. He had it all worked out. He would stay on the mountain until the first of October, and he would spend enough time in the sun to darken his flesh. He would also sport a clean shave. Very few people had ever seen him that way, and because he had worn a filthy, unkempt beard for nearly a decade, those that did had long forgotten him. He would also have to use his new alias—Al Joseph. Everyone in four states would be on the lookout for a bearded George Hendricks. George knew it. As far as he was concerned, George Hendricks would die on the mountain, and Al Joseph would descend it bearing a fortune in gold.

He took a large gulp of water from his canteen and then gazed into the distance. He could see the mountain range lining the backdrop just above the top of the canyon ridge. Its broad peaks were ringed with rocky cliffs that led down into shallow, twisting canyons. Those canyons eventually trickled into the confines of the Book Cliffs.

•

After five miles of rugged terrain and nauseating humidity, George came to another ranch. From the top of a ridge, veiled by the cover of a desert juniper, he watched a family of seven harvest potatoes. The mother and father dug them out of the ground while the children—two teenaged boys, two teenaged girls, and a young boy, roughly seven—were transferring them into large baskets. The oldest man, presumably the father of the family, removed his cowboy hat and wiped the sweat from his forehead. He then walked a few paces, dropped to his knees, drew his head close to an irrigation ditch, and splashed sun warmed water onto his soiled face.

George's eyes followed the irrigation ditch. He could see that it fed the property from the hills to the east.

•

It took almost a half an hour for George and his burro to loop around the property and find a secluded place to make use of the irrigation ditch. When he arrived, he stripped down to his undergarments and washed his boots, pants, and shirt in the water. Once they were clean, he put them on sagebrush plants to dry under the sun. He washed his face and his arms and then he dug into his pack and found a metal container that held his hygiene materials. There was a comb, a pair of scissors that he had used infrequently to trim his hair and beard, his straight razor, which he had not used in a great deal of time, and an old hand mirror that had been his mother's. He trimmed his beard as much as he could with the scissors and then used the straight razor to give himself a clean shave. Because it had been so long since he had used a straight razor, he cut himself a half dozen times. The largest cut of all was on his chin. He trimmed his hair a little, using the mirror to assess the movements of the scissors, and then he used the water to help comb his hair differently than he had ever worn it— parted on the right side and combed to the left. He then retrieved an Aura cigar and put on a fresh cotton tee and his new straw hat. He smoked the cigar and scarfed down a few slices of bread while he waited for the clothes to dry.

•

Sunset approached after four hours of walking, but George kept on. It wasn't until dusk that he decided to set up camp. He found a place on top of a canyon wall where a clump of pines concealed him. A bonus was that a small opening in the trees allowed him to keep an eye on the canyon below in case Wolf Blankston's goons rode through looking for him. He decided to build a fire so that he could enjoy a hot meal, but as soon as his dinner was made, he would extinguish the fire and sleep in absolute darkness in order to remain concealed. The summer heat would keep the night plenty warm.

•

As he was looking for firewood, he came across a petroglyph left behind by the Fremont people. It depicted a human being with their arms raised and a pair of horns fixed to their head. At the feet of this person was another human being. The second human appeared to be lying on the ground. There was a large spiral above both their heads, and the human with the horns seemed to be guiding the second human toward it. George presumed that it was some sort of death ceremony where the spirit was released into the place where spirits go, though he could have been wrong. Nonetheless, the petroglyph made him wonder if Joe's spirit had carried on after death the way that Mrs. Ambrosius' had. Maybe he had become a Tommyknocker so that he could help the living avoid the unpleasant conclusion of life that he had experienced.

A blood-red sunset hovered above The Mountain of the Owl in the distance until the darkness set in, though

George hardly noticed it. He was thinking of Remo and Joe. He also wondered about the status of Wolf Blankston. Was he dead, or wasn't he? George had fled the mine office so fast that he never did confirm the death. He assumed that he killed him, but the possibility that Wolf was still alive made him nauseous.

At least that part of his life was over. There would be no more goddamned dirty coal. He had come to hate it savagely over the preceding days. Coal was the color of death. It symbolized the end of his father and of his friend Remo. Coal was the darkness—an assemblage of ancient plants and animals long since gone. Coal was death and decay. Gold, on the other hand, was the color of life—thriving, boundless life. Gold was the color of the illuminant rays of the sun, and it was composed of the sweet nectar that pleased what burned within George's soul. It was the promise of fortune, and the ticket to his salvation. It was what he felt he deserved.

●

He filled his belly with warmed green beans, potatoes, and bread and washed it all down with lukewarm water before extinguishing his campfire with shovel loads of dirt. He felt much better after he had eaten, but he still couldn't shake his troubled thoughts. Regardless of whether Wolf was alive or dead, it was expected that a posse had been formed to track down Wolf Blankston's killer (or attempted killer). If they traveled through the night, then they would be approaching George's camp at any given moment. George clenched his father's rifle in his right hand while he stared at the canyon below, waiting for the galloping horses and burning torches to come around the bend.

The stars shone brightly overhead, and in partnership with the nearly full moon, the landscape was slightly visible, as it had been during the nights in Rainville. A coyote cried in the distance and reminded him that the night was ideal for predators. Soon after, a cool breeze picked up and carried with it the whisperings of a forgotten past. The Book Cliffs had once been inhabited by the Fremont culture, as well as the Ute. In the darkness, George could feel their ancient life swirling about. He started to think about the strange petroglyph. It made him wonder what those ancient cultures knew about life, death, and the afterlife. Because our society was convinced it had all the answers when it absolutely didn't, the secrets of the ancient Fremont were all but lost. But George couldn't help but think that the Fremont and Ute knew something that modern society didn't. Perhaps modern society had been too ignorant and self-righteous to listen and learn. Too many in this world felt they already knew everything there was to know about existence and the universe, or at least didn't care to investigate, so they instead concerned themselves with acquiring things—land, power, etc. But George knew there had to be more to life than that. He just couldn't figure out what it was.

He suddenly forgot about Joe and Wolf Blankston. Instead, his mind slipped into a chilling reverie. He could feel the presence of a hundred souls. Their balefire raged, casting an orange-red light on the surrounding canyon walls. His burro, which was tied to a nearby pine, started shrieking. George could hear the tribe's chants as he looked up at the stars that beamed overhead. He couldn't see anyone, but he knew they were there. He smelled the smoke of the fire, and he felt them grabbing at his shoulders and arms, as if trying to lift him up. His eyelids were growing heavy, and his muscles loosened. He sensed that he was attending an ancient ceremony and that the tribe was trying to guide him toward the balefire for some reason—perhaps to entice him into their world. He could feel the flame gradually become warmer. At the same time, the chanting of the tribe grew louder. Just as the balefire became unbearably hot, he lost consciousness.

•

He had fallen asleep near the witching hour and slept until a hint of dawn had risen from the east. He awoke feeling like something had used his body while he slept. The same way he felt after the owl had communicated with him the previous night. He felt the gripping hands of the ancient ones still fresh on his biceps, and the realism of it all frightened him. Strangely enough, he could not recall the moments before he had fallen asleep. He had been lying on his stomach with his father's rifle in hand, staring at the canyon below, but he didn't remember growing tired. In fact, he remembered being quite alert at the time. The wind was blowing a little, and then the smell of the ancient balefire had touched his nostrils. The next thing he knew, he was awake, and it was dawn. There were three hours that seemed unaccounted for.

As strange as it all was, he was still in danger of being captured by law enforcement. He collected his belongings, untied the burro from the tree, and continued on his way. It was the third consecutive night that he had been deprived of sufficient sleep, but he knew that he wouldn't be able to relax until he reached the cover of the timbered foothills.

He walked as fast as he and the burro could in the pale light of dawn. But without rest, his tired body ached, and his weary mind wandered in and out of reality. The events of the previous day were a blur to him. He wondered if it had all been a dream. The golden owl figurine, which he gripped tightly in his left hand, had driven him from his home and was now pulling him toward the mountain. He knew the golden owl contained some sort of power—the magnitude of which was unclear. It was much more than a piece of jewelry. It had mutated itself into a living creature. That creature had darted at him in the blackness of the Rainville No. 4 before it disappeared into thin air. If the figurine had the ability to manifest itself into something like that, then he couldn't help but wonder if it could have conjured the storm that ripped through Rainville and killed thirty-six coal miners. And perhaps it could have injected him with a violent rage—enough rage to kill a man. The owl had told George that it wanted him to scale the mountain, and that when he arrived, a fortune in gold would be waiting for him. But the rage was difficult for him to understand. The golden owl had brought out a mean streak within him...a bitter anger...a violent rage. It swelled and stirred within him like a growing beast—thirsty for redemption.

•

It was close to noon when he finally escaped the Book Cliffs. He then spent the greater part of an hour circling around the town of Rabbit Gulch to avoid being seen. By two o'clock, he made it to the shelter of the foothills where he knew he would be safe. He assumed that if a posse had been formed, then it would likely be probing the nearby towns, asking if a lone, bearded man pulling a burro had wandered in. Now that he was veiled by the wooded foothills, he was home free.

23

Volunteers from Helper, Red Flats, and Placerton swarmed into the Rainville camp upon hearing news of the explosion. It was the communities that had organized, and it was the communities whose hearts burned with anger, amity, and sorrow.

It was near eight o'clock, two hours after the blast had rattled the hillside, when Stanton Pierce was informed by members of the rescue team that three miners had been recovered from the wreckage with their lives intact. The townsfolk had been praying for such news, and finally, it had come. They all raced to the mine's portal and watched as the rescued miners were carried out of the darkness and into the muted daylight. When the men were discovered, only one of the three was conscious. All three of them had been moderately burned, and they were all caked with blood and soot.

The rescuers transported them down the hill on large, flat pieces of wood and into the infirmary where they were situated onto rigid cots. They laid in the vicinity of Wolf Blankston, who also rested on a cot, though he was veiled by a curtain. Behind it, he was being treated by the young camp doctor, Robert Harriman. Wolf's preferred doctor, Doctor Meyer, was still on a train an hour outside of Rainville. Harriman concluded that the blade of the pickaxe had missed Wolf's spine but had punctured a lung and scraped his liver. There was a small chance that he could survive, but Harriman assured Stanton Pierce that those chances were bleak.

The infirmary was a small building capable of treating only five patients at a time. Most of its use had been for the birthing of children and treating wounded miners. It smelled of multiple bodily fluids and of coal, and the pea green walls correlated with the vile stench. Half the town had packed into the small room against Doctor Harriman's request, and they waited there for the identity of the miners to be revealed.

Harriman was a short, squirrelly looking man who wore thick glasses and was generally passive and soft spoken. When he had asked for everyone to clear out, he was ignored entirely, and he was too afraid to ask again. He had only been employed at the camp for six months—after the previous doctor had died of old age. Wolf did not care much for Harriman. He thought he was too soft and that he lacked commonsense. The first time that Harriman walked into Wolf Blankston's office to introduce himself, he was very nervous. He spent the duration of the conversation making awkward eye contact with Wolf—afraid to look into his eyes for too long and even more afraid not to look into them enough. His mouth had become dry, and he was at a loss for what to say. It was all terribly uncomfortable. And to top it all off, on his way out of Wolf's office, Harriman turned the doorknob and pulled, but the door did not open. The knob seemed to be jammed and would not turn completely. Wolf had to stand up and open the door for him. That was the largest reason why Wolf disliked the poor doctor, who was actually an upstanding young physician.

"The son of a bitch can make it through medical school, but he can't open a goddamn door?" Wolf had said at the time.

Wolf tried to replace Harriman with another doctor, but after a month of trying, he gave up. No other doctor would accept the cut in pay and the less than desirable living conditions in Rainville. When he realized that replacing Harriman would be next to impossible, he expressed to Stanton that if he ever underwent a health emergency, then Stanton was to contact Doctor Meyer. Harriman wasn't to lay a finger on him unless it was an absolute necessity. Given the seriousness of Wolf's injuries and the fact that Doctor Meyer was a three-hour train ride away, Stanton had little choice but to have Harriman treat Wolf.

There was only one nurse who worked in the infirmary. Her name was Helen Laine. She was the wife of a miner who had been killed in a cave-in six years earlier. Her hair was wiry and silver, her lips were dry and cracked, and her soft, green eyes expressed that she was a kindhearted woman who had suffered a great deal. She was the one who cleaned the faces of the rescued men with a sponge while the herd of townspeople hovered over her shoulder. The vast majority of those packed into the room knew that none of the three men lying on the cots were their loved ones simply by their clothing or body type. But they stayed put nonetheless, hanging on to the slightest hope.

After Helen Laine wiped the face of the first man clean, he was revealed to be one of the new immigrants who had been hired the previous day. He was badly burned on his arms and on his neck, but the young Greek would be able to live out the rest of his life, albeit a little deformed. There was an utter silence in the room when his face was uncovered. It was no secret that the townspeople were a little disappointed. They had hoped for family member or at least a friend. But above all, in a camp laden with mindless prejudice, a young Greek was the last person they had hoped would survive. As brutal as that may sound, it was true.

The second face that was washed clean was the face of William Renald, who had lived in Rainville for nearly a decade. His unearthing had made dozens of people very happy. He was a likeable man with many friends—not to mention he was a Caucasian. But the excitement was short-lived. William Renald's wounds and burns were far worse than any of the other men. Two days after being pulled from the mouth of the No. 4, he was pronounced dead.

The face of the third and final man was sponged clean—the only one of the three who was conscious. Upon seeing the dark skin and black hair, the men began to grumble, and the women began to weep. They were upset that it was another immigrant whose life had been spared. But the more Helen Laine wiped the dirt and coal from his face, the more recognizable he became. The man was Remo "Shit-Pants" Parelli. And unlike William Renald, Remo had regained consciousness and was already slightly responsive. There was a large gash on his forehead just above his left eyebrow that ran all the way to his hairline, though he had somehow been spared of any severe burns.

After he was cleaned, the nurse dressed the gash with a bandage that wrapped all the way around his head. Slowly, Remo started to regain his strength. Even though he was conscious, he was quite disoriented. He had inhaled a great deal of carbon monoxide and was having a difficult time thinking and concentrating. Antonia and the children were by his side with wide smiles and teary eyes. Soon after Remo had kissed and squeezed them all, he fell into a deep sleep.

24

George found a place to rest in the comfort of the cool shade. He leaned against a large rock that had a carving etched into it, which read 1733. He marveled at the carving as he inhaled the sweet nectar of an Aura cigar. He presumed that the carving was likely a date, though he wrote it down in case it had something to do with the location of his riches. 1733, he thought to himself. That was a long, long time ago. Who could have scaled the mountain all the way back then? Did they know of the golden owl? It was a mystery to him, but he was intrigued by the mystery. Someone else had sat next to the same rock long enough to carve 1733 into it.

After he drank the warm water in the basin of his canteen, he took the reins of the burro and continued on, hopeful that he would find some water before he and his burro were reduced to a pile of bones roasting under the sweltering midsummer sun.

•

A golden sunset painted the western horizon and was reflected from the mountain lake—the same mountain lake
that had been the salvation for Esteban Garza and his expedition so many years earlier. The lake, as well as its various
channels, was a resplendent golden color from George's
vantage point, which was at the top of a ridge that sat high
above the lake—the same ridge that Esteban Garza had
stood on. George was drenched in sweat, and his flesh,
which rarely saw the daylight over the last decade, was
moderately sunburned. He panted heavily, his chest rising
and falling, and his parched tongue bonded irritably to the
walls of his dry mouth. A surge of relief overcame him as
he set his eyes upon the cool waters. His legs ached, as did
his arms.

The burro had all but given up. George had essentially
dragged the wounded creature the last mile.

The downward slope that led to the lake was relatively
steep. George and the burro descended it carefully to avoid
further injuring the burro's already wounded ankle. When
the terrain flattened out at the bottom of the slope, George
hurried his pace, as did the burro. It knew the importance
of the water just as well as George did.

•

The burro had its fill of water from a fast-flowing stream
that ran southeast of the lake. With its mouth dripping wet,
it watched its new owner stumble in the water. George held
his new gold pan with both hands while he tried desperately to gain solid footing in spite of the swiftly moving current. At last, he steadied himself and drove the gold pan
into the bedrock. His left foot slipped a little, but he was
able to catch himself and lift the pan above the water. He
examined what he had scooped up and then dipped the

earth back into the stream and sifted through the rock, allowing the dirt and residue to filter through and leave only the solid elements. As the pan re-emerged, he observed no evidence of glimmering metals. There was only moss and algae and various insects that may have been a pleasing find for a fly fisherman. He sieved through the solid matter for a full minute before discarding all of it and starting over. He repeated the procedure again, and again, and again.

•

By the time dusk arrived, he had made a dozen attempts without a crumb of gold to show for it. He threw the pan ashore and then waded toward the dry land in frustration. It would be much cooler on the mountain at night than it had been in the valley below. A fire would be necessary, not only for warmth, but for a much needed hot meal. Beans and bread were on his mind, though he would have preferred fish. Unfortunately, there wasn't enough daylight left to fish and collect firewood.

He had wasted far more time in the stream than he would have liked and was now burdened with fading light. He prepared a fire pit by putting several fist-sized stones in a circular arrangement, and then he readied his woodcutting axe and started for a neighboring clump of pines and aspens. His eyes darted across the trees in search of dead and dry branches, though the vast majority of them appeared to be green and healthy. As a light breeze swept over the lake, the scent of rotting trout slithered into his nostrils and made him a little nauseous. To cope, he retrieved a half-smoked Aura cigar from his pocket and lit it. After ten minutes of scouring through the thicket, he found a handful of pines that were dead and dry. He hacked away at the lifeless limbs, chopping them into foot long fragments until the light had faded so much that he could no longer see three feet in front of him. He would have liked to have chopped more, but he was optimistic that he had gathered enough to last throughout the night. He prepared his camp near a few sparse pines not far from the lake.

●

A fire blazed and heated George's soul. He sat on his flannel blanket devouring a warm slice of bread and a pot full of kidney beans that he had loaded with salt and pepper. The crisp mountain air hit his face while his eyes remained locked on the heart of the fire. High above, the stars were clear and crisp, like a massive window of the universe peering through to evaluate George Hendricks without him even being aware of their awe-inspiring appearance.

As he stared into the warmth of the fire, his heart ached with the realization that there was no longer anyone in the world who he loved. He was all alone now—a single man against a massive, hostile world. On top of that, he felt tremendous guilt for having murdered a fellow human being. That horrific moment continued to play over and over in his mind. He recalled the pickaxe. At the time, it had felt two times heavier than any pickaxe he had ever wielded. He could remember his slow, careful footsteps that caused the hardwood flooring to creak. Then, there was the bone chilling sensation that he felt in his hands and arms when the blade of the pickaxe pierced Wolf's flesh and dug deep into the muscle and tissue. There was also the expression on Wolf's face—shocked and horrified. It was burned into George's mind for eternity. Killing another human being was one hell of a thing. George may have disliked Wolf, but Wolf didn't deserve to die simply because George disagreed with the way he conducted his business. George wasn't thinking clearly at the time. It was a crime of passion, and he wished more than anything he could take it back. But he couldn't take it back. He was thief and a murderer, and the thought of it left him disturbed and alone. Now that he was on the mountain, he would be alone for a great deal of time—or so he thought.

A crackling noise sounded nearby and broke his train of thought. The wind circulated the burning embers, causing a few orange sparks and gray ash to trickle from the apex of the fire. The burro, which was tied to a neighboring tree, remained calm—until it heard the call of the Great Horned Owl.

"Hoot, hoo-hoo-hoo-hoo," sang the owl from somewhere nearby.

George could sense that the owl was close. He could feel the presence of it through his goose-pimpled flesh. The owl darted from one tree to another, causing the pine needles to ruffle upon impact.

"Hoot, hoot," sang the owl before two bright, golden eyes appeared from the top of a pine twenty yards off.

The owl's eyes were only open for a matter of seconds before they closed again. When they did, the sound of the owl ceased altogether. George was on edge, as though anticipating a sudden and violent death at the hands of some unfathomable entity. He was sweating, and his right hand was squeezing his father's rifle. He was afraid now, and that annoyed him. All he wanted to do was fall asleep and remain asleep for at least eight hours. Maybe even ten or twelve. He had not slept more than five hours in the last three nights combined, and now fear was cheating him out of sleep again.

He could hear something trekking through the underbrush. It was coming toward his camp. He picked up his father's rifle and moved out of the light of the campfire. He listened as intently as he could over the sound of his own heartbeat and trembling flesh. He was able to make out the sound of at least three pairs of footsteps drawing closer. He cocked his father's rifle, certain that he was about to unload all six rounds on whatever emerged from the blackness.

He had expected to see three men, but only two outlines approached the campfire and slowly began to take shape within the radius of the fire's glow. His finger tightened on the trigger when a man spoke in a deep, gruffly voice.

"Sorry if I frightened ya," said the man. "I saw yer fire. I was wonderin' if I might share a camp with ya."

The two dark shadows moved another step closer, revealing an old prospector and his ancient burro. George let out a sigh of relief and then came forth from the shadows with his gun lowered, sensing no hostility from the old timer.

"All right," said George timidly.

The prospector turned and tied his burro to the tree next to George's burro. He then took his blanket and one of his packs from the animal before settling into the camp. George's suspicious eyes were fixed on him. When the old prospector sat within the radius of the fire, George could see that he was incredibly pale and appeared to be frightened. He had long salt and pepper hair and a salt and pepper beard. He looked eerily similar to George's father. He kept looking around the area, primarily behind him, as though concerned that he had been followed.

Neither man desired conversation. They sat in silence for several minutes before the old prospector finally spoke.

"Prospector, are ya?" he asked in a dry, raspy voice that sounded like he had smoked heavily since he was five-years-old.

George didn't look up from the fire.

"Well if it's gold ya seek," the old timer continued, "ya won't find it up here."

This broke George free of his hypnotic state. He gave all his attention to the pale old man.

"Whaddya mean?" he snapped.

"Ain't no gold up here, son," replied the old timer in a matter-of-fact fashion.

George's first impulse was that the old timer was an adversary. He figured he was trying to force him off the mountain so that he could hoard whatever gold there was to himself. He could see the mining tools fixed to the man's burro—they had been used.

"That ain't what I hear," George challenged.

"Well yer wrong," the old prospector replied.

"I don't believe I am. I figure ya just ain't lookin' in the right place," said George, which amused the old man.

"Lemme guess," said the prospector as he removed a fifth of whiskey from his pack. "Somebody sold ya some phony Spanish writin' that led ya all the way uptuh this godforsaken mou'un, or maybe they even sold ya a map?"

George grew defensive at the allegation that he had been swindled. But what if it were true? For the past two days, he had worried about the maps legitimacy. Ultimately, he feared that he had been tricked by Edmond Kelly. The world was full of trickery. Perhaps he should have known better than to trust a lazy drunk.

"You wanna find mineral?" asked the old prospector. "I'd say travel east over to Winton County. That's some decent silver country. That's where I'm headed. If ya had any sense in yer head, you'd come along."

The latter part of the prospector's statement reminded George of his father during the twilight of his life. "If you had any sense in your head" was one of Joe's favorite phrases. It seemed like every other day Joe would question George's intelligence and even his judgment. But why had he been so vile toward his only son? George always assumed that Joe's indignation was toward life in general—for a lifetime of poor fortune—as opposed to resentment toward George. But George certainly caught the brunt of it. Joe had been far more pleasant to Remo and the other men. Well, technically he was never pleasant to anyone, but to the others, he was at least tolerable and from time to time made an effort to be decent company. He had never given that to his own son. The thought of it troubled George. Maybe, just maybe, Joe had wanted George to escape from the bonds of mediocrity all along. Maybe treating him with discontent was his way of driving him off. It was possible. But if it were true, then George only wished that it hadn't taken ten years for that message to take root.

"I ain't goin' nowhere," said George. "I suppose if I hadda mine up here, I'd be tryin' to drive off other prospectors, too."

George expected the prospector to become angry, but he didn't. His flesh was still as white as a sheet, and his demeanor was as serious as a heart attack.

"I'll admit that I'm tryin' to drive ya off," said the prospector. "But it ain't for no selfish reasons. I'm warnin' ya. You don't want no part of what's on this mou'un. Two weeks I been up here diggin', and two weeks I been seein' things—terrible things."

The old prospector took a sip of whiskey and then calmed a little.

"About ten miles off is the mouth of a canyon," he said cautiously, as if he thought someone was hiding nearby, listening in. "That's where yer map'll take ya, I'm sure of it. That's where my journal took me. Fella that wrote the journal talked a lot about the evil things that live in that canyon. Before I made this journey, an Indian fella told me that his people won't set foot there 'cause the land beyond it belongs to somethin' evil. 'People just go missin' up that canyon,' that old Indian toll me. He says that over time, whatever's up there keeps gettin' stronger. I tell ya, Mister, when I set foot in that canyon, I felt my heart sink into my stomach, and I couldn't help but feel like I was bein' watched by somethin' from all angles. When I gottuh the place my journal led me, I spent half the time pokin' around in the dirt and the other half lookin' over my shoulder. There's very little in this world I fear, but as I was diggin' this mornin', I turned and saw it. I dunno if it was a man or a beast or somethin' else. Whatever it was, it scared the hell outta me. It was as black as the night. It had the torso and the head of a man but...it only had part of its legs...it just kind of hovered over the ground, and I could see the terrain behind it. It was like a cloud or a mist." Tears of fright began to collect in the eyes of the old prospector. He began trembling. "It was lookin' at me—it didn't want me there— and part of me feels like it told me that, but I don't member hearin' no words. I just knew it didn't want me there. I packed up everythin' and got outta there as fast as I could. It followed me for miles. As soon as I got outta that canyon, it didn't follow me no more. But I feel it. I feel it still followin' me."

George looked on with frightened eyes. He could see that the prospector was rattled. Thus, he was likely genuine.

"I'm gettin' off this mou'un at first light," claimed the prospector. "Should I count on ya joinin' me er not?"

George tried to think, but his mind was scattered in a combination of uncertainty, anger, and fear. The story the old prospector shared was an unpleasant one, but it reeked of the same elements that George himself had been experiencing since he had acquired the golden owl figurine. There was the encounter with Mrs. Ambrosius, the strange, lingering presence of a real Great Horned Owl, and the mist-like entity that the prospector described sounded awfully familiar to the smoke and coal dust entity that was standing at the mouth of the Rainville No. 4 after the explosion.

George's tangled mind started to wander. He thought of Wolf and of Remo and Joe. He even thought of Jari Ronni, who had been relieved of his job two days before the Rainville explosion—the lucky bastard. He also thought of Edmond Kelly. Why did the owl not grace Edmond Kelly with its presence? Perhaps it did, and Edmond was too stupid to notice? Or maybe he had noticed and had chosen not to say anything in order to increase his chances of selling the golden owl figurine and *El Mapa del búho*? Or was it possible that the owl knew Edmond had no ambitions of scaling the mountain, so it didn't bother pursuing him? It was feasible that the owl knew Edmond wasn't the chosen one. Edmond was a lazy slug. George's heart burned with desire and passion. George was the chosen one.

But the physical appearance of the prospector told a different story. He had not been visited simply by a bird in the night but by something much more horrifying. His story had left George frightened. But was the fear enough to scare him from a potential fortune? What if there was no fortune like the prospector had said? If there was one thing that George had not prepared for, it was being afraid. Twenty minutes prior, there was nothing in the world that could have stopped him from discovering what was rightfully his. Now, his mind was clouded with apprehension.

"I suppose if there ain't no gold up here, then there's no use in stickin' around," said George.

Though, he had made no such decision. There was still a part of him that believed the old prospector was trying to scare him off. George couldn't blame him. He would have done the same thing if he were in the prospector's position.

"Good," replied the prospector. "We best get some shut-eye. We've gotta long haul ahead of us in the mornin'."

The prospector took another swig of whiskey.

"By the way," he continued, "I apologize for my poor manners. The name's Paige—Hunter Paige."

He extended the bottle to George, who took it and swallowed a little to buy himself some time.

"Al Joseph," George finally replied.

"Pleased ta meatcha, Al. Thanks fer sharin' yer camp."

George handed the bottle back to Paige.

"Don't mention it."

George then laid down and covered himself with his blanket. He looked over at Paige, who was staring into the surrounding darkness trying to spot the strange entity. George then looked up at the stars. They were crystal clear on the cloudless night. His eyes reflected the vast universe, yet his conscious mind would not allow him to appreciate the beauty. Instead, he saw only the dark matter—the blackness that could not be defined.

25

The mountain lake had earlier reflected the shining moon, but the clouds had rolled in and blotted out the sky—siphoning any visibility and conforming the surroundings of George's camp to a deep black. George's breath was visible in the chilled air as he tossed and turned, battling vainly against the bitter cold. He bundled himself with his flannel blanket, but it was hardly enough to keep him warm.

His eyes slowly opened to see a puny, dying fire that could no longer suffice a warm and comfortable slumber. Only faint blue flames danced across blackened logs. Within the logs themselves was a hint of orange radiance. Behind the fire, George could see the outline of Hunter Paige. He was asleep and snoring loudly. It was reminiscent of the way Joe snored every night in Rainville. In fact, it was so similar that when George initially awoke in a daze, he confused Paige's snoring for the snoring of his father. He almost felt compelled to blurt out. "Pop?"

George was a little surprised that Paige had fallen asleep after his story about the mysterious entity. Much like George, Hunter Paige had been rattled by a haunting experience, but the sleepless hours had tallied over the last few days.

As George sat up, he felt dizzy. He could barely see anything other than the feeble flame in the fire pit. As he became increasingly light-headed, his irises closed involuntarily, and the small amount of visibility that was present dipped into an ever deeper black. He forced them open again and tried to draw a breath of fresh air, but he couldn't. The atmosphere was thick with something that smelled like rotten eggs. He figured that it was probably the lake, which had earlier smelled of rotting fish; however, the atmosphere was much more than a murky haze and a nasty scent. There was some other potent thing present with it. George found that his senses were sharp, the way they had been during those two nights in Rainville when he encountered Mrs. Ambrosius and the Great Horned Owl. He could detect the presence of some influential force—the same way a shark smelled blood and knew that a delicious meal was in distress nearby. Only, the omnipresent force of nature was the shark, and George and Paige were the defenseless prey.

George could hear the gentle waves of the lake trickling onto the shore. His teeth began to chatter and goose pimples formed on his arms and legs as he felt the cold air hovering above the lake's surface. He reached for a handful of twigs and dry grass and used them as kindling to reignite the fire. Once they were lit, he gradually added some larger sticks and then some smaller pieces of wood, and finally, one of the logs that he had cut earlier, and then another, and then another until the flame began to flourish.

He pulled his blanket over him and laid back down. He turned his body to face the fire in order to warm his chilled face. Behind the blaze was Hunter Paige who, as the flame rose, became increasingly visible. George was about to close his eyes when he noticed something. Paige had taken a pack from his burro before he entered the camp earlier. George could see that Paige was using the pack as a pillow; however, the pack had toppled over, and some of its contents had spilled onto the ground. There, lying in the dirt, was a golden fragment that reflected the flame of the campfire.

George's eyes grew wide. He began to crawl toward the opposite side of the fire. His heart pounded wildly, *thump, thump, thump*. He could feel it throbbing in his arms, neck, and head. To him, it sounded plenty loud enough to awaken Paige. But Paige did not wake. He continued to snore loudly with his mouth wide open.

With his arm extended as far as he could reach, George seized one of the golden fragments and held it inches from his face. It was gold, and his eyes flushed with the brilliant golden color. Suddenly, his eyes were no longer tired, his muscles no longer ached, and all of his pain, suffering, and fear melted away with a warm, devious smile. All that was left was a desire for more. The small nugget he held in his hand would not be enough to start his own mining company, and it was certainly nowhere near enough to compensate for what had been taken from him in the past. He needed more, a lot more.

The dreaded sound of the owl's flapping wings emanated from a neighboring pine. The creature landed on the top of the tree where the two burros were tied. One of the burros was frightened by it and shrieked loudly, scaring the daylights out of George. Worse yet, it awakened Hunter Paige. As Paige's tired eyes eased open, the first thing he saw was Al Joseph, aka George Hendricks, kneeling down three feet away from him with a chunk of gold in his hand. He then looked down at his pack and saw that it had spilled open, and he quickly realized what was going on. He was afraid that George would probe through his possessions while he slept. That's why he'd slept with his head resting on his treasure. It was also why he slept with his pistol near his right hand. He gripped it and pointed it at George.

"Hold it there, Al," said Paige.

He sat up and began shoveling the gold into his pack with his free hand, uncaring that the majority of what he was scooping in was dirt. He stood slowly, lifting his pack with his left hand. The pistol was in his right. He then staggered toward his burro.

"I thought ya said there wasn't no gold up here," said George with wild, desperate eyes as he rose to his feet. "Where'd ya find that?"

"I ain't tellin' ya a word," Paige replied.

"Show me where ya found it," George pleaded.

"I'm afraid not."

George's desperation began to fade as it was replaced by a violent anger. "Why'd ya tell me there wasn't no gold up here?"

The moon was still blocked by the dense cloud cover. Paige looked around and realized that he couldn't see a damn thing. He removed a lantern that was fixed to the burro's harness and put it in the dirt while he fumbled in his pocket for a bundle of matches.

"I'm gonna set my gun in the dirt and light this lantern," said Paige. "You make a move toward me, and I'll pick it up and shoot ya, got it?"

George sat still, eyes burning.

Paige struck the match, ignited the lantern, and then shook out the flame.

"I'm tryin' to pertect ya," he said in a calm, genuine voice.

"Take me up there," George demanded. "I'll be your pardner. I'll do all the diggin'. Hell, I'll do everything, just take me with ya!"

Paige secured the pack to his burro and then looked intently at George.

"Git off the mou'un," he said. "Git the hell off!"

"I'll take a 30-70 split," said George.

"I wouldn't accept a 90-10 split in my favor. Now damn it, I ain't goin' back up there. If ya wanna stick round here that's yer business, but trust me, you'll regret it."

Paige took the reins of the burro in the same hand that he held the lantern, and then he was gone—headed southwest.

"Please, I need this!" George begged, yelling into the night.

The small flame within Paige's lantern came to a stop. A second later, it was hovering toward George. Paige returned to the radius of the campfire and then walked to the side of his burro and took something from his pack. He looked long and hard at George and then tossed something that landed at George's feet. It was a small burlap sack, roughly the size of an egg and secured by a length of twine.

"Take that with ya and git yerself some silver property in Winton County," said Paige. "But fer the love of God, git off this mou'un. It knows yer here, Al—it don't wantcha here."

"What knows I'm here?"

But he knew, and Paige knew that he knew. Paige turned once more and disappeared into the night, the faint glow of his lantern hovering away from George.

But George could not be swayed by a fragment of what could potentially lie ahead. He started to follow Paige. Paige stopped when he saw that George had left the radius of the fire.

"Stop right there, damn it!" cried Paige. He was unsure of where exactly George was. "Don't take another step!"

Paige began to walk sideways with his lantern leading the way while his eyes and his gun were intent on the darkness behind him. George remained veiled by the night. This made Paige nervous. He stopped for a moment and listened.

Nothing.

Wherever George was, he was standing still.

From the blackness, George watched Paige's lantern—the orange sphere of light—move further and further away, like a faint, drifting soul.

Paige walked about twenty feet before he stopped again. All he could hear were the gentle waves of the lake crashing against the shore. The second he started to move again, a loud shot rang out and pulsed through the night, echoing against the canyon walls and resonating for nearly a full ten seconds. The bullet had struck Paige in the neck. He dropped his gun and his lantern and reached for his throat. His hands were quickly drenched in blood. He fell to his knees and then fell backwards. His eyes were wide, and they saw nothing but the gleaming stars. The oil lantern had shattered on a rock, and the flame within ignited a set of dry bushes.

George, who was holding his father's rifle, walked into the radius of the burning bushes and found Paige gripping his bloodied neck with both hands, gasping for both air and life. George kneeled down and stared at him with cold, empty eyes.

"Where is it?" he asked.

Paige tried to speak but was unable. He closed his eyes, gritted his teeth together, and then tried again. "He..." said Paige.

"He what?"

"Hee-kee-ya."

They were garbled words, laden with blood. But George understood him.

"Who will kill me?"

The bone chilling hoot of the Great Horned Owl resounded, causing George to turn and face the campfire.

A dark figure moved directly in front of the fire, projecting the humanoid shape as a silhouette. It stood there for a moment, and then it moved away from the fire and into the night.

George stood frozen, unable to move because of the inexplicable terror. All that moved were his enormous eyes. They danced around the terrain, trying to watch and listen for whatever it was that had passed in front of the fire.

"Hoot-hoo-hoo-hoo," cried the Great Horned Owl.

George looked upward to see the golden eyes of the owl looking at him from the top of a pine.

26

Sunrise filtered through the trees, reviving the forest green pines and aspens that were scattered throughout the region. Birds were singing a morning tune from the treetops, welcoming the new day. At the lake, the fish leapt from the cool water to snack on the insects of the aurora. It was a beautiful morning on the mountain, through it was spoiled by the stench of blood.

George's arms, hands, and face were all covered in dirt and grime as he put the finishing touches on Hunter Paige's grave. He had hollowed out a hole three feet in depth, dropped the body of Paige inside, and then covered the remains with shovel loads of surrounding earth. It was the second human being that he had buried. The first had been his mother ten years earlier. After he finished Paige's grave, he scattered rocks over the top of it in an attempt to make it look as natural as possible. It may have fooled some unknowing traveler, but George wasn't satisfied. He thought he might as well put a sign next to the grave that read: DEAD BODY HERE. It was the anxiety talking. He had started to dig Paige's grave no more than ten minutes after he shot him, and it had taken him until daybreak to finish it. It was his fourth consecutive night without sufficient sleep.

After he finished the grave, he sat near the latent fire pit rummaging through Paige's possessions. First, he removed sixteen egg-sized burlap sacks, all of which were full of gold. It was now his gold. He was entitled to it. Part of him did not feel comfortable looting Paige's hard work for his own benefit, but what did it matter now? After all, the gold that Paige extracted was gold destined to be George's gold—gold that served the purpose of leveling out his calamity, or so he felt. Either he took it, or the wealth would be forever lost. Or worse, it would fall into the hands of someone less deserving. The alternatives were enough for him to justify his thievery.

He reached deep into Paige's pack once more and retrieved an ancient diary that was convoluted with Spanish writing. It was the journal of Father Rodriguez—the man whose head had been hacked off by Esteban Garza in 1733. How the journal ended up in the hands of Hunter Paige was a mystery, though it was probably similar to the way the golden owl figurine and *El Mapa del búho* found their way to George. Of course, George knew nothing of Father Rodriguez or Esteban Garza. All he knew was that the journal was written in a language that he couldn't understand. Paige, on the contrary, could speak and read Spanish, and now that he was dead, so were the secrets that the journal would be able to unlock—at least until George could find someone to translate it for him.

George took the Aura cigar box from his pack. Not the one full of cigars, but the one that safeguarded his treasures from the past. The Aura box meant a lot to him, as did the Aura cigars themselves, but the box meant more. It concealed all of his aspirations and ambitions. It was a place of solace—a dream keeper. As he looked at the Aura box, an idea came to him—a brilliant one that made his flesh tingle with excitement. When he opened his own mining operation, he would call it the *Aura Mine*. It would be a place of hope for everyone who labored there. An honest endeavor that treated employees fairly and afforded them the latest and greatest tools and safety precautions. It would be a dream manifested. *If only Joe and Remo were still alive to see it*, he thought to himself. He looked at the box again. *Aura Cigars*, it said. Aura Cigars—the Aura Mine. Then, he noticed the smaller print, which read: *"crafted the real way, the genuine way."* He would probably leave that part out.

He put the box back into his pack and then secured both his and Paige's packs to the two burros. He was happy to have two burros. Maybe it was fate. Maybe he would need two burros to transport his fortune.

•

He was mentally and physically exhausted, but he had to press on—mostly because he didn't feel comfortable sleeping in the vicinity of a dead body—a person that he had killed, no less. Before he continued deeper into the mountain, he spent nearly two hours at the lake where he hooked five good-sized trout that would serve as his breakfast, lunch, and dinner. He was so hungry that he ate two of the smaller trout that very morning. He fried and seasoned them with dried garlic and washed them down with a pail of cool water and a fresh cup of coffee.

He then took the reins of the two burros and moved toward The Mountain of the Owl. The sun was completely visible over the western horizon, and the temperature had climbed twenty-five degrees in the last hour alone. He knew that he might be pressing his luck by testing the higher mountain and whatever strange entities were present there. Nonetheless, the gold of the mountain had become an obsession, and the obsession had taken complete control.

·

A day that started with blue skies and warm sun had quickly become dull and overcast. And the higher he climbed, the darker the sky became. By midday, he arrived at what used to be the Spanish cairn stone. The cairn had been destroyed by someone, likely the native Ute, many years earlier. All that was left were scattered stones that looked as natural to the landscape as a grove of pines. It had once been the key to a considerable fortune. Now it was a pile of rubble. A secret forever lost.

It started to rain lightly. A crack of lightning flashed in the ashen sky followed by a rumble of thunder. A breeze wisped through the trees and underbrush and produced an odd resonance. There was also a strange scent in the air. It smelled faintly of blood. George couldn't help but believe he was nearing the domain of the creature Paige had spoken so fearfully of.

He remembered that Paige mentioned a canyon during his tale the previous evening, so he scoured the distance for such a canyon. He saw a canyon, and another, and then another. But there was one narrow canyon entrance where a mighty boulder rested—nearly blocking it. It was not, however, the boulder that had attracted George's attention to the canyon, nor was it the canyon itself. It was a man standing at the mouth of it. The man must have been a quarter of a mile off. George gripped his father's rifle and moved slowly and subtly against the tree line.

The man at the entrance of the canyon didn't move. When George finally got close enough, he saw that the man was dressed like a priest. He had a large gut, and he was rubbing the back of his neck. He seemed not to notice George, who was standing only seventy yards away. Suddenly, the priest turned and disappeared behind the boulder.

What was a priest doing all the way up here? George thought. He wondered if the priest was in some way connected with Paige.

He advanced cautiously toward the narrow canyon entrance. When he arrived, the priest was nowhere to be found; however, there was a carving etched into the large boulder. The carving read, "*Come No Further.*" The letters of the carving were tall and slender, and they were painted black with some type of manganese oxide or charcoal pigment that had faded a little due to sunlight weathering. The rainfall had moistened each letter, making the phrase much more pronounced visually. They were words written to heed warning—words that meant that this was the end of the line, and that by crossing such a line, one would be putting their life, and in George's case, their dream, in jeopardy. There may have been a great wealth to be attained beyond that line, but George had already stolen a great deal of gold from Hunter Paige. It was more than enough to ignite his dream of opening the Aura Mine. But he had come so far. Turning back could haunt him for the rest of his life. But so could going forward.

The phrase *"Come No Further"* was meant to scare wanderers away, but to George, they were an assurance that there was indeed something of value ahead. Hunter Paige had made it into that canyon and left with about eight thousand dollars' worth of gold. Why couldn't George do the same? He could, and he knew it.

So, rather than be thwarted, he stepped forward into the canyon. After all, the warning didn't apply to him. The riches of the mountain were destined to be his because the owl, a supernatural being, had told him so.

The burros slipped by without incident, as they were much smaller than the horses the Spanish forced through a century and a half earlier. After he passed the large boulder, the canyon opened up a little. The priest had disappeared without a trace. *Maybe it was another trick of the owl,* George thought. *Perhaps the owl had somehow shapeshifted into the priest in order to reveal the path for me. But why a priest?* He thought maybe that carried some meaning. The more these strange occurrences presented themselves, the harder he tried to derive meaning from them.

He had entered the region deemed *La Montaña de la Lechuza* on the goatskin map. The Mountain of the Owl. He was so close. All he could think about was the treasure that was waiting for him.

He suddenly realized why he had endured the horrid living and working conditions over the last decade in various mining camps—not to mention the depressing company of his father. It was a matter of fate—a destiny that could only be fulfilled when he had withstood just enough frustration and heartache. Those sentiments had instilled within him the tools to become a mine owner. But not just any ordinary mine owner. Mr. Al Joseph, aka George Hendricks, was to become a giant.

I'll find it, he assured himself as he sleepwalked through the canyon, the burros obediently following. A fortune in gold was waiting for him. He would use the fortune to open the Aura Mine—his dream.

27

Harvey Bloomstein, the state mine inspector, arrived on a train the next morning to compose an official report on the Rainville explosion. He also sat down for a lengthy meeting with Stanton Pierce, who had assumed full control of the operation given the perilous condition of Wolf Blankston. The two of them determined that the No. 4 mine was to be sealed, and the rescue efforts were to be called off as the levels of carbon monoxide had become increasingly virulent. It was incredibly unlikely that anyone else was still alive, but more importantly, it was in the best interest of Stanton Piece—who quite possibly would be running the Rainville operation from that point on—not to put the lives of the rescuers in peril.

There still was not a definitive answer as to what had happened, though it was assumed to have been a dust explosion. The newspapers never mentioned the possibility of poor conditions or insufficient ventilation in connection with the explosion. Instead, Harvey Bloomstein generated headlines that blamed the miners of the Rainville No. 4. According to Bloomstein's report, a dayshift team "had not given a dynamite detonation enough time to ventilate." It was declared "a tragedy that could have happened anywhere in the nation" and that "coal miners needed to be more attentive on the job." It was all a big steaming pile of shit spawned not only to thwart any ambitions of a union uprising but also to shroud the public from knowing the truth. Remo Parelli and the two others who were rescued with him would be the only ones found.

As Remo awoke that morning, he found Stanton Pierce, as well as August Donant, the County Sheriff, in his stone cottage. August Donant, or simply, Gus Donant, was a short, slender man with large ears and a round face. He wore a handlebar moustache and his light brown hair was slicked back—favored slightly to the right. He had recently come under scrutiny after he tried to appoint a well-known gunfighter and outlaw—who was linked to Butch Cassidy and the Wild Bunch—as his Deputy Sheriff. Most of the county believed that Donant was corrupt when it came to the affairs of prominent outlaws, and they had been pushing hard for him to be removed from office. George Hendricks was no outlaw, just a simple coal miner who was on the run. But not surprisingly, the newspapers had likened him to a mindless killer who had attacked the "caring and innocent" Wolf Blankston. For Gus Donant, finding and capturing George would be crucial in his attempt to keep his job as Sheriff.

Stanton and Gus Donant had tried to communicate with Remo the previous day, but Remo was far too delirious to provide them with comprehensible information, so they had come back to try again. Remo was feeling much better on this day. His head only hurt a little, and bits and pieces of the explosion were starting to return to him. Antonia was sitting in a chair next to his cot feeding him a bowl of oats while Stanton and Donant stood by her side.

"Do you know where he was going?" Stanton asked.

Just as George suspected, a telegram had been sent to every town within a hundred miles. The authorities had swept all the nearby camps in search of a bearded man with a stolen burro, but there had not been a trace of George. George had told Stanton that he was planning on prospecting, but that hint truly meant nothing. Stanton didn't know if it was for gold or for silver, and even if he knew the answer to that, it wouldn't really matter. There was both gold and silver to the north, south, east, and west.

Remo chewed his oats with slow, careful movements of his jaw. He swallowed and then feebly asked for a drink of milk. Antonia held the glass to his face and allowed him a drink.

"I don't know," Remo replied after clearing his throat. "I heard he stole a burro. Why don't you follow the tracks?"

"We tried that," said Stanton. "You can follow them for a good thirty yards before they reach the main road. After that, there's hundreds of horse and burro tracks. Plus, the rain sure made a mess of things."

It was late the previous night when Remo awoke in a clear frame of mind. Antonia had told him about the fifty dollars she found in baby Sal's crib, and immediately, Remo knew that George had left it. Not only because he knew of the money that George had saved over the years, but because all of Remo's other friends (the ones who weren't habitual gamblers) had perished in the blast. George had left the money all right, and Remo was indebted to him for it.

"He never told you where he was going?" Stanton asked.

"Not a word. I wasn't that close with George. Maybe his old man knew, but...I guess that secret is buried in the hill over there," said Remo as he lifted his frail arm and pointed in the direction of the Rainville No. 4.

Remo suddenly remembered the map that George had drawn for him, and he panicked a little. What if they had found the map in his pant pocket? What if they knew exactly where George was? Remo had been stripped of his clothes while he was asleep in the infirmary and had been in his underwear ever since.

"Okay, Remo," said Stanton. "If you think of anything that might help us find him, then let me know right away."

"Yes, sir," said Remo.

Stanton and Donant left the cabin.

Remo looked at his wife and spoke in Italian.

"Where are my pants?"

Antonia knew what pants he was talking about. They were the only pair of pants he owned. They were draped over a length of metal wire that ran just below the roofline.

"I have not washed them," replied Antonia, also in Italian. "Let me clean your bowl, and I will wash them."

"No, no, no!" Remo demanded. "Bring them here!"

Antonia retrieved the pants and sat them on her husband's lap.

Remo put his hand in the pocket and withdrew the folded map. A smile arose on his face.

"What is that?" Antonia asked.

"George gave it to me," replied Remo. "I know where he is, and I must find him."

•

Antonia, who had very little say in her husband's decision to leave, which was usually case with hard-headed Italian men, dressed the wound on Remo's forehead with a fresh bandage. To ensure that the bandage wouldn't slip as he sweat, Remo wore a white straw hat and secured the dressing by putting the hat on top of it, wedging the bandage between the band of the hat and his skull. He kissed his wife and children goodbye, and then he hopped on a train destined for Rabbit Gulch. From there, he set off on foot for the mountain in search of his friend.

PART FOUR

THE AURA MINE

28

Golden shafts of light poured through a broken glass window and projected ornate solar patterns on an old brick floor. The wells of tilted light were so definite that particles of dust floated in their wake like little angels—vacillating between the light and the darkness. The room was a small, cabin-like structure that seemed to have been abandoned long ago. A layer of dust had collected on the floors and windowsills, and spiders had conquered the entire ceiling by spewing their delicate silk from corner to corner. But the structure was not abandoned. It was occupied by a man who had traveled into The Mountain of the Owl and returned with an impressive fortune.

A clean stack of papers mirrored a clean-shaven and dapper George Hendricks, who sat behind a large oak desk with his polished black leather shoes kicked up on the desktop. His hair was slicked back, and an Aura cigar was lodged between his teeth. He took a drag and then exhaled a plume of smoke that wafted upward into the sunbeams.

He watched in a state of wonder as the smoke rose and entered the luminous rays and then vanished behind them. The longer he stared into the light, the more a faint buzzing sound grew audible. It was not an unsettling sound. It was a gentle, soothing drone that spawned a tingling sensation deep within his bones. The tingling spread slowly outward until it danced across his flesh. He was cognizant of his surroundings, and he was at peace with them.

He suddenly felt compelled to stand. As he did, his joints groaned and creaked, but once they were extended, they cried out in sheer ecstasy. It was good to be alive. He walked to the broken glass window, which was the only window in the room, and peered out—squinting to filter the fierceness of the beams. The desert showcased a mixture of red and tan sediment blended together with short, rolling hills and scattered desert juniper trees. The sky was a resplendent blue—what he could see of it anyway, as the view was hindered by the crippling sunlight.

It was midmorning, or at least he thought it was. He removed a bronze watch from his pocket in order to find out. His name was engraved on the front cover of the watch in tall, cursive letters. Though, it did not say GEORGE HENDRICKS; it said AL JOSEPH. He opened the cover and then grinned. It was 10:35 A.M. Perfect timing. He had an appointment soon, and his associate would be arriving any minute.

It seemed like a great deal of time had passed since he had scaled the mountain and returned with its finest treasure, though he couldn't be certain. A lot had happened since then, and trying to think about it made his head ache. In fact, it did ache. There was a sharp pain in the back of his skull that leaked down into his neck and shoulders. In an attempt to relieve the tension, he rubbed his neck with his right hand. The pain subsided a little, allowing him to redeem his train of thought. Oh yes, the past and the future. He had committed himself to addressing only the present—the task at hand, which was the Aura Coal Mine—owned and operated by Mr. Al Joseph and the A.J. Mining Company.

Hunter Paige, the man who George killed on the mountain, had told him to travel to Winton County in search of silver. But silver did not satisfy George's craving. Coal was booming, the country was booming, and the demand for fossil fuels outweighed the demand for silver. Therefore, he chose coal. It was an excellent choice. Profits were on the rise, and because he had invested sufficient funds into safety, there had not been a single serious accident underground since the inception of his mine. There were thirteen men working for him. They were paid well, and they were safe, and when word began to spread that Al Joseph was a fair and compassionate man, more and more families found their way to the Aura—slowly, but surely.

There was a knock at the door just then. George was still staring at the sunbeams, but the knocking snapped him out of it. The daylight crept from underneath the door and shone elegantly on the dust that floated above the brick flooring.

"Come in," said George with a smile on his face.

The door creaked open, swinging inward toward the room. A figure entered that was nearly solid black against the blinding white abyss of daylight. The figure took a step forward and then shut the door, causing the light to retreat. When the room darkened, it revealed the enchanting face of Remo Parelli. The wound on Remo's forehead had completely healed. In fact, it had healed so well that George couldn't even make out where a wound had once been, as though the injury had never occurred. Remo looked fantastic—just the way George remembered him during the Rainville days.

"My God—you found it," said Remo. "I can't believe you actually found it."

George's smile widened, and he embraced his old friend with a hug.

"Remo...I can't tell ya how happy I am you're here." George separated himself from the hug, though he kept both palms on Remo's shoulders. "How's Antonia and the kids?"

"Everybody is well. Thanks to you. We would have been in a lot of trouble without the money you left. I intend to pay that money back, with interest."

"Come on, Remo," said George as he waved Remo off with his right hand. "You don't owe me nothin'. You woulda done the same for me or Pop if it was the other way around."

"Well sure, sure, but really—I would like to pay the money back."

"You wanna pay me back? I may have somethin' in mind."

"Anything, George."

George dropped his hands from Remo's shoulders and then gestured his left hand at the chair in front of his desk. "Have a seat," he said.

Remo sat down while George walked to a tall walnut cabinet in the corner of the room where he kept an assortment of booze and drinking glasses. He withdrew a bottle of bourbon, two tumblers, and then he poured the glasses half full. He put one glass in front of Remo and then walked to the opposite side of the table and sat.

George raised his glass. "Before we talk business, I'd like to make a toast. First, to Pop. He woulda liked to have been here with us. He was in alotta pain near the end, but he never complained. His life was like...a hole. I know that don't sound good, but it's true. He dug that hole for fifty-three years, thinkin' for sure there'd be some kinda treasure in it that'd make all the heartache in his life seem worth it. He thought maybe he'd only have to dig three years, then eight years, then twenty. Fifty-three years he dug that damn hole—'til he realized it had nothin' but dirt in it. He's buried in the dirt now. I guess at some point Mother Earth swallows all of us. As for Pop—he was unlucky, and he never deserved to be. I hope wherever he is he can feel like he's part of this operation, as well as our lives."

Remo's eyes were closed, and he had nodded to everything that George had said.

"To Joe," he said avidly.

"And second," George continued. "To the Aura Mine. May its riches flourish so that the two of us can live long and prosperous lives. Salute."

"Saw-loot," Remo replied.

The two glasses tapped one another, *ting!* Then both men drank.

"All right," said George as he put his glass on the table and extinguished his Aura cigar in an ashtray. "The favor I'd like to ask is a big one, but I have a feelin' you'll accept." He grinned, then continued. "The operation here at the Aura is well underway. We're at roughly thirty-six tons per day. It ain't much, I know, but it's a good start. I buy the best timberin' in the state and have it shipped here. The men have access to all the newest equipment, the ventilation is top notch, and the pay is almost a dollar more per day than what we were makin' in Rainville. The only thing we're missin' around here is some experienced men. We got alotta good young workers but very few of the old timers like you and Pop who are more comfortable underground than above ground. I'm sure ya know what I'm gonna ask ya. I've hoped for this a long time. I wanna pay ya five dollars a day to be my foreman."

"I would be honored, George," said Remo with a smile.

"You'd be takin' a huge weight off my shoulders. I've had to spend most my days underground 'cause the men are all so inexperienced. I'll feel a lot more comfortable knowin' you'll be down there with 'em."

Remo shifted uncomfortably in his chair. His elated expression shifted to one of concern.

"Are they still looking for you?"

George's smile faded. He nodded his head. He had hoped to avoid the topic.

"I wouldn't want to draw any attention to you," said Remo.

"You won't. I'm prepared. My name is no longer George Hendricks. Legally, it's Al Joseph, and I got the papers to prove it. There ain't nobody who could come here and stir up trouble, not unless Wolf Blankston himself rose from the grave."

Remo smiled, making George feel a little more comfortable. "Am I going to be putting somebody out of a job?" Remo asked.

"No. I've already talked to the men. They know who ya are, and they're all thrilled to have ya as foreman. In fact, ya oughta head on up there now and introduce yourself."

"Sure, George. I'll go right away."

Remo drained the rest of his bourbon and then stood.

"One more thing," said George. "From now on, never call me George. George is dead. The name's Al Joseph. The future of the Aura depends on that."

Remo nodded and then extended his hand.

"Thank you again, Mr. Joseph—for everything. I won't let you down."

"I know ya won't, Remo."

George expected that his conversation with Remo had reached its conclusion. It hadn't. Remo remained at the foot of his desk with wondrous eyes.

"There somethin' else ya wanna talk about?" George asked.

Remo shifted his weight. "I guess I'm just curious about what happened up on that mountain is all, Geor...Mr. Joseph. I mean, one minute you're running out of town with nothing, and now here you are with everything you've ever dreamed of. You and I used to talk about this kind of stuff all the time. Boy, did we ever. Must be one hell of a story. Son of a bitch, I'd love to hear about it."

George forced a smile. This was certainly something he did not want to talk about. There was a great deal of shame associated with his fortune. It had been attained through theft and murder.

"Whaddya wanna know?" George asked, trying not to sound irritable.

"Anything, everything—I mean, what kind of mine was it anyway? Was it dug into the mountainside, or was it just out in the open—maybe hidden by a tree or a rock or something? I seen a coupla mines like that over in Summerville. Or hell, maybe you panned in a stream for all that gold. That'd be a lot of work—in the sun no less, too. At least underground you can keep out of the sun. I know a guy down there in Placerton...oh, hell no, can't be Placerton...where was that stout son of a bitch from? Mercer maybe...or Templeton. Hell no, wasn't Templeton...had to be Mercer. Anyway, that son of a bitch was up panning for gold some place near Sunshine canyon. He told me there were a lot of folks up that way prospecting and that they were all mean bastards carrying rifles and threating to shoot people who set foot on their claim. It's lucky for you there wasn't somebody else up there waiting to blow your head off."

George exhaled a lungful of anxiety in the form of a sigh.

"It was a small mine dug into the mountainside," he said. "It was pretty high up. I found it four days after I left Rainville."

His mind continued to race. His lips were about to open in order to continue speaking, but no more words came out. The truth was that he had never found the gold mine. He had searched for days on end until he nearly starved to death. He had stolen the gold from Hunter Paige and used it to start the Aura. How could he tell Remo a story like that? There was absolutely nothing to be proud of or passionate about.

"I guess I was lucky enough to pull a little color outta the mountain," George continued. "But the pocket ran dry. I had just enough to start up a coal mine of my own, and here we are. The future is bright."

"Well, I'll be damned," said Remo. "Maybe you'd like to take me up there sometime. There might be a few more pockets you haven't come across yet. I used to work hard rock over in Summerville some time ago. I did that for about three or four months, I guess, before I heard they were paying better at Rainville. Hard rock is hard work, but hell, you cut me in, and I'd be damn glad to give you a hand. I'd even take a lesser share, too—this being your deal and all. You never know. Might be a damn motherlode up there."

"I'll give it some thought," said George hollowly. "We can talk about it more another time. You oughta head up the mine. There's alotta work to be done."

Remo was taken aback. He recalled the days underground when George talked about leaving Rainville to prospect on his own. They had talked a great deal about prospecting, and they had talked passionately. Remo expected that George would share his tale with pride and passion. Instead, George was distant and evasive.

"Okay, Mr. Joseph. Thank you again," said Remo. He slapped on a fake smile, turned, and opened the door, allowing the white abyss to swallow him.

George withdrew a book of matches from his pocket and reignited his Aura cigar. He sat at his desk—puzzled and a little apprehensive. The emergence of Remo marked the first time that he had spoken of, or even thought about, the mountain since his unruly excursion. He was surprised by how much the topic had rattled him.

There was something else that George had not done since his time on the mountain. He suddenly remembered what it was. Remembered probably wasn't the right word. He felt it. He opened the top drawer of his desk. As he did, it let out a high pitched squeak as wood scraped against wood. He withdrew an object that was wrapped in a white handkerchief and sat it down on the surface of his desk. A square beam of light was pouring through the broken glass window directly onto the handkerchief.

He unfolded it and exposed the golden owl figurine. As the sunlight touched the vibrant gold, the dark, twisting force within the figurine came to life. George felt its potent energy stirring within him. Cautiously, he lifted his right hand above the golden owl and lowered it until his hand was hovering no more than an inch from it. He could feel an intense heat radiating from it, which was odd. He couldn't help but lower his fingers and touch it. When he did, his hand recoiled away as the heat singed his flesh.

He suddenly felt a strong emotion, something that he had never felt before in regard to the golden owl—fear. What was he afraid of? He did not know. Fear was a sentiment that he did not expect. In the past, the golden owl had been in his favor. It was a beacon of promise—a loyal and compassionate entity that was devoted to him, and only to him. But that devotion was gone now, and he didn't know why. It made him angry. The point of buying the golden owl was to help him become a fair and honest businessman. Instead, he was a liar, a murderer, and a thief. The thought of it made it hard for him to sleep at night.

He covered the figurine with the handkerchief and then put it back in the drawer. He closed the drawer, and it let out another shriek as the wood scraped together. With his right elbow propped on his armrest, his thumb placed against his jawbone, and his index finger rubbing against his upper lip, he began to be muse. Fear. Why?

Perhaps the golden owl resented him for giving up on it. But gold was in the past. Coal was his business again. Gold was life; coal was death. Maybe that angered the force that dwelled within the owl. Maybe it was not yet finished with him. *How silly*, he thought. Was it possible for a material object to possess such a level of petty jealousy? Yes, it was possible. If he had learned anything, it was that the golden owl was capable of anything from observation, manifestation, communication, and everything in between. But what did it really matter now? Everything was going according to plan. He had his mine, and he had his foreman. Every goal had been met, and the wheels of his illustrious operation were churning. His will was strong, but his mind was stronger. It was an elaborate, powerful organism capable of boundless lust and fantasy.

29

The chattering of pickaxes had come to a halt, as had the shovels, hammers, and bits. The ore cars were idle, and the stubborn burros stood next to their owners with empty expressions. Only thirteen men were employed at the Aura Mine, but that was about to change.

The coal-dusted men huddled at the top of a test shaft that had been drilled in order to measure the width of a newly discovered seam of coal. The measuring was being done by two men who had climbed down a wooden ladder to record the measurement with a tape stretcher assembly. George stood closest to the shaft with an oil burning lantern in his hand. He wanted to be the first to hear the much anticipated result. He could hear the two men below, tinkering about. With each passing second, he grew more impatient. He hoped that the seam would be a large one. The largest seam that he had ever worked in Rainville was twenty-five feet. Wolf Blankston must have made a fortune off that seam and others like it. A more realistic expectation for

George was to discover a seam in the neighborhood of six to eight feet; however, he couldn't dismiss the confident notion that the seam would be a momentous one. Fate had smiled upon him lately. He had found gold. Rather, gold had found him, and the Aura was up and running without a single hitch. Oh yes, his days of tribulation were a thing of the past. It was the time of redemption. It was the time of wealth.

"Wow," said one of the men from the bottom of the shaft.

"What is it?" George cried.

"Almost got it," replied the echoing voice.

There was a moment of silence that made George nervous and irritable. He was close to hollering at the men impatiently when one of them spoke.

"Twenty-two feet, Mr. Joseph. Twenty-two goddamn feet."

It was a monster, and deep down George knew it was going to be a monster. A smile grew on his face as he listened to the oohing and aahing from the small assemblage of laborers.

"Congratulations, men," said George as he turned to them. "This is one hell of a find."

He could see the wistful look on their faces. They all knew they had discovered a fortune in coal—a fortune that did not belong to them. They understood that such a find would benefit one man and one man only, Mr. Al Joseph, aka George Hendricks. Their lives would not change no matter how many twenty-two foot seams of coal they unearthed. Al Joseph owned that coal. He owned the land, the housing, the stores, the crops, and the trees. The coal miner owned nothing. But just as that harsh reality set in, George shocked them all.

"Every man here'll receive a bonus for this find," he said. "And from here on out, you'll all get a ten percent increase in pay."

The men could not believe it. They had never worked for a man like Al Joseph. The majority of the men couldn't help but smile. Two men began to clap, sparking the clapping of every other man. One man whistled, and another man hollered, "Yeah!"

What a joy it was to work for a man like Al Joseph! Al was fair and honest, unlike Wolf Blankston. The thought of it pleased George. Wolf was finished in the mining industry, and George's career was starting to bloom. A twenty-two foot seam of coal was his ticket to the empire he always dreamed of. It was the ticket to a booming population, a ticket to schools and stores, a ticket to fame, and most importantly, a ticket to fortune. If only he had a little more money. If only he had found the gold mine. He could hire more men, acquire more equipment, and instead of a slow, tedious process that would likely take months or even years to develop, his empire would blossom overnight. But George had no more money aside from his meager profits, the majority of which were being used on the necessities of good business practice, such as adequate tools and strong timbering. Being fair was too damn expensive.

The thought hit him suddenly. He had left Rainville with forty-six dollars, some tools, and the clothes on his back. He had transformed that into the makings of a wholesome living. But now that his dream had manifested into a reality, it wasn't enough. Why weren't the modest earnings of the Aura enough to satisfy him? He wanted more—a lot more—though, it would cost him. There was always a cost. He needed more money. Once he had more money, he would use it as a catalyst to make even more money. He would never be satisfied. Even if he owned every mine in the county, his hunger for more would continue to swell. He would want to own every mine in two counties, and then four. After that, he would want every operation in the state. When would the vicious cycle end? Would it end?

Perhaps that was how men like Wolf Blankston had spawned all over the country. Greed was prevalent, and every day a new spewing, slimy egg of gluttony hatched somewhere in America. From that hideous egg, a corporate slug would emerge hissing and snarling—longing, not for blood, but for the taste of prosperity. And once they delighted in their taste of fortune, the appetite for wealth—which was almost always obtained through the exploitation of others—would balloon into a massive snowball rolling down the slopes of a snow-covered mountain. Nothing would stop it until it came barreling into the communities, knocking over houses and schools, and killing and injuring countless people in the process. But that is what our society had created—a system where greed and materialism are rewarded, while truth, diligence, and kindness are trampled upon and even laughed at.

The fact that George had reached his new status by killing two men was a terrible burden that he carried. But then again, he promised himself that he would acquire what was rightfully his by the use of any means necessary. No one would stand in his path. Little did he know how widespread and destructive that mentality was. It had been for centuries past and would be for centuries to come.

There were people born with nothing, and there were people born with everything. When Wolf Blankston was born, he entered a world where he would hardly have to lift a finger throughout his existence, whereas millions who owned next to nothing spent ten to twelve hours every day underground just to feed and clothe their children. All men are created equal. In what way? Mentally? Physically? With equal opportunity? Bullshit.

George would not become Wolf Blankston. An appetite for more would not steer his every action. When it came to the twenty-two foot seam, he would be patient. He would make sure that the men who extracted the coal would be safe. When he could afford to do so, he would hire more men. He would nurture it like a budding plant. There would be no need to cut costs on timbering or cut wages in order to hire more men. Wolf Blankston would have done both of those things, and George was not Wolf Blankston—that was to be made abundantly clear.

George understood what Wolf never did—the miner was more valuable than the coal. The miner was a living, breathing organism that wanted nothing more than to provide for the people he loved. Through him, the miner's family was given a quality of life, and life was beautiful. Coal, on the other hand, was death—literally. How ironic it was to fuel life with death.

Meanwhile, the two men who had measured the seam of coal climbed from the shaft in order to shake George's hand. They slurred a few generic congratulatory remarks, and then all the men returned to wherever it was they were assigned. George made his way for the surface. A twenty-two foot seam. He couldn't stop thinking about it. Removing the coal would be tedious. He had not the tools nor the men to approach it the way he would have liked, which would entail appointing two dozen men to develop the seam around the clock. Only thirteen men labored at the

Aura coal mine, and now George needed to triple that amount. Triple the men, triple the tools, triple the animals, and triple the timbering. All in exchange for triple the output. Spend money, make money, repeat. Taste money, crave money, kill for money.

As he trekked through the dark passageway, he heard a distant hammer pounding away at a jack. Ting... ting...ting. It was odd because every man who was employed at the Aura had been huddled around the test shaft minutes earlier, and George was the first to leave. Apparently, one man had not been present. George held the oil burning lantern even with his chest. The further he walked, the more distinct the hamming became. Soon he arrived at a junction. The tunnel to his left led out of the mine. He looked down that tunnel and saw a sliver of daylight. The tunnel to his right was where the hammering was coming from. George took the tunnel to his right.

The hammering became more and more distinct. Ping! Ping! Ping! There was a slight bend in the tunnel. Once George passed it, a solitary light appeared about fifty yards off. It was a dim light. He could see only the silhouette of someone hammering away at the coalface.

"Excuse me," George hollered.

The man kept hammering.

George kept walking toward him. With each step, a little more of the working man was revealed. George stopped ten feet away from him.

"Excuse me," he repeated.

Slowly, the man turned.

It was Joe. His eyes were jet black in color, and his flesh was milky white. He stared at George, and George stared back, petrified.

Joe let out a loud, eccentric moan. It was the same moan that George had heard from the Rainville Tommyknocker. Soon after, a gust swept through the drift, and the flame of Joe's lantern began to sway violently. The flame flickered on and off Joe's pale face, until finally the lantern went out. When the lantern went out, Joe went out, too. He had dis-appeared altogether—simultaneously with the flame. George swallowed hard and took a few nervous steps for-ward. No one was there. It was just an abandoned coalface.

•

In his office, George sat in his chair with his feet kicked up on the desktop. He stared at the wall on the opposite side of the room with a troubled expression. He wondered how it was possible that Joe was in the Aura. He recalled Joe tell-ing him once that, "a spirit can wander." But why had Joe wandered to the Aura? Or did he? He couldn't make sense of it. Good spirits, evil spirits. Some warned the living of trouble, others knocked tools from men's hands and snick-ered about it. It was starting to be too much. He wanted it all to go away so he could focus on his business. In particu-lar, the twenty-two foot seam.

He exhaled a lungful of apprehension and then looked at the floors that were caked with dust and at the daylight pouring through the rusted cracks in the ceiling. It looked like the room had not been cleaned in thirty years. He would have to pay someone to clean it for him. After all, he had a mine to run. Not just any mine, but a mine that was on the verge of booming. A dream that was on the verge of booming. His eyes continued to wander around the room. He noticed his old mining tools hanging on the wall. There was his scoop shovel (or chair, as Remo called it) and his jacks. There was also his crude mining pickaxe. The same pickaxe that had pierced the flesh of Wolf Blankston.

30

A set of iron train tracks looped around a winding hillside on a vibrant summer morning. A whining horn from a steam locomotive echoed off the adjacent hills, escalating louder and louder with each passing shout. The singing of the birds and the humming of the insects were drowned out by the hissing of the train's boiler and by the powerful driving wheels that churned mechanically, allowing the great beast to progress.

The jet-black locomotive came to a stop at the town of Whistle Springs—just four miles northwest of the Aura Mine. It was here that a well-dressed man stepped off the train and boarded a horse carriage destined for the Aura Mine.

•

The ride lasted forty-five minutes. The carriage rattled and shifted through the duration of the trip as it crossed the dirty, rocky terrain. On top of that, the brilliant sun heated the landscape to a sizzling ninety-six degrees. By the time the well-dressed traveler arrived at the Aura, he was ready to vomit. He staggered off the carriage, wiped the sweat from his forehead with a handkerchief, and then brushed the dust from his tie and jacket.

He studied the domain that George had built with great disgust. It was clear that George had put very little money into the operation. Certainly it couldn't have been making much profit—just as the well-dressed traveler suspected. He saw the mine's portal crudely built into the hillside. How primitive it looked, like a clan of Neanderthal had hollowed it out to be used as a habitat. The tipple was substandard as well. It was a small, crumbling shack where the loads of coal were weighed and scanned for rocks. Beyond the shack was a newly built bridge that followed the natural incline of the hill. A single set of iron track ran from the portal of the Aura Mine into the tipple and across the length of the bridge. At the end of the bridge, roughly eight feet below, were the railroad tracks where the lumps of coal were collected and shipped. Last, there was the office. It was a pathetic pile of ancient stones in the eyes of the well-dressed traveler, and this pleased him. The corrugated iron roofing contained several rusted holes, and the lone window on the building was cracked like a spider's web.

The traveler smiled and then paced toward the office. He stopped in front of the door and read from a bronze plaque: AL JOSEPH. Above the door, stamped on a flat plank of wood in bold black letters was the title: A.J. MINING COMPANY. The well-dressed traveler knocked three times.

"Come in," shouted a muffled voice from inside the shack.

The traveler opened the door and walked in.

George was sitting in his chair with his feet on the desk. As the identity of the well-dressed man was revealed, George looked on in a state of shock. *It couldn't possibly be*, he thought. Standing in the doorway, holding a briefcase, was Wolf Blankston—healthy as an ox. The two men stared at one another in silence before Wolf put his briefcase on the ground and removed his jacket. He folded the jacket and hung it on the back of a chair in front of him with slow movements. He then loosened his tie and began unbuttoning his shirt. One by one, the buttons came loose, and after he removed the last one, he pulled the shirt from his flesh and turned his back to George, revealing a large, nasty scar under his right shoulder blade.

George stared at the scar in both disbelief and horror. It was a gruesome sight. He couldn't help but wonder how the man had survived such a heinous blow.

Wolf turned and faced George, eyeing him as he slipped his shirt back on. He buttoned it back up slowly to make George feel uncomfortable.

"As you probably know," said Wolf in a cold, raspy voice. "The Rainville operation is shut down for good—sealed off—never to be worked again."

George was still in disbelief. He had tried to convince himself that Wolf Blankston was dead, but there had always been a small amount of trepidation lingering within him. He had long feared that Wolf Blankston was alive, and if he had survived the attack, then he would stop at nothing to track George down. Now he had, but what confused George was the fact that he was alone. George expected that if Wolf ever found him, it would be with a dozen law enforcement officials who would kick his door down and haul him to the upstate prison. Something was up. George could smell it.

"I hadn't heard," said George.

Wolf stepped forward and then sat in the chair where he had draped his jacket. There, he sat opposite George with only the desk between them. He had succeeded in making George feel uncomfortable.

"Whadderya doin' here?" George asked.

"You left me in a pool of my own blood," Wolf replied. "Did you think you would never have to face the penalties that your crime warrants—for instance—life imprisonment for attempted murder?"

George was speechless.

Wolf sensed the minor victory and unleashed a devious grin. "Well, here I am, George. Your guilty conscience has led me to you. I know everything about your little operation here. Much to my surprise, you're having a little success. But, I'm confident that the success will be short-lived."

"I beg to differ," George retorted.

"Be honest with me," said Wolf as he sat up straight, grimacing at the pain that rushed through his upper back. "Your honest ways have left you with empty pockets in this barren desert, haven't they?"

George shifted in his chair as a bead of sweat rolled from his temple. Wolf was right to some degree. If George hadn't been so fair-minded, then there would have been more room for growth. Certainly he had no intentions of depriving his workforce to the extent that Wolf had, but he could have cut a few corners. If he did, then maybe he would have the necessary savings to invest in the twenty-two foot seam, and overall, in the growth of the Aura. But George remained vigilant. Wolf was trying to trick him. He would not be easily fooled.

"I dunno where ya get your information, Mr. Blankston," he said. "But if your sources were reliable, then you'd know the Aura was doin' quite well. Now cut out the games and gimme a straight answer. Whadderya doin' here, and whaddya want?"

Blood rushed into Wolf's head, causing the vein on his forehead to bulge. "I could have you thrown in prison in a heartbeat," he snarled. He was looking at George the way he did in Rainville right before he popped him in the eye with a right hook. This time, however, Wolf gradually calmed. "But, after I heard about your endeavor here, I began to consider the alternative."

"And what's that?"

"All I've ever known is the mining industry," said Wolf. "My father started in it. He was a prosperous man—a great businessman. It was my duty to build upon what he started. I guess it's fair to say that now that I don't have an operation of my own, I have failed."

It was strange, but George could see that Wolf was candid. If he were acting, then George was compelled by his performance.

"I often recall our conversation in my office that day in Rainville," Wolf continued. "While you were out of line, some of what you said wasn't completely off the mark."

George was baffled. Wolf Blankston was actually... apologizing to him? It was hard to fathom, but as much as George wanted to doubt Wolf, he could still detect genuineness.

"How about a drink?" Wolf asked, snapping George from his train of thought.

George looked at Wolf, then to the liquor cabinet, and then back at Wolf.

"Scotch for me," said Wolf.

George rose to his feet and walked to the liquor cabinet. He eyed Wolf, expecting him to withdraw a pistol and shoot him then and there. George grabbed a bottle of Scotch and a bottle of bourbon as well as two glasses. He tipped the bottle of Scotch, but because he was distracted by Wolf, he poured in too much and spilled some on the tabletop. He took a red handkerchief from his shirt pocket and wiped the Scotch from Wolf's glass and then from the wooden countertop. He discarded the handkerchief and then poured a perfect cup of bourbon for himself. He would need it now, perhaps even two or three glasses of it. He picked up both glasses, the Scotch in the left and the bourbon in the right, and handed the Scotch to Wolf before sitting down.

"I'll spare you a prison sentence," said Wolf as he sipped the Scotch. "You'll never be arrested, and you'll never be questioned. You'll be wiped clean of this incident entirely, forever."

"In exchange for what?" George asked skeptically.

"A fifty-fifty split ownership of the Aura Mine," Wolf replied.

George's heart sank into his stomach.

"You're serious?" he inquired.

"Of course, I'm serious," Wolf snapped. "You want out of prison don't you? Well, I want a shot at redemption. Perhaps I've been a little too voracious as an owner, and I believe that you've been far too liberal. But, if the two of us could join forces and find some sort of...middle ground, then we might be able to make some money."

George opened a drawer on his desk and withdrew an Aura cigar. He cut the tip, licked the barrel, lit the end, inhaled, and then exhaled a plume of smoke. "Everyone at Rainville was in a cloud of dust. You ain't got no witnesses. You ain't got a damn thing that'd stand up in a courtroom, so I'd appreciate it if you'd be on your way."

Wolf grinned then opened his briefcase. "You're still smoking Auras, are you? Why—you've even named your operation after them." He chuckled. From inside the briefcase, he removed three sheets of paper and slid them across the table. "Aura brand cigars...so poorly crafted they'll make you sick to your stomach. I'd say you've chosen a fitting name."

George glared at Wolf before picking up the forms.

"Three men watched you run into my office with a pickaxe," said Wolf as he watched George read the documents. "After that, they saw you steal a burro from my lot just before you fled town. These are copies of their testimonies. Do with them what you'd like; my lawyer has the originals."

George began to flip through the testimonies. As he did, Wolf continued his rant. "Not only that, but our little dispute in my office was witnessed firsthand by Stanton. He remembers everything that happened down to the last detail. He would have no problem telling the story to my dear friend, Judge Hanson. I tell you, George, I think you have it backwards. If there's anyone who doesn't stand a chance in a courtroom, it's you."

George tossed the testimonies across the table where they landed right in front of Wolf. George recognized all three names on the papers. Leonard Pearl, Carter Hirsh, and Walker Thompson—Wolf's top spotters. They were rats, and they were all loyal to Wolf simply because he gave them a little extra money. The testimonies had been fabricated in all likelihood, but what did it matter? There would be no way George could prove they were. It wasn't like anyone from Rainville would testify against Wolf Blankston on George's behalf. The only person that would was Remo. Unfortunately, he was trapped underground at the time. In an instant, the dream of the Aura had crumbled. He would have to accept Wolf's proposition.

"I'll tell you what," said Wolf as he withdrew a cigar from his shirt pocket. "I would be willing to contribute five thousand dollars to jumpstart the operation. I'd say that's quite generous, considering your alternative."

George knew that Wolf had a much greater incentive for joining arms with him. It was likely that Wolf would find a way to remove George from the equation entirely in due time. There would be no way that Wolf could ever open his heart to George, or visa-versa. Something would have to give eventually; however, Wolf had offered to contribute five thousand dollars. Perhaps he would be willing to invest more. Maybe it was too good to be true.

"I remember who ya are Wolf Blankston," said George with burning eyes. "Whadderya gonna do, have me sign some contract that says you own the mine then have me arrested so ya can take it all for yourself?"

"George, please," said Wolf calmly and confidently. "I don't want the whole operation. I'm too old for that now. I know that your men are happy working for you, and they'll stay that way. I can't run this operation without you, and, I'm sorry to say, you can't run it without me. But together, we could build a giant. Let's bury the hatchet. Let's put our mindless feud behind us and make some real money together. Who knows, perhaps I could even convince the Navy to rekindle talks of a contract. I'd say there's an excellent chance. They're always in need of more coal."

There was no use debating. It was either play Wolf's game or go to prison. It wasn't much of a choice.

"All right," George agreed.

Wolf grinned and extended his hand.

George felt his heart sputter in his stomach as he gripped Wolf's chunky mitt. The two men shook hands.

"Good, then," said Wolf. "I'll be departing now to retrieve my belongings and the money that I've promised the operation. I'll also have some contracts prepared to ratify our deal." Wolf closed his briefcase and stood. "Everything you do must turn a profit," he continued. "Regardless if it risks the lives of men. There will be more men. In this country, there will always be men looking for work. Some of them will lose their lives along the way, but there will always be more. They aren't worth the coal that's in that hill. Remember, there are those who collect heads and then there are the headless wandering around without a goddamn clue." Wolf turned and walked out of the office.

George watched, still in a state of shock. Wolf Blankston had stormed in and seized control of the Aura. It had happened in a flash. It was not what George expected. He expected to be behind bars. He always feared being caught, which was why he went to such great lengths to disguise himself. He knew that one day he would have to pay for his crimes. That day had come.

He swallowed his entire glass of bourbon with one gulp before standing and retrieving the bottle from the walnut cabinet. He filled another glass and took a sip.

What a helpless position he was in. Truly, he had no chance. More likely than not, the materialization of Wolf meant that the Aura would crumble, or that George would end up in prison. Perhaps both. Wolf wanted full control of the Aura, and he wanted George in prison or dead. There was no getting around that. Wolf had always been a vindictive man, and George had harmed him in a way no other human being ever had. It was time for the ultimate vindication. George was in the crosshairs now. There was nothing he could do but allow the booze to ease the tension. As he downed the smooth bourbon, he began to accept the fact that he had to kill the old bastard. Again. Otherwise, he was doomed.

31

George had consumed four glasses of bourbon—followed by another, and another, until his eyes were red and glazed and his muscles were loosened—at which time the day had faded into darkness. A moderate state of intoxication had dampened his anxieties, but the weight of it all still suffocated him. He was angry and hopeless. He thought about running away—back into the mountain. But he couldn't bring himself to abandon his dream without a fight.

A single kerosene lantern lit his filthy office. It was barely enough light to illuminate the journal of Father Rodriguez (which he had stolen from Hunter Paige), *El Mapa del búho*, and the golden owl figurine. The golden owl was still putting off an intense heat. George had tried to touch it again, but for the second time, it burned his hand. He couldn't figure out why the damn thing was behaving the way it was. It had him flustered. On top of that, he had drained a half dozen glasses of bourbon, which only enhanced his emotions.

George used to drink in his late teens and early twenties, but he gave it up after he saw how it affected his old man. Drink was always the catalyst for Joe's poor decisions, and it was the reason why his health had deteriorated so quickly over the course of a decade. But after George killed Hunter Paige and Wolf Blankston (or so he thought), he started drinking again. He found that he couldn't function or sleep unless he swallowed a glass or two of bourbon throughout the day. On bad days, he would have three of four. The smooth bourbon was his only escape from the crippling guilt and shame. Without it, he felt that his nerves would cause his heart to beat right out of his chest. The re-emergence of Wolf Blankston had triggered a feeling of anxiety that he had never felt in his life, and he compensated for it by drinking triple what he was used to. He knew that it was likely a poor decision. He was probably too drunk, but he didn't care. It shielded him from the horrors of reality. It also gave him a little spunk.

He had spent the last three hours probing the *El Mapa del búho* and the journal of Father Rodriguez for a morsel of information that might reveal the mine's location. Despite his efforts, it was a puzzle that he was incapable of solving. He could hardly reconcile the fact that he wasn't clever enough to unravel the secret of the map. It made his blood boil. He paced back and forth across the room, leaving a patterned wake of footprints behind him on the dusty brick flooring.

There were, in fact, two puzzles lurking above him like menacing shadows. The foremost puzzle was figuring out how to handle the cunning Wolf Blankston. George agreed to provide Wolf with half the Aura, but he knew that it was an agreement predestined to fall flat. Wolf had arrived with a scheme of deceit—principally, the intent to usurp George and proclaim the Aura and its riches for himself. Sooner or later, Wolf would reveal his true intentions. George would not give in. He had to be prepared for anything. Equally, he had to conjure up a recipe strong enough to eliminate Wolf before he was the one eliminated. That was the only way out.

A breeze surged through the room and caused George's skin to tighten and the flame of the kerosene lantern to sway. Up until that point, the night had been perfectly still. Now, there was a breeze strolling through the crack in the broken glass window, whistling an enigmatic tune as it entered. The breeze carried with it a thickness that George recognized, and therefore he knew that he was no longer alone. He stood still for a moment, taking a long drag from his Aura cigar before taking six dreary paces toward the door.

He walked outside and looked upward to see that there was not a cloud in the sky. The dazzling stars floated over the Aura operation like the burning lanterns of six thousand coal miners. The droning breeze picked up a little, causing the desert junipers to sway and the dry dust to swoop and stir. There was a carbon filament lamp overhead that lit the front of George's office. The inside of the bulb was spotted with soot, which diffused the light within. Moths and other insects were buzzing around the bulb—their navigation systems in dismay as the poor creatures confused George's industrial lamp for the moon and stars, which they depended on for travel. The bulb's dim light projected a shadow onto George's face, making his eye sockets appear as two black cavities—the depths of which were seemingly infinite.

A second industrial lamp brightened the portal of the Aura Mine one hundred yards from George. The portal was blacker than the night—an obscure subterranean chamber. There was something evil stirring in the night air. It was thick, and it was quiet, and it seemed to be abnormally cool for a midsummer's night.

"Hoo-hoo-hoo," cried the owl from the top of a nearby desert juniper.

The cry was met by George's frightened eyes.

What did it want now? He thought to himself.

The glowing golden eyes opened and met George's gaze. There was a demonic quality about them. They were two golden circles of light against a canvas of darkness. They looked as if they could belong to anything—man, beast, or something else far more terrifying. They slowly closed, and the owl's wings began to flutter. When the flapping stopped, a humanoid silhouette moved from out of the darkness and under the portal's industrial lamp.

"Hey!" George screamed.

But the figure did not stop. It drifted slowly toward the portal—not walking, but floating.

"Hey!!" George yelled again, this time at the top of his lungs.

The apparition continued to move until it disappeared into the mine. George's chest was rising and falling, and there was a collection of sweat forming on his brow. It was the same entity that had passed in front of his campfire on the mountain...the same entity that he saw hovering at the mouth of the Rainville No. 4 after the explosion...it had to be. Goosebumps formed on his flesh, and the hair on his arms and neck prickled. What was it doing in his mine? He wished that he'd had a better look at it. He had consumed far too much bourbon. It had clouded his mind and vision. *It was probably one of the men wandering back into the mine from the tipple*, he thought. It was only the goddamn bourbon talking. There was no apparition. The thought gave him enough comfort to walk back to his office.

As he reached for the door handle, he heard the sound of approaching footsteps. He looked toward the mine—the direction the footsteps were coming from. Whoever was walking toward him had already passed through the light radius of the portal's lamp and was trekking through the darkness. With each step, the sound of the footsteps grew louder and closer as they dragged through dirt and rock.

George swallowed hard and stared frightfully ahead.

"Remo?" he cried.

There was no answer.

"Who's there?" George hollered.

Again, there was no reply.

The footsteps came to a stop under the office lamp. George's eyes grew wide.

Standing in the light was absolutely nothing. At least, nothing that could be physically observed. The footsteps started again, walking slowly toward George. He found that he could hardly breathe. Whatever the invisible entity was, it was siphoning a great deal of oxygen from his proximity. The door of the office swung open by itself, and George nervously backed away. He could hear the footsteps walking across the brick flooring until they came to a stop in front of his desk where the golden owl figurine and the journal of Father Rodriguez rested next to the opened *El Mapa del búho*.

It isn't real, George thought. But it was. There was someone, or something, standing in his office. He staggered into the room and stood in silence, anticipating the phantasm's next move.

The stillness of the night crept through the cracks of the ceilings and walls. George felt completely helpless, and his helplessness provoked an anger that gradually dissolved his fear. This provided him with the confidence to wander further into the room. He went straight for the liquor cabinet and removed two glasses. He poured both half-full of bourbon and then put one of them on his desk in front of the apparition.

"I hope ya like bourbon," he said with a jesting smirk.

George drank his bourbon in two swallows and then smacked the glass down right next to the other. A curious grin formed on his face, and soon after, he released a bizarre chuckle. His eyes met *El Mapa del búho.* He knew the apparition was looking at the map, too. Why the entity was interested in the map, he didn't know, but the fact that it was interested in it meant something.

"You know where it is, dontcha?" George asked. "Tell me where it is!"

He lost his balance momentarily, catching himself on the corner of the desk with his right hand. Realizing that he was fine, he let out another offbeat laugh, one that seemed to be manipulated by some vile force. He then staggered to the opposite side of the desk and opened the top drawer. From inside, he removed a .38 caliber pistol. He then began circling the desk with his right hand squeezing the grip and the barrel resting on his shoulder.

"With your help, the two of us could be the richest men west of the Mississippi," he said in a slurred declaration.

There was no response.

George eyed the full glass of bourbon resting on the table. It hadn't been touched. Suddenly, he felt that he was being disrespected. With a violent swing, he smashed the glass tumbler with the barrel of his pistol. The bourbon, as well as shards of glass, spilled across the room.

George swelled with rage—the same rage that he had felt when he drove the pickaxe through Wolf Blankston's back and when he had fired the bullet through Hunter Paige's neck.

"I wanna be rich," George shouted. "No...not rich...I wanna be filthy fucking rich!"

His grin faded as he started to feel faint and nauseous. He tried to catch himself on the desk with his right hand again, but this time, his hand was occupied with the pistol.

With a loud thud, he crashed against the brick flooring. Around him, the room spun like a violent merry-go-round. He closed his eyes in an attempt to slow it down, but it produced the opposite effect. The room began to darken, and he knew that he was about to black out.

"Whaddya want from me?" George pleaded

Again, his question was not answered.

The footsteps re-emerged, though George couldn't discern where they were coming from. With all the strength that he could muster, he looked toward the door in time to see the dark entity walking out. He crawled on his hands and knees toward the door. As he looked into the night, he saw the mist-like entity floating away from the office. It disappeared as it left the radius of the overhead lamp but soon re-appeared under the portal's overhead lamp, then it floated into the mine.

No, George thought. No!

He then vomited all over the ground and fell face down into it.

What's that thing doin' in my mine—or in my mind? Damn it! Is it in my mine, or is it in my mind?

Darkness shrouded the office as he started to lose consciousness.

"I can't find it...I still can't find it," he mumbled.

His eyes fluttered, and then they closed. He was out of the light and into the darkness.

32

He was awakened by the sound of the office door, which was wide open and wavering a few inches back and forth due to the inconsistent breeze. The brick floor was cold and hard, and the lantern on his desk had gone out, reducing the confined office space to an ominous shadow. Only the weak moonlight shone through the broken glass window, gracing a world of darkness with a hint of radiance.

There was dried vomit on his face and hands, and his head ached. He was not used to drinking so much. Because he wasn't, the hangover had set in with great intensity. *Damn Wolf Blankston*, he thought. *Damn him for making me drink so much!*

As his eyes fluttered open, he was uncertain what time it was, or where he was for that matter. All he knew was that his head was pounding and that his stomach was sour. He looked up at the door and vaguely remembered the events that transpired earlier that evening. He had consumed far too much bourbon and passed out on the floor. He took comfort in knowing that much.

He rolled over to clear himself of the vomit and then rested his head against the brick floor. Just as he closed his eyes, he noticed a sound in the room that he was so accustomed to hearing that he had been ignorant of it entirely. It was the sound of heavy, raucous snoring. It was the snoring of his father. George sat up, and the pain surged through his head as he did. In the corner of the room was a cot that had not been there earlier. Lying in it was the shape of a person, snoring like a grizzly bear.

"Pop?" George asked nervously.

The snoring continued.

George struggled to his feet, grimacing in pain as both his brain and stomach were displeased by the sudden movement. Immediately, he felt lightheaded. He was about to black out again when he planted his buttocks on the desktop. Sitting, he closed his eyes and took a deep breath. The dizzy sensation started to fade. He removed a matchbook from his pocket, ignited one of the matches, and then set alight his lantern. He shook out the match and put it in the ashtray on his desk. He then picked up the lantern with his left hand and held it even with his chest. He walked slowly toward the sleeping person, whose snoring grew louder by the second.

"HAWNKK," and then a quiet "shhhh" followed as he exhaled lightly. "HAWNKK—shhhh."

The pain in George's stomach was nearly unbearable. He needed to either vomit again or lie down, but fear had put those necessities on hold for the time being.

He was within five feet of the snoring man when the light from his lantern finally lit the cot. Whoever was lying

there had drawn the covers over their head, veiling themselves completely. George stood next to the cot, prepared to
lift the blanket and see who was under it. It was undeniably
the snoring of his father, and the body underneath the
blanket seemed to be his father's figure. And yet, it couldn't
be. His father was dead—trapped forever under the hillside
of Rainville.

The old hinges on the door groaned as the wind swept
through and pushed the door open a couple feet. George
nearly jumped out of his skin. When he realized that it was
only the wind, he took a breath of relief.

With a rush of confidence, he reached for the blanket
and lifted it from the snoring person. It was the last person
he expected to find. It was Hunter Paige. He was no longer
snoring. He was no longer making any noise at all. He was
dead. There was a fresh bullet hole in his neck and blood
seeped from it like a faucet. His wide, lifeless eyes stared
heavenward, and his mouth was wide open.

What's the meaning of this? George thought. *It had to be
some cruel trick. The owl—this was the work of that goddamned
owl.* The vile creature had to be nearby. He could feel its
presence. He took a careful look around the room. Everything seemed to be in order (other than the corpse of
Hunter Paige), so he walked to the door and looked outside.
As his eyes surveyed the moonlit terrain, he saw that something was terribly amiss. The moon was full, and there was
not a cloud in sight. He could see everything—the rolling
hills, the junipers, the large tipple, the mine office, and the
residential cabins that belonged to Wolf Blankston and the
Rainville Coal Mine. He was not at the Aura—he was in
Rainville.

He turned around to see that his office was not his office at all. It was the stone cottage where he and Joe had previously lived. The same wooden door was wide open, swaying lightly in the evening breeze. *What an incredible trick this was,* George thought. *The power of the owl was truly infinite. But why Rainville? What does the owl want to show me here?* He grew frustrated. *Why am I trying to derive meaning from it? This is a figment of the imagination. The arrival of Remo and Wolf must have motivated recollections of Rainville.*

George could feel the wind brushing at his face. If it were a dream, it felt incredibly real. There were no lights on in the residential camp, and there was no light above the portal of the Rainville No. 4. The surrounding vegetation had grown in, filling the once tidy dirt paths with weeds. Some of them were as tall as George's hip.

Wolf had told him that Rainville was sealed off for good. Perhaps it had already been abandoned. He walked toward Remo's old cottage and opened the door. It was dark inside, but George could tell that the shack had been cleared of its possessions. There were no cots, there was no stove, and most importantly, there were no people. It was empty apart from the thriving weeds that had grown through the cracks of the brick flooring and conquered the room. There was also a large chunk of rusted corrugated iron roofing laying in the midst of the weeds. It looked as though the roof had collapsed long ago.

"Hello!" George yelled into the summer night.

Nothing.

How strange it was. Hundreds of people had once lived in the Rainville camp, and now it was deserted.

But then, from the southwest hills, appeared the woman in white, Mrs. Ambrosius, hovering across the weed filled landscape. She was the wandering spirit whose life had been ruined in Rainville, and because of it, she was there to stay. Her patterns were so well-defined. Every night, she would emerge from the southwest hills and approach the office of Wolf Blankston with tears pouring from her eyes. *What was her purpose?* George wondered. Perhaps she was determined to get a little money from Wolf Blankston so her child could eat. That's probably all she ever wanted. How tragic it was that Wolf refused to grant such a trifling request.

Come to think of it, maybe it wasn't money that Mrs. Ambrosius wanted at all. Perhaps it was vengeance. Who could blame her for that? The paltry lives of a family with nothing crushed by a man with everything. Wasn't that life in booming America?

Mrs. Ambrosius reached the bottom of the hill and was within thirty yards of George. Her movements, as well as her appearance, were a mirror image of what George witnessed during his prior encounter with the spirit. Her gown was white, her flesh was blue, and her eyes were full of tears. It was only a matter of time before she walked right passed him, completely ignorant of him, as she had been the last time he saw her.

She drew closer, though George felt no fear. She could not harm him. He did, however, feel sorry for the poor woman. If only there were some way to lay her soul to rest. Vengeance. If only he would have killed Wolf Blankston with that blow from the pickaxe, then maybe she would be at peace. On top of that, George likely wouldn't be in the mess he was in now.

Mrs. Ambrosius was within ten yards when she suddenly stopped. Her horrified eyes stared directly at George.

George's heart skipped a beat. The hair on his neck stood tall, and his eyes watered from the unthinkable fear. The sorrowful expression of Mrs. Ambrosius faded, and a smile bloomed on her pale face. She started moving toward him again, though she wasn't floating; she was walking. And as she drew near, George could see a little color in her face. She was less than an arm's length away when she stopped and smiled at him. She then took hold of his hand, raised it to her lips, and kissed it. George looked on in disbelief.

She let go of his hand, turned, and then walked back to the winding southwestern hills. There was one sound that George could perceive over the whistling wind and the ruffling trees. Thelma Ambrosius was singing something in Greek. Her soft voice bounced off the canyon walls and faded as she drifted further away. It was chilling, yet beautiful.

33

George was lying face down on the office floor, which was still peppered with shards of glass from the tumbler he destroyed the previous night. There was a heap of vomit four inches from his face and a .38 caliber pistol six inches from his right hand.

As the sunlight passed through a rusted hole in the roofing, it projected a circular pattern in the center of the room where George laid almost perfectly in its circumference. When his glazed eyes fluttered open, he was instantly struck with a sense of relief. He was in his office, and as he looked out the half-open door, he saw what was unmistakably the landscape of the Aura. It had been a terrible dream after all, just as he suspected. Thank goodness for that.

The hangover symptoms had lifted some, mostly in his stomach, but his head continued to throb. The stench of the vomit made him queasy, so he turned away from it. He tried to remember what had happened the previous night. He had drank too much; that was apparent. He couldn't remember throwing up or being visited by the ghostly entity minutes before losing consciousness. And yet, for some reason, he recalled the dream about Mrs. Ambrosius and Rainville perfectly. The dream had felt so real. Even as he sat on the floor of his own office, Rainville seemed more factual than the Aura. What a vivid dream it had been. It was so powerful that he had to look up and read the bronze name plate on his desk to verify where he was.

The bronze plate read: AL JOSEPH, and underneath his name it read: A.J. MINING COMPANY.

Good. Good, he thought.

His clothes were soiled with dust—the goddamn dirty floor. He brushed his shirt and his pants, and then he paused as he heard a commotion. Footsteps could be heard slogging through the dirt and rock outside his office.

He lurched to his feet. Immediately, he felt the impulse to vomit, but he was able to hold it in. By standing, he had doubled the pain in his head, neck, and stomach. How could he have been foolish enough to drink so much? He was angry at himself and embarrassed.

The light was so harsh when he stepped outside that he could barely open his eyes. He shielded the sun with his left hand, but it wasn't enough. The omnipresent rays caused his brain to throb and his stomach to turn. He battled through the affliction the best he could. It was his mine—his fortune—and he had to know what was going on. Little by little, he began to distinguish a large gathering of men standing fifty yards to the west of the Aura Mine's portal. The stragglers who had passed his office were just arriving at the assemblage. He couldn't identify what was going on, but as his eyes were given the opportunity to adjust, the picture became a little clearer. The men were huddled around a large wooden box. Next to the box was a hole in the ground. One fit for burying a human being.

Someone must have been killed in the mine, George thought. But why didn't anyone wake him and tell him? If someone had died, then George should have been notified immediately. This made him angry, and the anger surged as his pace toward the gathering quickened. It was clear that whoever died had been dead for a significant amount of time, simply because the men had taken the time to build a coffin and hollow out a grave.

George began to count the men who circled the gravesite. There were at least twenty-five of them, almost double what he employed. Just what in the hell was going on? *Perhaps Wolf Blankston sent them,* he thought. The assessment made him sick to his stomach. *Remo,* he remembered. He had not even spoken to Remo since he arrived. What would he think of Wolf Blankston's involvement? Wolf and his callous ways had almost killed him. George had planned to inform Remo and the other men at dawn of Wolf's involvement, but he had remained unconscious for far too long.

He began to wonder how late in the day it already was. He looked upward to see that the sun was almost directly overhead. It was almost noon. How sickening. The day shift had been underway for six hours while he slept like an infant on the floor of his office. The thought of it caused his anger to swell. Why didn't anyone wake him and allow him an opportunity to clean himself so that he could at least be presentable for the new men? What if someone had brought the new recruits to his office, only to find him face down with an empty bourbon bottle on his desk and a pistol and a pile of puke by his side? How pathetic. How could anyone respect him after a first impression like that? Furthermore, he had been lying face down on the floor all morning. What if something was seriously wrong with him? What if he was dead? Had anyone even bothered to check? His anger peaked. It was enough to become violent—enough to lose control, as he had in the past when he had killed.

The new laborers noticed George ascending the hill. As their eyes met his, George didn't know whether to feel anger or shame. There were far more men than what were visible from the bottom of the slope. There weren't twenty-five men at all; there must have been fifty-five. George didn't recognize any of them. He looked into their eyes and saw that they were frightened and disgruntled. They were all skinny, undernourished men who reeked of sweat and tobacco. Most of them had shaggy beards and crusted, oily hair. Their clothing was filthy and frayed, and their boots were tattered and torn. Their flesh was leathered, and their hands were worked to the bone. It was the only life they had known—the only life they were capable of living. Their dejected eyes met the gaze of their new boss. They had heard rumblings of how wonderful the Aura was and how well its owner, Mr. Al Joseph, treated his employees. But they had arrived on this day to see that Al Joseph was a broken man, and that his operation was just as dangerous as any other. It was only twenty-four hours ago that George had the unmitigated respect of thirteen men. Now more than half his workforce thought of him as weak, careless, and sloppy. Why—this wasn't the Aura he dreamed of. The Aura was a place where Mr. Al Joseph was a revered figure. Now, it was some hot and nasty place that reeked of Wolf Blankston's tinkering. It was a hard fact to swallow, but

George was certain that it was true: the Aura belonged to Wolf Blankston.

George very much wanted to say something, to explain himself, and to plead for their respect; however, one of the men was reciting a few words for the departed soul, and to avoid losing even more respect, George elected to keep quiet until the ceremony came to an end. He looked at the new men one at a time. They were also looking at him. He had no choice but to hold his head high and challenge the pain that pulsed in his neck, skull, and abdomen. Despite his efforts, he wasn't fooling anyone. His skin was pale, he was covered in a hot, sticky sweat, and a small yet noticeable amount of vomit was streaked across his chin.

The man finished his words to the departed. Just before another man spoke, George's anxiety peaked, and he blurted out: "Just what in the hell's goin' on here?"

The men looked at George like guilty children who knew they were about to be punished.

"What happened?" George yelled.

"Mr. Joseph," called a voice from within the slew of men. The crowd stirred, and then Remo emerged. Remo put his right hand on George's shoulder and then walked him away from the rest of the group.

"He was a tall, skinny son of a bitch. Name was Garfield," said Remo. "Just started here today. Poor bastard."

"Why didn't ya wake me up?" George snapped.

"What do you mean?"

"For God's sake, Remo. Somebody died in my mine. I shoulda been the first to know!"

All of the men could hear George clearly.

"I'm sorry, Mr. Joseph," Remo replied. "I was in your office about two hours ago. You went out on quite a bash last night, so I thought you'd want to get some rest. I didn't want to trouble you with this stuff."

"I'm the owner of this operation. If somethin' like this happens, ya tell me right away. I don't give a shit if I'm asleep or dead, you tell me what's goin' on in my mine!"

"Yes. I'm sorry."

"Maybe this was a bad idea," said George as he glowered at his friend.

"What was a bad idea?"

"I want ya to answer somethin' for me."

"What?"

"Are you gonna take some responsibly and be Remo the Foreman, or are ya just gonna be Shit-Pants Parelli your whole goddamn life?"

Remo looked up with a hurt expression.

George immediately felt guilty. "I'm sorry," he said. "I dunno why I said that. I dunno what the hell's wrong with me, I shouldn'ta said that."

"It's alright. I'm gonna be your foreman," said Remo. "I promise."

George felt much more nauseous all the sudden. He wiped the sweat from his forehead.

"You look terrible," said Remo in a voice so low that only George could hear it. "What's happening? Wolf Blankston has been crawling around here all morning. It ain't no good. Luckily, a lot of these men don't know who he is, but when they find out, they ain't gonna be happy."

George was speechless and disgusted with himself.

"Are you in trouble?" Remo asked. "Tell me if you're in trouble, and I'll help you."

George let out a frustrated sigh. "I'm in trouble, Remo. A lot of trouble."

"I can help you. Tell me how I can help you."

"What's happened here?" hollered another voice.

Climbing the hill awkwardly was the chunky Wolf Blankston. His carefully combed and parted hair was ruined by sweat that seeped from his forehead, and he was flush with the frustration and pain brought on by the short climb.

George and Remo looked at one another, and then Remo stepped forward.

"There was a minor collapse, Mr. Blankston."

"Remo," said Wolf with a dissatisfied gaze. "Oh, yes, I remember you." Wolf shifted his attention to George. He took a handkerchief from his front pocket and wiped the sweat from his face. "What is it that Remo does here at the Aura, Mr. Joseph?"

"He's my foreman."

Wolf's eyes narrowed as he looked at Remo and then back at George. "We'll have to have a little talk about that."

There was an uncomfortable silence as the three men studied one another.

Wolf took another step forward. "But for right now, let's talk about this collapse. What's the damage?"

"We lost a man," George replied.

"I asked about the damage," Wolf snapped, loud enough that every man heard him.

George put his hands on his hips and then looked at Remo. "How long's it gonna take to get this cleaned up?"

"Maybe a day or so," said Remo. "The fella was putting in some of the new timbering and the ceiling gave way—"

"What new timberin'?" George interrupted.

"The new timbering that I'm having the men install," said Wolf. "No more of your overpriced oak. I have a deal in place with Brigsby to provide us with Douglas fir. It will save us a fortune."

George said, "I don't have no problem payin' a little extra for oak."

"Let's not do this in front of the men," Wolf suggested. "What do you say we step into your office and have a little chat...Mr. Joseph?"

Mr. Joseph. The alias had always satisfied George. It was homage to his mother and father. But hearing the name mocked and soiled by Wolf Blankston made his skin crawl.

"Remo," said George. "After the service is over, have the men start cleanin' up the mess down there. I'll find ya later." George and Wolf walked down the hill toward George's tattered office. The eyes of Remo, and the eyes of fifty-five others, looked on with discontent.

34

The previous night, George had been studying the golden owl figurine, the journal of Father Rodriguez, and The Owl Map—*El Mapa del búho*. He had completely forgotten that these sensitive objects were still sitting on his desk as he and Wolf entered the room, stomping on the broken glass from the tumbler that George had shattered and around the vomit.

"What have we here?" Wolf asked.

George looked at his desk and saw the owl, the journal, and the map, as well as a nearly empty bottle of bourbon resting next to an empty glass tumbler. His cheeks grew flush when he realized that Wolf Blankston's wicked eyes had examined his most treasured possessions.

"My personal stuff," said George as he hurried and collected the artifacts and then quickly stashed them in the top drawer of his desk.

"Good God, it smells absolutely dreadful in here," said Wolf as he covered his nose with his sleeve and eyed the vomit on the floor. "How about we step outside?"

George deliberated for a moment, until his eyes met his old mining shovel hanging on the wall. He staggered across the room, took the shovel from the wall, and used it to scoop up the vomit and hurl it out the door.

He felt nauseous again, so much so that he needed to sit down immediately. He leaned the shovel against the door frame—the scoop facing the frame—then adjusted the angle to assure that the handle of the shovel wouldn't slip. Once satisfied, he sat down on the back of the scoop.

"What on earth are you doing?" Wolf asked.

"Little trick a friend showed me."

George took a deep breath. He felt a little better, so he stood. "That smell better?" he asked.

"I suppose so," said Wolf with an uncertain expression.

George put the shovel outside and then re-entered the room. "So let's talk," he said as he walked to his desk and sat down.

"That map and that golden figurine—"

"I told ya already; it's my personal stuff," said George.

Wolf chuckled. "Don't be ashamed. I've known all along."

"You've known what all along?"

Wolf walked to the liquor cabinet and helped himself to the bottle of Scotch.

"Drink?" Wolf asked, flashing the bottle at George.

"No thanks," George replied. Just thinking of another drink made his stomach turn.

Wolf said, "I'm well aware of your gold mine. Rumor has it that you struck it rich up there. But, if I had to venture a guess, I would say that you never found squat, did you?"

The question caught George off guard. He was appalled by that fact that Wolf had knowledge of his beloved gold. Unfortunately for George, his fragile state of mind rendered him incapable of thinking quickly and clearly. He sat hunched over in his chair while Wolf stood in front of him like a lion that smelled a wounded gazelle.

Wolf was right. George had never found the treasure of the mountain. He had spent days searching for it, though he wasn't sure how many days it had been. His time on the mountain was all a blur to him. He had been afraid of a search party tracking him down and killing him or throwing him in prison. His heart had been heavy with the death of his father, and he had been riddled with guilt for the slaying of Hunter Paige and what he thought was the slaying of Wolf Blankston. He went an entire week without sufficient sleep, on top of three days of tireless travel. Above all, he had been afraid. A nefarious entity had tormented him on the mountain. Whether it was real or not, he had encountered it on more than one occasion.

George forced a response from his mouth in an attempt to demonstrate some degree of strength. "I found what I found fair and square," he said defensively.

Sweat was pouring from Wolf's forehead. He sat down in the chair opposite George, removed a yellow handkerchief from his shirt pocket, and wiped the sweat from his face before sipping the Scotch. "I find that unlikely. Maybe you found a little gold, or maybe you stole it. But if you had found a gold mine, then you'd still be up there today digging it out. You're far too eager of a man to settle for coal when you had gold at your fingertips."

"I pulled out as much color as I could before it ran dry. Had the pocket held up, I'd still be up there."

Wolf's suspicion diminished for the time being as George's lie had sounded authentic.

"I'll tell ya about the map some other time," said George. "Right now, we've got more important things to discuss."

Wolf sipped from his Scotch and then nodded in agreement. "What do you suppose is the problem here at the Aura?" he asked.

George grimaced as the pain in his forehead suddenly amplified. "I really don't know what's goin' on," he said in exasperation. "Everything was goin' just fine 'til you showed up. I had a workforce that respected me, and there weren't no accidents."

"There are always accidents," Wolf testified. "No matter how much effort and money you put into safety, someone will still find a way to get hurt or killed. And, when that happens, it's not your fault—even though everyone will blame you. Do you remember what I told you back in Rainville? The working man is a careless man. It's just the way it is. I can't tell you how many times some idiot has hurt himself underground because he wasn't paying attention and tried to blame me for it. As long as you're running a mine, it will happen to you more than once. You better get used to it."

Wolf removed a cigar from his shirt pocket. He bit the head from it and spat it onto the ground. He then licked the barrel throughout, ignited the foot, and then rested the cigar comfortably in his mouth. "I'll be frank with you, George," he continued. "If you ever want to succeed in this industry, then you need to let go of the idea that you'll ever be able to do it honestly. Too many people in this world mistake honesty for weakness. They'll eat you alive every chance they get. You and all your talk of truthfulness and diligence, it's all a load of crap—a charade that has clouded your reason and crippled any realistic chance for you to succeed in this industry."

There was an awkward silence as Wolf waited for a response. George wasn't sure how to offer one.

"Are you familiar with Balzac?" Wolf asked.

"No."

"That's a shame. He was a fine writer. He said something that I have always found very intriguing. When it comes to the fortune you discovered, as well as your possibilities here at the Aura, I believe it rings true. He said, 'behind every great fortune lies a great crime.'" Wolf lit his cigar with a match, inhaled a lungful of the expensive tobacco, and then exhaled a cloud of smoke. "I don't mean that in a bad way; I'm just trying to prove my point. No one is honest in this day and age. Everyone steals a little. It's in our nature to steal—to survive—it's just a part of the game. I didn't make the rules. The rules were set in motion long ago, but I can assure you that if you don't play by the rules, then this world will swallow you whole. You do what you have to do to get ahead."

George dipped his head in defeat. He knew his righteous ways had amounted to nothing. He could preach honesty and strong values, but he had to face the harsh reality that the majority of those who were prosperous had not reached such a level of success without cutting a few corners, arranging a few favors, and even exploiting resources at the expense of others. All over America, businessmen preached honesty, but behind the scenes, there was corruption, fraud, greed, exploitation, and everything in between. It was wrong, but it was the way it was, and it had been that way for a long time. The extraction of natural resources had birthed scores of power-hungry, greed-driven industrialists, and if someone like George Hendricks wanted to compete with them, he stood little chance without practicing cut-throat tactics. Profit, profit, profit was all that mattered, no matter the cost. Were you willing to trade the life of a man for fifteen hundred tons of coal? The bulk of the mogul scum replied with a resounding yes. It was all true, and George hated it with a fiery passion. But it was simply too much for one man to fight alone. There are those who collect heads, and then there are the headless—the twisted rubric of a selfish and disconnected world.

George let out a frustrated sigh. "I—I guess I was out of line before. I wasn't thinkin' clearly. I've known for some time the timber company's been swindlin' me. I appreciate ya findin' a better deal for us."

Wolf smiled. "I'm not out to undermine what you have going here. I've been around mining all my life. The name of the game is profit—everything else is horseshit." Wolf's glass hit the table with a light thud. "Look, I know you're worried about the men. I learned a long time ago that men need to be held in check. If you give them something that they might consider a luxury, then they want more. And if you don't give them more, then they complain. On the other end of the spectrum, if you give them nothing, then guess what? They complain. You can't win. You have to have balance, but most importantly, you have to stop caring about them because guess what? They don't care about you."

George allowed Wolf's words to settle in.

"How long have you been running this operation?" Wolf asked.

George did not answer. He stared vacantly ahead as though under a spell.

Wolf watched him curiously. "George?"

George thought for a moment, though he grew confused as he brainstormed for an answer. "I...I don't know. I've had the worst pain in my head and in my neck and shoulders for a couple of days now and... I ain't thinkin' clearly... I don't think I'm well."

"Shall I call for a doctor?"

"No. I...I just need to get a little rest."

Wolf noted the empty bourbon bottle on the desk. "Well, it's clear to me that you're in no condition to make any critical decisions. I'll tell you what. Why don't you rest up, and we can meet later this evening? I wouldn't mind a little shuteye myself. I've been traveling nonstop for two days now."

George nodded.

Wolf stood and opened his leather briefcase. From inside, he retrieved a stack, roughly twenty-five pages thick, of contractual forms. "Here's our contract. I'd like it to be signed by the time I see you this evening. What time shall I return, seven or eight?"

"Better make it eight," George mumbled as he noted the thickness of the contract.

"All right." Wolf put the forms on George's desk. "Just remember," he continued. "You can't control everything that happens. There will be accidents, and there will be lives lost. Men go wandering into the unknown without a clue of what's waiting to swallow them up."

With those words, Wolf left the office.

George kicked his feet up on the desktop and closed his tired eyes.

35

He spent only a few minutes trying to sleep, but he knew damn well that sleep would be impossible given the circumstances. Time was of the essence, and every minute surrendered to sleep was a minute ceded to Wolf Blankston, who was surely plotting against him that very moment. It hit him suddenly—a burst of anger and disgust in himself. Here he was, moping around his office, feeling badly for himself, when he had Remo and twelve other men who would certainly stand alongside him. He had dropped his guard in a major way when he decided to drown his sorrows in the spirits. He had given up the same way his father had given up. He had allowed Wolf Blankston a stranglehold on the Aura, which was likely inevitable regardless, but either way, it was time to fight back if he wanted a chance to keep what was rightfully his.

He stood, and a burst of pain swept through his skull and shoulders and climaxed directly behind his Adam's apple. What terrible condition he was in. This was no ordinary hangover. He thought for a moment that he should take a carriage to Whistle Springs and see a doctor, but he hadn't the time now.

He staggered out of the office and re-entered the bright summer afternoon. When his eyes adjusted, he was dumbfounded to discover that the cemetery was abandoned. Five minutes earlier, two dozen men were standing around an unfinished gravesite. The coffin was still resting next to the open grave, and the shovels were thrown aside as if the men had all left in a hurry. *Perhaps there had been another accident in the mine,* George thought. That was the only explanation. He began to hustle toward the portal. The faster he moved, the more his bodied ached.

Fear hit him unexpectedly—like a jolt of electric current, forcing him to stop ten feet from the portal. *Don't go in there—you won't like what you find,* he thought to himself. Fear again. Why? Then, he remembered. The strange entity had disappeared into the portal just before he blacked out the previous night. He had forgotten. Did the creature have anything to do with the collapse that had killed a man earlier that day? The thought knocked the wind out of him.

He knew there was a slim chance that he could overcome the threat of Wolf Blankston. Wolf was a flesh and blood human being whose flaws were haste and greed and whose heightened age, pudgy, flaccid skin, and rigid joints rendered him ineffective in a tussle. But the threat of the mist-like entity and the Great Horned Owl made the troubled relations with Wolf Blankston seem trivial. The owl and the entity were so mysterious that George didn't even know what controlled what. Was the humanoid entity a minion of the owl, or was it the other way around? Were they separate, were they equal, were they even associated?

He strayed from the mine's portal and walked to where the dead miner's grave was being dug. He looked at the coffin, then at the hole, and then at the headstone that was already carved. He leaned down to get a better look at it. It read: GEORGE HENDRICKS 1865-1900. GONE BUT NOT FORGOTTEN.

George's eyes grew wide. He kneeled down and read it again.

RON GARFIELD 1865-1900. GONE BUT NOT FORGOTTEN.

What the hell? George thought. He closed his eyes, rubbed his throbbing forehead, and then read it again.

RON GARFIELD 1865-1900. GONE BUT NOT FORGOTTEN.

1865 was also the year George was born, which was odd. Still, he couldn't help but chuckle. *It was another one of the owl's tricks,* he thought. The damn thing loved to play games with his head.

He stood up and looked around. It was so quiet, so barren. As his eyes danced across the terrain, he noticed a coal cart resting halfway between the portal and the tipple. There was something unusual about the cart. It was rusted, and after a closer look, it appeared to be very old. He couldn't recall seeing such a deplorable cart being used inside the Aura, or even inside of Rainville for that matter. He had purchased new carts and new tools. A decrepit coal cart was inexplicable to him. *Someone should have reported the poor condition of the cart,* he thought. By the looks of it, it was virtually unusable.

Speaking of the men, something truly disastrous must have happened if it caused them all to abandon a funeral ceremony. And where was Wolf Blankston during all of this? He had left the office minutes before George did. He must have seen something. Perhaps the men abducted him and threw him down the test shaft that was dug for the twenty-two foot seam? It was an amusing thought, but it was unlikely.

He had to venture into the mine; there was no other choice. He took a step toward it, when—out of the corner of his eye—he saw someone slip behind a desert juniper.

"I saw ya," George cried. "Come out from behind there."

There was no answer.

"You there. Get out from behind that tree."

Nothing.

"What's goin' on here?" George shouted.

Again, it was silent and still. Not a single insect made a peep. He looked at the desert plateaus, the resplendent green trees, the snow white clouds, and the radiant blue sky. The colors of the environment were hyper saturated, almost unrealistically so.

"What's goin' on here?" George yelled once more, this time ubiquitously to the desert. His wide eyes danced around the terrain as his chest rose and fell and his lower lip trembled. "Did ya hear me? I asked—" His words faded midsentence, and his own voice was fully replaced by the voice of Remo, who finished the sentence: "—asked you what's going on here?"

George turned and saw Remo standing in front of the grave. There were two men lowering the coffin into the hole, and there were another fifty men staring at George. The old, rusted coal cart was being schlepped toward the tipple by two of the new men. Oddly enough, the old cart rolled along the track without a flaw. It barely made a peep, and suddenly, appearance wise, it looked much more serviceable than it had previously.

"What's going on here?" Remo repeated. "Everybody's saying that Wolf Blankston is here because you asked him to be here. They said you made him co-owner of Aura. Tell me that ain't true, George. That crooked son of a bitch. You ain't sold out, have ya?"

Remo had called him George, and several of the other men heard him. But what did it matter now? Wolf Blankston had found him, which meant that he no longer had a reason to conceal his identity.

George turned and looked at the desert juniper that the strange figure had disappeared behind. He began to walk toward the tree at a wide, circular angle so that he could see behind it from a fair distance. When he drew close enough, he looked behind the tree. There was nothing there.

George turned to Remo and waved him over so that the two of them could talk in private. Remo reluctantly obliged. George was drenched in a cold sweat, and his pale skin reflected the rays of the sun.

"He's tryin' to push me out and take the mine for 'imself," George whispered. "I didn't have no choice but to give him half the Aura, otherwise he'd send me up the river."

"Son of a bitch, George," said Remo.

"Stop callin' me George."

"I'm sorry, it's hard for Christ's sake. I've been calling you one name for the last two years and now you want me to call you something different. It's going to take some getting used to."

"Forget it," said George. "Look. I need your help." He took a deep breath in an attempt to slow down his swift beating heart. He looked around at some of the other men, and then he took a step closer to Remo. "I'm gonna kill him," he whispered.

"When?" Remo asked.

"Tonight."

Remo was speechless—dumbfounded by everything that had happened in the course of twenty-four hours. There had been no Wolf Blankston or demoralized men the previous day. Now there were both. It was difficult to accept.

George put his hand on Remo's shoulder. "After it's done, you, me, and all the men will get paid the way we deserve to get paid. Wolf's puttin' up five thousand dollars for split ownership of the Aura. We'll invest it in the twenty-two foot seam, and then we'll start makin' the real money."

Remo looked into George's crazed eyes. He could see the passion swelling within.

"I can't be involved with a murder," said Remo. "Maybe I don't understand the kind of mess you're in, but I got a wife and kids that depend on me. I can't just leave them out here in the desert. Think about what happened to Thelma Ambrosius. I almost put Antonia and the kids through that once already."

Remo looked at George and saw the desperation in his eyes. He felt guilty all the sudden. George had been so gracious to his family. He owed him a favor. "Wolf Blankston is the worst damn thing that could have happened to this operation," he continued. "Between you and me, do whatever needs to be done to get rid of him—just don't ask me to pull no triggers."

"You won't have to. Near sundown, you'll accompany Wolf and me a little ways into the desert. I have a plan to get 'im out there. Once we're far away enough from town,

I'll take care of it. I just want ya to be with me in case he has similar ideas."

"You want me to have a gun on me?" Remo asked.

"Yes."

"So what if he does try something? What if he tries to kill you? What am I supposed to do?"

"I'll take care of it, trust me."

Remo scratched his stubble beard. "All the men already know about Blankston. What are you going to tell them when he's not around tomorrow? Or how are you going to explain how you have all this new money?"

George suddenly felt defensive. He was the mighty ruler of the Aura Mine, and he didn't like his actions to be questioned. "Just go along with it," he said. "I'll figure out what to tell the men. Let's not forget that their job is to pull coal outta the hill over there. If they wanna question me, then we'll find somebody who'll mind their own business."

Remo dipped his head. "I'm not proud of it," he admitted, "and your old man wouldn't be proud of it neither, but when you call on me, I'll be ready."

Remo turned and walked toward the newly constructed cemetery.

George watched him for a moment, sensing the bitter disappointment, and equally, musing over his own concern of Remo. *He better keep his mouth shut, and he better follow through,* George thought. He couldn't help but note the tension that arose at the tail end of their discussion. Remo was clearly disappointed in George, and George was losing patience with Remo. After all that he had done for Remo, George was annoyed that Remo was so reluctant to protect him.

George followed Remo and joined him at the burial site. Many of the men were praying for the departed soul. Prayer did not serve much of a purpose to George. He had prayed for his livestock to survive the spring of 1889, and soon after, he had prayed for his mother to pull through after she came down with pneumonia. The livestock died, as did his mother, and he had since regarded prayer as a useless practice. As he looked around, he could see how faithful the men were, reciting prayers to themselves—prayers they knew by heart. *What the hell,* he thought. It was a thoughtful sentiment. He touched his forehead, his navel, and then both shoulders. He folded his hands and closed his eyes.

He found that it was impossible to pray for the man who had just died because he had no idea who the man was. He had already forgotten his name. What else could he pray for—aid in murdering Wolf Blankston? That didn't seem extraordinarily Christ-like. *What am I doing?* He suddenly wondered. He was standing at a burial pretending to pray and pretending to care for a man who he truly did not care about. Wolf Blankston had put on the same charade countless times, and the men had despised for him for it. What was happening to him? Was he turning into some heartless monster like Wolf Blankston? Or perhaps...no...he couldn't think of it. But it was true. Sometimes you just had to walk in someone else's shoes to be able to understand. Maybe, just maybe, he had been wrong about Wolf Blankston all along.

36

George made himself comfortable while he read through Wolf Blankston's contract. It took him nearly two hours. It was all a bunch of legal gibberish—stuff that he hardly understood. It made him feel weak. His livelihood was on the line when it came to this contract, and signing it without being conscious of the repercussions would be absurd. So he read it again, and again.

•

Three more hours passed. He had scanned the entire document meticulously, certain that somewhere, buried within the fine print, was some misleading clause that would put him behind bars and forfeit the Aura Mine to Wolf Blankston; however, after reading it three times, he had not found anything that aroused his suspicion. Much to his surprise, it appeared to be a legitimate contract with genuine intent.

It couldn't possibly be, George thought. Could it? He began to wonder if killing Wolf Blankston was the right idea or not. Wolf had said something the previous day that George couldn't help but replay over and over in his head. When it came to running the Aura, Wolf had said: "I can't run this operation without you, and, I'm sorry to say, you can't run it without me. But together, we could build a giant." A giant. Deep down that was exactly what George wanted. Maybe he was being too hasty. So far Wolf had given him little reason to doubt that his intentions were sincere. Killing him right away might be a serious blunder of his judgment. But, on the contrary, waiting might be an irrevocable mistake.

George opened his watch to see that it was almost 7:00 P.M. Wolf Blankston would be arriving at his office in one hour. George needed to make a decision, and fast. His plan was to retrieve Remo from the depths of the Aura so that he would be present for Wolf's arrival. George would already have the contract signed to appease Wolf; that way, it would be less obvious that something was awry. Once the three men were in the room, George would suggest that they all go look at an encouraging new prospect that was discovered a few days earlier. Its location would only be a short walk from the Aura camp. Of course, such a prospect didn't actually exist, so the murder would have to take place before they arrived at the fictitious location. The midsummer sun would not set until 8:30 P.M., and it wouldn't be dark until 9:30 P.M. He would have plenty of time to kill Wolf and hide his body.

George opened the top drawer of his desk and removed his .38 caliber. He opened the chamber of the pistol to make sure it was loaded. He assumed that it was, but his state of drunkenness the previous night warranted it to be checked. Before he slid the drawer shut, his eyes met the white handkerchief that concealed the golden owl figurine.

The golden owl. Why had it betrayed him? He needed it more than ever. He felt lost and alone without it, and he was desperate for its assistance. He retrieved the handkerchief and sat it on the desk next to the pistol. He unfolded the cloth and allowed the sunlight to reflect upon the golden owl figurine. He looked at the gun and then at the owl, and then at the gun and then at the owl. One of the objects held the answer to his future. He lifted his right hand and held it inches from the golden owl. Much to his surprise, it wasn't hot. He lowered his hand and touched it gingerly. It wasn't hot. A smile grew on his face, and he picked up the owl and felt it with both hands. There was neither heat nor fear radiating from it.

It's back! My God, it's back! George rejoiced to himself. He gripped the owl with his right hand and held it inches from his face. "Tell me what to do! Please, tell me what to do!" He was so desperate...so hungry...so credulous.

He felt a pulse of energy trickle through his hand and race through his whole body. It was a very subtle feeling, and it lasted for only a second. But after that second had elapsed, the answer was clear. But should he trust it? He didn't know when it had happened, but he had fallen out of the owl's favor. He wondered why it would suddenly embrace him again. Perhaps it was another trick?

To kill Wolf Blankston, or to let him live? The weight of the decision could have crushed him like a small insect.

He decided to put his confidence in the golden owl. What other choice did he have? It wasn't like he could raise his fists and combat the owl as if it were some mortal, flesh and bone creature. He was helpless against it—like a man standing alone against an empire. He had to trust the owl, whether it led him to his fortune or to his doom.

He put the golden owl on the desk and then returned the pistol to the drawer. He then folded the figurine into the handkerchief. He was about to return the handkerchief to the drawer when he remembered that Wolf Blankston had watched him conceal his treasured items within that compartment earlier that day. He scoured the room for another hiding place, but the office was so bare of furniture that he didn't feel comfortable stashing it anywhere else. He put the owl in his pocket and then he retrieved the map and the journal of Father Rodriguez from the drawer. He put the map in the same pocket he put the owl, and then concealed the journal in his belt above his buttocks. He untucked his shirt and then tucked it in again to cover the journal. He then stood and hurried for the door.

•

He put his hand over his eyebrows as he paced toward the entrance of the Aura. As he walked, he couldn't help but notice the hypnotic, rhythmic chatter of his footsteps. With each one, they grew more distinct. It brought to light just how eerily silent the desert was. It made him feel alone. Though, despite the credible feeling, George knew that he was not alone. He could still feel the presence of the owl. He had felt it the previous night, and it had lingered since. Somewhere, the Great Horned Owl, or the force that controlled it, was watching him—peering into his thoughts and evaluating his actions and emotions. It was as if he were a lone stage actor performing in a large, empty amphitheater. The only person in the audience was the astute ruler, who enjoyed a bird's-eye view of the tragic monologue.

The silence of the desert was gradually replaced by a squeaking sound. Two men emerged from the mouth of the Aura Mine pushing a cart full of coal.

"You there!" George yelled, as he hurried toward them.

The two men stopped and waited for George to climb the hill.

George didn't recognize either one of them. They were both Hispanic men wearing black pants and tan boots. Their faces and clothing were dusted with coal. One of the men was almost two feet shorter than George. He wore a long-sleeved button up shirt that was gray, and he sported a thick, bushy moustache. The other man was nearly as tall as George with a clean-shaven face, a white button up shirt, and striking amber eyes.

"Will one of ya fetch Remo for me?" George asked. "Tell 'im to meet me in my office."

The two men looked at him blankly.

"Do ya understand?" George asked.

The two Hispanic men looked at one another, then the tall one spoke to the shorter man. "Ir a buscar al capataz."

The short man nodded his head and then walked briskly toward the mine.

"He gettin' Remo?" George asked as he looked into the amber eyes of the tall Hispanic man.

The Hispanic man nodded his head.

"Much obliged," said George.

The Hispanic man smiled and nodded his head again, and then he continued to schlepp the coal cart toward the tipple, though he struggled as he was now doing the work of two men.

George watched him for a moment. *How strange that man was,* he thought. There was an air of confidence about him that George recognized, though could not comprehend. All day long, he had seen only the distraught faces of men who were reluctant to enter what they thought was a dangerous mine and who were unsure if they were being led by the careless Al Joseph or by the reckless Wolf Blankston. And here was this Hispanic man with a smile stamped on his face and an air of serenity about him. He wasn't worried about the condition of the mine or the precarious state of the mine's ownership. He was in complete control of his environment, as though he knew something no one else did.

A bead of sweat rolled from George's temple, passed his eye, and trickled down his cheek. He wiped his face with his sleeve and then turned and walked down the hill.

•

George was sitting at his desk with a pen in his right hand and Wolf Blankston's contract turned to the last page when Remo walked in. He was covered in sweat and coal, and his troubled eyes told George that he was wracked with anxiety.

"I'm ready," said Remo as he lifted his shirt, revealing a Colt Derringer tucked into the front of his belt.

"Are ya all right?" George asked.

"I've just got a bad feeling about this, a real bad feeling. I'm gonna follow through with it for your sake, but I just wish there was some other way to get rid of that son of a bitch. I know I ain't a very smart man. I haven't got the brains that you or your Pop had, but I tell ya, George. Boy, do I tell ya, this feeling I got is real bad, like nothing good could come from this."

"I agree," said George. "That's why I'm callin' it off."

Remo exhaled, forcing the distress from his lungs. He wouldn't say it, but he was relieved.

"What will you do instead?" Remo asked.

"I dunno," said George plainly. "I just gotta hunch this is the right thing to do for right now. In time, the answer'll come."

Remo would never know what made George change his mind. Hours ago, he had spoken passionately about killing Wolf Blankston. Now, he wanted him to live. Wolf was going to have his hand in the day-to-day operations of the Aura Mine. It didn't feel right. None of it felt right. Whether they killed Wolf or let him live, there was a strong sense of an impending dire outcome.

George looked through the broken glass window to see a blanket of dark cloud cover moving in, hovering over the arid desert, foreshadowing the imminent doom.

"You're sure about this?" Remo asked.

"Yes," George replied. "I'm afraid there ain't much choice other than to put our trust in Wolf Blankston."

Trust in Wolf Blankston. That was what the owl had told him to do. Deep down, George knew that the owl was the greater threat. Trust in the owl, that was more like it.

"How's the cleanup comin'?" George asked.

"Almost through. We'll be up and running first thing tomorrow morning."

"Good. Why don't ya go back up there and forget about all this other stuff. I'm sorry for the stress I've caused. I'm also sorry about the way I've treated ya the last coupla days. Ya came here to be my foreman. Ya didn't come here for this."

Remo looked at George like a puppy that sensed trouble. Foreman—as long as Wolf Blankston was around, he wouldn't be foreman for long. George and Remo both knew it. Remo nodded his head and then turned and opened the rickety door, allowing the white abyss to flood the office. The door closed, the light faded, and George was alone.

He took a deep breath, ignited an Aura cigar, and then signed Wolf Blankston's contract.

37

A purple and orange sunset painted the western sky, sucking the hellish heat from the land and allowing the desert birds a comfortable atmosphere to feed and to sing their evening tunes. The male crickets had already started rubbing their forewings together in an effort to attract their female counterparts, and to establish and protect their territory against competing males. George had also prepared himself to defend his territory against a competing male. But unlike the crickets, he had not mustered a defense mechanism of his own behest.

He was sitting behind his desk when Wolf Blankston entered the office wearing a fresh suit. It was clear that he had recently bathed and that he had lathered himself in fine cologne. George could smell it from across the room. His hair was parted and slicked back with a comb and his shoes were polished. He looked like he was ready to dine at a fine restaurant or attend a theatrical performance, as opposed to hashing out business parameters in a crumbling shack in the middle of the desert.

"Are you feeling better?" Wolf asked as he shut the door behind him. He then sat in the chair opposite George.

"Much better, thanks," George replied.

"Good. Were you able to look over the contract?"

"Yes."

"Excellent, George," said Wolf with a cunning grin. "You don't mind if I call you George, do you? After all, as of to-day, George Hendricks is officially exempt from any crime that he may have committed in the past."

"Is that right?" George asked suspiciously.

"That's right. As long as you've signed the contract, of course."

That was a question, and Wolf expected an answer.

"I've signed it," said George as he picked it up and tossed it to the other side of the table.

"I tell you—I can't wait to get started," said Wolf as he flipped to the final page to confirm that it was signed. "I have a little surprise for you. I was going to come earlier and tell you, but I had to see it through first. I contacted Lieutenant W.H. Adams of the U.S. Navy, and it sounds like he's interested in a contract with the Aura operation. In fact, he's so interested that he wanted to travel here right away to discuss it with you face to face. I hope that's all right."

George leaned forward in his chair. "Where is he?"

"He's waiting outside. Shall I call for him?"

"Yes, of course," George replied.

Wolf smiled, and then he stood and opened the door. "He's ready," he said, speaking to Lieutenant Adams who was allegedly standing outside.

From the blinding white void, the foreman of the Rainville No. 4, Leonard Pearl, along with Carter Hirsh and Walker Thompson, stormed into George's office. George quickly opened the top drawer of his desk and reached for his pistol, but he was too late. Leonard Pearl grabbed him by the collar and pulled him violently from his chair. Soon after, he was completely overwhelmed. They took hold of his legs, and then they dragged him out of the office. He kicked and hollered, but it was three against one. Leonard Pearl alone counted as three men. They dragged him across the rock and dirt face down. He felt scrapes and cuts forming on his hands and forearms, and he clenched his teeth in a vain attempt to absorb some of the pain.

He looked up to see Wolf Blankston exit the office. Waiting for him outside were Stanton Peirce, Wolf's protégé, and Harvey Bloomstein, the corrupt mine inspector. The sight of those men brought to light just how insignificant George was and how little of a chance he stood against those with real money—real power. Even if he had decided to kill Wolf that evening, he would have been too late. The mongrels were ready to pounce on him then and there, and there was nothing he could have done about it.

He heard an iron door squeal open. The next thing he knew, he was being hurled onto a rough cement floor—his ribs crashing hard against it. The iron door slammed shut. They had thrown him in the camp jail, which was a small stone structure meant for holding only one prisoner.

"George," called a voice, though he wasn't sure where it was coming from. He tried to look for it, but the movement caused his bleeding arms and damaged ribs to cry out in pain.

"Up here, George," called the voice again.

He looked up to the single window in the jail. The window was barred, and the opening itself was no bigger than a standard textbook. When his eyes adjusted, he saw Wolf Blankston's chubby mug peering into the cell. He was already sweating like a pig, though he wore a wry smile from ear to ear.

"You goddamn mutt!" he stated victoriously. "Did you really think that I would partner with you? You tried to kill me. The magnificent Wolf Blankston, cut down my some peasant trash! I have no interest in your mine. What you've built here is an absolute travesty. I do, on the other hand, have an interest in the land. You've given me the land by signing the contract. I'm sure that you're completely unaware. You're no mine owner. You're no businessman. You're a peasant. That's all you've ever been, and that's all you'll ever be. I've paid the men four-hundred dollars apiece to fix every inch of this mine with dynamite so that I can blast it to kingdom-come. After it's gone, Stanton and I, as well as the men, will start a new operation. I'm going to call it New Rainville. What do you think of that?"

George grimaced on the floor like a worm that had just been stepped on. No wonder so many new men had found their way to the Aura. They had not come to help him—they had come to destroy him.

"Whadderya gonna do to me?" George asked.

Wolf chuckled. "Why—I'm going to keep you here and make you watch the detonation, of course. After that, you'll be sent upstate to serve a lengthy prison sentence for attempted murder."

What could George say? What could he do? He had no choice but to remain vigilant.

"So long, George," said Wolf before moving away from the window.

It was the lowest that George had felt in some time. Perhaps this was what Joe the Tommyknocker was trying to warn him about. He could suddenly hear the bitter words of his father echoing in his mind: "You don't have any sense in your head. You're a goddamn stupid bastard for trusting that Wolf Blankston." It was true. He should have never trusted Wolf, and he should have never trusted Edmond Kelly. He should have stayed by his father's side and died with him in the Rainville No. 4. He would have never killed Hunter Paige or Wolf Blankston, and he wouldn't be in the mess he was in now. But George didn't want his father by his side. He didn't want him to be a part of his dream. There was nothing he could do about that now.

George's right hand slipped into his front pocket and felt the golden owl as well as *El Mapa del búho*. They were still there, and the shape of Father Rodriguez's journal was still in his belt. His most cherished items were still in his possession. That meant something; however, it would only be a matter of time before Wolf came looking for them. He knew the objects were important to George, and he knew about the gold that was tied to them. There would be no way he would let George keep them. He would either take them for himself or have them destroyed. George had to hide them somewhere.

The only furniture in the cell was one small cot tucked into the corner of the room. It was far too obvious of a hiding place. There had to be a better spot. Fortunately, George was a tall man, and he was able to reach up and put his hand against the corrugated metal roofing. He stumbled around pressing upward on the metal, hopeful that a section would give way. Finally, in the corner, one did, though it let out a loud screech as the metal scraped against a protruding nail. He released the roofing, expecting that someone had heard the ruckus.

He waited a full minute standing still, but no one came. During that time, he thought maybe he would be able to escape through the roof later that night, though it would be difficult given his physical condition—that, and the certainty that Wolf Blankston would have armed guards appointed to the jail. Wolf would never allow him to escape. His life depended on it. Still, it was probably worth taking the chance. It might be his only shot at freedom.

He cautiously lifted the corner of the metal sheeting again, this time with his left hand so that he could withdraw the map, the owl, and the journal and put them on the roof of the building. He put the map on the bottom of the pile, the journal on top of the map, and then the weighty golden owl, which was wrapped in the handkerchief, on top of the journal. He hoped that the order would hold the objects in place in case of wind.

He lowered the corner of the metal roofing. Much to his delight, it didn't make a peep. He moved across the room and sat down on the hard, springy cot. There wasn't much he could do now but wait and hope. He had put his trust in the owl. He had to believe that the owl would come.

38

The dark storm clouds lingered, blotting out the yellow moon and the brilliant stars. It was so dark that George could not even see the brick walls of the jail, which were no more than three feet from him in every direction. He could hear whoever was standing guard in front of the cell. Every couple of minutes, the guard would walk all the way around the building and peer through the window to make sure that George was still there. George couldn't tell who the man was because it was too dark. All he could see was the shadow of someone's head appearing and then disappearing in a flash.

He could hear the thunder stirring in the distance and the gentle, gusting winds ruffling through the nearby juniper trees. It made him nervous. He knew that if it started to rain, he would have to retrieve the map and the journal from the roof or else they would ruin. But the wind was the greater threat. If the wind began to howl the way it was capable of in the high desert, then his treasured possessions could easily be blown from the roof and onto the ground to be discovered by the jail guard.

George was lying on his back, staring up at the small portion of night sky that he could see through the tiny opening of the window. No one else had tried to speak with him since Wolf's tongue lashing, and he found that to be rather odd. Where was Remo or any of the other men who had been so loyal to him and he to them? Why weren't they making an effort to help him? Wolf mentioned that he paid the men four hundred dollars to plant dynamite throughout the Aura. George wondered if Remo was among the men underground sabotaging his dream. It was hard to believe that his only friend could have abandoned him in exchange for a little money. But then again, money—substantial amounts of it—had the power to make otherwise good people do rotten things.

Throughout the last hour, George had heard men shouting instructions. No more than ten minutes earlier, he overheard a great deal of bickering between the men as well as what sounded like a carriage arriving. Based on their dialogue, George assumed that the carriage was loaded with boxes of dynamite—dynamite that would blow the Aura sky high.

He wobbled to his feet and groaned and cursed at the pain in his ribs and neck. As he looked out the window, he could see only what was taking place under the industrial lamps, which were located above the door of the mine office and above the portal of the Aura. Under the mine office's bulb, he could see Wolf Blankston and Stanton Pierce speaking with a third person who George did not recognize. Under the other lamp, he could see a half-dozen men hauling boxes of dynamite into the portal. The boxes were almost the size of a coffin. It took two men to carry one.

George returned his attention to the office. He watched as Wolf Blankston signed something and then handed it to the third man, who then departed. Soon after, George heard the carriage pulling away. *The third man must have been the carriage driver,* he thought. Wolf was puffing away at a cigar—Stanton, a cigarette. They were speaking to one another, though George couldn't make out what they were saying. Whatever it was, it appeared to be enormously pleasing to Wolf.

Stanton opened the office door and then the two men disappeared inside, shutting the door behind them. Under the lamp of the Aura's entrance, the last set of men disappeared into the mine. There was nothing to see now other than the scores of moths writhing against the lamps, so he slipped back into the room and took a seat on the springy cot, which creaked under his willowy frame.

Remo... George thought. He was beginning to consider the possibility that Remo was being held captive separately, at least until George was dealt with. That was the only reasonable explanation. If Remo were free, then he would have tried to help him somehow. Or would he? A dreadful thought entered George's mind just then. He recalled that Remo and Wolf had arrived on the same day. What if Remo had a hand in capturing him? What if Wolf Blankston had paid him a great deal of money to track him down? It was possible. Anything was possible. Remo was the only living connection to George, so it would make sense that Wolf would try to entice him to track George down. Remo had a wife and children to think about, after all. It would be next to impossible for a poverty-stricken man to turn down a handsome offer. From that moment on, Remo could no longer be trusted.

Footsteps materialized in the still night air, growing louder as they drew closer to the jail. George's heart started to pound. He wondered if Wolf had lied to him. Maybe he wouldn't be going to prison after all. Maybe Wolf's goons were on their way to kill him right then and there—to end the Hendricks-Blankston feud once and for all. If they were going to do it, it made sense that they would do it while the men were occupied. They could simply tell them that George was transported to the prison while they were underground.

George grimaced in pain as he rose to his feet. He slithered to the corner of the room so that when the iron door swung open, he would be hidden behind it—that way he could attempt to slither out, get his items from the roof, and then make a run for it.

The stomping drew closer, and with it came a strange dragging sound, as though the men were dragging some piece of equipment. With a thud, someone put their hand on the iron door. George could hear them fumbling with a set of keys. Soon after, the iron door swung open, and someone was hurled into the room, crashing hard against the concrete the same way that George had earlier. Three men then stormed into the room. George leapt from the shadows and tried to make a run for it. He was halfway out the door when someone grabbed hold of his shirt and pulled him back into the jail. The man staggered a little. George seized the opportunity and clocked him with a hard right. Whoever he was, he was a brute of a man. George's fist swelled with pain. He knew right away that he had afflicted himself with more pain than the brute.

He was then restrained by two other of Blankston's henchmen. They held him while the man who George hit retaliated with a hard right hook across George's left cheekbone. George dropped like a brick, and then the men began to pat him down. A fourth man entered the room carrying a lantern, and the light revealed to George that these weren't just men—they were Rainville men, Wolf Blankston's dogs.

"Where are they, Hendricks?" grumbled one of the men.

As the man entered the radius of the lantern, George saw that it was Leonard Pearl. It was he who George had struck and who had retaliated with a blow of his own. It was the wrong guy to hit. The other men, including Walker Thompson and Carter Hirsh, began probing the cell. They turned over the cot, looked behind the door, and searched the roof trusses. Those were really the only places that something could be hidden within the room itself. The roof, on the other hand, was a hiding place far too inventive for the witless swine to think of.

"Where are they, Hendricks?" Leonard repeated.

"Whaddarya talkin' about?"

"The map'n that little figurine. Where are they?"

"They're in the office," said George.

"Like hell they are."

"If they ain't in there, then I don't know where they are."

"Yer a goddamn liar."

"There ain't nothin' here, boss," said Walker.

Leonard leaned in close to George's face. "I'll give ya one last chance. Where are they?"

"I swear on my life. I don't know. If they ain't in my office, then I dunno what to tell ya."

Leonard stood up straight. All the while, he maintained a steadfast gaze on George. "We turned that goddamn office upside-down. There ain't shit in there!"

"Well I don't have 'em, do I?"

"All right," said Leonard in a governing voice. "I'll see what Mr. Blankston wantstuh do 'bout it. I can't guarantee we won't be back."

Leonard and the others left the room and slammed the metal door behind them. George heard the sound of metal on metal as the iron key rattled into the lock, and then he heard their departing footsteps. He looked across the room to see the vague outline of the man who had been thrown into the cell. He was sitting up with both knees lifted, his arms resting on them.

"Remo?" George asked quietly.

There was no response.

"I'm sorry, Remo. I don't even know what to say."

Again, there was no answer.

After a moment, whoever was seated began to move a little. A small burst of fire sparked as the other inmate scraped a match against the coarse side of a matchbox. He used the flame to ignite a candle that he retrieved from his pocket. The man stood up and stepped forward.

It wasn't Remo after all. It was the Hispanic man who George had encountered earlier that day.

The Hispanic man spoke with broken English in a deep, raspy voice. "Are you all right, Mr. Joseph?"

"Yes. Why'd they throw ya in here?"

"They wanted me to put dynamite in the walls. They wanted me to destroy the Aura. I said no. I told them that I wanted to leave, so they took me here."

"What's your name?"

"My real name?" the man asked with an odd grin. "Aldric...my real name is Aldric."

"I feel like I know ya from some place."

Aldric's smile faded a little. "I overhead those men talking about the objects they seek from you. Once they find them, they're going to come here and kill you."

"Then I guess I can't let 'em find 'em," George replied.

"I heard them talk about a map, a journal, and some kind of figurine."

"That's right," said George with questioning eyes.

"I don't think it is wise to keep them on the roof. The rain will fall hard tonight."

"How the hell you'd know they were up there?"

"That's where I would have put them."

George studied Aldric for a moment, and then he asked, "Can I trust ya?"

"Yes."

George eased his way to the corner of the room. There, he cautiously lifted the corrugated metal roofing and retrieved the journal, the owl, and the map, and then lowered the sheet of metal into place.

"This is what they were after," said George as he presented the objects to Aldric.

Aldric traded his candle for George's possessions. He looked them over. First, the journal of Father Rodriguez. He opened the journal and began to skim through pages. "This is written in Spanish," he said.

"Can ya read it?"

"Yes. I can read it for you if you wish."

"Please," said George with a surge of passion.

Next, Aldric looked at the owl, which made him smile. "This is gold," he said.

"Yes."

Last, Aldric looked at *El Mapa del búho*, though he chose not to unfold it. "This leads to gold, yes?"

"It does."

"If you know where it is, we can burn the journal and the map. That way they can never find it."

"I can't do that," said George. "I need 'em still."

Aldric nodded his head. "Then I know what to do."

"What?"

"I will hold them for you. They have already searched you and the jail. They won't search me. They have no reason to."

"That ain't too bad of an idea," said George. "But I think I'll hold on to 'em myself. I know it's risky, but they've already searched me once. I doubt they'll do it again. Either way, I'll take my chances."

Aldric nodded and smiled, knowing that deep down George didn't really trust him. How could he? He just met the man.

"Shall I read from the journal?" Aldric asked. "This candle won't last very long. It's the only one I've got."

"Then let's hurry."

"Please, lie down on the bunk. You've been through a lot."

"Thanks," George replied as he sat down on the bunk.

Aldric sat against the stone wall with his legs extended. He held the candle in his left hand and the journal in his right. The candle burned for nearly two hours. Leonard Pearl and his goons did not return. By the time the candle died out, George learned a great deal about Father Rodriguez and the Spanish expedition of 1733—their hardships and their victories. He learned of the merciless Esteban Garza and that the Spanish had encountered the same mist-like entity that George had during his first excursion—the same entity that was now present somewhere within the Aura. But above all, George finally learned the secret of the lost Spanish gold mine. At long last, he knew where he had been turned astray. He had been so close. Now he knew, but it didn't hold much significance seeing that he was imprisoned by Wolf Blankston. He needed a way out. He needed the owl to set him free.

39

George awoke to the sound of rainfall dribbling onto the corrugated metal roofing above his head. Water was dripping from the various rusted cavities, causing the dust on the ground to coalesce into a sooty mud. His left eye was swollen halfway shut, and there was dried blood that ran from his nose and caked onto the left side of his upper lip. The pain in his neck was still present, as was the pain in his head from being smacked around by the thunderous fists of Leonard Pearl.

Aldric was already awake. He was looking out the window—eyeing the cool morning overcast—unaware that George was conscious.

Metal clanked on metal as a key was inserted into the iron door. Wolf's goons entered, led by the boneheaded Leonard Pearl. Leonard grabbed George's right arm, and Walker Thompson grabbed his left. They dragged him out of the jail and into the clammy dawn.

Outside, all of the Aura's laborers as well as their families—which together tallied nearly one hundred people—were arranged in a semi-circle facing the entrance of the mine. There seemed to be mixed emotions emanating from the crowd. There were those who seemed thrilled by what was about to happen, and there were others who were downright disgusted by it. In the middle of the semicircle were six wooden blasting machines that were all linked together with insulated copper wiring that trailed all the way from the gathering to the entrance of the Aura like six infinitely long snakes. It was detonation time.

Leonard Pearl threw George to the ground ten feet behind the blasting machines but in front of the townsfolk. George sat up on his knees while Leonard withdrew a Schofield revolver and held it to the back of George's head.

The rain was only trickling down, though a rumble of thunder roared in the distance. The dirt, rock, and trees were the same shade as the stone-colored sky. There was a great storm approaching. It, too, had come to witness the destruction of the Aura.

Wolf Blankston emerged from the crowd with a wry smile and a cigar wedged between his teeth. He took a long drag and then spoke. "Good morning, George. It sure is a wonderful morning, isn't it? Two days ago I promised you five thousand dollars to jumpstart your operation. Well, I've gone ahead and spent that money on dynamite." Wolf chuckled and then turned to the laborers. "The time has come men. You'll all be receiving your four hundred dollars at the conclusion of the blast—assuming that it goes off without a hitch. Then, as promised, you'll all be employees of the Wolf Blankston Mining Company. In a couple of hours, our new mine, New Rainville, will be underway."

The majority of the men cheered, though the men who were originally employed by Al Joseph looked on with desolate faces.

George turned toward the crowd in an effort to spot Remo. As his eyes looked over the crowd, he saw a lot of familiar faces. There was Helen Laine, the nurse from the Rainville infirmary. There was Martin Paulson, the old man who rang the bell. There was the six-year-old boy who smiled at George the day before the blast—a smoking pipe was in his mouth. There was the old man who was always singing in the mine, and there was the always dapper Stanton Pierce. He then spotted Jari Ronni—the Finnish man who had lost two brothers underground. *What was Jari Ronni doing helping Wolf Blankston?* George wondered.

Suddenly, Leonard Pearl kicked George between the shoulder blades. He fell forward but caught himself with the palms of his hands.

"Keep yer eyes forward," Leonard grumbled.

Wolf took another drag from his cigar and then nodded toward a section of the men. Six coal miners emerged from the crowd. Each one settled in front of one of the detonation boxes. It was time. The miners put their hands on the blasting handles.

Wolf started to count down.

"5... 4... 3... 2... 1..."

The six miners plunged their respective handles downward simultaneously.

With a thunderous crash, the ground began to rumble, causing many of the townsfolk to stumble and the women and children to cry and shriek. A stream of black smoke belched from the mouth of the Aura Mine. George dipped his head in defeat. He could hear the cheers of some of the men, and the laughter of Wolf Blankston. But above everything else, he could hear, and feel, his drifts and tunnels collapsing. His beloved twenty-two foot seam was forever lost.

Black smoke started pouring from the entrance of the Aura and brought on painful memories of the explosion at Rainville—ultimately, the death of Joe. George recalled the fierce rattling of the ground and the billows of thick, filthy smoke that teemed from the portal. It was the same vision that he was watching now. It was a collapse that was so catastrophic that, in all likelihood, his father's mortal remains would be forever sealed in the Rainville hillside, as so many men had been before him. What was it like being crushed by thousands of pounds of dirt and coal? What did Joe go through on that horrible day?

George's mind began to drift toward oblivion—a place where his haunting past fused with a vivid fantasy. He began to imagine himself moving through the dark tunnels of the Rainville No. 4. He could hear the echoing hum of the hillside above him and the distant, raspy singing of the battered miner:

> *"You could look at the rib or the face or the top,*
> *Never a sign or a laggin' or a slap or of prop;*
> *Someday I expect that old mountain to drop*
> *And come down, down, down."*

He moved through the tunnel then down the ladder into the No. 2 drift. At the end of the drift, he could see his father battling his marred knees as he shoveled coal into a coal cart. Remo was already hauling the first loaded cart to the surface, so there was only Joe and the new guy—the name of the man had slipped George's mind. Little Lemon, their trusty canary, chirped and chirped while his little black eyes looked around. Then George heard a sound that made his skin crawl. It was a strange moaning sound. The sound of a Tommyknocker. Joe and the new guy didn't hear the cry of the Tommyknocker, only George did. From the darkness of the No. 2 drift, the shadowy Tommyknocker came forth into the dim radius of Remo's work lantern.

George tried to shout in order to warn Joe about the Tommyknocker, but he couldn't. His lips moved, but no sound came from them. He tried again, and again—deep, bloodcurdling screams, but no sound could be produced, as though he were in some sort of vacuum.

The Tommyknocker took another step forward. The shadow faded a little, revealing the soft, humanoid features of the wandering soul. It had a sturdy chin and a protruding cheekbone, and after it took another step closer to the light, the man's amber eyes became discernable. George looked on in disbelief. It was Aldric, the man he had shared a jail cell with the previous night.

George's train of thought was severed as his mind began to show him more of what happened. He saw the man that had been hired earlier that day. The man drove his shovel into the pile of loose coal, causing a flurry of orange sparks to jump from the shovel and cascade onto the ground. Because the ventilation was nowhere near reliable, there was a large coalescence of coal dust clinging to the air from an earlier dynamite blast. A spark from the shovel had ignited the coal dust, which ignited the crate of dynamite, causing the massive blast that killed Joe Hendricks and thirty-five others. Neither Joe nor the new guy had an opportunity to react. They were both, along with poor little Lemon, blown to smithereens. The substandard timbering throughout the Rainville No. 4 had given way, trapping the majority of the men underground. Thirty-six men had died because their owner had denied them the proper safety measures.

Rage began to swell through George the way it did before he drove his pickaxe into Wolf's back; however, this time, he was unable to act. He had no weapon, and he was gravely outnumbered by men who were loyal to the man who was paying them. Leonard Pearl, on the other hand, did have a weapon, and if George were to move a muscle, he wouldn't hesitate to use it.

"Should I put the prisoner back in the cell, boss?" Leonard asked.

"Not yet," said Wolf as he walked toward George, taking a drag from his cigar. He stopped in front of George and looked at him with wrath. "Where's the owl?" he demanded.

"I dunno," said George.

"Put your arms in the air," demanded Wolf.

George hesitantly raised his arms.

"Walker, hold his arms."

Walker Thompson came forth and held George's arms while Wolf leaned over and reached his hand into George's pocket. When he withdrew it, he held the golden owl figurine in his avaricious hand.

"There it is," he said triumphantly. He then eyed Leonard and Walker. "I told you he hid them somewhere in the cell you goddamn mutts!"

He returned his attention to George and reached his hand into George's other pocket. It was empty. He then began to pat George down. Much to Wolf's dismay, the golden owl was all that George had.

"Where's the rest of it?" Wolf growled.

George remained silent. It was an excellent question. Last he knew, the map was in his pocket, and the journal was in his belt. They were both gone now.

Wolf was about to strike George with his fist when Walker spoke out: "What's goin' on over there?" He was looking at the jail.

Every pair of eyes turned toward the jail. There was a stream of smoke trickling from the window and blowing toward the assemblage.

"Hold him there," Wolf commanded. "Carter, open that cell."

Carter Hirsh materialized from the crowd and hurried toward the jail, fumbling with a set of iron keys in the process. Carter was an older man who had a blonde handlebar moustache and a messy goatee. He was very thin—so much so that it looked like his flesh was clinging directly to bone. He ran as if there were a pole jammed three feet into his rectum.

Wolf followed him. When they entered the jail, they found Aldric standing near the window. On the windowsill, El Mapa del búho and the journal of Father Rodriguez were burning to a crisp.

Wolf bolted into the room and tried to salvage the items, but he was too late. They had both already been reduced to a pile of ash. With an enraged swipe, he knocked the residue of the map and the journal from the windowsill and onto the ground. He then turned to Aldric.

"What in the hell did you do that for?" Wolf snarled.

Aldric looked at Wolf with a blank expression.

"Do you understand English?"

Again, Aldric's face was vacant.

Wolf hurried to the door and stopped underneath the frame. "Stanton, come over here," he hollered.

Wolf turned and glared at Aldric. Soon after, Stanton entered the room. "He doesn't speak English," he relayed to Stanton. "Ask him why he burned those items."

Stanton took a step into the room and noted the pile of ash on the windowsill. He asked Aldric, in Spanish, why he burned the objects.

Aldric spoke.

Stanton echoed, "He says he found them hidden in the room. He didn't think they were important."

"If he didn't think they were important, then why in the Christ did he burn them?" Wolf scoffed.

Stanton looked at Aldric and asked him that question.

Aldric replied.

"He says that his hands were cold and that he wanted to warm them," relayed Stanton.

"What a load of shit!" yelled Wolf in a furious rage, frightening everyone else in the room. He calmed a little and then said, "Ask him if he read them."

Stanton asked if he had read them.

"Si," replied Aldric with a smile.

That one Wolf understood. He dipped his head in frustration. "Damn it," he grumbled. He then looked out the door. "Bring George here," he yelled.

Seconds later, George was dragged into the cell by the brute strength of Leonard Pearl.

"Close the door," Wolf instructed.

Like a puppet, Leonard obliged, sealing them all within the confines of the tiny jail.

Wolf stepped in front of both men. "All right, George," he said with a distressed look on his face. "I guess I don't have much of a choice but to fill you in on something."

He took a deep breath and then looked toward Stanton, who nodded his head in support.

"We came here to take the land and to destroy the Aura," said Wolf. "But those were secondary objectives. The biggest reason why we came was for that golden owl figurine and the map. I know all about them. You know Edmond Kelly, I presume? He's the one who sold them to you, wasn't he? Well, before he sold them to you he tried to sell them to me. I didn't believe anything he said, but after I recovered from a terrible incident that involved a pickaxe"— Wolf's eyes narrowed—"Stanton and I conducted a little research. We found that Kelly's claims were actually legitimate. But, by the time we figured that out it was too late. Kelly had already sold the objects to you, and you were long gone."

Wolf puffed from his nearly depleted cigar. "I have a vague idea of how much gold is in that mountain. If I'm right, the value of that mine is worth tenfold what Rainville was worth—a hundredfold what your shithole mine was worth." Wolf gestured at Aldric. "But, it appears this man has destroyed two valuable pieces of the puzzle." Wolf walked to the windowsill and picked up a pinch of ash left behind. "Believe it or not, this stupid mutt spared you a prison sentence, at least for the time being." He threw the ash on the ground. "You've been on the mountain. You've even memorized the map, haven't you?"

"I know it pretty well, yes," George admitted.

"Good, then," said Wolf. He looked at Aldric and then back at George. "That leaves us with our pyrotechnic. He claims to have read the journal, but how could he have possibly read the entire thing without you knowing about it?"

George took a moment to manifest an answer, one that would keep him and Aldric alive. "I let 'im read it," he said. "I couldn't understand the Spanish. He was gonna translate it for me."

"So, you do speak English?" Wolf asked, glaring.

"A little," Aldric replied.

Wolf returned his attention to George. "Has he translated it for you?"

"Not yet," said George. "He was about to when your men came in."

Wolf nodded. "So you know the terrain, and this man understands the content of the journal."

He stared icily at both George and Aldric for a moment, and then he turned and walked out of the cell without saying another word. His goons followed him like sheep, closing the door behind them and locking it.

George put his hands on his head. The golden owl—of course Wolf wanted the golden owl—why wouldn't he? *Oh well,* he thought. Wolf Blankston needed him now, which gave him an opportunity to live. George looked across the room to see Aldric looking back at him.

"Thank you," George said.

Aldric nodded and then turned and looked out the window. There was smoke pouring from the Aura Mine. On the horizon, just to the left of the smoke, was The Mountain of the Owl.

40

Black smoke was still pouring from the mouth of the Aura when the key was rattled into the jail door—granting entry to Leonard Pearl and his emptyheaded sidekicks. The demeanor of Leonard was much different from what it had been during his previous visits. He seemed to be holding something back, as though subdued—likely through the instruction of Wolf Blankston—and there was nothing the inane brute hated more than being told to restrain himself from conflict.

"Mr. Blankston wantstuh see ya—hurry up," Leonard grumbled.

George was lying sideways on the cot with his knees bent so that he would fit on the stumpy mattress. It was close, but his toes were still hanging off the edge. He lengthened his feet, slid to his side, and then pushed himself up to a seated position with his right hand, causing his ribs and neck to cry out.

Leonard took hold of George's bicep, though it was a gentle grip, and led him out of the cell.

The rain was still falling softly but seemed to be picking up. The clouds had darkened, and there was a light breeze blowing from the east. It was only a matter of time before the skies opened wide and soaked the desert.

Before George's eyes could adjust to the dim afternoon sunlight, which was twice as bright as his cell, he was led through another door—a wooden, creaking door—of what was once his office. Gradually, the muted vision of the room began to manifest itself—the stone walls, the brick flooring, the corrugated iron roofing, and the large, oak desk. Wolf Blankston was seated behind the desk smoking a cigar. Stanton Pierce and Harvey Bloomstein were standing on both sides of him smoking cigarettes, leaning over the desk and inspecting some sort of canvas that was draped over the desk's surface.

George instinctively thought of something that Remo might say: *"Two gangly sons-a-bitches and one fat son of a bitch."*

Wolf, Stanton, and Harvey had been drinking George's booze. The doors of the liquor cabinet were open, and there were three glass tumblers on the table as well as a bottle of Scotch and a bottle of bourbon. There was also coffee and black tea for Harvey, and on top of all that, they had smoked enough cigars and cigarettes to fill the room with a blue haze. Booze, caffeine, smokes, rolled up sleeves, loosened ties, and sweaty foreheads. And here it was, barely noon. It was the sign of men in distress.

All three of them sat upright when George walked into the room, and their eyes widened like the eyes of errant children. They all gaped at George's swollen eye and bruised cheekbone as if they were the ones responsible for it. In a way, they were. The bastards.

"Sit down, George," said Wolf with a serene tone, trying foolishly to make George feel welcome.

George wondered what would happen if he sat down. He knew they needed information from him, but once he gave it, would they kill him? As long as he refrained from divulging too much, they would have to keep him alive. He sat down.

George couldn't help but notice the paper canvas resting on the table. It was a map of what appeared to be a mountain region—*the* mountain region—though George couldn't help but relish in the fact that the gold-bearing country was not pictured. Either that or the geography was not plotted correctly. It looked to be freshly drawn, as if Wolf had been drawing it based on his faint glance at the map the previous day. Wolf was totally blind without George's map. Unfortunately for him, the map was now a handful of ash scattered across the desert.

Wolf extinguished his cigar in George's ashtray—his stubby, sausage-like fingers prodding away at the bottom of the glass vessel. "We have a serious problem on our hands," he said. "You know something that we need to know. Therefore, you are of tremendous value to us. What I want is no longer a secret. I've been mining coal my entire life, but the promise of a gold mine—owned and operated by the Wolf Blankston Mining Company—why, it doesn't get any better than that."

"Where's Remo?" George asked, ignoring what Wolf said.

Wolf smiled. "I thought you knew," he replied. "He fled town yesterday with his family. Normally, we would have stopped them. But, we decided to let them go."

"Why?"

"I think the two of you being separated is a substantial victory for me. Sure, Remo is probably on his way to communicate with the authorities. He'll tell them that I've commandeered the Aura Mine and that they should have me arrested at once." Wolf chuckled. "If the authorities do show up, then I'm afraid you'll be the only one arrested." He smiled, then the smile faded, and he began to shake his head. "But, let's get back to it. Stanton, Walker, and I are scheduled to leave here in one hour. Harvey here"—he gestured at Harvey Bloomstein with his thumb—"is going to run the operation in my absence. It was my intention that we would climb the mountain to the north under the supervision of your map and the direction of your journal. I was going to navigate from the map, and Stanton was going to translate the Spanish. But now the journal and the map are both gone. Your friend claims that he burned them because they were useless, but I don't believe him. I think he burned them because he knew how important they were."

Wolf began to twirl his chubby thumbs in an attempt to calm himself. It didn't work. Sweat continued to flow from his hairline, and the flesh underneath his clothing was clammy and almost unbearably warm. "I want you to tell me the truth," he continued. "Did you find the Spanish mine or not?"

George looked at the other men. They were all anticipating his answer.

"I found it."

"You swear it?" Wolf asked.

"I swear it."

"Then I'm afraid there's no other alternative. We're taking you with us. You'll be shackled at the wrists, and someone will be assigned to keep a constant eye on you."

Wolf allowed George a moment to let the information sink in. He reached for the glass tumbler in front of him and sipped from the Scotch. He then continued his statement. "I know what you're probably thinking. What's to stop you from leading us astray, far from where you found gold? Well, the answer to that question is nothing. We've done what research we could, but we know very little about it. Therefore, you must be provided with some incentive. This may be against my better judgment, but if you can lead us to the gold mine in one week—one week from this very moment—you'll be set free."

"And if I don't find it?"

"Why would you be worried about that? You just swore to me that you already found it."

"I ain't worried about it. I'm just askin'."

Wolf looked long and hard at George. "You wouldn't be lying to me, would you?"

The others looked intently at George, their cigar and cigarette smoke climbed into the air.

"I ain't lyin'," George replied.

"Good. Because if you drag us all the way up there for no reason, then I'm afraid the penalty will be worse than prison. Is that understood?"

"Yes."

Wolf eyed George, and then looked at Leonard Pearl. "That Hispanic man in the cell, we're taking him too. I have a hunch he may know something that George doesn't."

It was another trick, George thought. Wolf wouldn't let him go. Even if George found the gold mine, then Leonard Pearl would put a bullet through his head. He knew that now more than ever. But again, as it had been since he fled Rainville, he was at the mercy of Wolf Blankston. It was one week—plenty of time to orchestrate his final escape from what seemed like the eternal bonds of Wolf Blankston.

"If you can round up the horses, we might be able to make it by tomorrow," said George.

"We won't be riding. We'll be hiking," Wolf replied.

A hike? George thought. There was no way Wolf was fit for a hike.

Wolf glared at George as though reading his mind. "You don't think I'm physically able to hike?"

"Not really, no," George replied, feeling confident with the new circumstances.

"Like hell I'm not," Wolf snapped. "We aren't riding horses because a horse would make it awfully simple for you to escape, wouldn't it? Besides that, a little exercise and fresh air will do me some good. It will do the lot of us some good."

What Wolf failed to mention was that he had never ridden a horse in his life. Ever since he was a child, there was always a carriage driver to chauffeur him wherever he wanted to go. He was terrified of them—not only horses, but any animal that was larger than he. That's why killing deer, elk, and the occasional buffalo, bighorn sheep, or black bear brought him a great deal of pleasure. Mighty beasts slain—from a distance—by the great and powerful Wolf Blankston.

Silence overcame the room. Wolf retrieved his cigar from the ashtray and reignited it with a match. He wanted to discuss matters further. He wanted to know more about the terrain and more about George's previous outing, but the realization set in that George may have taken the upper hand. He couldn't cope with the frustration.

"Return him to the cell," said Wolf disgustedly. "Feed him and the other prisoner some of the lamb and potatoes. The men are almost finished rounding up all the necessary provisions. After the prisoners have eaten, we'll be on our way."

Leonard dragged George to his feet.

"Remember, George," said Wolf, which stopped Leonard and thus stopped George. "One week is all you have."

"We'll be there in three days—no more, no less," George affirmed.

Wolf nodded in acknowledgement, and then Leonard led George out of the room, through the moist desert terrain and into the small jail.

The metal key rattled into the lock, and George was again imprisoned. Aldric was still standing by the window as he had been before George was taken from the room. Even after the metal door squealed open and slammed shut, his amber eyes remained fixated on the smoke pouring from the Aura Mine and The Mountain of the Owl.

George sat on the cot and removed his boots before lying down on the rigid springs. He had a long and difficult adventure ahead. Some rest as well as some food would do wonders for his hangover symptoms, which—because he had barely eaten—were still present from the previous day.

He watched a black widow spider crawl from underneath the door and creep across the floor until it found a housefly imprisoned in its gluey web. Two of the spider's legs held the fly in place while its sphere-like body moved from side to side. Its mandible prodded at the quivering fly. The prey was being devoured so helplessly, and George couldn't help but to sympathize with it. But unlike the fly, George had a chance to break free.

The fire was burning once again within his soul. The treasure of the mountain was calling him. He had fled Rainville some time ago because the golden owl had represented a fortune that was inherently his—compensation for years of turmoil and sorrow. At long last, the burning sensation had returned. This time his back was against the wall, but he was certain that somehow, some way, he would finally claim his fortune.

41

Leonard Pearl unenthusiastically brought George and Aldric a plate of roasted lamb and potatoes and a pail of lukewarm water to wash it down with. The feast had been prepared by one of the Greek families as part of the celebration ceremony that Wolf requested. It was a celebration to rejoice in the inception of New Rainville.

George inhaled the food as if the plate itself would vanish into thin air after one minute and take the food with it. He hadn't eaten in two days, which certainly didn't help his already fragile mental and physical condition. The lamb and potatoes were perfectly seasoned, albeit a little cool because the food had been served an hour earlier. Aldric also cleaned his plate, but he took only a few sips of water before instructing George to consume the rest of it. He knew that George needed it more than he did. The meal caused the pain in George's brain and stomach to melt away. It even gave him a little energy, which was critical because he had three days of harsh terrain ahead of him.

The metal key was forced into the lock, and the iron door scraped opened. It was the colossal nincompoop Leonard Pearl, and behind him were Wolf, Stanton, Carter, and Walker. The spotters—Leonard, Walker, and Carter—were dressed in what they wore everyday underground—filthy black boots, black pants, and thin white t-shirts. Wolf and Stanton were both wearing brand new hiking boots and clean pairs of khaki slacks with suspenders that ran atop white button-up shirts. Wolf's suspenders were red, and Stanton's were blue. Wolf was wearing his black top hat and his horn-rimmed spectacles. Stanton wore a gray Homburg.

Walker and Carter entered the room. They were both carrying huge packsacks that were bloated with picks, shovels, hammers, bits, lanterns, pots, pans, and whatever else made Wolf Blankston's excursion into the mountain as harmless as a stay at a rustic resort.

The packsacks were fixed to George and Aldric, and then Leonard came forth holding two pairs of iron shackles. The shackles contained only four links of chain so that George and Aldric would be limited in their movements. They were bound with their wrists in front of them, and then they were led out of the cell and into the afternoon gloom.

Outside, Walker, Carter, and Leonard picked up packsacks of their own, though they were much smaller, lighter, and less hindering than what George and Aldric carried. Wolf and Stanton also carried small packs, though the contents of their packs were their personal effects—water canteens, medicine, fresh clothing, compasses, and binoculars. In their left hands, they both carried brand new walking sticks. And on their right hips, they both carried a pistol. In fact, they were all carrying pistols.

Judging by the position of the sun, which was barely visible through the overcast sky, George assumed that it was almost 1:00 P.M. It was a late start.

The seven men departed the Aura and hiked north through the soggy desert terrain. George was ordered to march in front so that he could act as the navigator and so that his back would always be turned to Wolf. Leonard Pearl and Walker Thompson were assigned to watch over George. Leonard marched a few feet behind him with his pistol readied on his hip. Walker marched side by side with Wolf and Stanton in the hindmost position. Aldric, under the supervision of Carter, walked in the middle.

George could see The Mountain of the Owl on the horizon. He always believed that he would return with a better understanding of the map and a translation of the journal, though he had not anticipated a return under such peculiar circumstances.

The golden owl was now in Wolf Blankston's possession. He wondered what that meant. Would the owl favor Wolf now, or would it be indifferent, as it had been to Edmond Kelly? All that mattered was whether George was in the owl's favor or not. It was one final excursion into The Mountain of the Owl. It was all or nothing—life or death.

PART FIVE

DISCOVERY

42

An hour after the men left the Aura, the trickling rain graduated to a full-fledged downpour. As they walked, their boots splashed in pools of water that formed in various low spots throughout the flat desert landscape. Birds were drinking from the pools that the travelers had not disturbed, chirping at one another as they drank. A thin layer of fog collected at the tops of the jagged plateaus, and a light breeze from the west brought with it an icy chill. The dark clouds had followed them all the way from the Aura, showering them and perhaps testing their endurance to gauge whether or not they would be able to withstand the trials ahead.

Physical endurance was a crucial variable in George's quest to discover the mine in under a week, and what he had long feared was already starting to manifest itself. As he looked behind him, he could see Wolf Blankston gasping for air, and despite the fact that the group was still treading on flat terrain, and even with the aid of a walking stick, he had already found a way to injure his left ankle.

How in the world will we ever reach the mine in a week with Wolf in such poor physical condition? George thought to himself. He knew all along that Wolf would never be able to make the climb in three days. It was going to take four or perhaps even five days to reach The Mountain of the Owl at Wolf's pace. That would give George very little time to locate the mine, which he had never found in the first place.

Every time George looked back to catch a glimpse of Wolf, he was scolded by Leonard Pearl, who instructed him to face forward. It was five against two. That was the way George looked at it. But maybe he should have thought of it as six against one, seeing that Aldric had been walking stride for stride with Stanton Pierce for the last half hour, exchanging information in Spanish—information that probably related to the journal of Father Rodriguez. There was a cloud of mystery that shrouded Aldric. George assumed that Aldric's allegiance was with him, but perhaps Aldric was loyal to no one.

●

The rain only seemed to fall harder as they moved along. The sky darkened, and the wind picked up, as did the rain. From the back of the group, Wolf yelled for everyone to stop, demanding that they take a break and allow the storm to pass. His excuse was that the rainfall was too harsh, but as George observed the way the fat man was panting and wheezing, he knew the break had a lot more to do with his conditioning, or lack thereof.

They situated themselves under a desert juniper where they warmed their pink fingers with their breath. Through the falling rain, George couldn't help but gape at the Book

Cliffs. The jagged slopes, the scent of wet sagebrush and junipers, and the tiered inclines that had formed from centuries of water erosion. The gorgeous imagery brought to him a sense of connectedness, as though the mighty Book Cliffs had been, and always would be, a part of him. He had traveled the Book Cliffs several times, and as he glared at them on that soggy afternoon, there was the evocative feeling that he would travel through them many times in the future.

•

The desert sun materialized from behind the cloud cover and began to beat down. The mixture of heat and rainfall created a mugginess that made it difficult to breathe. Few words had been spoken since the group left the Aura outside of Stanton prying Aldric for information and Wolf's groaning and complaining.

There was still a great deal of pain in George's face where he had been struck by the fists of Leonard Pearl. His eye was black and blue, and his cheekbone was red and swollen. It was also difficult for him to massage the back of his aching neck with the hindrance of the shackles and the bulkiness of the packsack, which extended well over the top of his head. Though, he had been able to squeeze his fingers in and rub the vertebrae sporadically throughout the day.

"How much further today, George?" moaned Wolf from the back of the group.

George squinted and looked up at the sun. Judging by its position, he estimated they had another three hours of daylight remaining.

"Couple hours yet," he replied in a tone that suggested he was annoyed by Wolf's complaining.

Without another word, Wolf, who was covered in sweat and was panting heavily, retreated for the shade of a Russian olive tree. When he arrived, he plopped down on his fat buttocks and closed his eyes. The rest of the group looked on with concern.

"We ain't traveled but seven miles," said George, catching the attention of the others. "Ain't no way he'll be able to make it."

The look on the faces of Wolf's men suggested that they agreed. Leonard took hold of George's arm and jerked him toward the Russian olive, but before they reached the tree, Leonard stopped and stared into the distance.

"Looks like we got comp'ny."

George and the others tried to spot whatever it was Leonard was talking about. The moisture in the valley below had formed what looked like a thick sheet of white mist from their vantage point. It looked as if all the distant terrain was gradually being swallowed by it. George's eyes moved left and right until he spotted what it was that Leonard was talking about. With his first glance, he had mistaken it for a juniper tree, but with the second look, he could see that it was moving. It was a man, he realized. Whoever the man was, he was about one thousand yards behind them.

"One of the men from town, you think?" Stanton asked.

"Could be," said Leonard. "Coulda followed us out here."

"Maybe he's tryin' to tell us som'in'," Carter suggested. "Suppose som'in happen at the mine?"

"I say we shoot the son of a bitch," said Walker with a wad of tobacco bulging from his lower lip.

"We're not shooting anyone," said Stanton. "Here." He put his pack on the ground then kneeled and began digging through it. Eventually, he retrieved a pair of Dolland London binoculars. He stood and faced the valley and lifted the binoculars to his eyes. The vision of the man was distorted due to the rippling heat waves, but despite the distortion, Stanton was able to confirm that it was a man wearing a white hat. Stanton lifted the strap from his neck. "You know the men better than I do," he said as he put the binoculars in the bulky hands of Leonard Pearl. "Maybe you'd be able to recognize him."

Leonard took the binoculars and lifted them to his blue eyes. He was silent for nearly a full minute as he lowered and raised them in a ritualistic fashion. But the man was simply too far away, and the heat waves, as well as the fog that stretched across the valley, made it too difficult to recognize anything other than vague characteristics.

"I don't have a clue," Leonard grumbled. "Might be a man from the Aura, might not be." He returned the binoculars to Stanton.

Wolf Blankston struggled to his feet, intent on having a look for himself. It was a sad sight to behold. He looked like a pig bogged down in a heap of mud, wincing and snorting as he battled his fat for the luxury of standing. Finally, he staggered to his feet and waddled toward the others. He ripped the binoculars from Stanton's hand and held them to his wet, pudgy face, convinced that he possessed some gift of vision far superior to what Leonard and Stanton had.

As he held the binoculars to his face, a breeze picked up and ruffled the neighboring pine trees. Walker spit out a chunk of tobacco grit onto the ground, and Carter unbuttoned his fly so that he could take a leak on the opposite side of the Russian olive. Wolf held the binoculars to his face two times longer than Leonard had. But despite the extended look, he didn't have a clue what he was looking at. He lowered the binoculars in frustration.

"Care if I have a look?" George asked.

Wolf deliberated for a moment and then passed the binoculars to George, who grabbed them awkwardly because of the limitation of the shackles. He held the binoculars to his eyes and looked through the broad lenses. After only a matter of seconds, he lowered the binoculars and stared into the distance.

"Ya recognize 'im?" Leonard asked.

"No." George replied.

"Let's keep moving then," Wolf demanded.

The group waited for Carter to finish pissing. When he was done, George led them toward what looked like a round mountain island above a sea of pine trees. George had lied. He knew exactly who the man in the white hat was. How Wolf Blankston didn't pick up on it was a mystery, but it gave George a great deal of pleasure. The man in the white hat was Remo. There was no doubt about it. If there had been a thousand men standing next to Remo, even at a mile away, George would have been able to determine which one was his savvy Italian comrade. Remo was a unique human being. He walked like no one else, talked like no else, and the physical shape of his body was unlike anyone who George had ever met. It was Remo, all right. At long last, Shit-Pants Parelli was on his way to help.

●

An hour passed. Much to the delight of Wolf Blankston, they had not seen the man in the white hat since. Either they had lost him, or he had not been following them after all. At least that was Wolf's explanation.

The expedition started its ascent from the south side of the mountain. The promise of gold was already motivating each step they took. The higher they climbed, the stronger their obsession became.

The men looked like mere atoms in comparison to the towering mountains. And to put their insignificant lives in prospective, the mountains were only a dot on a small blue planet, the small blue planet was a dot in the solar system, and the solar system was virtually invisible compared to the massive universe. Yet, despite being so inconsequential, here were seven human beings whose minds were contaminated by certainty and entitlement. They were certain that their morals, values, and ethics were valid, that their religions were indisputable, that their prejudices were justified, and that their hard work, or God given status, or past suffering, was enough to entitle them to the sweetest fruit that Mother Nature had to offer.

George's hair was soaked in sweat. The perspiration was trickling down his forehead, and to prevent it from running into his eyes, he wiped it clean with his forearm. He heard a wheezing sound from the tail of the group. He turned around to see Wolf Blankston sucking air, as he had been all day. As for George, carrying the heavy packsack had done a number on his neck and back. The strength he had gained from the lamb and potatoes he ate hours ago had worn off, and he was starting to feel weak and nauseous again. He decided to slow his pace and see if Leonard would kick up a fuss or not. He didn't. In fact, he welcomed the interruption in progress.

George stopped at the base of an aspen and assessed the terrain ahead. In the foreground, there were fir and aspen trees blotched erratically throughout the uphill slope. In the background, he saw a wall of what looked like impassable ponderosa pine trees. Beyond the pines were the blue peaks of The Mountain of the Owl.

Although it was near day's end, it felt hotter than it had all afternoon. The smell of heated dirt and vegetation climbed into George's nostrils as he watched the rippling waves of the sun distort the landscape ahead.

The others hovered in George's radius—their chests rising and falling as sweat poured from their faces. None of them looked as haggard as Wolf Blankston did. Wolf's face was bright red, and he was sweating so severely that it looked like he had jumped into a swimming hole somewhere nearby. Wolf dropped to his buttocks and then lowered himself to his back and stared upward at the sky. Stanton knelt down to make sure that he was all right, but Wolf waved him off in frustration.

"We've got an hour to go before we oughta set up camp," said George as he looked at the pathetic sight that was Wolf Blankston, though Wolf ignored him.

The others nodded their heads, but as George read their faces, he could tell that none of them wanted to take another step. They were men who were in excellent shape, but toiling in an underground mine was far different than a dozen miles of uphill hiking through drapes of humidity.

George looked into the rippling distance once more. This time it wasn't empty. Roughly one hundred yards ahead, he saw three dozen men walking on foot—a few of them were leading horses. The whole group was caught in a torrent of heat waves from George's vantage point.

"What in the world..." he said as he stared into the distance.

"What?" Leonard Pearl asked.

George pointed at the larger expedition. The others shielded their eyes and gazed into the faraway terrain.

"Them travelers up ahead," George explained. "Must be two or three dozen of 'em."

Leonard looked at George, then at Stanton, Carter, and Walker. They were all just as perplexed as Leonard was. "There ain't nobody up there, George," said Leonard. "I think the heat's gettin' to ya. Drink some wadder."

Leonard extended his canteen to George, but George remained fixed on the larger expedition. He finally took the canteen and swallowed a healthy swig of water. When he looked into the distance again, the larger expedition was still there, though gradually, it was disappearing into a thicket of trees. *It was no mirage,* George thought. He could see them as clear as day.

Wolf Blankston was lying on his back, fiddling with his belt that was now loose around the waist. Due to the heat and the strenuous physical activity, he must have shed ten pounds. "George, I can't go any further," he proclaimed. "We're camping here for the night."

"We've still got an hour-a-daylight," George replied. "Got at least another mile to go if we wanna stay on course—"

"To hell with your course," Wolf interrupted. "I'm physically unable to do it. We're stopping here, and that's that."

George looked into the distance. The larger expedition was gone, but it was still troubling him. For some reason or another, he had been the only one to see it.

"If he can't do it, then he can't do it," said Leonard, interrupting George's train of thought. "Wouldn't mind callin' it a day myself."

"All right," said George halfheartedly.

43

A camp was set up in a clearing with tall pines and under-brush surrounding it. Two tents had been erected, one for Wolf and the other for Stanton. Within the tents, they each had four blankets—two for lying on, one for pulling over themselves, and another just in case it got too cold. Of course, such comfort wouldn't be complete without a feath-ered pillow to absorb the weight of their weary heads. The other men were to sleep outside with only one blanket—half to lie on and half to pull over themselves.

Leonard and Carter were already asleep outside Wolf's tent like dogs. Walker was to stand guard for three hours before waking Leonard, who would serve three hours be-fore waking Carter.

Wolf, too, was already asleep and had been for over two hours. Building Wolf's tent had been prioritized over the construction of a fire and the cooking of a hot meal. Wolf had vomited three times due to dehydration and sunstroke.

He had no appetite, so he skipped dinner and fell asleep well before the sun went down.

After the fire had been kindled, the men prepared and then devoured plates of beans, corn, bread, and a small portion of pork. Carter and Leonard had fallen asleep minutes after shoving the food into their mouths. The others were seated around the campfire. Walker and Stanton were sitting opposite one another between George and Aldric. Stanton passed around a small bottle of bourbon, and the others took a few nips at it. The bourbon eased the tension, and for the first time since arriving at the Aura, Stanton had the opportunity to speak to George without the presence of Wolf Blankston.

"Are you feeling well?" Stanton asked as he was looking at George. George was pale and sweaty, and the bruises on his face were swollen.

"Doin' the best I can," George replied.

He was being modest. He was in a great deal of pain, and he was physically and mentally drained. There were scrapes on his arms, bruises on his face, a buzzing sound in his head, and a sharp pain in his neck.

"You know," said Stanton. "I don't exactly agree with what's gone on the last few days. If I had been allowed a say, we would have come to a more civil resolution. I just don't have much of a choice other than to go along with whatever Wolf wants. My future depends on it."

"When Wolf wants somethin', he gets it. No matter what," said George.

Stanton nodded and then took another hit of bourbon. Both Walker and Aldric seemed uninterested in conversation. They were both staring blankly into the fire, allowing the cold night air and the fire's warmth to work in harmony against their tired flesh.

"That's true," Stanton said finally. "We've certainly had our differences. But my father taught me to support those who support me. I wouldn't be where I am today without Wolf's guidance. I'm indebted to him for that. But that doesn't mean that I always agree with his methods."

"What are your methods?" George asked.

Stanton smiled. "I suppose they aren't much different from your methods. I believe in the safety and the education of the people. If our laborers are safe and educated, then we can only benefit from that. But Wolf doesn't much care for the idea of educating people. He fears that if they learn too much, they might grow up wanting more with their lives than spending twelve hours a day in a hole." Stanton took another pull from the bottle. "You know those damn deer heads he has hanging in his office?"

"Yes."

"Well, in regard to those, he often says: there are those who collect heads—"

"And then there are the headless," George finished.

A breeze picked up and sifted through the tall pines. The two men allowed a silence to settle in. George watched the tops of the shadowy pines sway against the dark sky. The stars appeared more definite behind them.

"It's hard to admit," said George, "but sometimes I think he's right."

Stanton chuckled. "I would agree. You know, I don't want to sound rude or cold-hearted. Our men are good men. But if I had to venture a guess, I'd say that over three quarters of them are no brighter than the deer hanging in Wolf's office. That's the way Wolf wants it. Twelve hours a day those men spend underground, and for what—a loaf of bread, a bottle of whiskey, and a lifespan cut in half? And they just let it happen. Sure, there have been a few weak attempts at a union uprising, but nothing that's made Wolf sweat. People put too much trust in those with power. All it takes is some authority figure, whether in their government or their church or even in the newspapers, to tell them what to do, or what to say, and even how to think. And that's the way people live their lives—doing what other people told them to do. I commend you for being an exception to that. Perhaps you're a collector of heads after all."

George remained silent. He may have strayed from the pack, but he remained unfulfilled—therefore, he didn't feel obliged to accept the compliment.

"What do you think about it, friend?" Stanton asked as he turned to Aldric.

Aldric raised his head and pondered for a moment, drawing the undivided attention of George and Stanton. "Some may think they are the 'collectors of heads' as you say, but I believe they are wrong. I think that, in the end, we are all headless."

George and Stanton began to consider that possibility. Walker, on the other hand, was not a philosophical man. He simply shifted an empty gaze between George and the fire.

We are all headless, George thought. That was certainly a possibility. Everyone is in search of something, but most people either die before they're able to figure out what they want or they spend their existence looking in the wrong places—and maybe, just maybe, they continue to strive for those ambitions in what some call the afterlife, especially if those ambitions go unfilled. George knew dozens of men who had lived their entire lives without ever attempting to do what they were passionate about. Instead, they simply lived the way that people told them to live because "that's the way it is" and "this is how we're supposed to be."

Before wealth ever entered the life of George Hendricks, he had been in search of contentment, and he had spent the last fifteen years trying to find it. From his late teens to his early twenties, he believed that contentment would come through the act of sharing his life with another person. This may have worked for some people, but not for George. He had been engaged three times from age eighteen to age thirty and had dated countless other women. But no matter who it was he cared for, and no matter how close he was to commitment, his intuition would always tell him that something was wrong. The void in his soul was not being filled. What was this void? He didn't know. All he knew was that something burned within him—a fire of some kind— something he yearned for that would fulfill his existence on Planet Earth. He understood that all people required some measure of Nirvana in their lives, and that their interpretations of it were all different. He had known men whose fulfillment came through adventure and tireless travel and others who discovered it through stability and repetition. No one was right or wrong. Different people had different needs. George's problem was that he didn't know what he wanted. There were times when he thought he would be fulfilled by a wife and a couple of children—anchored to the same place for the rest of his life. But then there were times when he felt he needed to roam freely through the world exploring places like Los Angeles or New York City in order to culture himself. He was like a teeter-totter— swaying back and forth—striving for something one day and something else the next. It was the curse of the Gemini, his mother had told him once—an indecisiveness that was as frustrating for George as it was for those around him.

After his third engagement, he vowed that he would not break the heart of another woman until he was able to find his own enlightenment. He spent years contemplating what it was and what it would take to satisfy it. Was it the camaraderie of family and friends, or was it an achievement attained only through one's personal trials? For a considerable amount of time, George thought his fulfillment would come through strenuous labor underground—a measure of self-satisfaction that, with any luck, might result in a promotion to supervisor or perhaps even foreman. Hard work always made him feel content, but it wasn't enough to satisfy his troubled heart and mind. Something else was missing.

The pain that had formed through the death of his mother and the deterioration of his father was far too earth-shattering to be dissolved physically. He also needed to combat it mentally. He once spent a month attending various churches in an attempt to find salvation through the Lord God. He did not grow up religious, but nearly everyone he ever met claimed that God was watching over them, intervening in their lives and directing their fate. God was good, and God was loving. Best of all, God was constantly looking out for the well-being of their wives, husbands, and children. But where was God when George's mother died at the tender age of forty-seven or when his father's cattle became contaminated with disease? Both things had propelled Joe Hendricks into a downward spiral that he never recovered from. *God works in mysterious ways,* they told him. But if God loved everyone and had a plan for everyone, then why was the plan so joyous for some and so horrible for others? Why were kind and honest people trampled upon and stolen from while liars, murderers, and thieves ran wild, reaping rewards for their devious actions? Why did children starve to death in coal camps while Wolf Blankston gorged himself with the finest wares of existence each and every day? Something wasn't right.

One day, George became compelled by the idea that what he really sought was fortune. Wealth attracted everything; friends, leisure, women, opportunity, luxury, respect, and most importantly, power. Yes, it was a fortune that George sought, and once he attained his fortune, then everything else would fall into place. It was time to stop being one of the headless. He would not be conned every day of his life simply because "it's just the way things are." *To hell with that,* he thought. It was time to collect heads. But what if what Aldric said was true? What if everyone, or at least the vast majority of people, were headless? It was a hard idea for George to swallow after everything he had been through.

He looked across the fire to see Aldric marveling at the sky above. George looked upward, too. Immediately, he was captivated by the radiant cosmos. He realized in that moment how much he had taken the beauty of the world for granted. His angst and despair had suppressed him so much over the years that he could no longer appreciate a tall, jagged mountain, or a babbling creek, or a soaring owl, or even the magnificent view of six thousand gleaming stars.

Somewhere along the way, George had lost sight of his dream. He lost sight of who he was. The promise of wealth, along with his anger and frustration with the world, had turned him into a man willing to steal and murder for his own personal gain. Maybe he was one of the headless after all.

When George looked down, he saw that Aldric was looking at him. His amber eyes were glowing. They were strikingly familiar to the eyes of the Great Horned Owl. They were the eyes that had darted at him in the depths of the Rainville No. 4, they were the eyes that had investigated him from the tops of the trees, and they were the eyes that had once told him that the gold of The Mountain of the Owl belonged to him.

Aldric looked at George knowingly, and a wicked smile grew on his face. In that moment, George realized that he had not seen or heard the Great Horned Owl since Aldric was hurled into the jail cell with him, though he had felt its presence.

Stanton rose to his feet, unnerved by the silence. "I think it's time I turn in. Sounds like we have one hell of a hike on our hands tomorrow. Goodnight." Stanton disappeared from the fire's light and into the darkness. His clomping footsteps softened as they grew distant.

A coyote howled somewhere far off while the fire cracked and popped, providing a little noise to disguise the silence.

"There's just one thing I wanna know, Hendricks," said Walker Thompson, breaking the silence. "What the hell'd ya go 'n hire old Shit-Pants Parelli as foreman for? I don't reckon that's too swell an idear. Hell, I been workin' mines since I's eight. I'd make a hell of a foreman. Now instead men is gonna come 'n ask me, 'Where's the foreman?' 'n I'm gonna havetuh tell 'em the foreman's gone 'n drank too much 'n shit hisself."

"You played cards with 'im in Rainville," George stated. "I thought ya got along."

"Hell no, we didn't. Old Shit-Pants was a dirty cheater, yer old man, too."

"You watch your goddamn mouth," George threatened.

Walker was quick to draw his pistol and aim it at George. "I'll say it again...yer old man and his buddy Shit-Pants were goddamn cheats, and so are you, Hendricks. I know ya stole the gold ya used tuh start the Aura. You ain't foolin' nobody."

"That's a lie," George rebutted.

Walker smirked. "That ain't the way I see it. Yer some kinda moron if ya don't think I know 'bout Hunter Paige. Old fella went missin' on this mou'un same time you was up here. Those that knew 'im said he pulled gold outta this mou'un all the time. What'd ya do, kill 'im and take 'is gold for yerself?"

"I never came across nobody else up here," said George, trying to sound sincere.

"Yer lyin'. I know it. But fer some reason Mr. Blankston and Mr. Pierce believe ya. They think yer gonna take us tuh gold, but I think yer full o' shit. Yer a liar and a cheat, just like yer Pa."

George wanted to grab Walker by the throat and rip out his esophagus, but he couldn't without being shot first. He sat quietly with burning eyes.

"It came back to bite ya in the ass, didn't it?" said Walker. "Ya really are a stupid bastard—'specially if ya really think we're gonna letcha go after ya find the mine. Hell, I plan on puttin' the bullet in yer head myself."

"Do it now, Walker. Make your boss proud."

Walker put his finger on the trigger and gritted his yellow teeth together. "The both of ya better get tuh sleep," he said. "We need our mules well rested."

The two men glared challengingly at one another before George lowered himself to a comfortable position and pulled his blanket over him.

The wind picked up suddenly. The force of nature was drawing closer to the encampment. It knew that George and his expedition had encroached upon its land. The creatures of the mountain cried out in terror, as did the trees and the underbrush.

A deep, reverberating hum was drawing closer. Aldric had read the journal of Father Rodriguez to George. It contained, in detail, several accounts of "the force of the mountain," or "Nature's Wrath." It was exactly how the journal had described it.

"It's here," George thought.

He let out a sigh and then closed his eyes. There was no use fretting about something he could not control. It wasn't the first time that he had encountered the strange force, nor would it be the last.

44

The grotesque image that George witnessed when he punctured the back of Wolf Blankston with a pickaxe was nothing compared to the sight he was about to observe. As his tired eyes eased open, he felt an icy chill rattle through his bones. Not only was it twenty degrees cooler than it had been the previous night, the dawn carried a dense fog that consumed the woods, restricting visibility to a radius of ten yards.

The campfire was all but extinguished aside from a few faint embers that sent a trail of dark smoke into the air. The cries of the mountain wildlife had been resonating through the foothills for nearly an hour, trying to inform George of the horrifying act that had been committed at some point during the night.

It was blood that he first noticed. It stretched from the front of Wolf Blankston's tent and disappeared into the underbrush. He rose hesitantly—afraid that whoever, or whatever, had spilled the blood was still present...still hungry.

But even more troubling was the fact that Leonard Pearl, Walker, Carter, and Aldric were all gone.

George watched the fog move above the underbrush as he walked to Wolf's tent and looked inside. Wolf was gone. He walked to Stanton's tent. He, too, was missing.

"Hello?" George hollered.

Nothing.

With cautious steps, he followed the dappled trail of blood that looked black in the dull morning light. The trail gradually intersected with a second trail of blood. The two trails had led into one, and where the blood joined, it formed deep, oozing puddles. As his boots moved through the underbrush, he was struck with a feeling of dread. He was about to abandon his search and return to the camp when he saw them. There were two bodies in the underbrush, mangled and maimed, a massive pool of blood underneath them. He could tell who they were simply by the clothes they were wearing, even though the clothes were soaked in blood. It was Carter and Walker, lying side by side.

At first, George's theory was that the men had been killed by a bear or a mountain lion and dragged away from the camp. But after a closer look at them, he realized that their deaths were brought on by something much different. Their bodies were almost entirely flattened, as though they had been crushed by some massive object. But how could that be? There were no large objects around...no fallen trees or runaway boulders. Perhaps they had been beaten profusely by someone and dragged into the underbrush, but by whom? Remo? George had a hard time believing that Remo could be responsible for such carnage. *My God,* George thought. *Aldric must have done this.* But where were Leonard, Stanton, and Wolf? Had Aldric killed them, too?

A twig snapped. George stood still and listened. He could hear footsteps clomping through the underbrush. The hair on the back of his neck stood as the outline of a human being started to manifest through the fog.

"Who's there?" George cried.

There was no answer.

George prepared to defend himself, but when the figure finally became visible, he froze. He had seen this man before on his previous outing, but he didn't know who he was. The black eyes of Father Rodriguez looked at George with desperation.

"Who are you?" George asked.

Father Rodriguez put his hands on George's shoulders and began to sob. His hands were like icicles against George's shoulders, and his brown fingernails felt like daggers driving into his flesh.

"¡Ayúdeme," said Father Rodriguez.

This man is a ghost, George thought. There was no doubt about it. He shared the same characteristics as the ghost of Mrs. Ambrosius: bluish, translucent flesh, dark eyes, and the behavior of someone riddled with apprehension and confusion.

"¡Ayúdeme," Rodriguez repeated. "Yo no pertenezco aquí! He confundido a Dios por algo más."

Again, George looked at him without comprehension. Father Rodriguez could see the confusion on George's face. He dropped his head sorrowfully and then walked away, convinced that George was unable to help him.

"Who are you?" George inquired again.

But Rodriguez did not stop. Seconds later, he was swallowed by the mist.

"George," cried a soft voice from behind him.

George almost jumped out of his shoes. He turned to see the distraught faces of Wolf, Stanton, Leonard, and Aldric. Realizing who it was, George let out a sigh of relief.

"I'm sorry to have frightened you," said Stanton.

"What happened?" George asked.

"You saw them?" Stanton asked.

"It looks like somethin'...crushed 'em."

"We don't know what happened," said Wolf Blankston. "We found them like this. I would have guessed that you and your friend here"—gesturing at Aldric—"were the ones responsible for this, but I don't understand how you could have committed such a heinous act without getting a single drop of blood on you, and in the dark, no less."

Wolf was sunburned, but he looked much better than he did the night before. Ten hours of sleep and five canteens of water had done wonders for him. Still, it was clear that he hadn't recovered one hundred percent.

George was about to ask the others if they had seen Father Rodriguez wandering through the underbrush when he suddenly had a change of heart. He knew the others hadn't seen him, just like they hadn't seen the large expedition the previous day. These were images that were only perceptible to George, or maybe they were images created by his mind.

The men stood within the wooded grove in silence. The trees amongst them looked like slender ghosts in the thick, sprawling fog. There were no birds or small animals or insects, and there was no wind or sunlight.

George proposed, "What about that fella that's been fol-lowin' us—maybe he did this?" He tried to act as though he didn't know who the follower was.

"That's what we thought, but it ain't no good," said Leonard, whose face was as white as a sheet. He was clearly afraid and also saddened by the loss of his friends. "There ain't no fog back the way we came. I went and checked it out myself—took Stanton's binoculars with me and spotted him. He's still followin' us all right, but he ain't responsible for this. I reckon he's about forty minutes back."

"It just doesn't add up," said Stanton. "Carter was supposed to be awake and on duty, but even if he hadn't the chance to cry out for help, then I don't understand how none of us could have heard anything. How could anyone, or anything, unleash that kind of hell without making a peep?"

"We're not alone up here," said Wolf as he pointed behind George, peering at a spectacle that rattled even the audacious Wolf Blankston.

George followed Wolf's finger and saw a ridge nearly fifty yards off that sat higher than the fog. Hovering on top of the ridge was the black, mist-like entity. It was the first time that George had observed the figure with the aid of the daylight. Of course, the daylight was diffused by a mixture of fog and an overcast sky, but it was daylight nonetheless. The figure was black in color and appeared not to have any feet or hands. It hovered above the ground as if a million locusts had united as one to create a single entity. It remained still for a moment, staring down at the group of mortals. Then the black mist began to stir. Suddenly, without being aware of how it happened, George saw that there were two entities. They hovered there for a moment and then began to float away from the expedition until they disappeared behind the opposite side of the ridge.

Wolf turned to George, giving him a withering look. "You claim to be familiar with this mountain. Would you like to tell me who those people were?"

"I've seen 'em before," said George. "But I—I dunno what they are."

"I know what they are," said Aldric, drawing the attention of the others. "They are spirits—vengeful spirits. Men possessed by greed."

"Spirits?" Wolf queried.

"That's right," said Aldric with an unyielding expression.

Wolf frowned. "If you're going to tell me that those two...*things* standing on that ridge weren't living, breathing human beings and that they slaughtered these two men like pigs at a goddamned slaughterhouse, then you're simply insulting my intelligence. I don't know what's going on here, but I certainly don't believe in ghosts or spooks, so someone better come up with a more rational explanation."

Stanton said, "I'm just as skeptical as you are, but let's look at the facts here. We checked everybody's supplies and ran the camp for clues. There wasn't a trace of anything. How could anyone pull that off in the middle of the night?"

"I wasn't implying that it was any of us, you half-wit," said Wolf, clearly offending Stanton with the remark. "I, for one, firmly believe that the men who were standing on that ridge were two human beings, and I believe they've just relayed a very gruesome message to us. Now, we can either run home with our tails between our legs, or we can find those bastards and put their heads on pikes. I, for one, prefer the latter."

354 *Michael Zaccaria*

"I don't think they were human beings," said George. "Hell, ya saw 'em—they were at least two feet off the ground."

"It may have looked that way," said Wolf. "But there must be some kind of...optical illusion. Perhaps the fog is to blame for the anomaly."

"Even if they are real people," said Stanton, "then I suggest we heed their message and get off this mountain while we still have the chance. We've already got an operation to run. The gold up here doesn't mean a damn thing if we die before we get to it."

"You can all forget the idea of going back," said Wolf. "We're not leaving here until we find what we came for. That was the deal. Besides, there are only two of them and five of us."

"We don't know that," said Stanton. "There might be more of them further up for all we know."

"There might be, but I find that unlikely."

"Come on, Wolf," said Stanton. "Two good men are dead. What does that mean to you?"

"It means we have two less indolent bodyguards. I'll be honest with all of you...I never cared much for Carter or Walker. They weren't the brightest men, and come to think of it, they were lazy, and they tended to complain a little too much for my liking. But I'm confident that Leonard can handle it from here on out. This travesty would have never happened on his watch. He's the best man I have working for me." Wolf smirked at Stanton, who was clearly unimpressed, and then he patted Leonard on the back. "You're with me, aren't you, Leonard?" Wolf asked.

Leonard nodded halfheartedly.

"Good then," said Wolf as he sized up George and Stanton. "You two aren't going anywhere." He glared at Stanton. "Unless you're no longer interested in becoming the heir to my corporation." He switched his gaze to George. "And as for you, a prisoner is a prisoner— that goes for your friend here, too," he said, nodding at Aldric.

George and Stanton looked on with defeated expressions.

"Let's bury these men," said Leonard.

"We're not going to bury them," Wolf affirmed. "We don't have the time with that stranger following us."

"Like hell we ain't," Leonard scoffed. "I say we wait fer that bastard and kill 'im. It ain't no secret he's followin' us."

Wolf pondered for a moment. "I suppose you're right. Very well, we'll kill him and bury him with Carter and Walker. That way we can have a hot breakfast and some coffee before we push out."

Leonard withdrew his pistol. "Will you two be all right alone with them prisoners?" he asked.

"We'll be fine," said Wolf as he withdrew his own pistol. "Make it quick. I'm starving."

Leonard took two paces before George stopped him in a state of panic. "Hold on," he said. He had to do something. He couldn't allow Remo to be ambushed by Leonard Pearl. "We don't know who's followin' us. Killin' 'im's a lousy idea. I think we're better off hidin' the bodies, coverin' up this blood with some dirt, and gettin' the hell outta here soon as we can."

"We have to do something," Wolf retaliated. "If he keeps following us, then eventually something has to give. I don't plan on sharing my gold with him or with anyone else."

My gold? The words made George cringe. It was his gold, not Wolf's.

"If we leave right away, we'll be able to lose him in the fog," said George. "We can bury them bodies on our way down in a coupla days. Plus, we're already behind. Buryin' three men might take half a day. We've got alotta ground to make up."

"I'm with George," said Stanton. "It's in our best interests not to kill anyone. Could be law for all we know."

"With all due respect here, boss," Leonard pleaded. "These men were good men. They deserve a Christian burial."

Wolf pondered the dilemma. "Damn it," he said finally. "If we don't lose him in the fog, then we kill him first chance we get—no buts about it. Leonard, we'll find the bastards that did this and get even. Then, as soon as we locate the mine we'll come back and bury these men. Now, let's get going."

The men hurried back to the camp and packed everything up as quickly as they could. Leonard was clearly angry, so much so that he didn't bother to say a word while he and George dragged the lifeless bodies of Carter and Walker to a perfect hiding place deep in the underbrush. While they did that, Stanton and Aldric used shovels to cover the blood with dirt. Wolf, meanwhile, sat under an aspen and scarfed down half a loaf of bread and sucked warm water out of a canteen.

It took them only ten minutes. Much to their delight, the concealing fog hardly wavered. Leonard, Stanton, and even Wolf were forced to carry the supplies that had originally been appointed to Carter and Walker. With clouded minds and a cold, lingering fear, the five men moved toward the higher mountain.

45

After they freed themselves of the fog, their pace throughout the day was relentless in an attempt to gain on yesterday's lost ground—and to outhustle the man who had been following them. The exhausting pace wreaked havoc, both mentally and physically, upon every man. Wolf Blankston, in his poor physical condition, had taken the brunt of it. During the first few hours, he forced the group to stop a handful of times for a brief rest. But as the day progressed, the quieter he became. He simply pushed on unconsciously without saying a word. It was apparent that he was in a great deal of pain. George feared that it would only be a matter of time before the fat man collapsed to the ground in need of multiple days of medical attention and recovery time. But much to George's bewilderment, Wolf's pace somehow remained stable for hours on end.

•

The dry heat of the desert was in their wake, but by midday, the five travelers had to endure another miserable condition. Higher altitude meant thinner air, and though they were fifty-two hundred feet above sea level, in the peak of summer, it was still eighty-seven degrees on the mountain. They walked with their eyes shielded from the sun by their hands and forearms, and they walked in an unbearable silence. No one had said a word since they left the foggy clearing. Worse yet, George had still not eaten anything other than a few scraps that Stanton had given him. Wolf, Stanton, and Leonard had snacked on bread, peanuts, and red apples throughout the day—only rationing a small amount to George and Aldric when it looked like they needed it. George's stomach rumbled with a ferocious hunger, and his throat was as dry as an arid desert. Worst of all, the large, awkward packsack that he was forced to carry had strained his neck into one inflexible position, amplifying the searing pain that was already present.

As for all the men collectively, dirt and sweat had invaded every pore, and they felt their skin burning and stinging under the intensity of the sunrays. They were soaked in sweat, their joints ached, their bones trembled, and their lips were cracked and desiccated.

When they had first left the Aura, George thought he was walking into a trap set by Wolf and Stanton. But much to his surprise, there was just as much tension between Wolf and the other men as there was between George and Wolf. Wolf was starting to question Stanton's loyalty after disagreeing with him earlier in the foggy thicket. The two had hardly looked at each other apart from the sharing of snacks. Wolf had also grown wary of Aldric after the sighting of the mist creatures. The fact that Aldric possessed knowledge of them made Wolf think that Aldric knew something the rest of the men didn't, and he didn't dismiss the possibility that Aldric was in some way involved with the killing. Then there was Leonard, who was visibly upset by Wolf's decision to leave the bodies behind without a proper burial. Wolf could sense the resentment; thus, it gave him a reason to distrust Leonard.

As they pushed up a steep ridge, a sense of familiarity came over George. He had been there before, and he knew that whatever was beyond the ridge was something important. The top of the ridge overlooked the mountain lake. The same lake had been the salvation for Esteban Garza and his men over a century and a half ago.

•

Aldric sat under an aspen tree near the stream with his hair soaked. Wolf laid down next to him and waited for Leonard to retrieve a container of water. When Leonard handed him the dripping canteen, he chugged the whole thing. He then puked it all up and fell asleep with his mouth encased in vomit.

Leonard refilled all of the canteens. When he finished, he took the keys from his pocket and unlocked George and Aldric's shackles so that they could relieve themselves of the massive packsacks. As soon as the packsacks hit the ground the shackles were reapplied. George watched as the keys found Leonard's pocket.

George stepped into the water and knelt down in it, soaking his pants and half his shirt. He dipped both of his hands in the water, making a bowl shape with his palms and fingers, and then he threw the water on top of his head. As the water dripped from his face, he heard footsteps approaching. It was Leonard Pearl, holding one of the smaller packs.

Leonard threw the pack on the ground. "It's the clothes Mr. Blankston and Mr. Pierce wore yesterday. Wash 'em in the stream and leave 'em out in the sun to dry."

"We shouldn't stick around here too long," said George.

The second he finished his sentence, Leonard kicked him in the chest. George fell backwards into the water, causing a large splash that drew the attention of Stanton and Aldric.

"Mr. Blankston needstuh rest fer at least an hour before we go anywhere," Leonard commanded. "So wash them clothes-n-dry 'em before I blow yer goddamn head off."

Leonard was serious, judging by the look on his face. George expected Leonard to be bitter about Wolf's decision not to bury Carter and Walker, but he didn't expect the wrath to be aimed at him. He thought it would have been directed toward Wolf for electing George's plan instead of his. George should have known better. Brutes never seem to retaliate against the correct person.

Without a fuss, George stepped out of the water and picked up the laundry pack. He opened it and removed the shirt that Wolf had worn the previous day. It smelled awful. It was already crusty with dried sweat. George walked to the area of the stream that he had just left when Leonard stopped him.

"Don't wash it there, ya idiot," Leonard grumbled. "Wadder's all stirred up there. Wash it further upstream."

George stepped out of the water, took the laundry pack, and began to walk further upstream—away from Stanton, Wolf, and Aldric. This made him nervous. Leonard walked alongside him with a stupid glare. After twenty yards, George tried to re-enter. But again, Leonard thwarted his efforts.

"Keep goin', Hendricks, 'til the wadder clears up."

The water had cleared up ten yards back, but George reluctantly continued along the stream. He watched the suspicious demeanor of Leonard Pearl, whose gun was visible on his hip—his right hand near it. All the while, the rest of the group became increasingly distant. George stopped again after another twenty yards, well aware that something was up. He took a step toward the water when Leonard stopped him for a third time.

"Keep goin', for Christ's sake, 'til I tell ya when yuv gone far enough."

"Water's crystal clear," George replied. "Ain't no reason why I can't wash 'em here."

"You can't wash 'em here 'cause I said ya can't."

Leonard backhanded George across his already swollen and tender cheek, causing him to stumble into the stream. Leonard laughed. "Wadder's all stirred up there now, too. Best keep movin' along, ya son of a bitch."

George staggered out of the water and gave Leonard a knowing look. There was a bend coming up in about forty yards that was concealed pines. It would be the perfect place for Leonard to shoot George and claim that he had done so in self-defense because George had tried to attack him. It was such a stupid and simple plan, but it was written all over Leonard's face.

"If ya kill me, Wolf'll never find the mine," said George.

"So what? I'll kill all you bastards-n-find it myself."

George needed to think quickly. He looked up at the tall ridge—the same ridge they stood on when they first spotted the lake. Suddenly an idea came to him.

"Hey," he said.

"What?" Leonard asked, and then he followed George's gaze to the top of the ridge.

"That fella' that's been followin' us. I just saw 'im come over the ridge and duck behind a tree up there. He musta seen the others at the lake."

"What tree'd he duck behind?" Leonard asked.

George approached Leonard and pointed. "That tall one, just to the left of the peak."

Leonard gave George a questioning look. "Yer sure?"

"I'm positive."

"Follow me. Stay close. I don't think he seen us." Leonard charged up the hill like a rhinoceros. George followed.

They stumbled over rocks, bushes, and weeds as they climbed the ridge under the cover of the pines. The higher they climbed, the higher a ledge to their right became. It sloped downward into a ragged basin of arbitrarily placed pines and fallen rock. Leonard stopped thirty yards from the tree he believed Remo was hiding behind. He, too, took cover behind a pine and withdrew his pistol.

"Ya see 'im?" Leonard whispered.

"I saw the brim of his hat. He's still behind that tree there."

"Yer sure bout that?" Leonard asked.

"I'm sure."

"All right. Soon as he moves away from it, I'll take the shot."

Ten feet to their right was the ledge. From where Leonard and George were standing, the drop off was about one hundred feet. Leonard was focused on the tree he thought Remo was hiding behind. As his finger tightened on the trigger, George lifted his shackled hands and interlocked his fingers to create a powerful weapon of iron and bone. With all his might, he slammed them downward onto Leonard's skull. Blood gushed from Leonard's head, and the brute just about went down. George gripped his hands on Leonard's shirt and hurled him toward the cliff, causing him to drop his pistol and fall hard to the ground. With every ounce of strength that Leonard had, he kept himself from sliding off the edge. That was, until George kicked him square in the nose, shattering it. The blood from Leonard's head and nose covered his entire face in a matter of seconds. It was running into his eyes, making it difficult for him to see. George drew his right leg back once more, this time striking Leonard in the stomach, knocking the wind out of him. Leonard was inches from the cliff now. With one final kick to the midsection, he rolled off the edge and tumbled one hundred feet to his death.

George smiled wickedly. The mindless brute was finally out of the equation. There were no more bodyguards. Best of all, he now had a weapon—Leonard's pistol. He picked it up and held it in his right hand. He then looked over the ledge and saw what was left of Leonard Pearl.

Remo, he suddenly thought. He ran to the top of the ridge and scanned the valley below in an attempt to find him. His heart was pounding from the adrenaline of killing yet another person. He needed the companionship of the only friend he had to his name.

Nothing in the distance moved but the swaying trees and a moose that George could see rummaging through the underbrush about two hundred yards off. He scanned the terrain for a full three minutes before he finally gave up. His plan to lose Remo in the fog had worked. Now that George was in control, he wished it hadn't. He could have used Remo. It was still two, or possibly three, against one.

He hurried down the slope and then wandered off the beaten path to track down the corpse of Leonard Pearl. He had never seen so many protruding bones in his life. Leonard must have broken every single bone in his body. Half of them had penetrated through the skin. George could see Leonard's brains and his guts. One of his eyeballs had even popped out of its socket, and his jawbone sat in the dirt about ten feet away. The stench was horrific. George covered his nose, reached into Leonard's pant pocket, and retrieved the bloody set of shackle keys. He used them to remove the shackles from his wrists. Once free, he draped them over his left shoulder and hurried toward the lake with Leonard's pistol in his right hand.

After only a few steps, he stopped and leaned against the trunk of an aspen. The pain in his head, neck, and shoulders was unreal. He felt weak, both mentally and physically. The booze had weakened him, as had the sleepless nights and the lack of nourishment. For a moment, he completely forgot where he was and what he was doing. He had killed again. He had killed two men and had tried to kill three. It didn't feel real. Nothing felt real. Wolf Blankston, Thelma Ambrosius, Rainville, Joe the Tommyknocker, Father Rodriguez, the vision of the Spanish expedition. It all felt like a terrible dream. There was blood on his hands and blood on his shirt. His throat was dry, and his head was pounding. The pain, the hangover, the fatigue, the blood, the history—all of it worked in harmony to shape his reality. The terrain started to spin, and the trees seemed to inch closer. The buzzing in his head returned, and this time, it was louder than ever. He dropped the gun and cried out in pain as his hands gripped the back of his neck. He then dropped to his knees and started to vomit a green and yellow bile that clung to his lips.

•

Wolf was still asleep, snoring loudly in the shaded grass. Stanton was resting his head against the trunk of an aspen with his eyes open. When he saw George coming, he could tell that his shackles were gone and that he was holding a pistol. But strangely, as George approached, Stanton looked on with intrigue, as though he somewhat favored the new circumstances.

Stanton lifted his left hand as a symbol of submission. He then removed his pistol and handed it to George, who tucked it into his belt behind him. George then took Wolf's pistol from the holster and tucked it into the front of his belt. He then pressed the barrel of Leonard's pistol against Wolf's forehead.

"Wake up."

Wolf's eyes eased open.

"We've got ground to make up, you mutt," said George mockingly.

Wolf was as red as a lobster, and his eyes were as wide as the moon.

"Where's Leonard?" he asked.

"He's gone," George replied.

Wolf swallowed hard and then struggled to his feet. Once he gathered himself, George grabbed one of the massive packsacks.

"Put that on your back," George demanded.

"You'll pay for this," Wolf threatened. "You lay a finger on me, and you're a dead man."

Wolf's attempt to intimidate was frail. The climb had reduced him to a fraction of his former self.

"You don't got no power," George boasted.

"Don't got no?" Wolf mocked. "You think you're really something, don't you? But you can't even speak proper English. People like you will never amount to shit in this life. You're too stupid. That's why you were a coal miner for so long—a slave for those with real promise—people like me. You're nothing but a piece of trash blowing in the wind. You're a peasant, George Hendricks, the lowest kind of low. That's all you've ever been, and that's all you're ever capable of being in your meaningless life."

"I'm sure you think I'm gonna kill ya, but I'm not," said George. "I got somethin' much better in mind for you. We're gonna find that gold mine, and when we do, guess who's gonna work it?" George grinned wildly, and his eyes glistened with passion. "That's right. You're gonna crawl into that hole with a pick and shovel and work the walls until you can't lift your goddamn arms. You'll only work under candlelight. The ventilation won't be worth a damn, and you'll be usin' old tools. You'll just have to deal with it, the same way your men have had to deal with it for the last twenty years."

"Just remember," said Wolf. "The Aura belongs to me, and it always will be whether you kill me or not. And if you try to leave this mountain, then you'll be caught by the authorities. I sent a telegram to every lawman in the state in case you were able to escape. They've been instructed to arrest you on sight. So keep smiling, you mutt, because you're damned to this mountain."

"I don't think you get it," said George. "You're the mutt now. Now get your fat ass goin' up that hill. We gotta mine to track down."

Wolf glared at George. He then bent over and picked up the large packsack. Stanton came forward and helped him with it, lifting it so he could get the straps around Wolf's broad shoulders.

George took the shackles from his shoulder and gave them to Stanton. George didn't have a say a word; Stanton knew what he wanted.

"Hold your arms out, Wolf," said Stanton.

"You're a weak son of a bitch, Stanton," said Wolf bitterly. "You could have done something about this. You can kiss your share of the Wolf Blankston Mining Company goodbye."

The two men glared at one another while Stanton applied the shackles.

"Now unlock him," said George, looking at Aldric.

Stanton removed the shackles from Aldric's wrists and then handed the keys back to George.

The group that had started with seven was now four, and the four departed the lake and walked northwest toward the gold-bearing highland. At long last, George was once again in control. Best of all, Wolf Blankston was at his disposal. He couldn't wait to reach the mine so that he could give Wolf a dose of his own medicine. He was certain that Wolf would find toiling underground to be comparable to Hell on Earth. How sweet victory was. The owl, some way, somehow, had freed him from the bonds of Wolf Blankston, just as it had promised. There was only one thing left to do.

46

The setting sun painted the mountaintops a lurid pink behind a wall of seemingly impenetrable pines. In front of the pines was the flourishing underbrush, which was peppered with large stones that also absorbed the soothing pink of the waning sun.

The four diverse yet equally gold-thirsty travelers arrived at the place where the secret of the Spanish gold mine, a cairn stone, had once stood but had since been reduced to a pile of rubble.

They made excellent time during their second day of travel. They had caught up to and even surpassed George's initial goals. They would be within the proximity of the gold mine early the following day—the third day, just as George promised.

The Mountain of the Owl was a place of exceptional isolation, mystery, and trepidation. It was a place that not even its native people dared to set foot for fear of being consumed by the elemental powers that lived there. They were powers that were separate from living things yet innately connected with them through some level of expanded, or extended, perception. Whether it was something tangible or something imagined, the malevolent force of nature was as real to the native people as the bark on the trees or the clouds in the sky. When the wind blew and the pines began to hiss and sway, the mountain came to life. The sound was unlike any other. It truly sounded alive, like the inhalation and exhalation of a thousand giants breathing synchronized breaths. It was a place where wise men were deterred and foolish men were attracted—a place where greed outweighed a violent warning, where wealth meant more than life, and where power trumped serenity. Naturally, that was the heart of the issue—power was confused for serenity. Power comes, and then it deteriorates, like trees in the height of autumn, into a dull and barren state of its former self.

Deteriorating faster than anything else on the mountain was Wolf Blankston. He had been pushed far too hard for too long. The others knew the repercussions would be severe. Stanton and Aldric had been holding Wolf up by his biceps for the last hour and had gradually felt the burden of his weight increase.

George was also in rough shape. His footsteps staggered, and his eyes fluttered. His fine dress shirt was covered in sweat and dirt, and his once combed hair looked like it did after a day underground. He looked like he might collapse at any given moment.

As they stepped over the toppled stones that were once part of the cairn, Stanton realized that Wolf's eyes were closed and that they were carrying his dead weight.

"Hold on a minute, George," said Stanton as he and Aldric stopped. "I don't think he's conscious."

The men dragged Wolf's limp body to a thicket. They laid him down in the shade and removed his shackles and packsack. Stanton knelt down beside him and began repeating his name and slapping him gently on the cheek. Wolf did not respond. In desperation, Stanton sifted through his pack and discovered one of the water canteens. He poured the contents onto Wolf's face.

Wolf opened his eyes to a world that left him baffled.

"Where the hell am I?" he asked.

"You're all right," Stanton replied as he removed the top of another canteen and handed it to Wolf.

Wolf's eyes danced across the landscape while he chugged the lukewarm water. The more he saw, the more confounded he became.

"Where are we...what's happening here?"

George noticed that Aldric had wandered away from Wolf. He had removed the large packsack and was kneeling down near some of the stones that had once been part of the cairn. He began unearthing some of them. He looked a few over before discarding them.

"What's the last thing you remember?" Stanton asked.

Wolf's face was empty, as though he was unable to recall a single memory of his past.

During the pause, George returned his attention to Aldric, who had taken one of the shovels from the pack. He was using it to pry up a large, flat stone. It aroused George's curiosity. He walked a short distance to give Aldric a hand with unearthing the stone. With their combined strength, they were able to lift it out. They lowered it to the ground and began to rub it clean with their hands.

The stone was red shale that had since collected blemishes of brown and black from its century and a half underground. One of the sides contained Spanish writing as well as a small indentation of the golden owl figurine. At the bottom of the stone was a large N, depicting the direction north.

"I remember pouring myself a drink," said Wolf finally, attracting George's attention. "The mine...my God. There was an explosion...a terrible explosion." Wolf's eyes grew wide and his lip trembled as he recalled the horror. "There was black smoke pouring from the mouth of the No. 4. There were women and children crying and screaming. My mine...destroyed. I needed a drink to cope with the devastation. I remember pouring myself a Scotch. That's when I felt the pain in my back. I hit my face on the desk then I fell to the ground. That's when I saw him. I saw him just before the darkness came."

"Who did you see?" Stanton asked.

"George..."

Stanton and George both found it odd that this was Wolf's most recent memory. It felt like an eternity since George had stormed into Wolf's office with a pickaxe.

"I want you to find him," Wolf continued. "I want him alive...I want to rip his goddamn heart out of his chest!"

Stanton looked at George for a moment before returning his gaze to Wolf. "Sure, boss. Get some rest, and I'll take care of it."

"Good," Wolf replied, and then he closed his eyes.

Aldric patted George on the shoulder. When George faced him, Aldric withdrew the golden owl figurine from his pocket. The crafty devil had stolen it from Wolf while he was asleep at the lake. Aldric put the golden owl into the crevice on the keystone.

"El ala derecha de la lechuza muestra el camino," said Aldric, reading both the phrase on the keystone and the phrase on the back of the golden owl together. "The right wing shows the way."

The right wing of the owl was pointing toward the narrow canyon entrance where Father Rodriguez had appeared during George's first outing.

"I don't think we can go any further," said Stanton as he joined George and Aldric around the keystone. "Wolf's in lousy shape."

The men could hear Wolf coughing. They thought nothing of it at first, until the coughing transformed into a violent choking. Wolf's eyes widened as he gagged and struggled for air.

They all hurried to him. George and Stanton took hold of his arms and raised him to a seated position. As soon as they did, Wolf spit out a large amount of blood. George and Stanton both noticed blood on their hands, then they noticed a massive pool of blood underneath Wolf. Before they could even begin to comprehend what was happening, Wolf Blankston was dead—gazing lifelessly at the orange sky above.

"What in God's name?" Said George with wide eyes and a colorless face.

There was a long silence as the men looked at one another—unsure of what had happened. Stanton's face was as white as snow. He looked like he was about to start crying.

"What is this?" George asked. "What's happening?"

He looked at Aldric, but Aldric just kept looking at Wolf with a concerned expression. He then looked at Stanton.

Stanton looked back icily, and then stood up and stormed off in the wrong direction. George and Aldric watched him, confused by what he was doing. The sun was setting on the western horizon, and Stanton paced toward it.

When he was fifty yards away, George stood up and ran after him.

"Stanton!" he yelled.

Stanton kept walking.

As George stumbled along, his vision started to betray him. Everything turned blurry—Stanton, the trees, the orange sun in the valley below. It was hard for him to see anything but distortion.

Finally, he got close enough to grab Stanton's arm and stop him.

"Where ya goin'?" George asked.

"I'm not going with you," said Stanton. "I'm going back down the mountain."

"I dunno what's happenin' here...but we're gonna find it, I promise. I'll share it with ya."

Stanton gave George a withering look.

"I'm sorry about Wolf," George continued. "I know what he meant to ya."

"Wolf never meant shit to me. I'm glad you killed him."

George's expression was empty. "I didn't kill 'im...you saw...I don't know what the hell happened to 'im." George's voice was shrieky, hysterical.

"I found Wolf in the office—face down in a pool of his own blood. I called for Harriman right away, and he had some of the men carry him down to the infirmary. He died three days later. After that, the company became mine. Fifty-seven years I ran that company, but as you can see, I'm still a young man—that's the way you remember me."

George couldn't wield a response.

"I'm just a branch on Wolf Blankston's tree," said Stanton. "I only existed here because I'm a small part of your memory of Wolf."

With a tear streaking down his face, George said, "Why don't we rest and have a drink and talk this over? I think the heat's gettin' to the both of us."

"I'm perfectly well," said Stanton. "And I'm afraid I haven't got time for a drink."

"I've gone mad, is that it?" George asked with a little smile.

"You're perfectly well, George."

"Please just tell me what's happening...I'm beggin' you."

Stanton put his hand on George's shoulder. "I'm sorry, but I can't do that. It's something you have to find out for yourself. Those are the rules, and they apply to everyone, no matter what. All I can say is that you shouldn't be afraid."

Stanton took his hand off George's shoulder and then continued, "Your reality is no different than an ordinary dream—thoughts, images, sensations. People you've met and people you haven't, people you want to remember, and people you want to forget. They can be your fears, weaknesses, victories, and desires. They can be whatever you want, and they can also be furthest thing from it."

"You're telling me that...but what about Leonard, Carter, and Walker?"

"Carter and Walker died in the same blast that killed your old man."

"...Of course..." There were tears in both eyes now.

"As for Leonard, he survived the blast."

"I remember seein' 'im..."

"Well...about three months after that, he slipped and fell down a shaft we were digging in one of the new mines. Poor bastard must have fallen one hundred feet."

"I don't believe it," said George as a smile grew on his face. The smile gradually transformed into hysterical laughter.

"You know what to do, don't you?" Stanton asked with a grin of his own.

"Yes..."

"Godspeed, George."

Stanton and George shook hands, and then Stanton turned and walked toward the massive sun that was setting on the western horizon. He looked like a lone cowboy wandering off into the sunset. George watched him with a little smile and tears rolling down both cheeks. Suddenly, from his viewpoint, Stanton walked directly in front of the sun, causing him to disappear into a nether of orange light.

Tired, hungry, and confused, George staggered back to Aldric and the toppled cairn stone.

When he returned, he found that the corpse of Wolf Blankston was gone. So, too, was the blood or any indication that anyone had been lying there.

"You know where it is?" George asked as he looked at Aldric.

"Yes," Aldric replied.

"You've known all along?"

"Yes."

"Whaddya want with me?" George asked.

Aldric grinned. "Now we can claim what is rightfully ours."

"How close are we?"

Aldric took the golden owl figurine from the keystone.

"We'll be there by morning." He then handed George the golden owl. "This belongs to you," he said.

When they arrived at the mouth of the strange canyon, both men read the phrase, "*Come No Further*" carved into the massive boulder that nearly blocked the canyon's entrance. They were words written to heed warning. Words that meant that they had reached the end of the line, and that by crossing such a line, they would be putting their lives in jeopardy. But even as they rode tirelessly on the median of life and death, the hunger for a glimmering mineral outweighed the hunger for understanding.

47

A campfire raged against a rocky wall in the strange canyon. George and Aldric sat on opposite sides of the fire, which projected them as two ghostly silhouettes against the jagged walls. Billions of stars hovered overhead, worlds that an insignificant being like George Hendricks couldn't even begin to fathom. In the previous days, the stars had represented a window to the soul—a massive organism—that permeated through him and around him. But his interpretation of the stars was different on this night than it had been the previous night. On this night, the stars were a treasure map and a compass—a reassurance that he was drawing closer to his greatest desire.

"I found this today," said Aldric as he retrieved a quartz arrowhead from his pocket. "The people that used to live in this region believed gold to be very powerful. They felt that it was capable of powerful things—evil things. There was a time when they would stop at nothing to protect it—to keep it out of the hands of bad men."

Aldric closed his eyes and inhaled the bracing mountain air. He opened them again and looked at George. "May I see the owl?" he asked.

George retrieved it from his pocket and passed it to Aldric, who held it in front of the fire so the orange light could reflect on it.

"This owl," said Aldric. "It is incredibly mysterious. It sees all from a high place. It waits patiently in the tops of the trees, and when the time is right, it swoops down and strikes with such a vengeance—such a swift and powerful vengeance. The prey is pinned to the ground—calling out in desperation. It's frightened...it doesn't know what's happening or why. But before it can find out, the prey is eaten, and always, it is eaten head first."

"Sounds barbaric," George replied.

Aldric lifted his gaze from the golden owl to George. "We are all barbaric, both animals and humans. We are one in the same."

"Maybe we ain't got no choice but to behave like animals," George intervened. "The rules of the world were set up a long time ago. We have to follow the rules, or else we don't stand a chance of makin' somethin' of ourselves." Immediately, he hated what he said. It reeked of Wolf Blankston's philosophy, not his. He was too easily swayed.

"That's one man's theory," said Aldric. "But if you ask me, I say there are no rules. True happiness blossoms when one forges their own path—when one is a creator of ecstasy, not a consumer. If I have learned anything during my time on this mountain, it is that."

"If ya don't mind, I'd like to ask ya somethin'," said George.

"Please," Aldric replied.

"I know this might sound crazy...but...you're the owl, ain'tcha?"

"No," Aldric replied with a smile. "The owl is an owl, just like a deer is a deer. But I do know what you're referring to."

"What?" George asked, unconvinced by Aldric's words.

"The wind and the trees, the lakes and the seas. She is a very powerful thing. Her purpose is much greater than the trivialities we seek, and her wisdom is that of a trillion souls. She is God and Satan. She loves us and loathes us. She gives and takes, though one thing is for certain, she'll always be there, bearing beauty and chaos. She is that which gives us life and that which takes it away. But to her, death is life, for she is fueled by our essence and us by hers. When we depart from being, all that's left is a content or bewildered soul. The bewildered souls are destined to search and repeat until they find the answers they seek. You must understand, George. The gold of this mountain does not belong to the native Ute, or to the Spanish, or to the prospector who bears this golden owl. It belongs to her. It is a valuable part of her. We must stop for a moment and relish in her beauty and listen to her gentle language."

George's eyes burned as he looked across the fire at Aldric. Though, despite their burning, they remained empty. "You're sayin' that 'She' is the one who controls the owl—she directs its every action?"

"Something directs all of us," said Aldric. "I suppose it's up to us to recognize it before it's too late."

"I'm afraid," said George. "I know I ain't supposed to be, but I am. I wish Pop was here."

"You didn't want him to be."

"I know..."

"Don't let it bother you. Things are this way for a reason. You and I will meet at this campfire again. We'll meet here hundreds, if not thousands of times. We'll share the same stories, we'll feel the same emotions, and we'll hear the call of the owl. This mountain has become us, and in turn, we have become the mountain."

George stared into the golden eyes of Aldric as though hypnotized by some ancient spell. An eerie silence set in as the flames of the fire raged on. The silhouettes of George and Aldric wisped and swayed against the canyon wall.

"Fear not," said Aldric. "For the dawn will yield gold."

48

A thick fog once again consumed the high mountain and swallowed the forest green pines that looked black in the dawn's early glow. The mountain peaks jutted from the fog like little islands in the clouds. The sun had not yet risen, and the bluish-gray dawn carried an icy chill that forced George awake, shivering. He looked around and noticed that he was strangely alone, as he had been the previous morning.

He staggered to his feet and stumbled around the terrain in search of his dubious friend, though the fog made it difficult. *At least there's not blood all over the ground today,* he thought.

His head was throbbing in pain. He lifted his arm and began to massage his neck.

"Hello?" he yelled.

A strange shrieking came from the northeast. George's head turned sharply in that direction. His eyes widened as he sat and listened, watching the white fog comb through the pine trees as if it were alive.

He walked hesitantly toward the northeast, hunched over and with his left hand on the back of his neck. He stopped for a moment and listened...nothing. Then he started walking again.

The fog wavered slightly at the base of a rounded hill. The top of it was slightly visible, as the fog thinned at that height.

He cried out once more and was granted with another reply. It sounded like the cry of a human being and the screech of an owl merged into one. It was a terrible, disturbing sound.

At the top of the hill, the outline of a human being emerged, though the thin fog rendered it as a dark, misty figure. George took a cautious step toward it, certain that it was Aldric. Then he noticed that there were two of them, as there had been the previous morning when Wolf discovered them standing on the ridge above the foggy thicket.

"It's all right," said the creature closest to him.

The entity then started down the slope, hovering toward George. It disappeared altogether for a moment when it entered the thick fog and then reappeared as it reached the bottom of the hill. George's heart was racing uncontrollably. He felt like he was going to pass out.

The black shadow moved closer and closer, and as it did, more and more was revealed. Suddenly it stopped about five feet away. It was Aldric, clear as day, though his appearance was much different. His hair was longer, and he wore a thick black beard. He was missing a portion of his left arm—in its place was a metal hook. He also wore an eye patch that covered a nasty scar over his left eye. Aldric grinned from ear to ear. But Aldric was not Aldric. Aldric was Esteban Garza.

"We made it," said Esteban. "The mine is just beyond those trees."

George stared at the golden eye of Esteban Garza, unsure how to respond.

"Aldric?" George asked.

Esteban nodded and grinned.

"Who's that?" George asked, pointing at the top of the hill.

Esteban turned and looked. The second black, misty entity was standing at the top of it.

Esteban turned back to George and smiled.

"Now we can claim what is rightfully ours," said Esteban.

He turned and faced the second apparition again. George's wide eyes looked up at it, too.

Suddenly, the second apparition started to move. It was floating down the hill toward them. It disappeared in the thick fog for a moment and then reappeared and verged toward them.

When the second apparition came forth, an expression of shock and horror filled George's face. His eyes began to water—not due to sadness, but sheer fright. Standing in front of him was himself—the version of George Hendricks that never made it off The Mountain of the Owl after he killed Wolf Blankston and Hunter Paige.

The earlier version of George was also frightened. The two just stared at each other in disbelief—unwilling to accept the existence of the other.

Then, footsteps materialized behind them, slogging through the underbrush.

The earlier George, with black eyes and pale skin, pointed in the direction of the later George—not at him, but behind him. The later George turned around to see who, or what, was coming.

"Come now, George," said Esteban Garza. "We must hurry."

When the later George turned around again, he saw that he was the only George. He looked down at his shaking hands to see how pale they were. A tear sprang out of his eye and rolled down his cheek.

"...Am I...?"

"We have to hurry," said Esteban.

All the while, the clomping through the underbrush grew louder. Whoever was coming was close.

"The mine is all ours," said Esteban. "Don't be afraid."

George looked at Esteban and then smiled. Esteban smiled, too, before hurrying up the hill. George followed.

The two spirits reached the top, followed the tree line about fifty yards, and then ducked into an opening in the pines. The closer they got to the mine, the more their mortal features faded and the black, misty form started to take shape.

George hurried through the passageway in the trees, no longer walking, but floating, and emerged into a small clearing. He stopped in his tracks. There it was...the legendary Spanish mine—blacker than the night—a faint layer of fog hovering around it.

He looked at Esteban, who still had a grin on his face.

"Go ahead," said Esteban.

George looked at the mine, then back at Esteban, and then at the mine again. He smiled wickedly and then hovered toward it. Gradually, he started to become transparent.

The closer he got to the mine, the more he faded. He looked down at his hands again and saw that he didn't have any. Despite this, he wasn't afraid. Whatever was happening, it felt right. Just as he reached the entrance, he disappeared altogether.

•

Back the rounded hill, the clomping footsteps continued. From the sprawling fog, Remo Parelli emerged. He was wearing a white hat. Underneath the white hat was a bandage wrapped around his head.

"Oh God," said Remo, spotting something on the ground. Then, he fell to his knees.

There were not mist-like spirits in front of him. There were only the decomposing remains of a human being, though an incomplete one. It was missing its head. Remo recognized the attire of his friend George Hendricks. He had worn those same clothes to labor side by side with Remo for the last two years. It was George, all right. He had been cut down by someone, or something, less than a hundred yards from the King's Crown, and thus, the legendary gold mine.

•

A place where one finds a decapitated man and two dead burros is not a place where one wants to spend too much time. Before Remo left, he skimmed through George's possessions in case there was anything of value. He found a pocket watch, a letter, a spinning top, and a photograph of George's mother—Joe's wife. He also found the golden owl figurine, *El Mapa del búho*, and the journal of Father Rodriguez. But the biggest prize of all was eight thousand dollars' worth of gold, which was packed into little burlap sacks. Why George's killer had not taken any of the valuable possessions would always be a mystery to Remo, but the fact that they hadn't would be a miracle bestowed upon himself and his family for decades to come. Remo said a prayer for George and then descended the mountain.

•

Two days later, in the back of a horse-drawn carriage, Remo, along with a carriage driver from Rabbit Gulch, transported what was left of George's fetid corpse to Rainville. The body had been decomposing for more than a week, and Remo, as well as the carriage driver, had to stop a half dozen times to vomit. When they arrived in Rainville, they were met by Stanton Peirce, the owner of the Rainville Coal Mine.

That very day, George was buried in the Rainville cemetery, despite the fact that Wolf Blankston, the man who George killed, was also buried there. Though, Wolf was buried in a private section far from the commoners with a fenced off memorial fit for a king. Remo paid for George's headstone. It read: GEORGE HENDRICKS, 1865-1900. GONE BUT NOT FORGOTTEN.

•

Remo retired from underground mining and used his new fortune to open his own grocery store in bustling Helper. It was hard to believe. Old Shit-Pants Parelli, from deprived coal miner and laughing-stock of the Rainville Coal Mine to prosperous and well-respected business owner. No one ever knew how he did it, nor would he ever tell anyone. He didn't want people ending up like his friend George. Remo's establishment, Parelli's Market, would thrive for nearly a century.

49

Golden shafts of light poured through the broken glass window in George' office at the Aura coal mine. George was sitting behind his desk with his feet kicked up on the desktop and an Aura cigar in his mouth. His face was cleanly shaven, and his raiment was fresh and fancy.

He stood suddenly and approached the broken glass window while his right hand rubbed the back of his aching neck. Why it hurt, he did not know, but it was a menacing pain. As he looked out the window into the sunlight, he removed a luxurious brass watch and checked the time. 10:35 A.M. Perfect timing. He smiled and closed his watch. There was a knock at the door just then.

The building suddenly grew dark, and its true nature began to reveal itself, although George was unaware of it. He was in a different world. The office building of the Aura Mine, in its actual state, resembled the broken glass window, which George had busted himself the day of the Rainville explosion, more prominently than anything else. There was no roof overhead, and the stone walls of the building were almost entirely destroyed. On the walls were amateur graffiti and bullet holes, and on the ground were shattered glass bottles, beer cans, and shotgun shells.

George was totally ignorant of the fact, but his mine office was no office at all. It was the stone cottage that he had lived in during his stint in Rainville. Rainville was abandoned now. The entire camp, what was left of it, at least, was overgrown with sagebrush. The roofs had collapsed, and the entrances of every mine were sealed off.

The Aura was a place where Al Joseph called the shots—a place where no one like Wolf Blankston could invade. The truth was, he was wondering through the ruins of Rainville. Rainville was a forgotten place, a figment of the past, and George's final resting place. But in George's world, he was climbing the hill at the Aura, on his way to the Aura Mine. That was his world. That was his pattern. But the Aura was not a blossoming business endeavor established by the ambitious Al Joseph. It was the broken and tattered ruins of a dream that never was.